RUBY
RIVER

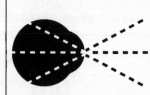

This Large Print Book carries the
Seal of Approval of N.A.V.H.

RUBY RIVER

Lynn Pruett

Thorndike Press • Waterville, Maine

Copyright © 2002 by Lynn Pruett

Lyrics to "Hi-De-Ho Baby Mine" written by Alton Delmore, copyright © 1963 by American Music, Inc., reprinted by permission of Sherry Bond and Debby Delmore.

Grateful acknowledgment is made to the editors of the following magazines in which sections of this novel first appeared: *Limestone*: "Another Kiss"; and *The Louisville Review*: "Breathing in Darkness."

Published in 2003 by arrangement with Grove Atlantic, Inc.

Thorndike Press Large Print Americana Series.

The tree indicium is a trademark of Thorndike Press.

The text of this Large Print edition is unabridged. Other aspects of the book may vary from the original edition.

Set in 16 pt. Plantin.

Printed in the United States on permanent paper.

Library of Congress Cataloging-in-Publication Data

Pruett, Lynn.
    Ruby River / Lynn Pruett.
        p. cm.
    ISBN 0-7862-5144-1 (lg. print : hc : alk. paper)
    1. Mothers and daughters — Fiction. 2. Women — Alabama — Fiction. 3. Single mothers — Fiction. 4. Truck stops — Fiction. 5. Alabama — Fiction. 6. Widows — Fiction. 7. Clergy — Fiction. 8. Large type books. I. Title.
PS3616.R84R83 2003
    813'.54—dc21   2002042967

*For my great-aunt
Frances Fricia Ross of Dexter, Kentucky,
lifelong reader and inspiration*

Dip him in the river who loves water.
— William Blake,
The Marriage of Heaven and Hell

— the wild dark eyes like rubies in the
fire.
— Thomas Rabbitt,
Abandoned Country

I

The Ladies of the Church of the Holy Resurrection

The ladies of the church often noted that Hattie Bohannon appeared taller than she really was. They regretted that she took a tan well and looked fashionable, while most women her age, raised on the class/color quotient, had shied from the sun to maintain their perch above the rising tide of social democracy. However, current fashion equated tans with health and youth. So these same women drove first to the tanning salon on the town square, where they burned for $15 an hour, and then trudged to a pink gym twice a week so they could jiggle in pastel sweatsuits, like fruit-and-butterscotch swirl puddings, in front of a huge mirror. They drew the line at the sauna. Diseases lurked there.

What disturbed them even more about Hattie Bohannon was her ease in handling orphanhood, widowhood, and de facto single parenthood. Hattie had no breakdowns or depressions or weight gains or drug dependencies. Equally disturbing was her smooth clear skin that hinted of expensive treatments, old Atlanta, and inner peace. There was no Christian way not to admire her.

She was friendly and moral — the kind of woman you could trust with your husband — but come to think of it, that was a little peculiar. Did she think she was too good for their husbands? Impossible. She was from Brentone, the resort town on the other side of the mountain, where questionable things went on. Northerners vacationed there, demanding foods with foreign names. They spent the evenings splashing nude (it was reported) in the natural springs. As a girl, Hattie Dameron had waitressed at the resort and snagged Oakley Bohannon, a man twice her age, for a husband.

In truth, the Resurrection ladies claimed they rarely thought of her, except on the few occasions when they emerged from aerobics, sapped and glowing, and spotted her coming from the bank, dry in a cotton print dress, another transaction mastered and satisfaction reflected in her calm smile. That woman could flatter a pair of overalls, they'd think, and wonder what they were doing wrong — not that they'd be caught dead in overalls.

They watched her new truck-stop venture with more attention. Even went up there and ate and were surprised that the grubs — truckers — it was designed for had not made the place grubby. It was okay for a *cheap* meal, say on a Wednesday night before church, but not the place to go for a nice dinner out.

This gossip that clogged the telephone wires at the Maridoches exchange drove Jewell Miller, telephone operator and police dispatcher, veteran of World War II, absolutely mad. Was this the democracy she had fought for in the Women's Army Corps? Was this why she had lost her left leg below the knee? More than once she'd misconnected parties only to have the conversations flow smoothly into one another without a pause for subject-verb agreement.

Hattie Bohannon

In the blue light of the dawn, Hattie Bohannon held her hand out to feel the air. She stood in shadow on her porch and leaned over the rail, testing the darkness. In it she smelled heat, the tips of summer's fingers creeping into the valley. From now on, whatever drifted into Maridoches would wallow there until football season began.

Hattie licked her lips. It would be her truck stop's first summer. Fifty yards below her house it gleamed, an island of light in the Ruby River Valley. She had created a world bigger than the dark mountains outlined across the highway, a world as vast as the brightening sky. Seeds planted in distant soils, in arid climates and in cold ones, grew into vegetables and grains, were harvested, packed, and sent in cool trucks to her address, where they nourished thousands of customers, who, in her mind's eye, became a sea of different-colored bill caps bent over Coca-Colas. Mississippi catfish slinking along muddy river bottoms, Iowa beef grazing dumbly near corrugated steel sheds, Florida oranges fluorescent against their green foliage, crisp apples from Delaware, Kentucky raspberries so lusciously red she always wanted to plunge her hands into the containers. Her heart beat with awe at the world she had spun around her.

She tested the cup of coffee cooling on the rail. Mornings like this made her miss Oakley. The big sign over his former fields, Bohannon's, would have pleased him. But this was not his world anymore. She'd razed his tobacco barn to make room for the truck stop. The dark wood had heaved and groaned before collapsing into the sweetest-smelling lumber she'd ever known. She was glad he'd been in Walter Reed Hospital in Washington, D.C., the last four years, spared the upheaval of the interstate. But he'd always imagined coming back home. She sighed. A year after his death, his body was stuck in beaurocratic limbo. The good people at Walter Reed had lost his remains. She drained her coffee and went inside to rouse her daughters.

When she came out, dressed in her uniform, ready to lead her parade of girls to work, she saw a tractor trailer, sporting a logo of vegetables doing the can-can, park behind the truck stop. Hattie leapt off the porch and ran down the driveway past the bank of wild roses, scattering gravel, until her sneakers smacked the flat blacktop parking lot. As the truck's accordion back door squealed open, she picked up her pace. She flung herself across the delivery entrance. Her breath was hot.

A trucker in wide-hipped jeans backed toward her, balancing a box in his arms.

"Open that box," she said. A broom leaned against the wall, just out of reach.

He swung around and stepped toward her. Two drops of sweat peered, like the eyes of a field mouse, out of his mustache. She didn't recognize him — probably an independent, gotten cheap. His box of Florida Sun-Ripened Tomatoes rested in his arms just inches from her nose. Flattened against the closed door, she looked beyond him into the yawning trailer full of gassed vegetables. Once he got the box into the truck stop, she had to accept this delivery.

"Open it." A small crowd, witnesses, had come out of the restaurant. She pushed the box back at him.

He staggered. "Lady, I'm not going to unload every tomato by hand."

"Open the box."

The box slid down to the shimmering pavement. He ripped the cardboard and, with a grin, raised a pink tomato above his head. The crowd booed. He hitched his pants, paused, hitched them again, then strutted toward the loaded dolly.

"Don't unload another one of those things." Hattie picked up the broom and stepped into the lot. She tossed the firm tomato high above the truck, a pink ball brilliant against the blue sky. As it fell, she swung. A solid hit on the broom straw. The tomato careened off the shiny truck, barely missing the trucker's head, and landed in the parking lot.

Gee Sullivan, a regular customer who was half deaf, hollered, "It ain't even split."

"Hit another one, Hattie, to make sure," said Haw, Gee's twin.

She rested the broom against the wall and waved the customers away. "I got business to take care of." Not a bad swing for a forty-two-year-old, she thought. She yelled to the trucker, who shoved the box with his foot. "I won't buy shoddy produce. This is the third shipment in a row of substandard vegetables. Tell Mr. Ranford I wouldn't take them."

"I'll save him some trouble. This is the last delivery you'll see for a while," said the trucker.

Hattie turned on her heel and strode into her restaurant, where the steady sound of silverware and the intermittent flutter of napkins was all the applause she needed. The place was clean and comfortable. She conceded one small aisle to the right of the cashier for chips, candy, cigarettes, and cold drinks. A red arrow glued to the cash register directed customers down the long counter that swept into a curve, opening up a large room lined with padded booths and private phones, the preference of truckers and travelers. In the center of the room, beneath a shower of country songs, round tables spun with local romance.

The decor did not look like it belonged in a truck stop. Hattie refused the deer heads, stuffed fish, and presidents' portraits suggested by Kenny Ranford's salesman. She believed people wanted to eat in comfort without something dead looking at them. She painted the walls sky blue, chose dark blue seat covers, and placed seasonal flowers in thin juice glasses on the tables.

Weaving through the breakfast crowd, Hattie smiled as she recalled her interview with Kenny Ranford two years ago. He'd said, "You are doing this truck-stop thing because you have no other way to make a living. You are a desperate woman."

Desperate as Hank Aaron, she thought. Desperate as Babe Ruth. In her office, she opened the ledger to the savings account and felt a quick rush of pleasure. The balance always gave her a lift, not that she had extravagant plans for the profits she made. Only to send Heather, who was seven, to college when the time came. The other girls, Connie at sixteen, Darla, eighteen, and Jessamine, twenty-one, were too old to benefit from a savings plan. They thought she ought to get a new car. She had no use for a new car. True, Oakley's Jetstar 88 was an antique, having passed its twentieth birthday. But it was a large steel machine and it gave her a tremendous sense of security as she drove on the highway. Let those expensive toys cruise by but they'd better not hit her. The Jetstar would squash them flat. No, she'd tell her girls, I don't need a new car. This one is in prime condition. No sense replacing steel with fiberglass. Kenny Ranford wanted her to be a showy success. He'd cook up something like a gold Cadillac with a vanity plate proclaiming EATS.

She picked up the mail, half sorted. A pink envelope from North Carolina topped the stack. Inside was a matchbook. Printed in red and black letters, its cover read: FULL-COLOR PHOTOS OF BEAUTIFUL MODELS ON ADHESIVE-BACKED DECALS. Its small print said, *Apply to automobile dash or locker door or carry in wallet.* She unfolded the matchbook. A naked woman stretched diagonally across the yellow one-by-one inch square. Her glow-in-the-dark red mouth was open, her eyes shut, one hand on a bent knee, the other cupping her thigh underneath her very white buttocks. She was wearing short black heels. The photo was out of focus. Dixie Nudes, indeed.

Hattie threw it in the trash. She was amazed by the amount of creativity that went into the advertisement of condoms. Scented ones she could not fathom. If you had to scent the condom, you shouldn't be near the man who needed it. Naturally, Kenny Ranford had told her nothing about the disgusting machines that could junk up her rest rooms if she let them. Instead, he delighted in annoying her and began their conversations with his private secret of success. "I offer truck-stop franchises to single mothers. Divorced women. I do not mean the women with gold bracelets on their arms and booze on their breath. I mean women who fall into bed every night and sing hallelujah for the soft cushion of their pillows."

She thought of Kenny's saying on nights when she found the softness of the pillow too oppressively nonhuman. Then she'd get furious. If the Veterans Administration returned Oakley's body, she could forge a new social life. With, perhaps, the sheriff? She flushed. He was due at ten o'clock with his squad for breakfast.

"I am not desperate," she announced to herself. Adversity was an old defeated friend, and Hattie, who believed she operated best under duress, looked forward to beating the business odds in the same foolish perverse way she had looked forward to the labor and delivery of her first child.

Jessamine Bohannon

The red-orange soup puckered then popped loud kisses as I bent over the cauldron, a two-gallon can of kidney beans digging into my hip. If I hurried the simmer, I could add cayenne before Gert, the day cook, returned with the meat for her special spaghetti sauce. Even though I was the kitchen manager at the truck stop, she and I fought all the time over the recipes. Gert thought there were three food groups: sugar, salt, and oil. If I cooked up a vegetable, she slipped a slab of bacon into the pot. I preferred food to taste like itself.

I tipped the can and stirred. The beans settled like silt. Strips of jalapeños, seeds intact, and sliced red onions bobbed in the thickening stew. I picked up the pepper sauce and shook it into the pot. That would give truckers a wake-up call before they hit the road.

Gert said that's not our job. They got drugs for that.

She came back overloaded with packages of ground beef. Because she forced all her thick hair into a hair net, her nose gained prominence, arching forward like a dolphin diving into the spray. Her head looked unbalanced. Gert dumped the packages on the counter, then knifed each one before skinning off the plastic and cracking the Styrofoam backing. The meat hissed as it hit the hot griddle. I shuddered to imagine her with a fresh-shot deer.

When the ground beef turned from pink to brown, Gert took up her dicing knife and quartered a dozen garlic cloves. She scooted the shavings into a pile. "When is your mama going out with the sheriff?"

She liked to bring Mama into our arguments. It was her way of saying if I wasn't the owner's daughter, she'd be the manager and I'd be the cook. "Sheriff Dodd's a regular customer, that's all."

"She ought to be looking somewhere else for happiness," Gert said.

"She's not dating him, okay?" I scraped

the cauldron hard to drown out what she might say next.

"Your mother's been off her feed of late." Gert moved down the grill and poked the warming sausages with a giant prong.

I glanced at the clock. My heart picked up a beat. Soon Richard would arrive and I would go on break. I pictured him like he was the day we met, standing on the deck of a speedboat, the wind whipping around his tanned chest, the flecks of gray in his hair like the rifts of foam on the dark lake.

"It's hot as hell," said Gert, as she threw open the back door. Late spring's languor was starting to build on the blacktop.

A drop of sweat formed on my forehead and fell toward the chili. I lifted my head to brush it dry and saw Richard staring through the EMPLOYEES ONLY door. I blushed to my roots because I knew from his crooked grin that we were remembering another drop of sweat and how it came to be, he and I so close we shared it. I watched the drop spread on the edge of the pot and vanish.

Even without looking I knew his shirt was tucked crisply into his ironed khakis. He had a nice face, with just enough cheekbone to offset his blue eyes. He was forty-seven but still built, square shouldered, kind of shy in public like me. Our bodies talked best for us.

Gert peered down her arched nose at me. She knew the air had changed and she seemed to have got a whiff of why. She shook her head and went *harumpf* and muttered some evil little prayer, but I did not care because I knew what Richard and me did was absolutely right.

I tasted the chili and it was perfect, full-bodied and peppery.

Gert took off her apron and freed her thick dark hair from the hair net. Swaths of flesh fell from her shoulders and gathered neatly like balloon drapes above her hard round elbows. The rest of her looked solid, shoulders and legs muscled for action. "I'm going to ask your mother to come to church with me."

She was gone before I could answer. Richard said Gert's church, the Church of the Holy Resurrection, was like the kudzu weed overrunning the South. His wife attended services there daily. Mama would never brighten their door. Richard's clean plate came in on Connie's tray, the circle of crab apple placed dead center, like a bull's eye.

It was cool and dark in the storeroom. I lingered in Mama's recliner, soft gold, worn corduroy. It reminded me of the rows of corn across the valley in the fall, burnished and even. I leaned back, cradled by the soft cloth, and smiled. It was all I could do. My clothes were here and there and Richard had left me glowing again.

He had held my breasts as if they were precious and fragile, then caressed them with his mouth as if they provided succulent necessary nourishment. He did this before and after and during.

The chair felt to me like the hand of God. I was held in His great palm, the golden light of His approval washing over us as we made love. There was nothing else that feeling could be but holy.

Richard had left me a bag of chocolate kisses and I ate them one by one, letting each pyramid melt to a small spoonful of sweetness before sliding down my throat. I was insatiable for chocolate after we were together. I traded with him. He gave me silver-coated kisses and I gave him quarters for his trips to Mississippi, where he played the slots.

The door banged open and in came the cart of cleaning supplies, buckets rattling and rags swishing, followed by Gert's heavy footsteps. I held my breath and hoped she'd leave the cart and go back to the kitchen.

She huffed loudly, paused to look back down the hall, then pushed the rear of the cart into the room. She skirted it, cursing as her hip hit the Lysol dispenser, which sent out an antiseptic spray. Off balance, her behind swished around aimed at my chair. I shouted, "Holy Moses!"

She dropped a cigarette pack and gasped, covered her mouth, and crossed herself like Catholics do. Then she lunged toward the light switch and turned it on.

"Thanks, I needed that." I crossed my legs.

Her face was dark red and she collapsed into a swivel chair that bucked like an unwilling horse. I dared not move.

We sat a minute or two staring, me getting paler and more naked than I'd ever been while her face shifted through all the shades of the color spectrum. When we discovered neither was going to yell again, we relaxed, breathing in tandem. Gert picked up the pack of Marlboros she dropped. "Could you reach me them matches?"

They had fallen underneath my chair,

too far back for her to reach without some major contortions of the flesh. Her knees loomed like white boulders. She ought to be required to wear pants. I tucked my feet under my butt and posed my hands as if they were fig leaves. "Could you wait to have a smoke until after I leave?"

Gert tapped the cigarette on her knee. It bounced up and down as she sucked her cheeks between her teeth and began to chew them. She was addicted. I would have to move first, before Mama came down the hall wondering where the kitchen staff was. Our restaurant was smoke-free, no smoking allowed. None. Mama was willing to lose a customer here or there to keep her restaurant clean. My father had smoked all his life and it had killed him, so she was zero tolerance on cigarettes. Gert knew her job was in danger.

My lavender bikinis dangled from the knob on the closet door. A sigh heavy as an old woman's came from my lips. Would Gert tell on me?

I reached over and palmed the underwear. As I inched them up my thighs, they rolled into a stretchy string. I flushed. My movements were obscene, as if Richard were still there while Gert occupied a ringside seat.

I tossed her the matches. She lit up, inhaled, and blew the letters of her name in smoke at the ceiling, a hazy E dissolving on the too-bright bulb.

I smoothed out my underwear, taking time to line up the small triangles in the front and back before skittering over to Gert's chair and snatching the bra from its leg. I fumbled with the bra's front hooks. Richard preferred that kind. None of his passion put on hold while he clawed at fasteners he couldn't see.

"Pretty titties," Gert said.

I blushed and retrieved my uniform.

"Cigarette?"

I shook my head, then said, "Sure." I'd smoked until Richard complained about my breath.

"You know, girlie, you're going to hell in a handbag." Now that Gert had had her fix, she puffed up, lording the situation over me, her usual grand toady self.

"That's my business."

"You're screwing a married man. You're twenty —"

"I'm twenty-one."

"You done had a baby."

"I did not. I did not have a baby." No one, not even my friends, had ever guessed the truth about Heather. I inhaled, my fingers shaking. The smoke came back up through my nose.

Gert took a long slow draw, her eyes shutting as she relished the pleasure of nicotine hitting her cranium. I thought of dinosaurs, grand in body, tiny of brain, settling for so little.

Gert smiled. "You think I don't see them stretch marks on your titties?"

The overhead bulb was unbearably bright, highlighting in pale purple the faded darts along my breasts, indelible reminders I'd take to my grave of a pregnancy I had to forget. In private I sometimes looked at them because they were proof that I had borne a child. Deep down, my body remembered the stretch, the way my hips opened, the pain of milk not drunk. Wasn't skin supposed to replace itself every seven years?

No one else had noticed. Not Richard. Maybe only women would know. I finger-combed my hair. "At least I won't end up working as a go-go dancer."

Gert laughed. "No, but you could end up with a can of Lysol as your best friend."

The phone rang, the sound I'd been waiting for. Richard's call that came after he got back to work. I lifted the receiver after the fourth ring, wishing Gert was

27

gone so I could tell him about my bizarre experience with her, when he blurted, "I'm getting a divorce," and hung up the phone.

Gert saw my face, its sudden dark tinge, and walked out. My break was long over but I couldn't go back to the heat of the kitchen. I picked up the bag of chocolates and ate five or six kisses, chewing and swallowing without tasting. I wanted to go to Richard and say, Don't get a divorce. Think of us. We are fine. I'd almost told him the truth about Heather, but keeping secrets from my secret lover added a sweetness that was almost unbearable.

I folded the pants of the blue uniform, then the pebbly top, and dropped them into the laundry basket. In the closet, I found my white blouse and khaki shorts. If Richard got a divorce, his wife would reign as pity queen until the next man threw away his worn-out wedding vows. Everyone would know about us. And what about us? Was there any kind of future for Richard and me?

I went outside to finish the chocolate. Heather was jumping rope on the blacktop. She'd tied one end to the door handle of a patrol car and had a trucker turning the other. Soon I was turning the rope and she was chanting, "My mother and your

28

mother hanging out clothes/My mother punched your mother right in the nose," her blond hair flipping up and down at the ends. My little lie had gained fifty pounds.

My virginity vanished quickly, not in a progression of stumbling steps but suddenly one night, at the river, with a boy I barely knew. It was the last weekend before ninth grade. Already the water had started to cool but Darryl, my cousin, dared everybody, even us girls, to go skinny-dipping. Darryl stood on top of the big rock, silhouetted against the red sky, and hollered like Tarzan, beating his chest and making his other parts shake. Right then a boy I did not know slipped a Styrofoam cup into my hand and wrapped his fingers around mine. I smiled and he smiled back. We gave each other sips of peach brandy, our hands twined around the warm cup. Soon I was giggling. When the brandy was drunk, the boy pulled his white T-shirt over his head, then stepped out of his jeans. Without a word he walked up to the big rock and dived. Minutes passed, it seemed, before I heard his splash.

Behind a thicket of junipers, the other girls giggled as they stripped. I picked up the boy's clothes. His shirt held the faint smell of tobacco. I undressed, crossed the small beach, and walked straight into the water, as if nudity was my common appearance. The other girls followed, running, laughing loudly. The boys hooted.

My skin tingled as water crept up my thighs and on up over my shoulders. The others were swimming further out, where several rock islands formed a cove. I parted the water with my hands and let the ripples break coolly on my breasts, frog-kicking shivers all the way to my toes.

On the far bank, fireflies blinked like a thousand tiny lighthouses, fluid and various, a thousand destinations. The boy appeared silently from underwater, the sudden gleam of his limbs beneath the surface a shock. I treaded water. He swam on. His arms, white in the moonlight, rose up and beckoned with each arc of the crawl. I soon matched his strokes and we crossed the current, heading for the rocks. I veered toward a willow. The long wet leaves brushed over me like fingers as I glided toward the trunk. Overhead, the branches rocked in soft rhythm, a murmur of river and cove. The boy slid close. His warmth surprised me but my skin welcomed it. He kissed me and I kissed him while my whole body shivered from the cold, the warmth, the water, the night air.

Heather is my baby. I feel she is only mine. The boy faded distantly until I couldn't remember the color of his hair, the slant of his shoulders, if he was tall or smart or fun or cute. I couldn't see him in her at all as she tired of jumping and raced into the truck stop for a drink. I left the rope dangling from the sheriff's door and picked up my bag of chocolate.

Even Darla and Connie don't know that Heather is mine. That was the first lie, or the beginning of it. I ate another kiss. One lie led to another. It was an addiction, perhaps as great as that to cigarettes, just as deadly, accumulating like tar in the lungs. Soon breathing would be impossible. Soon speaking would be impossible. I'd suffocate myself with my own lies, my mouth clogged with fabrication. My body could function and I'd smile, plastic as a TV actress, desirable, of course, because of what I presented. But I'd know I was dead.

I passed the cash register in the dining room and snuck breath mints from the candy shelf. Heather and Mama shared a booth with Sheriff Dodd. A bowl of chili and a half-drunk sweet tea sat in front of each of them. Mama's spoon was coated with the greasy red residue but Sheriff

Dodd's was licked clean.

Mama laughed, at some stupid joke no doubt, the lines around her eyes transformed into good-humored crinkles. She had naturally curly brown hair and smooth skin that she maintained with Dove soap and lots of cold cream. She liked clear nail polish, nothing tacky, and had this air of aboveness, like she was running the truck stop out of the goodness of her heart, not economic necessity. The truckers said "Ma'am" when Mama walked by and put their napkins in their laps and never ever made any lewd suggestions to her. I should be so lucky. Heather lounged on Mama, a wet Sugar Daddy in one hand.

Sheriff Dodd's cropped hair slowly came to attention on his pinky clean scalp. His cap hung on the corner of the table, above Mama's knee. "That's a mighty big girl to be sitting on her mama's lap," he said.

"She's my baby. When she's fifty years old, she'll still be my baby and she can still sit on my lap," Mama said.

Heather smacked her lips.

"I wasn't allowed to eat candy before supper," I said, feeling the dig though Mama didn't mean it. That's what got me angry. Once Mama took over Heather, she didn't seem to think I had any feelings for the baby. It was like giving birth was an anonymous act. "You must be getting soft in your old age."

"You need glasses, honey," Sheriff Dodd said. "That's one firm woman."

A faint blush appeared on Mama's face, as if she and Sheriff Dodd shared a common cord.

I couldn't believe it.

I stood above her brown, softly waved perfection of curls and aimed nasty thoughts at them, snarls to catch her comb on. She slid Heather off her lap and turned toward me, giving him a better profile. He reached toward her chili with his spoon and said, "May I?"

She nodded as he dug in, with the manners of a cur.

I had to get out of there.

If I could get quarters, I would take them to Richard, and we'd talk about our future. Having something to offer seemed necessary. We were in new territory now, him and me. The truth would spread like wildfire and torch this place Mama had built. Unless I stopped it now. "Mama, I need ten dollars for the rest of the day."

"It'll come out of your salary."

"I know." I resisted saying, What salary?

"Take a ten and mark it down in the ledger."

"Can't I have quarters?"

"We're low on quarters in the register." Mama's voice was so even, I couldn't help but be impressed. But her cheeks rose and deepened past a pleasant blush. Her eyes were blue flint. "Ten dollars is ten dollars."

"Don't be a grump," said Heather.

I went to Mama's office, knowing she'd be out front with Sheriff Dodd long enough for her skin to fade to a more pristine shade. I used the tiny key to click open the cash drawer, took out a roll of quarters and put in the ten. I had to have them. They were my reason to call Richard, which I never had done before. We had to talk. To protect us from the people we feared so much, our customers and friends in Maridoches. The quarters fit into the valley between my breasts.

Richard was not taking any calls, I was told when I phoned Logan's Yard, which meant he was probably at home. I headed out toward his house but my stomach got queasy, too much chocolate rush. So I cruised off the highway and headed up an old road and thought about glasses of milk. Soon I passed brick houses with mowed yards and old tires planted with marigolds. I drove higher and higher up a mountain that began in Georgia clay and rose over the state line, combs of southern pines spiking its soil.

A vaguely familiar scent drifted in the window, the smoky scent of damp wood and pine needles untouched by the sun. It was the same thick air that had surrounded me in the days after Heather's birth. Mama had arranged for me to wait out my pregnancy with Aunt Leola up on Sand Mountain. That year, Daddy was in and out of the Birmingham hospital, so he did not see my shame, but he wrote me funny notes about his confinement. Mama ate herself fat to convince everyone at home that she was pregnant.

My birthing screams were partly anger, partly pain, but they marked the end of my bliss. Mama made me walk every day, even those first days when walking and sitting were so painful. She made me walk until we flattened a path through the broom sedge to a granite slab jutting over the valley. Then she made me sit flat on the warm rock for fifteen minutes morning and night.

"Help you heal," Mama said, as she nursed my baby.

It is seven years and I am not healed. Shame hovers around our front door, threatening to come in and break up our house, if I dare say what is in my heart. When I see my little girl hugging Mama tight and hear her, every night across the hall, praying to keep Mama safe, my stomach churns like a washing machine. She is pretty and has hazel eyes. Her light hair is like mine. I am so close but I can never hold her like I want to.

Eventually the afternoon heat reached the pines and filled the car. I had to do something. I knew what lying felt like, invisible ankle cuffs weighing me down. But telling the truth would be freedom to own my life. Mama was wrong to lie about Heather. I would tell the truth about Richard and me. Then watch me fly! It was strange to think what I needed really mattered. I mashed that pedal to the floor before I could chicken out and start to consider everyone else first, as Mama had taught me to do.

Richard's house squatted on a shallow plateau in the middle of a steep hill. Fresh yellow paint around the door reflected, like flames, two geraniums placed below the slim windows. I remembered a dab of paint on Richard's neck, a yellow spot at the base of his skull after he'd tossed me the chocolate kisses, just before he stepped into the hall.

I rapped hard on the door, wondering why it was closed in the heat. I didn't hear an air conditioner. It was too quiet on the steep hill, in the clipped yard. Nothing moved. I swung my purse against my thigh to hear my keys jingle.

"Come in," a woman called. Richard's wife. I didn't think she'd be here. Before I could run, she opened the door.

I stepped through the doorway into the dark living room. Gradually I noticed the floor-length drapes drawn closed, the sand-colored carpet, two stuffed chairs upholstered in cool violet chintz, the sofa print, geometric birds in chocolate, violet, and teal. It was a desert effect, the desert at night. I shivered. The woman held some mending, a thread between her front teeth, her eyes looking up under shy, lined brows.

She tied a knot and deftly snapped the thread. "May I help you?" she said, with the brittle veneer that passes for politeness to strangers.

We were the same height but Mrs. Reynolds's coloring was brown, a surprise. I expected a pale, puny woman. I spied the beauty mark Richard had mentioned, a dark mole on her cheek, framed by a stiff curl. Her other moles were hidden in lingerie. "I'm Jessamine Bohannon and I've come for Richard."

Mrs. Reynolds's face froze. Her mud-colored lips blanched. She stretched her mouth wide several times and coughed. "Oh, do you work with him? In accounts? Purchasing? You're from Logan's Yard?"

Mrs. Reynolds's voice did not change pitch, her face stiffened. She knew. That kept me planted firmly in the heavy carpet. Richard had always assured me that no one, especially his wife, knew about us.

"It's not my fault," I said, and, realizing my sentence lay there like a lit match, added, "your divorce."

Mrs. Reynolds closed her eyes. Her chest heaved but her mouth stayed firmly clenched.

On my right was a china cabinet full of religious figurines. Porcelain scrolls offered scripture lessons in fine-lettered gold.

"Taking inventory?"

I turned back to find myself pinned by Mrs. Reynolds's eyes.

"Deciding what you want when I'm gone and you live here?"

"No," I said. "I don't want your things."

"No. Merely my husband." Mrs. Reynolds paused. A short whistling came out of her nose. "I suppose I should give you a tour. Please come to the kitchen." She gripped my elbow with strong fingers and guided me into the next room. "The oven" — she banged open the door — "cooks twenty-five degrees higher than its setting. I asked Richard to fix it but he never did. *You* should have no problem getting him to do what you want." She opened all the blond cabinet doors, letting them swing into each other, showing every box and bag wrapped in plastic and secured with a twist tie at the top. "It's cockroach free. The chill keeps the vermin away." She slammed back a wooden lid. "And here you'll store the potatoes. And here." She dumped a bucket of garbage down a chute.

"Mrs. Reynolds, Mrs. Reynolds, please. Richard hasn't asked me to marry him." I shrugged my arm loose and did not add *yet* because she was already in a frenzy.

"Live in sin then as you already have been!"

"Mrs. Reynolds, he's just leaving right now. That's all," I said, and realized that was the kernel of it all. He'd promised me nothing.

"Oh, no, you don't, you little bitch." Mrs. Reynolds's mouth stopped as if to taste a new forbidden flavor. "Bitch!" she screamed. "Bitch!"

She lunged forward and ripped my blouse open. Her hands so adept at knots were equally skilled at ripping, knowing a garment's structural weaknesses. In a single yank, my bra was unhooked. "Look at them! Look at them! Perfect! That's what he wants!"

Mrs. Reynolds tore open her blouse and unsnapped her bra. "Look at mine!"

I backed to the door and ducked my head. "No," I said.

"Look!"

Mrs. Reynolds had only one breast. Where the other had been, a ridge ran, raised and pink against her brown skin.

I covered my bosom with my arms. The swift memory of Richard's obsession with my breasts made me gag. I leaned into the refrigerator with my eyes closed, hoping the coolness would keep me from getting sick. My knees gave way and I sank to the hard floor.

"Too ugly for you, my dear?" Mrs. Reynolds stepped closer.

I saw Richard in my mind. His chest sagged, and he was brown and wrinkled on his torso but he'd never been ugly before. Tits, that's what I was to him. A pair of tits. "I have to leave."

"Oh, no," said Mrs. Reynolds. "It's too soon." She shook out her hair, took off her blouse and folded it into a square, then took off her bra and hung it on a cabinet door. Her breaths gradually became silent. "Well. You can't leave looking like that." Lightly touching my arm, she helped me stand up, then led me to a closet and took out a navy cardigan. She held it open for me and I forced my arms through the sleeves. Inside the big sweater, I shrank. I was a puppet being pulled along by Mrs. Reynolds.

"You must have some tea. It's already made." Before I could escape, Mrs. Reynolds said, "I insist."

I sank into the sofa while Mrs. Reynolds poured iced tea. The cubes were large and square and had sat in the glass unmelting for as long as I had been there. The tea was the kind Mama served at the truck stop, sweet and sticky.

"When is your wedding day?" Mrs. Reynolds said.

Her words poked my bruised heart. Richard never intended anything but sex, but for me it was holy. My fingers numbed

41

around the glass. I hated her suddenly, this strange ugly woman. I wanted to leave but she had me cornered with her one brown breast staring like an accusing eye. "There isn't one."

"So he's plain leaving me." Mrs. Reynolds sipped her tea. A change passed over her eyes. The iris and pupil blended into one dark hole that gave off only the impression of energy. There was no spark of intelligence, no hint of expression behind it. She set her mouth in a line that could have been called a smile if it wasn't for the paralysis of her eyes. She opened her sewing box and took out a pair of large new shears. The blades, ten inches long, shone too brightly to have ever been used on the thick material they were designed for. Mrs. Reynolds slowly rubbed each blade with a scrap of corduroy.

"You know," she said. "Richard gave these to me at Christmas." She opened and shut them. Then, as if fascinated by the shirring sound, she clapped the handles faster and faster. Holding the flashing shears above her head, she stepped toward me.

I slipped the quarter roll out of my purse and wrapped my fingers around it. I climbed over the couch and scooted backwards toward the front door, bumping the china cabinet and rattling the contents.

"Are you afraid of me?" Mrs. Reynolds gave a short spurt of a laugh.

I slammed the front door. At the end of the driveway I stopped the car, stripped off the sweater, and threw it in the ditch. My burning fingers fumbled to button the one button remaining on my blouse.

Mrs. Reynolds moved from window to window, shearing the drapes in half. The sashes fell first; the heavy fabric curled slowly toward the floor; the half curtain swayed uncertainly.

I sped up and down the hills and caught sight of Richard's red Oldsmobile rolling toward home like a marble in a trough. I pulled over behind a rotten barn and watched him drive by. He was singing; an arrangement of daffodils and glads was propped up in the passenger seat.

The car dipped out of sight. I imagined Mrs. Reynolds with her scissors tearing into Richard, slamming his head with the flat of the blades, jabbing him, until he felt like I did.

Richard Reynolds

Richard Reynolds touched the yellow paint on the door frame. It was dry. He gathered the daffodils and glads from the steps where Ann had thrown them. Squatting on the porch, he could see, beneath the clipped drapes, the strange shapes of his living room furniture revealed like internal organs normally covered by skin.

An unpleasant odor rose from the limp flowers. He squeezed the stalks. A gummy residue oozed between his fingers. He switched hands and squeezed again. The sky was cloudless and deep. Huddled in the sliver of shade that cut across the steps, he held out his hand and felt the immediate burn of the sun. His car shimmered red, a mirage of escape. Sighing, he pushed open the front door. From upstairs came Ann's crying.

He blinked. The living room was hard on his eyes, the lower regions bright, the upper dark as if a cloud covered the ceiling. He opened the slashed drapes. Sunlight streamed in. He slipped quietly across the carpet.

All the kitchen cabinet doors were open. It was easy to locate a glass vase. He filled

44

it with water and carried it out to the living room and set it on the table. Light caught in the glass. The flaming red glads and yellow trumpets arched out of the vase like sparklers.

Richard sank onto the sofa and marveled at the southwestern look of the room. Aqua and purple and muted orange, sand, prints of stylized birds, all angles. He'd never paid much attention before but he saw the room now. It was not a room that belonged in Maridoches, yet it was what Ann had chosen. Now he saw it needed light to be beautiful. But she had not wanted the sun to fade the fabrics.

Ann's sobs continued steady as rain. How could he ever face her or anyone again? He hated his smallness — he had no idea what to do. Fixing food didn't seem right. He couldn't turn on the TV. Talk to Ann? He'd wait and let her come to him.

He hoped she'd look at him and simply listen. He wanted to tell her the truth — to reveal himself as it had been with Jessamine, how scared he'd been that Ann would die from breast cancer and he'd be lost, alone at his age, and how there was Jessamine who made him feel young and untouchable. He recognized how cowardly he'd been, how in his forty-seven years he'd never faced such a difficult thing as Ann's illness, had never felt so impotent because he could not cure her, could only bring her food she didn't want or pace uselessly in his office the days they waited the results of the biopsy, the radiation, the prognosis. He wanted to tell her how blamed he felt when she undressed in the bathroom, and how admonished by the bra she always wore under her nightgowns. He was ashamed of how he had fled her illness, how weak his faith had been.

He wished she'd look at him calmly and let him say those things, let him be the struggling boy he felt he was. Oh, if there is a God, then there can be this intimacy between married people — for if not, why are we bound together?

His chest shook. His hands trembled. To ask and be forgiven, that is all he desired.

When Ann came down it was early morning. He heard her bang into the wall at the bottom of the stairs, then run water for coffee.

Richard was stiff. At some point the air conditioner had clicked on, and he felt beneath the sharp-feathered birds that he was sleeping in the desert. He ached all over for having slept huddled up, hugging himself.

46

Ann appeared, ghastly in the morning light. Her brown hair was mashed against her head. She'd slept with her makeup on. Her eyes looked like large puffed bruises. She carried a cup of coffee. Only one.

He sat up.

She lowered herself into an armchair. "Your acts are reprehensible."

Richard nodded.

"Take those flowers out of my house."

Richard picked up the vase and walked through the kitchen past the coffeepot, which was empty and burning. He turned it off. He opened the back door, lifted the lid of the garbage can on the porch, and threw the vase into it. It shattered. He smiled.

He went back into the kitchen and made himself coffee, six cups. He waited for the pot to fill, then selected their largest mug, an orange bowl with a smooth handle. He found a pint of whipping cream, took out the mixer, and beat the cream to a froth. He shaved chocolate from a Dobler bar Ann kept in the freezer — for eons, it seemed. It was always there, that whole chocolate bar. Into the mug he poured a shot of bourbon, the coffee, the whipped cream, and sprinkled on the chocolate shavings.

He carried his creation back to the couch and sat down. "Done," he said.

"Richard, I want you to confess."

Richard started. Could his prayers be answered? "I'll tell you all of it, Ann."

"I do not want to hear all of it. I have seen enough."

Richard drew in a mouthful of coffee and licked the whipped cream off his upper lip.

"I do wish you would at least pretend to be grown up," Ann said. "I have seen her beautiful breasts."

Richard felt a stab in his stomach and tried to wipe out the image of Jessamine's breasts covered with whipped cream, the nipples peeking through like cherries on top.

He'd never felt worse in his life. *I'm sorry*, the truest words he could ever speak, stuck in his throat the way *I love you* had for so many years. The words ached to be said but they grew and choked him. I am so sorry, I am so sorry.

Ann's face was set. How could he make her smile? She would never forget. Was this the face he'd see every breakfast and dinner for the rest of his life, this face of pain hardened to disgust? He drank more coffee, appreciated the bourbon bite.

"I want you to confess in church," Ann said. "In front of God and the congregation so your soul will be cleansed."

Richard felt light enter him and yet he shrank from it. Confession to God would clear his conscience, but he was frightened. He imagined the shocked faces of the others in the pews, their wagging tongues, Ann's embarrassment, his own shame. A church confession would not draw the two of them closer; it would not open the door to the closeness of their souls as he wished, had once hoped that that was what marriage meant. He blurted, "But I want to confess to you."

"You must confess to God in God's house. Then I can forgive you too."

He saw she needed that religious force to get her through this, just as she'd needed that faith to help her through the cancer. But his soul, twisting in his gut, still cried out for the hope of intimacy. He gulped the coffee, let it burn, burn all the way down. He looked around at his absurd living room, imitation desert, yet the sand so gritty he felt it on his lips. "I'll do it for you, Ann."

Reverend Martin Peterson

Reverend Martin Peterson and his wife, Stelle, lived in a modern home on Lake Cherokee. One plate-glass wall two stories high faced the lake. In the living room was a fireplace of stone; on the walls, Stelle's paintings of apples and pomegranates and Old Testament women in shades of blue. Often, after a heated church service, Stelle retreated to the living room, blasted it with fluorescent rays, and took up her brush. Martin, damp as a dishrag, would go upstairs to the bedroom and stuff towels along the bottom of the door to block out Stelle's light.

They had a deck off the plate-glass wall where Martin wished she'd paint but she said the trees, which he admired for their height and the restful sound of pattering leaves, broke the light and made her palette muddy. They also had a dock and a dock house, which he imagined would make a nice studio for her, a place to store her smelly oils and turpentine. But the dock rocked with waves from motorboats. Motion was the problem there, not light.

Martin never went to the dock. He could not swim. He was fine in the baptismal pool. It was only waist deep. But the lake was vast, dark, and bottomless.

He liked to sit on the upstairs balcony outside the bedroom among the treetops. He watched birds and squirrels and listened to the oaks and enjoyed the scents that swept across him. He wrote his sermons there. Often he was amazed at how inflammatory his words became when he preached, considering the peaceful circumstance of their conception. Repetition, tone, and pitch could change an innocuous phrase into a violent one. Whispering, which he learned from the pines, was a good sound for lulling the crowd, but too much of it, seven minutes to be exact, and the congregation grew impatient. Invariably someone burst out in tongues. So he'd learned to coax the spirit by speaking softly, with a continuous modulation — and then like the shrill cry of a bird caught in a cat's grip, a voice from the congregation would shout out in inspired sound.

That was a different music, brasher, to hear; speaking in tongues. The speaker impassioned, the syllables unknown, the phrasing and cadence suggesting a grammar, a language. The congregation listened reverently. The translation would come at times through Martin, vessel of God's Word. The messages were as new to him as to the congregation. Sometimes Stelle would translate. Her interpretations applauded creativity, expression, and nurture. Occasionally something doctrinal would creep in as an afterthought. He was grateful for her interpretations though he didn't listen carefully when she spoke. He watched.

Stelle had long thick black hair with a skunk's streak running from her forehead to the middle of her back. Her face was bony and tanned. Perhaps there was some Cherokee in her family line. She was tall and slim and not particularly feminine. He liked her strength and assumed they were to be together always — their passion put into their ministry.

But this night, Tuesday, he fretted as he lay in their dark bedroom and watched the pines. Beside him Stelle slept. She wore Egyptian cotton pants and a red T-shirt and rested flat on her back, arms crossed across her chest as if for burial. Most of their marriage she'd slept in the nude.

He sighed. Nothing was automatic for Stelle anymore, not since she'd been to a folk art sale and bought small paintings of snakes and black angels and seen in them a new way of looking at God. Something as simple as making tea seemed to require her avid concentration. The choice was more than boiling water and pouring it over a bag of orange pekoe. Now she paused to listen to the kettle's whistle or to the rumbling of the preboil as if there were some mystic message in the utterance of steam. She breathed in the aroma of the new tea and tossed sticks of cinnamon or sassafras or rosemary into the cup.

Martin had learned to sieve his tea. Otherwise he'd have to fish out the debris and litter his saucer before sipping.

The leavings Stelle would study. He was relieved she never asked if he could read them. What would they portend, this pattern of flat flecks and sticks?

The demise of their marriage?

It had already fallen someplace dark beyond his grasp. If he pushed the tea remnants around they would not cling or reform. He did not believe in signs. He believed in God.

Or so he had before Stelle had moved into a new zone, painting, or standing up in church, her eyes glazed, her mouth silent, the hush of the congregation expectant, then pregnant, then stillborn as no sounds came forth from her mouth, no speaking in tongues.

He prayed but found only silence, and

then his mind would wander.

It always went to the dark tunnel of Hell. Faster these days, automatically, as soon as he said, "Dear Father." After these words, darkness, and then he'd burst into a heat so southern his insides burned. Sweat popped out on his forehead as he disconnected from his body and tasted cinnamon on his lips, on the lips of a woman full of flesh, ample, wide, pressed up against him, hot Hell, and then he'd go blank in his mind, and worse. When it was over, his hands, long unclasped from prayer, unclean.

And worse, the worst sin: he did not feel guilt.

In rational moments, on days he made his own tea and the leaves were clamped inside a tea ball, he'd wonder who that demon self was. On days when Stelle was back to normal, visiting parishioners, keeping the church books, he'd sigh and try, "Dear Father," and pure true words would flow uninterrupted. Grace was granted him on those days.

He plumped his pillow and closed his eyes. In his mind he saw a sky of heavy clouds with sun streaming down from Heaven. Gert Geurin nude in a field of snow. Screeech! The barn owl — thank God.

Martin shuddered, thinking where his dream might have gone.

Stelle did not stir but her eyes were open in sleep, dark brown spoonfuls of medicine.

A sudden rage locked his jaw, and his breath shot loudly in and out of his nose. He lay tense. He did not touch her. I am a man of God but I am a man, he thought. He braced his hands against the bed. "Dear Father," he whispered, and waited for the rush to the tunnel.

But it did not come. He gritted his teeth and went back to the heavy skies, soft lavender clouds with streaks of Heaven slanting down, a field of yellow hay stubble in the snow, and Gert Geurin, gray-haired and gargantuan, dancing nude. Her buttocks were so pink and broad he put his thumb in his mouth and bit it until it hurt. Her breasts swung to her navel, pink pendants tipped with heavy brown jewels. He imagined them swinging above his mouth. He felt her weight on him, making him sink and rise at the same time. Oh, to be smothered by such largesse!

Stelle sat up, straight as a board. "Who's here?"

"Me," Martin squeaked. "It's just me."

"No, there's someone else in here with us."

"Look, Stelle, look." He flicked on the light and turned toward her. "No one else, unless you mean —" He pointed with his palm toward his erection.

"I am losing my mind," said Stelle. Martin reached over and switched off the light. His penis stood like a hopeful prairie dog.

"I wish this wasn't happening," said Stelle, "this awareness of spirit. It's exhilarating but scary. I think I'm learning about Eve."

"Eve who?" said Martin.

"Eve in Genesis." Stelle drew the covers up. "She was very powerful. She told God where to get off."

"She told God to get off?" The rage returned to Martin's body. He was furious with her casual heresy. And mad at God, too. Mad that he was supposed to dictate doctrine when what he needed right now was to cleave. "I wish you'd help *me* get off," he shouted, loud, as if he was shouting at God and not Stelle, who was lying right next to him.

She stiffened. "Martin, you are so thick sometimes."

Martin rolled back to his side of the bed and made an odd sound. It sounded strange to him, not merely a sigh but a sigh infused with anger — a grunt. Disappointment became rejection and pain and then anger. How could Stelle be so in tune to his fantasies but so cold to his real touch? He prayed plainly and clearly for God's help. Stelle needed an intervention. Often a lost soul suffered mightily and publicly before being brought back to the fold. They'd never suffered a crisis of faith, he and Stelle. They'd been rock solid.

Gert Geurin

Jessamine had been stirring cayenne into the chili when I arrived at the truck stop kitchen the Tuesday morning that turned X-rated. Her blond hair hung like a suspended waterfall above the pot.

Because cigarette smoke was so fresh in my mouth, I said nothing until I'd donned my apron, affixed the hair net, and drunk half a cup of burnt coffee. "I hope you're not using hair for protein this time."

She ticked her head like a bird does until her hair righted itself. I fried up the eggs and hash browns, looked up from the grill, and caught sight of Richard Reynolds peering through the square window of the EMPLOYEES ONLY door. Blockhead, I

57

thought, seeing his face planed off like a square. He had a strange twist to his lips, as if he was starved for what we offered in the kitchen.

I glanced at Jessamine, about to make a joke about my fine cooking, but she was returning the starved look, and her surrounded by mounds of food.

I waved the spatula to cut the invisible cord between them. His face disappeared. Jessamine remembered to chop tomatoes.

"If he wants cooking lessons, he can pay extra," I said, "or he can ask his wife. This is not a peep show."

The deep blush of vanity spread across her face. Youth, I thought. This too will pass. I opened the back door and was met by the lazy swell of April. The air moved in, slow and thick. Summer's the most dangerous time of the year when it comes to desires of the flesh. Even if you are sitting still, the air rubs up and down your little hairs, like a cat in full purr. I stood upright in the doorway until the sheriff's patrol car passed by, leaving exhaust trapped in the heat.

I thought when I got this kitchen job that my duty was to help Miz Hattie Bohannon, a widow with four daughters, raise those girls right. That's how Reverend Peterson put it to me when he suggested I apply to be the day cook. But when the sheriff became a regular feature of the dining room, I sensed that Miz Bohannon herself needed surveillance. With summer coming, Miz Bohannon was moving toward the sheriff ignorant as a fish on a line. It thinks it's got the worm, all the sweet eating and a whole lake to swim in, but it's hooked. The sheriff was reeling her in and letting her out, making her think she wasn't caught. She needed a little spiritual shock treatment.

I found her at her desk, smiling at the ledger as if it was a mirror, raising an eyebrow, then letting it slide back into place. Then she lifted the other eyebrow. I cleared my throat.

"Miz Bohannon, on behalf of our Savior, I ask you to attend our revival service next Friday night."

Her eyebrows shot up like two mountain peaks. "Oh, Gert," she said, "I'm afraid I have a date Friday night."

"I see," I said, and walked into the dim hallway. *Afraid* was right. She'd chosen the wrong path. Her refusal left me gloomy. I'd failed Reverend Peterson. I went to have a cigarette in the storeroom when the Lord stood up and slapped me in the face with

Jessamine's problems.

There she sat in a gold chair. Naked. Spouting about holiness. I dropped my pack of Marlboros and for once I felt like total liquid, a mess about to flood the floor. I was grateful a rickety chair leaned against the wall. Sometimes you need the slightest support, a little touch to get you going in the right direction again. That swiveling chair swung me around to Jessamine, bare as when she was born but grown up, sitting there like in a trance, and then I recognized the smell: spent man.

This was sin but I went on and tapped out a cigarette and proceeded to go down the wayward path myself by asking her to fetch me the matches that had fallen under her chair, which she did, making sure I got an eyeful, as if she was something special. Once the smoke curled down my throat, I felt right again and yet I knew this was not right.

I offered her a cigarette and she took it and smoked it like a pro so I knew that this was a sign. One of us was here to redeem or corrupt the other. I waited and watched while she pranced around finding her undies flung in unlikely places. No shame at all.

"Your body is a temple," I said.

"Making love makes God happy," she said, flouncing into her clothes and tossing me a wicked smile as she left. I sat under its spell while I smoked three cigarettes.

I don't judge but sometimes I am God's mouthpiece.

Open up to the world your wholesome heart, is what I say. Close your legs. Clothe your behind. Your body is a temple.

I have built my body into a temple, solid and round like temples in the Holy Land. American churches are all steeple and points, nothing substantial. When I was a girl, one blew down all around me, though it was sturdy and over a hundred years old. I would not lose an ounce of me for anybody but God.

I smoke to keep from getting too big. I have to be an up-tempo temple, sharing the Lord's word and exposing the little lies that tarnish otherwise sacred lives.

Ann Reynolds is cursed with a fallow womb. But that does not mean her husband can spread his seed in the willing soil of a young girl's heart. I could see Jessamine was all heart about him. She said it's holy but there's no spirit in it if you aren't free to give your whole self.

It was a burden I did not want to take.

But I was shown knowledge, and when you are called forth by the Lord to tell the truth, you must. Because things happen for a reason. I puzzled on this reason for a while, thinking maybe I needed to quit smoking, and somehow one thing related to the other. But I do not like being a trumpet — a mouthpiece, yes, in small ways, but not one to blare a naked truth.

I started out in Arab, Alabama, so named because my mother's people, who settled the town, resembled Arabs. Maybe we are Indians, or Spaniards' bastards, the leftover trace of Hernando de Soto who passed through Alabama four hundred years ago, fighting Indians all the way. Tuscaloosa is named after a great Black Warrior who wasn't an African at all. So maybe we come from his stock. My skin is light, diluted by generations of mountain Christians, though I have a large curved nose that caused me lots of agony when I was a kid. One girl, Patty Jordan, my best friend anyway, was the only kid besides my sister Herma who didn't call me Honker.

Patty Jordan was pale with white hair and eyes touched with just enough blue to keep them from being white. She was thin, rickets probably, though she had clean new clothes and her father was the deacon of our church. In the sixth grade Patty and I were chosen to recite a Bible verse during Sunday service. Her father was displeased. Deacon Jordan didn't think it right a girl should speak in church. I mean, I could, but he didn't want his daughter to do anything unseemly, but he relented under pressure from our Sunday school teacher, Mrs. Killian.

We practiced our verses while I helped Patty execute her cheerleading routines. Even then, I was big and strong. I'd kneel and she'd step on my shoulders, our hands locked as I slowly rose, holding my breath until I was upright. She'd let go one hand at a time and balance until we were both standing straight up. Patty'd extend her arms, making us a human cross. We'd shout our verses as if they were cheers — *"For God/ so loved/ the world/ that He gave/ His* own/ *lee Son,"* — thrilled by any wobble that threatened to topple us. I'd lift my hands and she'd lower hers, grip, then dive head first into a flip, and I'd let go as she swung toward the ground.

The Sunday of our performance came, dimmed by October rain. Patty and I were dressed alike in white dresses and white tights. Her father had pinned a corsage to each of our bodices, mine a single pink rose that bobbed as I breathed. I could not look out at all those eager faces in the congregation. Instead I studied the poplar floor and Patty's pale blue satin shoes. Mine were my usual saddle shoes, scuffed with mud from the parking lot.

We sat in the choir loft, just us two. I kept saying my words over in my head and reading the program, marking off the events before we spoke: Call to Worship, Hymn Number 257, Prayer, Litany. We were to speak right before the collection plate went around. Rain beat hard against the stained-glass window behind me. The wind howled like a locomotive bearing down. The organist pumped up the volume. Deacon Jordan nodded toward us. Patty stepped forward, and as she opened her mouth the roof blew open. Patty, thin little stick in white tights and pale blue shoes, flew up from beside me and into the power of the prevailing winds.

I grabbed the sturdy loft bench, closed my eyes, and said loud as I could, over and over, *"This is the day the Lord has made, let us rejoice and be glad in it."* I could not hear my words through the storm of wind, the gusts strong and swirling as rapids gone airborne. I heard the splintering scream of the roof as it was ripped off, the cries of people as it crashed and the walls twisted away, the voice of the organ, violent and discordant, when wind rushed through the pipes in the wrong direction.

When it was over, I opened my eyes. I was still standing, still hugging the curved arm of the choir bench. The church was gone but for the wall behind me and the brass pipes of the organ, plinking now like common gutters. I kept saying the words over and over. Groans came from where the sanctuary had been. The walls had fallen in. The sky was black and heavy with clouds but a strange red line appeared in the west, a band of yellow-tipped clouds floating below the darkness fiery as living coals.

Twenty-seven people from our congregation died because of the tornado. My sister Herma survived but was crushed by a stained-glass window that broke her ribs and splintered across her body. She had to lie still, barely breathing, while the medics suctioned the tiny shards of colored glass off her body. They didn't want to cut her or press any slivers into her eyes. When the glass was removed, her body was green, blue, yellow, and red as if stained. She stayed in the hospital for weeks.

My mother had a broken leg. She said she could hear me through the storm, shouting over and over again, "This is the day the Lord has made, let us rejoice and be glad in it," and that sustained her because she could not fathom so ugly a thing as destroying a church full of worshipers. My father, who didn't often go to church, lost faith in his job, which was selling insurance. He saw that no amount of insurance money could compensate for disaster.

The sign to me was clear. God's words had saved my life. Them and my bulk. Patty had been reciting too, but she had not made her body substantial, and she had blown away like a mustard seed fallen on a rock. I had rooted and stood tough. I understood then how the body and spirit were related, how it took both to live a full life in God. So I set about making my body substantial and my spirit as well. I have been guided by God's words ever since and I understand my responsibility in this life. I am a mouthpiece. I was spared to share what is right, and so when I see a person living in error, I sigh and say, Yes, Lord, You have put her in my way and I understand it is my duty to set her right.

So I sighed when I caught Jessamine in

the room with the smell of spent man. I'd seen the way Ann Reynolds's husband had spied on her through the kitchen door that morning, so I knew it was him.

I tried to get out of it. Jessamine held my job in her hands. There aren't many places to work in the county, none at the eye of the storm as often as the truck stop. Reverend Peterson had put a lot of faith in me and I did not want to fail. So I said, Lord, instead, I'll give up smoking.

The first day it felt like a meat tenderizer was drilled into my skull. I could not work. I went to bed but the drill got sharper. I walked around my room, seeing nothing but the floor, then closing my eyes to ward off light. I smelled smoke in my clothes and sheets and curtains. I escaped but it was too hot outside. I vomited like a dog in the yard. Still the drill pounded. I went to the river and entered the water, in my clothes. I put my wet shirt up to my eyes. The drill drove deep and hot to a place in my head I could not touch. Under the shade of a willow, I cocked my head backwards and found mild relief, less pain. I held myself up there for a while, but soon my body was exhausted and I had to head home or drown. The sun was so bright I could not bear to look at anything but my flowered tennis shoes. I concentrated on small things, the eyelets the strings passed through, the strangely sharp way I saw each blade of grass, the clovers my feet would cross before I got sick again.

I exhausted myself trying to find a way to hold my head so the pain would subside enough for me to tolerate it, for it to ease so I could lie down and rest. I saw the hand of the Lord in my pain. I wanted to ask for help but knew I could not, since this was of my own making. That night the headache got so bad I wanted to die.

In the darkest hour of Friday morning, I got out of bed, got down on my knees, and said, "I accept my mission." I got back into bed and laid my head gingerly on the pillow but my mind raced as I thought of the pain I was about to cause Ann Reynolds, and I wondered how to tell her and not get Jessamine in trouble with her mother, and then I thought maybe I should tell Miz Bohannon, and then I remembered that Jessamine knew I smoked. Had smoked.

A lightness came through the buzz in my head. I hadn't had a smoke in three days. I still could not function. My hands shook too much for me to trust myself around the grill but I was getting over cigarettes;

the Lord was sending me a ray of hope, a blinding ray to let me know I was within reach of the kingdom. I just had to give up my bullheaded ways. So I lay still as I could and began relaxing each muscle starting with my toes and getting up to my neck before I fell into blessed sleep.

Friday afternoon I was back at work and everyone, except Jessamine, looked happy to see me. Miz Bohannon had dragged Darla in to help out, though she's not much for work in a kitchen. She did say, "Thank goodness you are here," before stripping off her apron and bolting out the back door.

Jessamine was edgy around me as always, contradictory — you know, one salt and two peppers when I'd do it the other way, but I was feeling better in my body. My breaths reached to the bottom of my lungs. I smelled broccoli! Astonished, I lifted the lid of the steamer and savored the aroma, green with a bit of iron. So that was broccoli. I opened the oven for a better whiff of biscuits and bent over the chocolate sheet cakes so long I almost swooned. Jessamine put her hands on her hips and asked if I was on medication.

Before I could answer, Miz Bohannon dropped in, dressed for her date. She had on a nice blue drop-waist jumper, nothing provocative, although her lipstick was a deeper red than I'd seen before. She might have done something to bring out her blue eyes because they were sparkling. Jessamine didn't say anything to her but I allowed as she looked nice. She smiled and went outside, where I heard the guffaw of the sheriff's pick-up truck as she climbed in.

I unboxed Rice Krispies to prepare for Saturday's breakfast and set them on the counter near the refrigerator. I checked the milk supply. "We're out of oatmeal," I said.

Jessamine shrugged. "It's too hot to eat oatmeal anyway. Come with me to the storeroom."

Guessing it was confession time, I prayed for the fortitude not to start speaking before she was done her piece.

"I've got something for you." She flung open the door and turned on the light.

On the gold chair lay two cartons of Marlboros, opened, the packs still stacked. The silver rectangles were wrapped in cellophane, shiny and magnetic. My brain did a little tick. My fingers touched my lips. A gush singed my windpipe. I walked toward the cartons and slipped into the rickety chair without making a squeak.

Jessamine was gone.

I sat as if in worship. I knelt and reached out for one pack. The crinkly paper rustled like a Christmas package and my mouth watered. I lifted the box to my nose and sniffed. Tobacco, rich and brown. All that stood between me and pleasure was a thin skin of cellophane, a wafer of cardboard — and a lack of matches.

I searched the storeroom, the cabinets, the closets. I went through all the waitresses' dirty uniforms, but found none. I went out to the dining room, searching for an ally. Instead I saw Reverend Peterson, so I retreated to the kitchen.

"Well," said Jessamine, jiggling silverware on the drying tray as if it were a haul of herring, "happy now?"

"I came for matches," I said. My voice was so frail I didn't recognize it.

She tossed me the big box of matches we keep on the windowsill for lighting birthday candles. They came at stomach level. I felt as if I'd caught a log in my gut. Jessamine began to burn with the power of lies; it looks white and healthy in the beginning but it heats too fast and too bright and cores you from the inside. I knew her soul was on my conscience.

I went back to the storeroom and sat a

long time, my mind in turmoil. I opened one pack and broke a cigarette and rubbed the brown crumbs on my fingers, then pressed them to my nose. This heavenly smell was the aroma of my descent into Hell. So delicious, the temptation.

I sat there a good hour in the fading light, breathing in agony, then just breathing, breathing in darkness. The sun's last rays caught the slick wrappings and made the chair glow as if in flame, smoldering, as Jessamine had when she'd sat there all high and mighty with adulterous sin. And then I understood her wish. She was giving me the chair as she had been in it. Lusting. But I knew better. This was my chance to show her the way.

The smell of the devil was there with me, crisp to the touch and papery. I breathed loudly against him, against sin. Tough and hard air rushed through my passages. I felt my lungs inflate and grow, become large beating wings, and then the smell was gone and words came to me.

Now my lungs are clear. Now I am in the light. Whatever befalls the Bohannons and the Reynoldses cannot touch me, for it is ordained.

I am in the light.

Relief broke like sweat in my heart.

I loaded the golden chair onto a flat

docket, pushed it into the parking lot, careful not to spill its precious cargo, held my breath as I dipped up a bucket of discarded cooking oil from the vat near the Dumpster, then poured that rancid slime over the Marlboros. I stood back a piece and tossed lit matches onto the chair. The oil ignited. Flames spread over the crackly curling cellophane. The boxes roared; then the cigarettes caught, but they were too few to send up a tobacco-scented cloud as I wished. I wanted to see the ghost of the tobacco devil shoot out of that chair. I wanted an angel to appear at my bonfire, something grand to acknowledge acceptance of my mission, someone I could thank for my new fresh breath.

Reverend Martin Peterson

On Friday, Reverend Martin Peterson stood in his living room in front of a canvas twelve feet high, speechless. Stelle applied red paint to the canvas with a cleaning brush as if trying to scrub through it. It was dinnertime and, as far as his nose could discern, nothing was cooking.

She said, "When I speak in tongues, I see visions."

"Visions of what?" he asked, regarding the zigzags of red and black and white from a distance.

"Visions of spiritual truth, like this," said Stelle, standing somewhat in awe of the gory thrusts of oil.

"I see," said Martin. This was not art but slashing with paint. "What's for supper?" he asked, hoping to move back to familiar territory.

"I haven't thought about it. I guess there's some leftover lettuce and peas." Stelle seemed to have slipped into one of her trances that brought forth strange syllables in church. When Stelle spoke in tongues, the language flowed like a cool stream through the congregation. Silence followed, a still harmony in the wake of beauty. Martin did not feel serenity in her paintings, though. They were angry and ugly and formless. She was talking of hanging them behind his pulpit, but that he would not allow.

He stood with the refrigerator door open and saw that the peas she'd mentioned were field peas, brown and mushy with dark eyes in their center, not green and sweet as he'd hoped. He'd already reconciled himself to fixing a salad, the leaves ruffly with red edges, a mountain of peas capped with creamy hollandaise.

Before she began painting, Stelle had loved to cook. Not only had the food surprised his tongue but the beautiful arrangements pleased his eye. There had always been something warm and bright — red beans or roasted red peppers or shaved yellow squash or darling sugar snap peas perfectly blanched. But Stelle never planned meals for him anymore. She barely talked to him except about the sermon and her paints. She did her minister's wife's duties without comment. In the past she'd fill him up with entire conversations she'd had with people in the church, all their foibles and motivations and needs. She was so empathetic. She could lay her finger on someone's heart. Yet she'd held her distance, too, so that their house was not overrun with parishioners. They felt administered to when Stelle listened and therefore did not bother him, as he was struggling through his sermon or analyzing the budget or corresponding with other ministers about the embarrassing sex scandals of some of their national leaders. She was then the perfect minister's wife in a state where people were busybodies and liked to visit.

With their sex life dwindling to nothing

and her forgetting to shop or cook, Martin did not know what to think. He was forty-six and, until last fall, a youthful-looking man. Age appeared suddenly, sagging the skin beneath his chin, dragging down the corners of his mouth. At breakfast one morning, Stelle had said, "So you look your age. Finally."

All his adult life, he'd been caught up in his career, practicing the delivery of God's words. He'd been a firebrand, solving problems, raising money, leading trips to disaster areas. In Alabama, where tornadoes rushed through twice a year, these became annual treks for the Church of the Holy Resurrection. Back then, Stelle had not denied him. She was still beautiful, still the woman of his choice, still the woman he loved. But every evening now he had to negotiate a blind maze and if he took one false step — then no sex.

"I do not want to eat cold field peas," he said glumly, loudly, but she was too enamored of her painting to hear.

He marched over to the front door and jangled his keys.

"I'm going out for dinner, to the truck stop," he said.

"Have a good time," she said.

Have a good time! What did she think he

was going to do? He hadn't had a good time in years, it seemed to him. She'd been so cold so long, so very long. He'd tried prayer but he had the nagging fear that Stelle was praying too and it was her prayers that were being answered.

He floored the gas pedal. Chunks of gravel bit the bottom of the car as he peeled out without looking. At the truck-stop exit, he had to mash the brakes to avoid rear-ending a red Oldsmobile that belonged to Richard and Ann Reynolds. As he was getting out of his car, they hailed him, so he went inside and joined them for dinner.

Hattie Bohannon

God was the last thing on Hattie Bohannon's mind when Gert Geurin caught her in the office and invited her to church. She'd been having murderous fantasies about Kenny Ranford over late shipments of beef: Kenny Ranford, sprig of a man, chilled in a meat locker until inert, released onto blacktop so steamy it shifted when trod upon. That'd give him the fantods, the same flutter of anxiety he gave *her* when the food supplies didn't arrive on schedule.

"However, I am not an evil woman," she'd said, glanced up from her ledger, and seen Gert, pious as a bull, filling the doorway.

"Miz Bohannon," said the cook, "on behalf of our Savior, I ask you to attend our revival service next Friday night."

"Oh, Gert," Hattie said, "I'm afraid I have a date Friday night." So Hattie accepted Paul Dodd, the sheriff, by way of refusing Gert. Until that moment she had turned him down. A man who dangled handcuffs from his belt made her nervous. Yet he had a pleasing protective shape, a barrel chest, and thighs, she supposed, bigger than hers. Her heart began to pound a little, just thinking about him. I am silly, she thought, but she couldn't keep from smiling. It was no big deal, really, just a trip to the drive-in theater to see a movie. But something had changed. Fresh blood seemed to flow from her heart and she felt as if its old husk was splitting and falling away.

On Friday night, Hattie shook the enormous tub of yellowed popcorn on her lap. It had sat, a barrier between herself and Paul Dodd, on the seat of his truck. He had neglected to buy her supper. The snack crunched like Styrofoam, and on opening night, too. She munched a handful as yet another preview showed men in combat, this time using tanks and a radar screen to blow up an enemy. Yay, team! Oh, a mistake. It was an ad for the army. They could spend a million dollars in advertising but they couldn't tell her where her deceased husband was. Oakley Bohannon, Missing in Traction. How could they lose a body from a hospital bed?

She forced her attention to the screen. She wanted to have fun tonight. She watched the opening credits and absently let her hand sift popcorn. If she placed the tub on the seat or offered it to Paul, they would have an awkward moment of speech. The silence in the cab loomed large as a cave. Perhaps he had bought the big tub because he hadn't eaten supper either. Perhaps he had expected her to offer him a meal, since she owned a restaurant. Perhaps he thought she was a pig.

She had thought the drive-in romantic but now everything about it irritated her: the perspiration on her neck, the dust on the windshield, the squawky box she jarred loose trying to swat the mosquito biting her knee. It was smelly and dusty and the movies moved fast and too many people got killed in them. She glanced across the seat at Paul, enthralled in the now-rolling murder-chase adventure. Why had he worn setting gel on his hair? Short and stubby, it looked like a fresh wash would make it stand up.

Paul's arm reached out and lay across the trickle of sweat on the back of her neck. Her jaws clamped down on two kernels of popcorn. She stared hard at the screen. His head drew close. He planted a kiss, half-on, half-off her mouth. Before she had time to think, she wriggled her shoulders out from under his arm. He slid away, his chin resting on the steering wheel, eyes glued to the hero's mad escape in a Land Rover.

She choked, then coughed the chewed corn into her hand. Paul slapped her back where her bra hooked. The bra was old and one hook was bent and sharp. It jabbed with each blow of his hand. She felt the hook lose its grip. She sat back, squashing his hand against the seat. "I'm fine," she gasped.

He slipped his arm free. "Didn't mean to give you a scare, old gal."

Old gal? When her breathing calmed, she stole a look at his rigid profile. She retrieved the tub and hugged it to her chest. He was a nice man, well-meaning. Could she tell him that sitting in a pickup truck on a warm evening with half the county galumphing by for peanuts and Sno-Cones was not the ideal spot for stealing a kiss? It was nothing like she'd imagined, the first kiss of being single again. She pictured herself sitting on an overstuffed couch covered with soft peach fabric, leaning forward, hand closed around the slender stem of a crystal wineglass, her knees comfortably together beneath a striking but tasteful marine-blue evening gown. The man was a bit amorphous. All she'd imagined was a dark suit and a dark head bending to meet hers.

Paul broke out laughing. All the trucks around them seemed to be shaking with laughter as well. On the screen, the red cherry of a patrol car slowly emerged from a shallow lake. A fat sheriff's face sputtered a soggy oath.

This felt like a charade of a date, all wrong. As if she was an alien, not a native. Who did she think she was? A model in a magazine, a movie star, a doctor's wife? Her sojourns to Washington to visit Oakley had changed her. She'd always gone alone and enjoyed being anonymous in the city.

Yet her trip last fall to find Oakley had been fruitless. She'd come gladly home, where her name meant something. But did it mean she had to fit in to be happy? She looked at Paul enjoying the action. Maybe he would like to drive his patrol car at fast speeds chasing criminals across state lines.

The more he laughed, the more alone she felt. She studied his lips, features she hadn't considered before. It seemed important to fix them in her head in a pleasant way. At the truck stop, she reduced men to a single characteristic — a chin, a chest, a pair of knees. It made them less intimidating.

Paul's lips were uneven, ragged. The right slope trailed longer into the corner than the left, and the lower lip rolled forward like a fat caterpillar. No. No. Positive. It must be positive — an ocean wave to buoy her with tingles and goose bumps. There, that was right. His lower lip was like a cresting wave.

Slowly Paul turned, as if beckoned by her probing eyes.

"You remind me of Clint Eastwood," she said.

He swung his head back to the screen.

Good Lord, Hattie thought. Would he take that as a compliment? She hadn't paid enough attention to know if Clint Eastwood was in the movie or not. But there was something about Paul Dodd that reminded her in a vague way of Clint Eastwood: his silence and the craggy brows over his eyes that seemed to know more than he would ever say.

So she simply reached across the seat of his pickup truck, took his hand, and squeezed it.

He sighed and returned the squeeze. On the screen the hero and a starlet fell to the ground and began rolling in wild passion. Paul talked over the window speaker. "These young girls today don't even fight. They want it, and that turns me off like a hard freeze. I like a gal that resists." He pointed to the screen. "We are of the right generation, Hattie. No kooks."

Hattie leaned against the headrest. This was going to be all right. They'd go just as slow as she wanted.

On the way home, Paul's police radio squawked. A woman had died on the other side of the county and he needed to go right away. "Let me show you how a real cop works, honey," he said, and squared his shoulders.

Hattie sighed and watched bugs swirl in

the headlights above the back road they took to Nougat, a tiny community that still wasn't hooked into the county water system. The window was down. They drove through a tunnel of heavy-scented pines. Despite the circumstances, it was nice to be out and away from work and her daughters. She moved her face into the wind.

"You know," Paul said, "I could set up a radar team at the truck stop. Tennessee and Georgia cops don't mess much with speeders so I'm sure the cars are flying like bullets into Alabama."

"If you get to be a regular, you won't have to wait for your food," Hattie said, and looked away to hide her smile.

Paul stopped in front of a small house. Hattie waited until he joined a huddle of people on the lawn before she fixed her bra. She felt like a voyeur. The people gestured toward the house and a car parked on the road where others hovered and tapped its windshield.

Hattie got out of the truck. Honeysuckle grew like grass in the yard and made the air sweet. The vines rooted a stack of cascading tires to the ground, a statue of movement. Hattie wondered where the dead woman was.

Paul was still writing on his tablet when the ambulance and the news reporter arrived. A spotlight swept over the parked car, revealing, in silhouette, a woman sitting in the driver's seat, glaring down the beams flaring in her face.

Drawn, like Paul, to the car to watch the medics ridiculously shine a flashlight in the dead woman's wide-open eyes, to see them push back a dozen layers of sleeves to find her thick wrist, to check her pulse, to hear them shout, "Stretcher and a sheet!" and then to feel her own way backwards to the pickup truck, to lean against its breathing warm metal with her breathing warm skin, Hattie wished for the antiseptic deaths of the movie screen.

A tottering old man at the edge of the crowd collapsed. The neighbors tugged his shoulders but he was too weak to sit up. They put a flask to his lips. He rinsed the liquor through his mouth, then spat it on the ground. "I never drank a drop in my life and I am not going to start now on account of Dovie Mae."

Dovie Mae was hemmed into the seat by several blankets and an old fake fur overcoat. Her fingers had to be peeled off the steering wheel. Finally the medics pulled her out and laid her on the stretcher. She'd been dead since morning and her husband had discovered it only when he got in the car to sleep with her that evening. Now lying on her back, her fingers curled, her knees resting on her stomach, her right foot extended, Dovie Mae gave the impression both of mashing the gas pedal and of bracing herself against a crash. She looked the picture of terror, as if she had seen Death in her final moment and fought it with all her might.

Hattie began to get queasy, not over Dovie Mae but over Oakley. Had he, lying calmly in an oxygen tent, died in fear? Or had he thrashed around, tangling himself in suffocating sheets, like Dovie Mae's husband wrapping himself in ropes of honeysuckle? Hattie longed to roll around on the ground in grief, surrounded by kind friends, but she could not without her husband's body.

She still felt Oakley's presence. There were times when she seemed to catch him standing at the bedroom window, the scent of smoked tobacco lingering in the air. She wondered what he wanted, maybe nothing, maybe just to be in the place where his things promised him a long life: the hickory chest that had come down the backbone of the Smokies in a wagon to rest in this house in Maridoches County, Alabama; the patchwork quilt, its cloth spun by his great-grandmother from the first cotton grown by his great-grandfather; the stoneware churn purchased with hemp eighty years before. It was no wonder he wandered away at times from the steel and concrete and speed and sterility of Washington, D.C., to stand in their bedroom and gaze out at the rolling hills, to hold for a few minutes the life promised him by his land. He never looked at her; she was sure of it. He'd already lived forty-one years when they'd married. She was a small part of his life, the bright explosion of a firecracker in an otherwise steady whistling ascent.

The medics loaded the ambulance, then hooked Dovie Mae's car to a tow truck. The car's two front tires were flat. The reporter gathered the story from the neighbors.

"Her husband never did give us a good answer," said a broad man who was supporting his slight wife, a combination of shapes that made Hattie think of a house and a lean-to.

"I don't know why she done it," the wife said. "She kept a clean house."

"It was six cars in the last ten years. First

a green Hornet, but I guess it was too small —"

"Hornets get lousy mileage," said another.

"Oh, Raymond. Mileage don't matter to her. She never went nowhere."

"And then there was an Oldsmobile, a black LTD, early model, and then it was a red car, a red Chevy."

"Yeah, Dovie Mae warn't loyal to no one company, but she surely didn't buy no Japanese cars."

Paul waved at the reporter and nodded at Hattie. "We can go."

"Good." She climbed into the truck. The neighbors abandoned the reporter and piled the husband into a car to take him to the hospital. The air was heavy with fragrant moisture, too cloying to breathe. Hattie felt tears roll down her cheeks.

"A strange pair," he said.

Hattie nodded, then had the vague idea he was talking about her and Oakley, then about her and himself. She quit nodding.

"Everybody in this side of the county knew about them living in cars. They weren't breaking any laws. It was just something they decided to do." Paul drove at a steady pace, grinding through holes and over broken knobs of concrete with equal disregard. "Don't take it so hard, Hattie. They wanted to sleep in the car. You saw their house. It was pretty nice, considering."

Considering what? Dovie Mae Jarboe looked like she wanted to get out of there as fast as she could. Maybe that was the trick. Be the first to die. "I'm sorry. Death affects me in funny ways."

"Well, in my job, you see it often enough that you get hard to it," Paul said.

At a stop sign, he opened the glove box and took out a handkerchief. "Cry the clouds out of your eyes. They're way too pretty to be hiding."

Hattie took the handkerchief and dabbed her eyes.

"It's your husband?" Paul said.

"Yes," said Hattie.

"Let the dead lie and the living keep moving," Paul said. "That's my philosophy."

How simple that was. How clear and utterly irresponsible, she thought. The gulf in this cab is wide. Though she ached to hold and be held by this man who was causing her nerves to thrill in fits and bursts, the bag of grief she carried was heavy. But maybe, maybe, this blue-eyed man was the one who could pry it loose.

Jessamine Bohannon

I didn't care that Mama was out on a date on Friday night and I was at work adding up the receipts. She could be at the drive-in eating fresh popcorn and laughing, not a thought in her head, while I was keeping an eye on the truck stop. It wasn't like I was the grown-up and she the daughter, nothing like that.

I dumped the week's coins into the sorting machine, ratcheted it up, and covered my ears. The machine clanged so loud the noise jarred my bones. I hollered to drown it out. Richard had not called me. I had dialed his number and hung up more than once. I didn't want to talk about Mrs. Reynolds and her half tit. But how could I pretend I had not seen it? I screamed like a train tearing through a tunnel.

When the sorting machine stopped, the silence hit like withdrawal. My voice sounded pathetic, a snaky wisp of whine. I hoped no one in the restaurant had heard me. Since no one came to the rescue, I guessed I was safe. I pinched open an orange quarter wrapper, slid my forefinger inside, stuck it under the quarter chute, and released enough coins to fill it — forty, ten dollars. When the quarters were done, I did dimes and nickels, scooped up the odd change, and dropped it in my purse.

I went to the kitchen and made pancake batter. The mixer was on its first revolution when Troy Clyde, Mama's brother, ran in shouting that the truck stop was about to blow up. His eyes were shiny and his hair crackling with electricity. He's like a walking lightning rod. Everything is a crisis.

"You're not in Vietnam anymore," I reminded him. "This is Maridoches."

"Look out the back window, little sister," he said, as he ran into the dining room.

I saw the light before I reached the back door. The vat of waste oil was burning to Kingdom Come. Flames flew up like hands trying to touch the sky. I walked — walked! — to the fryer and saw that the switch to the grease pipe was off. Outside, voices howled for water. Everybody knew it took the Gadsden fire department forty-five minutes to get here.

I dialed 911. Jewell Miller had already tried to reach the sheriff but he was unavailable.

"He's at the drive-in," I said, "with my mother. It's a date."

"I'll note that," said Jewell Miller.

I went outside. My sister Darla aimed our hose at the fire but its tiny silver stream evaporated in the heat. Customers stood, watching. Their faces glowed orange while their backs were black, half-people, half-night, half-fire. Smoke spread out in the air like a rug, rolling farther and farther into the night. I could see where the stars were bright, and that was at the far horizon.

Voices buzzed with causes, a careless cigarette tossed into the trash, the No Smoking policy, what was a customer to do? I moved closer to the fire to tell Darla to quit with the hose. It was a waste of water. Against the Dumpster rested the charred husk of my gold chair.

I shouted. Dark faces turned toward me, Reverend Peterson and Gert. She'd done it — she'd burned my chair. She'd lit the cigarettes I'd given her at dinnertime, I knew it.

I'd push the witch into the fire, push until she roasted and her fat had spit itself out.

I stormed over to scream at her oily face when I saw Richard watching our chair burn. His face sagged like melting wax. He looked desolate, his mouth downturned, all his happiness drained out. I wanted to bare my breasts and put his head between them and say, It's gone, the chair, not us.

Yet as I watched I felt his despair myself, and I could not move. It's the only thing that saved Gert from boiling in oil.

Reverend Peterson climbed into the truck bed of a Chevy and asked everyone to pray. All the noises stopped as he insisted in a fairly fine voice for us to be calm and to rely on God. Darla watered the parking lot. Puddles pushed the crowd back, their shoes soaking.

Troy Clyde jogged up, arms waving as if each new thought jerked them in a different direction. "Dirt's the answer, Jessamine," he said. "We need the trucker who owns that Coe." He pointed to a semi loaded with dirt.

I ran back inside — good thing; the mixer had about frothed the pancake batter into a beehive — and shouted into the men's room for the Coe's owner, but no one came out. Back outside, Troy Clyde and the reverend announced that the men would form a line and move dirt from the Coe onto the flames, but first the driver needed to back the truck closer. But he could not be found. The men stared as the metal walls of the Dumpster glowed red. Do something, I thought. Don't just stand there like a bunch of huddled cows in the rain. The Dumpster surged as if to burst. It would catch us in its river of heat and cascade fire over the truck stop.

"Maybe he's sleeping," I shouted. I beat Troy Clyde across the parking lot to the Coe's cab and flung the driver's door wide open.

The trucker lay back across the seat, pants around his ankles, a woman's massive brown hair covering his privates. On the dash was a ten-dollar bill.

"Lordy," said Troy Clyde. "I knew it."

The woman's head lifted. "You got to pay more for a party."

"Get out," said the trucker, as he sat up and raised his knees.

Troy Clyde, bless him, was cool. "Wake up and smell the smoke, brother. We need your dirt to smother that fire."

The trucker slipped his pants on, caught the fire's sheen on his face, and nodded. The woman moved into the passenger's seat. Her breasts stood out as if gravity didn't exist.

Reverend Peterson appeared behind me on the running board and looked into the cab. He gasped, then his face froze to stone.

"Move," said Troy Clyde to Reverend Peterson. "I'm putting out a *real* fire." He pushed me into the cab and pulled the door to. Squashed between Troy Clyde and the trucker, I was overcome by the strong smell of aftershave. On the floor, the woman thrust her arms into a stretchy gray top. Her breasts jiggled like water balloons as she fought to bring her shirt down over her head. The trucker leaned forward and bit the closest nipple. Her right hand sprang free and smacked his face.

The truck had not moved an inch since we'd come inside. Troy Clyde, too, had been caught up in the show.

"Goddamn," said the trucker. He scrambled over me and Troy Clyde into the driver's seat. I scooted to the passenger window, leaving room for the woman to climb up next to me, but she didn't get off the floor. The trucker backed the rig up.

I rolled down my window and peered out as we closed on the Dumpster. Richard was the first man to climb into the truck bed. He sank to his calves in the dirt. Soon he was swinging shovelfuls of soil onto the fire. Our chair collapsed, then became debris. I watched Richard bend, sweat, and turn, saw him remove his sodden shirt and fling it into the flames. He stood out, in silhouette, a smith slick with heat. My body has a memory way across the river from good sense.

I felt my heart beat hard in my ears. The rhythm drummed all the way down my arms and legs and every place in between. I was pulsing.

"Come on, little sister," Troy Clyde said, opening the door of the cab, "we need to get away from all this sinning."

When I stepped out, high beams blinded me. Reverend Peterson shouted about sin, prostitution, adultery, and fornication. I stood on the running board, stunned. I must have looked guilty. I stood there as if his words were true — of course they were, but only I knew that. I looked up into the truck bed where Richard was, and saw him hot and dirty. Oh, I loved him. I wished he'd reach down and pull me up there with him. We'd stand there together for everyone to see.

But he merely squinted in my direction as if the glare was too much.

Troy Clyde hustled me off the running board. The fire began to die. In the distance came the wail of sirens, useless now.

I walked to the back of the semi as Richard climbed down. A woman burst from the crowd. It was her, glassy-eyed, hair leaking from a bun, dress hanging loose as an empty sack. "Are you all right?" Mrs. Reynolds asked Richard.

He nodded and wiped his face. She offered him a glass of water, stolen from our dining room. I could see beads of sweat on his forehead and bubbles in the glass. He put his arm around her.

How could he? She was so weak and damaged and crazy. But there she was, wiping his brow and then — goddamn! — his chest. If I had a knife I would have cut her arms off for touching him. My breath came so fast I was panting. The smoke caught in my lungs like a solid and I coughed hard. I could not stop.

Sheriff Dodd was suddenly bending beside me. He got a good grip on my elbows. "You're a witness. Come with me."

I coughed my lungs clear, crossing the lot. Then the trucker and the woman and I were all seated in the patrol car, me in the front, them in the back. I didn't care what happened. Sheriff Dodd asked their names.

"You know my name," said the woman. She was younger than me and had big blue eyes and crooked buck teeth. Not pretty, all eyes and mouth.

"I'm arresting you, sir, for solicitation

and a lewd act and you, Miss Ash Lee, for prostitution."

"My understanding of prostitution is that money must exchange hands," said the trucker. "You can search me and my cab and you will see that I am broke."

Ash Lee said, "You can search me and you won't find one red cent."

Sheriff Dodd grimaced as if he'd swallowed nails. "Jessamine, did you see a lewd act?" He asked delicately, like I might not know what he was talking about.

The trucker and Ash Lee were watching me. I could feel their breath and smell their heat. I leaned against the window as if this whole thing was unsavory for me. Wouldn't they be relieved to know I'd palmed the ten bucks when I slid across the cab? Wouldn't they be grateful? "No, I didn't see a lewd act."

The trucker said, "Listen, sheriff, if your boys are finished pillaging my goods, I'll be on my way."

Dodd nodded.

The trucker said to Ash Lee, "You need a ride, darling?"

She put her head right up behind Sheriff Dodd's and said into his ear, "I'll let the law take care of me."

As if her breath were red paint, color

spread from the back of the sheriff's neck to his forehead.

Suddenly I was sorry for him. He knew Ash Lee but didn't want me or Mama to know it, and yet he couldn't turn her out to the wolves — Reverend Peterson and Gert — who were waiting near the patrol car.

"Where do you need to go?" I asked.

"Not far if I cut through the woods," Ash Lee said.

"Oh," I said in a normal tone of voice, "I can take you."

"Thank you, Jessamine," said Sheriff Dodd. "Your mother's occupied with other things right now."

I nodded at him as I got out of the car. Of course I could be in charge. I'd been in charge all evening.

Red lights spun on the fire truck and there was water in the air and water underfoot. Everything that had been oily with heat now dripped. The night was still pale above us. Troy Clyde shooed the crowd away and almost got into a shoving match with Gert when he came a tad too close to Reverend Peterson.

Ash Lee and I sloshed across the parking lot together. I felt so gracious to be helping the poor girl out of this embarrassing situation.

She plunked down in the passenger seat of my old VW and said, "Hand over the ten dollars, bitch."

Hattie Bohannon

When she stepped out of the sheriff's truck into the smoke, she almost swooned. He caught and steadied her. She pulled away and was rude, holding her brow, shouting out "Thank you!" and then dashing to the center of the disaster. Through the haze, the truck stop looked like a circus shutting down. Revolving red lights illuminated active dark figures. The fire truck's long gleaming ladder was strapped in travel position. A row of tail-lights marked the exit lane. She found Gert and Reverend Peterson holding a prayer meeting near the smoldering Dumpster. Troy Clyde was sweaty and shaky. "The fire," he said to her. "The fire."

She hugged his warm shoulders and said, "Go home. It's out. We'll be all right."

She was sprayed then with the hose.

"Stop it!" Hattie yelled. "Stop it!"

Darla's voice came back. "Sorry, Mama, Troy Clyde said to drench him."

"Tell me what happened," Hattie said.

She and Darla rewound the hose as the girl recounted the night's events, her voice pitched high, her eyes blazing.

"Where's Jessamine?" Hattie said.

Darla shrugged. "She's around here somewhere. The truck stop's okay. Nobody got burnt."

Queasiness rolled over Hattie. She needed fresh clean air. She went into the truck stop and washed her face again and again in the sink. She had to function, despite the illness she felt, memory flooding through every nerve.

A fireman came in and asked her to sign their report. They'd be there a few more hours until they figured out the source of the fire. He seemed awfully calm, Hattie thought.

"It got contained mighty quick," he said. "At least there were no deaths."

Hattie sat down at her desk and read the black smudged report. She checked the electrical systems and revved up the air-conditioning to prevent the burnt smell from settling inside. After a few hours, everything she could do was done. She had to go outside to get home.

The air was still a veil of smoke. Hattie staggered away from it, up past the house,

101

fighting memory as she breathed it in. She scrambled through the garden and rushed to the rise of the mountain. She needed air. Her feet slipped on pine needles but on she climbed until the scent of evergreens cut through the smoke. She lay down on the soft piney blanket and closed her eyes. It was her childhood home she saw, conjured by the smoke.

Winter had always come to the Dameron house before it reached the other homes in Maridoches County. Red leaves still clung to the maples when the cold wind sought out the water pipes, freezing the flow in them that it could not wholly staunch in the valley. The house, with a two-story wraparound porch, had been a river captain's dream turned into siding and lattice and oak shingles. He'd cleared all the trees between the house and the cliff so he could walk as if on the deck of a steamship and look out over the swirling waters of the Ruby River.

As clearly as Hattie saw the home, she saw her father on the upstairs porch, fist raised, a flow of hot words aimed at Heaven for sending droughts and bad market prices and cold weather down on him personally, a sight so familiar she could never think of going off to school without recalling it. She'd imagined her friends' mothers sending them out the door with a kiss on the forehead, an admonition to be good, a habit she'd created for her own girls. But she and Troy Clyde and her little sister Lucy were used to seeing their father wave his fist in the air, talking at God. Since God never struck Daddy with lightning, they had wondered about His existence. It was the main topic of their conversation on the walk to school. Why didn't He answer? was always the thought that occurred to Hattie.

One day in early winter, the year she was fifteen, as she trudged home from school up the mountain, Hattie sensed something was happening at the house. There was, all through the woods, the steady unseasonal sound of locusts gnawing through leaves and a soft rushing undercurrent that was neither rain nor the river. A film of smoke rolled down to greet her. She ran over ice-crusted leaves, past a mule train hauling barrels of water up the path. Her house glowed from the inside. The ice on the leaves in the yard had melted into a glassy brown lake that reflected the brilliant shoots of color dancing inside the windows. She watched the first bucket of water tossed onto the fire. It made a pitiful *psst*.

At once, she felt powerless, and a calm detachment took over. She became absorbed in watching the house and fire work in accord to complete their task of destruction. The house sighed; the fire kept its voice to a throaty whisper. It moved as if stroking the posts and walls, as if the black crust it left were a new coat of paint. The house acquiesced; the muslin curtains in the living room, sibilant couriers of flame, gently stretched to place red-tipped wisps on the windowsills, the pine floors, the lace tablecloth, the woolen slipcovers. The fire swirled with the leisure of a connoisseur, examining everything in its path, touching, peeling back wallpaper, leaving powder-smudged kisses, wrapping the railings in gray blankets. It was a friendly blaze until it reached the slate hall floor, where it was forced to leap like a tiger to the staircase. Then it stripped and blistered the steps, scorching a tunnel up to the second floor. It consumed, its tongue hot, hungry; the banister snapped like a matchstick. The second floor blazed hotter than poppy, shuddering in the instant before the shotgun-blast explosion hurtled glass. Searing red and yellow arrows hissed out in the brown lake, which grew deeper and wider as the men tried to keep the fire from spreading. Acrid smoked jetted out of the blackening window crosses, draping Hattie in a cloud. She ran to the back of the house and threw herself on the slick black ground.

A voice the timbre of fire made her open her eyes to search the flames. Black against the brilliance of orange heat, her father roared, his hair white and wild. His familiar ire reached a pitch stronger than the raging red tongues feeding around him as he yelled, "These pipes will never freeze again!" In the glimpses Hattie had of him through the forest of yellow and orange waves, she saw him shoot blue flames from a blowtorch at a teetering maze of pipes, now free of plaster and lath. His internal rage now consumed him and her home. A chill came up from the icy leaves. She felt the cold fingers of death around her heart and a cold pain in her head and chest, as if they were turning to ice too.

Then all went black and suffocating. She clawed at the blanket dropped over her head, fought against the arms carrying her away; she kicked and struggled, knocking her abductor down so the two of them rolled down the bank through frosty black-berry fingers that slapped against her face. She landed looking up at the underside of a white mule, who moved its delicate white legs off the trail to make room for her.

"Get up, Hattie," said Troy Clyde.

She stood. Behind her, Jake Hiler was brushing leaves and mud from his coat. He snapped the blanket, tossing sticks and plastered leaves into the air, startling the mule Troy Clyde and Lucy rode. Troy Clyde settled his mule and repeated, "Get up, Hattie."

She mounted the other white mule. Jake Hiler slid up behind her, wrapping them both in the blanket. As Troy Clyde passed, Hattie saw Lucy's feverish pink face and remembered that Lucy had stayed home sick from school that morning. Hattie collapsed back against Jake Hiler's sturdy chest.

"We're going to the mill to tell Mama," Troy Clyde said, his grayed eyes on the path ahead, unflinching when the crash of the house rushed through the woods.

In the following years, when, at night, the last horrible image of her father appeared and she'd waken, her mouth open, her throat constricted, her scream unscreamed, she would hate Jake Hiler for not letting her see the end of it. If she knew there was some end to her father's burning, if she'd seen a beam fall on him or, better, a maple branch heavy with snow — she could imagine the hiss — then she could return to sleep. Instead she lay petrified and became aware of the room, the night sounds, of Oakley's breathing, so regular and calm. She'd get up and walk the house, check on the girls, look outside at the yard, the large purple sky dotted with stars. These dreams usually came in winter when she could see skulls where the snow had melted, black eyes staring up through white bones, tree branches covered with ice rattling their death rattle. She felt that if death was as peaceful and still as the night, she would not mind dying. She'd lean against a cold window until her head ached. With a start she'd notice the etchings of Jack Frost that appeared, beautiful and mysterious, in the space of two breaths. She found comfort in them and went back to bed.

Tonight there was no comfort, and though she cried until her head ached and then slept shrouded by the pines, she felt not rested but uneasy when she woke. It was quiet under the trees, the stillness unfamiliar. She was not eager to go back to the house. So she took off her shoes and buried her feet in the needles, taking pleasure in rubbing pine gum on her fingers and scenting her arms and neck with it.

This perfume would get her down through the smoke to her house.

As she descended, she still felt uneasy. To dismiss the smoke was to dismiss her father — and Oakley too, she thought suddenly. The two men she'd loved were gone but she held on to them as if they could still love her. *They are my definition of love, and it is all in my memory.* She stopped short.

She thought of Paul Dodd, his half-kiss, the sturdy way he'd helped her out of his truck, and something flip-flopped inside her. For that rush, she thought, *I will bring Oakley home this time.* Her father was a spirit, probably roaming the world, beyond her reach. In the dim light, she watched her footing as the slope took a steep turn. Her feet bumped an outcropping of shale hidden beneath the needles. She lurched from tree to tree until the path smoothed out and the decline became more gentle. The closer she got to home, the stronger the odor of the fire became. Fat and full, the smell could linger in the humid Alabama air until fall, when tornado season would sweep the mountain clean. She could be in for days of fire memory. In the glimpses between the trees she saw a halo of smoke above the truck stop.

The Ladies of the Church of the Holy Resurrection

The news of Hattie Bohannon's date with Sheriff Dodd rescued the children of Dovie Mae Jarboe from a permanent cloud of infamy, despite the front-page article and dim night photograph of her car ascending to Heaven. The black cable suspending the front bumper blurred, out of focus, into the background trees.

Hattie's confident stand on Dodd's running board, poised to move on into the driver's seat, was a detail the ladies found particularly distressing. They thought of all those career women at the courthouse who had had their eyes and — pause — unmentionables on Dodd for years. Plenty of men came and went at the truck stop. Plenty.

To be charitable to Hattie, who after all had survived some dreadful ordeals, they suggested it was Dodd's uniform — and not the man himself, adeptly removing it from him — that attracted her, an idea that lead to chattering plausibilities. The unstated: Sheriff Dodd was remarkably fit and square. He had the muscular bulges for khaki. The much considered and revised: Hattie's husband served in World War II. Her brother ran the Viet Vets branch of the NRA. Her father, they knew, must dictate something of her taste. Yet they discarded this notion, aware that they had somehow failed in the psychological quest. Her father had died heroically, trying to save the ancestral home from burning to the ground. Which led to the speculation that the truck stop would also fail and that Hattie Bohannon was desperate for a man, a thought they all skirted as slightly vulgar to state but one they sincerely believed. That Dovie Mae Jarboe's psyche may have excited far more possibilities for examination did not occur to them.

What occurred to Jewell Miller became a full-blown memory of Oakley Bohannon, lean and impressive in his uniform, leaning toward her. She felt some pain in her leathery heart. Time to take her daily constitutional, the cure for all forms of heartache. As she marched through the woods behind her apartment, she wondered if all her former power had deserted her or if, indeed, she still had some pull with the Army.

Gert Geurin

I love getting ready for church. I'm a greeter. I stand at the entrance to the sanctuary and shake hands with everyone. This is how I prepare: I sprinkle Lily of the Valley talcum powder in my brassiere for the huggers. There are not many huggers, mostly the old widowed men, like Gee and Haw, known as Gerald and Harold at church, and a couple of the ladies who are very outgoing, the kind who put people off of hugging. But I hug them anyway and they seem pleased that there are others of their tribe.

The powder rises during a hug and leaves a pleasant dust. Perhaps that is what we huggers know and others don't. I also scent my gloves on the inside with powder and hope the bare-handed reap the benefits of Lily of the Valley when they pray.

After my greeting duties the Sunday after the fire, I selected a good pew up near the front next to Baker Thomas and his sorely tried wife. I intended to reveal my sacrifice regarding cigarettes and to expound about the great good Lord. But church service was intolerable. The air conditioner gave out so we were reduced to waving Jesus fans in front of our faces while the reverend warmed up to prostitution in our community. Reverend Peterson was nervous from the Call to Worship.

He said, "Today the sermon is on the subject of infidelity, whose root word is *infidel*, of which there are many in our midst." He said the word so low it was hard to hear, though he blushed to his roots so we all picked up on it.

He said infidelity separates a body from its spirit, and when you split the spirit off from the body you are in living death. That is why he worried over the souls of men who had relations with women other than their wives, to whom they had promised themselves before God. Because it mattered to your spirit, even if it didn't to your body, and that is what infidel men were finding out. People should have relations when they cared spiritually, not genitally, for each other.

He said that right. I wished Jessamine had been there to hear those words of wisdom.

Reverend Peterson allowed as how some members of our church had been tempted but were now remorseful and ready to confess. He railed on about women without men, and then about women with too many men, then about women who trafficked in men. It was hard to keep up with his groups, and soon they all swarmed together in my head and I found myself calling silently to the Lord to keep my mind's eye straight and pure. After the offering plate made its rounds, Reverend Peterson asked us to ponder a situation where many men came and went from an establishment that ministered to their physical cravings and asked us to condemn such places. Naturally I was sweating more than usual and wanted to get baptized just for relief but then I saw where he was talking about the truck stop — or was he? He was very confusing and I was so over-heated I could not think straight. I wanted to confess to starting the fire and to wit-ness that I was cigarette-free thanks to the glory of God but I never got my chance.

The first to the altar was Richard Reynolds and did he ever lay it on about laying with a prostitute and the wrong path and breaking his vow to God and his wife and Lord what a humble man he became.

I was shocked that he'd been after prosti-tutes. He must really be a horny old goat because I realized he and Jessamine had clearly been together for some while. You don't glow like she did if it's a one-time mingling. Poor Ann Reynolds was staring at Richard as if he'd just hatched out of an egg. But I knew why his guilt had got him up off his hind end.

Next to me Baker Thomas yawned and yawned. He is a man I believe who is here for appearances, not for sustenance. His wife has a grim look. She is skin and bones and he's a shoat. But that is not an uncommon sight in Maridoches, especially among people with more than their share of money. When Richard Reynolds came forth and announced he'd been with a prostitute at the truck stop, Baker Thomas leaned forward. What a pervert. Or maybe, I thought, as I faced him and stared, he was feeling guilt himself.

Next came Ann down the aisle, looking like a beatitude in a holy blue dress, and she had a confession to make. She said she'd lost a breast.

As if it was a nickel or something — lost it, as if it disappeared while she was watching a soap opera — and she took the blame for Richard's errant ways and was ready to forgive him for seeking out a prostitute. It had been a rough time but the two little love lambs were back together, and she hoped we'd all boycott the place of ill repute and not let harlots live easy in our community.

I thanked God with the rest of them. Now Jessamine would be safe from the old goat. Her heart would break, but it had to so she'd be out of that unholy alliance. I offered to God my services along these lines because, though she is contrary, she is a very young woman. I felt as if my own trial of quitting cigarettes would be a good model. It would give me strength and knowledge to help her through her time of need. I felt so chosen that I sang loud and clear and caught up with the tune the last three verses.

Reverend Martin Peterson

After the sermon, Martin wiped his brow. He was wet under his robe. When he lifted the garment off, he felt shorn of a sheep's coat. While preaching, he'd been unaware of his rising temperature.

He washed his face and dried his fingers one by one, changed into a pressed white shirt, added a dark-colored tie. A charge still tingled from the words he'd flung from the pulpit: infidelity, licentiousness, multiple partners, wantonness. They'd seemed lightning bolts as he'd shouted them. In a fresh shirt and tie, he was a little bewildered by the fervor that had inhabited him.

As he opened the door to the Men's Sunday school class, he heard a shout and felt the rumble of movement inside the room. The men, already seated in a circle, eyed him as if he were not one of them but a prairie schoolteacher who carried a big whip.

Martin launched into a long rudimentary prayer about the Power of God, and that seemed to settle the men. They took off their ties and their suit jackets and loosened their belts and bent over blue books that looked tiny in their large hands.

He opened a folding chair. After an inordinate amount of noise, chairs bumping and screeching, Martin's place was secured within the circle. The men squeezed their knees together to avoid touching their neighbors. Sandwiched between Baker Thomas and John Walker, Martin asked, "Is there a topic we need to talk about this week?"

"We were — uh, just getting ready for the Wheel of Gratitude," said Baker Thomas, whose heavy side abutted Martin. He raised his right hand. "I'm grateful that my appeal last week for some poured concrete was answered by God and Toller Odom."

"Praise be to God," said the group.

Martin smiled. Often the Wheel of Gratitude began and ended with Toller Odom. He was a warden for the state prison and was blessed with an endless supply of free labor.

Toller Odom's faded blue eyes crinkled. "I'm grateful Baker Thomas allowed some troubled young men an honest day's work. I am grateful they learned a new skill. Education is a precious thing."

Martin listened abstractly to the sounds of their voices, exuberant, energetic, too loud, the voices of boys. His practiced voice was stern and patrician. At church, the men relaxed. A Higher Power was on call. They were off the hook of authority, at least for a little while. But Martin had no chance to let the tensions loose. He had to represent — even for these men — God. It was why they came regularly, Martin was convinced.

His thoughts went elsewhere, as they often did, while the men shared thanks. He wondered if the young prostitute, the one with the amazingly lively breasts, was the one Richard Reynolds confessed to knowing. Richard's sins would be forgotten, but his own desires, if acted out, would be unforgivable. A twinge of jealousy galled him as the others shared a joke.

Without him, a direct descendant in the religious faith from the disciples of Christ and therefore from Christ himself, there is no Father, no church of comfort. He only felt vulnerable in Stelle's arms, when she held him and stroked his head. Then he could give up God and be a man. Her recent coldness unraveled him.

As the men laughed, he remembered with distaste the hunting trip they'd taken him on to Dollarskin Lodge. The men woke early and went out and shot deer and stayed up late drinking and talking. They were like boys then, too. The wives might say their husbands were children and roll their eyes, but they expected them to be men, and men they could be: earn the money, discipline the children, teach the boys to hunt and the girls to love football. At church they could be repentant boys. Because of him, of the power invested in him by God the Father. Martin laughed out loud and felt silence like a chill all around him. Someone had addressed him directly. He hadn't been paying attention.

Richard Reynolds was standing outside the circle, a folded chair leaning against his legs. He looked pale and shaken, a man who needed something strong like an electric shock to revive him.

The other men sat like boulders that would just as soon roll over Richard Reynolds as acknowledge him.

Martin held his tongue to see if someone else would come forward and take charge: Baker Thomas, the banker; Toller Odom, who commanded hundreds of criminals. No one moved. The sounds of the women's class, a muffle of changing cadences, could be heard. A car door slammed. Someone outside shouted, "Dixie Creme!" A trickle of sweat ran from John Walker's hairline down to the tip of his bony nose, but he did not even blink.

Inside Martin felt a swelling discomfort, then almost tangible pain, as if God had grabbed his heart with a fist and was squeezing it, telling him to stand up and steer this group of sinners straight.

At first, he resisted. His solace came from Stelle, and since she'd withdrawn he was left with only God's strict words. The pressure of the men's heavy eyes bore down. Inside, habit of authority rose like a volcano. The words crowded his throat. He stood up and practically vomited them into the room.

"Richard, the Lord will make His forgiveness known."

"I just hope my wife will," Richard said, and beseeched the other men for a laugh. A few chuckled in relief but quickly turned the chortles into coughs. He took off his tie and was beginning to lay his jacket on top of another's when Baker Thomas said, "Keep that tie on. You already done hung yourself."

Richard crumpled. "I had to say it. That girl came to my house, came into my house and talked to Ann. I had to say it."

"It is a brave thing to admit adultery in church and we are to forgive him," said Martin to the class. "Richard Reynolds has set a good example. Our community would be a much more Christian place if others bared their souls as Richard has."

"See, Reverend, there's something you do not quite understand —" began Baker Thomas.

John Walker broke in. "I think we should concentrate on Reverend Peterson's sermon and consider what he has said about a business that thrives on transient men. I think we ought to hold that truck stop accountable for those crimes such as Richard has told us about. I eat up there, and I do not want my food tainted by whoring hands. I do not want my wife and children to go up there and get exposed to what some of us saw on Friday night."

"He's right," said Toller Odom. "Prostitution at the truck stop is a community ill, and something should be done about it."

"Yes," said Baker Thomas. "Maybe Richard's wife ought to talk to our wives and give them a lesson about forgiveness."

"Ann would feel blessed and relieved" — Richard Reynolds choked — "so happy if that could happen."

"And maybe you could pray on how to get back on the Wheel of Gratitude," said Toller Odom. "Like, seeing about some mitered top-grade scrap lumber Baker's been needing for his new sunroom."

Richard Reynolds smiled as if his own request had been granted.

Ed Wohlgemuth, a stringy older man who'd lost most of his voice to cigarettes, erupted. "Let's get up in their face at that truck stop — bringing prostitutes and sick trucker trash into Maridoches."

"Eventually," said Toller Odom, "that place will be closed down and Maridoches will be pure again."

It had been years since one of Martin's sermons sparked enthusiasm, let alone action. He felt rejuvenated and secretly relieved. For now when he thought of the truck stop, instead of Gert Geurin and her sumptuous potato cakes, he saw the young prostitute, her nubile breasts in the glare of the Dumpster fire.

Martin stood but remained silent and oddly calm. He was in balance, having given in and spoken. He was simply a vessel now, and if words were to come they would. He could wait forever on God.

"I shall miss the chicken-fried steaks," he said out loud, remembering with a stab of pain in his gullet that Stelle had become a vegetarian. She'd been driving behind a steer bound for the stockyard and she swore she saw, in its bewildered brown eyes, a soul.

"A steak house," said John Walker, "is a noble idea."

"Yes," said Baker Thomas. It would keep the truckers out but draw families in."

"Hooters is a family restaurant," said Toller Odom.

"We're getting away from that," said John Walker. "A steak house for families administered by Christians."

Martin sat back and let them work their evil — using church fellowship to shut down a business. It was being done in God's house, and if God objected He could send a tornado crashing through the roof. He could give Baker Thomas a heart attack or let the prisoners revolt at Toller Odom's. I am a child of the bride of Christ, the Church, not a man, and so I shall not act as a man.

Richard Reynolds was still standing outside the circle.

"Have my chair," said Martin.

Baker Thomas put his arm around Richard. "You put us in the pickle, but I think we've found our oar."

"Praise God. Praise, praise God!" Richard Reynolds's face was pink as if suddenly flooded with oxygen.

"Richard, doesn't your daddy still raise beef?" said Toller Odom.

Martin closed the door. He went outside and followed the path of stones to the huge cross mounted against the church's wall. It was electric, made up of rows of lightbulbs. Extending above the roof, nightly it burned, a white cross in the midst of a barren landscape. After the service this morning, Gert Geurin had informed him that several bulbs were burnt out. He went back inside and brought out the ladder, climbed it, and screwed in fresh ones. Let there be light, he thought ironically. The sun's glare against the white concrete made him tipsy.

He was sweating again. Late April

hugged with its lubricious humidity, which he did not need. To be aware of his body every second, to remind him of carnality, of his manhood. But an Alabama spring did that. Every move he made was uncomfortable. He felt wet heat on body parts he never thought about: the upper thigh below the buttocks, the backs of his knees, the skin beneath the hairs of his toes. Sweat collected in the hollow above his clavicle. His bones sweated, and probably his internal organs too. Moisture wrapped his waist like the sodden band of his underwear. Worse to come was summer, when vanity was a luxury. Big bellies, blisters, and behinds shook free of clothes. Acres of Alabama skin was exposed, the flesh sensual and slick. He could not fight it, this man of spirit; he was already deep in the body season.

A lightbulb slipped from his fingers and splattered below. The ground wavered. He held on to the ladder with one hand and wiped sweat from his left eye, but then his right filled. The men came out, their faces distorted and run together, and Martin tried to keep his balance, grabbing the rung with one hand, wiping his stinging eye with the other, alternating hands and eyes, until the ladder began to hop. His sweat fairly poured down his forehead. The men stood in a respectful silent circle and finally Toller Odom steadied the ladder, but Martin did not come down.

After a while they moved to their cars. "Good preaching," called Baker Thomas. Another said, "We'll let the ladies lead," which Martin decided later, when facing his supper — cold cereal in a plastic bowl — was a bad idea in life and the topic of his next sermon.

II

II

Hattie Bohannon

She was sipping an early morning sweet tea at her desk when a stack of mail arrived. She sorted the junk from the business and paused when she read the return address of the Veterans Administration. She slit the envelope. The letter stated that Oakley's records had been located. His "disposables" had been sent. She should expect them soon.

His disposable what? His clothes? His body? There was an 800 number to call, which she did while drinking the sweet tea. Soon she was crunching ice to the tune of "The Dance of the Sugarplum Fairies." Soon after that she was disconnected.

Was she waiting for old socks or ashes? A hospital gown, his last uniform? If it was him arriving, she should stop everything and prepare the girls. But really, she couldn't prepare until she knew what was in the package. So this is how it ends, she thought. With a slip of paper.

With Oakley, life had promised to stretch green and everlasting as the hills outside their bedroom window. In the morning before the sun rose, she'd wakened just to hear him leave for the fields. She listened to him move through the dark house, heard the trickle of water in the sink, the soft scraping of the razor against his skin, then his voice low as he hummed a song that ended abruptly when the words became loud enough to hear. The scratch of his first match, the kettle's rattle in the kitchen. Off he'd go across the squeaky porch and call, "Dog, dog!" If she listened real hard, or maybe she just imagined it, she'd hear them head down the trail, the dog rooting in the cane and Oakley singing loudly, *"Apples on the table, peaches on the shelf, I'm too good a-lookin' to be livin' by myself."*

She dialed again and this time reached a live person who found that Oakley's remains had been mailed to his widow and she should have them soon. She breathed easily and felt relief stretch to her fingertips. Still, she'd wait before telling the girls. She pushed the junk mail into the trash and plucked up the top letter, a note from her accountant to file her quarterly taxes. She expected sadness to come down on her like a heavy curtain, but instead what she felt was curious elation.

There was a loud knock at the open

door. Gert loomed in the doorway. "Miz Bohannon, the Inedible Fat man is here."

"Oh, dear," said Hattie.

He bumped up next to Gert, a short man with round cheeks and a burnished but shiny complexion. Gert stood as if enduring the eager tail-wagging of a puppy.

Hattie rose and shook his hand and explained the fire in the vat. Gert led the procession down the hallway. At the kitchen door she announced over her shoulder, "I'll shut the hatch."

The man, whose name Hattie had forgotten, watched Gert through the window, a look of longing on his face. Men never ceased to amaze her. This little man always made an excuse to come to the kitchen and gaze at Gert. He often wanted to inspect the deep fryer and the hatch to make sure there were no leaking joints in the pipe that fed into the vat. Gert tolerated these interruptions grumpily, often tapping her large spatula on the edge of the grill, jarring everyone's nerves.

Hattie walked him outside. Troy Clyde and his son Darryl had cleared the vat and Dumpster of goo: dirt and grease. The man climbed up the side of his tanker, which was labeled INEDIBLE FAT in case of accident, and peered into the vat. "Shell's still solid," he said. He climbed down and thumped the walls. "Fireproof coating worked fine." He opened its door and slopped around inside, inspecting the pipe's opening and declaring it tight. "I'll just treat it as normal," he said, and unhooked a black hose from the back of the truck, affixed a clear plastic mask to his face, and sprayed the vat with a mist of cleaning agents, which oxidized. "Squeaking clean," he announced.

Hattie took his log and added her initials next to his entry: *No fat on account of a lit butt.*

"Why don't you share the good news with Gert," Hattie said, "and have a slice of pie."

"Well, actually," he said, "I thought I'd have some french fried potatoes, stick around awhile, and see that everything's in working order."

"Go on then," she said. Git along little dogie. She touched the warm sheet metal of the Dumpster. Soon the smell of ash would thin to nothing. Above the mountain, the sky was pure blue. *Sweet home Alabama, Lord, I'm coming home to you.* She smiled and felt a sudden tear in her eye. Oakley was on his way.

"Mama," called a sharp voice coming out of the vent in the men's rest room.

"What is it?" Hattie frowned and crossed the blacktop until she was standing under the vent. A diesel pulled up to the pump, snorting and rumbling. They yelled over it.

"There's writing all over the stalls again." Darla hesitated. "It's the Mad Queen."

"Clean it off."

"Why bother? Next week it'll be back for all the world to see. That stupid Mad Queen."

"What are you standing on?" Hattie said.

"The sink."

"You'll muddy it with those boots."

"Oh, Mama, the sink's the cleanest thing in here. Men don't wash their hands."

"Your weight will tear it out of the wall." Hattie heard Darla thump to the floor and the swishing of the mop begin. Darla was too thin to damage the sink, but at eighteen she was taking absurd stances on things.

The Mad Queen made Hattie's blood boil. Whoever the misguided soul was, she suddenly found his vandalism, this deliberate destruction of her property, a personal affront. At first she'd been appalled by the vulgar invitation he offered truckers,

133

but the content bothered her less and less as she grew accustomed to the obscene scrawlings and phone numbers inside the johns. She believed it was people traveling through, adding to what was there, or maybe some of the high school kids that came up to eat every once in a while. In truth, she resented the problem of cleaning up after the Mad Queen more than what he wrote. It would be so nice to establish something, like pleasant color on a stall wall, and have it respected. But no. Someone was always putting another obstacle in her path. All she wanted was clean rest rooms and a safe place to raise her daughters. She tried to rid her mind of the Mad Queen but found it impossible.

Darla Bohannon

Inside the bathroom, as Darla sent the last wave of mop water rolling toward the drain hole, she savored her assault on the Mad Queen's black scribble. She'd found a super cleanser that claimed it would eat Magic Marker and pen ink but leave paint intact. Industrial-strength Blister came in a can that looked like a steel drum. She wrung the mop out in the bucket and donned her outfit to repel noxious fumes. She fitted a white cone over her nose and mouth. Then she put on plastic goggles — stolen, she suspected, by her sister Connie from biology class — and, last, pulled on the yellow rubber gloves to prevent dishpan hands. With her long-sleeved shirt, jeans, and green rubber boots, every inch of her skin was covered.

She treated each toilet to a dose of Lysol then went into the first stall with Blister. On the walls some idiots from Virginia had written they'd been there and the date. Whoopee, big deal. What did they expect? Someday they'd be famous and this wall would go in a museum because they had scrawled their names on it? She could imagine Mama's billboard reading BOHANNON'S FAMILY RESTAURANT, JUNIOR JOBES PISSED AND WROTE HERE. Blister wiped that possibility out. Above the dispenser in very small letters someone had written a message that you had to be reaching for the paper to read. As Darla bent closer she hoped it was not one of those stupid poems some people thought were so funny — no, it was a high school cheer: *People in the front, let me hear you grunt!* Some idiot from school had done that. He'd probably come back. She Blistered it good. Foam moved like a small white avalanche onto the toilet paper roll, which soon sagged in two pieces, the edges of the cardboard core jagged and wet. Mama would get mad about this. Darla leaned out the stall door and made two good shots into the gaping mouth of the trash can, which was never used. It looked sad, standing there doing its duty for nothing.

It was crazy how things like toilet paper were so important. She and Mama kept a close guard on it, especially in the fall since so many people around here were Crimson Tide fans and loved to watch football games, raising toilet paper in one hand and a box of Tide detergent in the other. Roll Tide! The truck stop was on the road to Birmingham and Tuscaloosa, and sometimes people forgot to get their toilet paper before they went to the games. Why didn't they just buy the old scratchy generic kind?

In the other stall, she rubbed out several insult wars and some silly rhymes, a couple of War Eagles and Big Orange Crushes. Then she shut the door and faced the black hand of the Mad Queen. A whole week had passed and not a word from him, but here it was again. It appeared in time for weekends. Why then? The Mad Queen must know his message got erased every Saturday. Could she catch him somehow if she just left it up? She couldn't patrol the stalls. There had to be some way to stop this. What if there were no Mad Queen and it was just a joke? Just somebody who was leaving her messages, or somebody who wanted to make her work hard? She thought of all the time she invested in keeping the walls clean and of the collection of rejected cleansers in her closet at home. She stepped out of the stall to get some fresh air before spraying his message.

A man stood at a urinal, his head resting on the white porcelain. He slumped. The creases in his ruddy neck were dark with dirt, his sleeves rolled up past hairy arms. Without turning, he nodded in her direction. She knew she should move back into the stall. He held his penis with both hands, aiming it carefully at the sink. The stream stopped and he slowly raised his head. "Let me alone, you queer mother."

He shrieked and faced her, holding his penis straight out. It looked like a pink toadstool on a thick stem, sticking out of a thatch of dark hair.

"Mother of God! It's the goonies!" He stumbled as he zipped his pants and crashed through the door. Darla heard the

CAUTION: CLEANING sign hit the floor.

She ripped the nose cone off and gulped the lemon-flavored air. She had seen a penis. It was an odd-looking thing, so smooth and pink but sprouting from a nest of briary hair. Her breathing slowed. She mixed a heavy solution of water and Lysol and poured a bucketful down each urinal. Even though she wore gloves, she could never bring herself to swab them out by hand. Mama never seemed to notice. As she worked, she began to feel like she'd been given one of those boxes with a coiled snake inside. First she was shocked and then pissed off, like when you realize the snake is just wire. She took a squeegee mop and washed down the walls around the urinals because there were yellow streams where some men had missed, although she didn't know how they could be such lousy shots. They held the things in their hands.

Then she remembered the Mad Queen's message. The letters seemed to float at her, squiggly and black like the man's hair. FOR A HOT BLOW, COME TO THE HOLIDAY HOUSE. Blister, white and thick, foamed noisily as it obliterated the invitation.

She rinsed her gloves in the sink. A voice growled through the door to the bathroom.

"I'm almost done," she yelled, and quickly removed all her protective clothing.

Hattie Bohannon

Back at her desk, Hattie signed the official letter from the high school confirming that Connie had dropped out and was working as a waitress. At this time in her life, working suited Connie better than school had. She'd always been too energetic to sit down eight hours a day. There'd been no slack for her so-called behavior problems, which, Hattie knew, stemmed from a simple need to stretch her legs. Connie's time-out was an experiment. Right now it was going well.

Next she opened the *Maridoches Ledger* and found her ad in the Church of the Holy Resurrection Bible Contest. Whoever correctly identified the book and verse would win a Bible from her. It was extremely easy to win; the hint — the name of the biblical book — was as large as the logo above the quotation. The winner also had to submit a one-page testimony explaining how the Bible improved his life, which limited the contest to those who already owned Bibles. Hattie resented the business compromises she was forced into to appease the church — like running this ad and hiring Gert Geurin. But Gert was good; the most irritating part of the contest was the winners who felt inspired to read their prize-winning essays to the customers in her dining room. Haw Sullivan had won her ad twice, which was against the rules. She reported him to the church. It was discovered he'd won forty-one Bibles under assumed names and set up a Bible booth at Tannehill Trade Days. He was disqualified.

She scanned the paper. Below a picture of a platter of fried chicken and mashed potatoes ran this week's Bible verse:

Now she that is a widow indeed, and deso-late, trusteth in God, and continueth in supplications and prayers night and day. But she that liveth in pleasure is dead while she liveth.
— 1 Timothy 5:5–6

She felt her face burn. Was this a coincidence or true divine intervention? A widow indeed: well, she'd been a widow in fact for nearly five years, ever since Oakley'd gone off to Walter Reed. But she was not deso-late or desperate as Kenny Ranford had claimed. Why is a woman alone considered depraved or devastated? She'd read an article that said unmarried women were by far healthier and happier than married women. Maybe that accounted for her sense of relief rather than despair at the news that Oakley was returning. The last half of the quotation ate at her, though. Was this a reference to Jessamine? No, she thought. *Widow* could only be herself. Herself and Paul Dodd. Pleasure. If they only knew it wasn't pleasure but experiment, dipping her toe into the vast chilly river, recognizing that a plunge promised exhilaration and danger. And this verse was here to remind her of it, of the danger.

She glanced over the verses running below the other merchants:

For in much wisdom is much grief: and he that increaseth knowledge increaseth sorrow.
— *Ecclesiastes 1:18*

Clearly a dig at the proposal to raise taxes to improve the schools, a perennial argument in Alabama. But it could also refer to her own testing of the waters. Oh, what a day. First the letter about Oakley, then the strange quotation, and at ten o'clock she'd heard a newsman report matter-of-factly that the sexual revolution was over, as if there had been a wall map dotted with colored pins charting advances and retreats, as if another small island had been brought to its knees. Having missed the revolution due to wedlock, Hattie wondered how she was supposed to act. As a single mother? She rejected that tag with its suggestion of looseness. Certainly not desolate. Widow sounded so old and dry. The revolution over, the social codes broken and in disarray, what was left? And why must she name herself something that had to do with her sexual activity or lack of it?

She next opened a letter from Vegetables of the South, Inc., informing her that they would no longer send her tomatoes. She reached Kenny Ranford after four tries. His voice could sweat through phone wires.

Kenny Ranford shouted, "One of my deliverymen almost beaned by you because you want to put on a show for your customers! What if you had missed?"

"I never thought about it."

"You are either arrogant or a lucky fool."

"Or else I am a good softball player."

"Yes. Okay. You are a genius about the

people you sell food to, but do not harass my workers."

"Kenny, I am not going to buy gassed tomatoes."

"You opened the box first. That is a violation. Before you see the tomatoes you are refusing them."

"When I see Florida connected to tomatoes I know they are hothouse, not vine-ripened, no matter what the package says."

"What is the problem with Florida Sun-Ripened Tomatoes?"

"Everyone knows it is too hot in Florida to raise tomatoes unless they come from a hothouse."

"Oh? How does Carolina Sun-Ripened Tomatoes strike you?"

"Strike me?" Hattie could never get a good fix on Kenny. "Do you own those tomato hothouses?"

"I do not have to answer that. You could have asked me before you signed the contract, but now it is too late for that kind of impersonal question."

"Look, Kenny, I have my own problems. If we run out of gassed Florida tomatoes in the next two weeks, I'll serve fresh local tomatoes, fat and juicy."

"That's your funeral," he said. "Expect no more tomatoes from me. I must go now.

It is time for my four o'clock pill." He gulped. "Digitalis. This business of business is bad for the heart."

Hattie called Troy Clyde and told him of the tomato problem. He promised to go to Gadsden and buy as many flats as he could. He'd have Darryl till manure into the short field near his bean hills and then later on, after supper, he'd be ready to plant. Hattie sighed. At least there was someone she could count on.

She snuck into the storeroom looking for the gold chair so she could take a rest. It was gone. She went to the kitchen and asked Jessamine about it. The girl cast Gert a pointed look and said she needed privacy, so Hattie led her back to the office.

Jessamine began talking about the chair in a strange way. Somehow it related to Gert smoking and to Richard Reynolds and to an affair. She was spiteful, unrepentant, not sorry in the least. She stood there, her chin thrust forward, her hand sweeping and resweeping her fine blond hair, a gesture practiced to draw attention to it. Hattie wanted to pull her hair out by the roots, shout in her face, and tell her how egregious her mistakes had been. She wanted to shake the girl until she understood that she had committed social sins.

Hattie actually sat, quite shaken, in her chair behind the desk, growing paler and paler as Jessamine's words came out. How could her daughter do this? To her, Hattie, who had scrambled and sacrificed in order to save Jessamine from shame. Had given up so much to be a mother again. Had covered all the bases and made the lie a truth. Jessamine was the last person she expected to betray the lie.

The longer she listened, the more her mind turned to Jessamine's accomplice, Richard Reynolds, married and quite a bit older than her daughter. He was the one at fault and, should anything come of it, he should be the one to hang by the heels. She felt like searching the Bible and supplying her ad with a verse about adulterous men. Fidelity was one thing Hattie felt keenly about. It was why she hadn't gone out with anyone but Paul Dodd since the telegram came. She believed in until-death-do-us-part. If Richard Reynolds were divorced, she had no problem — well, a little problem — with Jessamine and him getting together. But this was just a case of sex. It always was. Lust. Despite protestations of love.

Then Jessamine said, "He's going to get a divorce."

"Don't hold your breath," said Hattie.

Jessamine said, "Oh, Mama, he loves me. When I was with him, I was so happy."

"Did you do anything other than have sex?"

Jessamine sucked on her lips. "If you only knew what it was like, you would understand completely."

Hattie cracked her jaw. She stared hard at Jessamine. Inside, though she was appalled. I am not this hard person. I know love and joy. Knew love and joy. Or did I? In those faraway nights she rode with Oakley to honkytonks scattered like debris across the lush mountainsides. When a shack, strung with blue lights, popped up unexpectedly among a forest of Georgia pines, she always asked herself, What does not belong in this picture? Today her answer was different. Then a newlywed, she'd matched Oakley beer for beer until, after several months, her skin plumped out. Often she was the only woman in the place. Late in the evening, if Chet Atkins was playing on the jukebox and if she'd drunk enough, Oakley'd call her his guitar and stretch her body across his lap. "Fellas," he'd say, "I'm goin' to play y'all a tune." He'd hold her left breast in his left hand and run through several chord changes. His right hand strummed invisible strings between her hipbones. With her head flung back, barely brushing the raw pine planks, and the room too dark to tell the ceiling from the floor, she'd felt giddy and terrified, spinning and falling, held by a pair of sturdy hands.

"Mother," Jessamine said, "you're frowning. Quit thinking about work and listen to me."

Hattie would call someone else, with such carrying-ons in her past, cheap. She knew on one level that her memories pointed out giant flaws in her relationship with Oakley. But on a deeper level she could not label that young woman in her memory, her former self, cheap. She'd been carefree and in love. She remembered the many mornings she awoke to a shifting sky of green leaves. Her legs carried the earth's imprint to Oakley's jalopy, where she shook sticks from her hair. Oakley's eyes said, What fun, while he walked like he wished he were a feather that could float home. Instead, they'd climb into the car and grit their teeth as they bumped their way back to Maridoches.

That was how she lived her days until

Aunt Leola drew her aside and left an indelible fingerprint on the inside of Hattie's arm. "You're a mother now," Aunt Leola said. How magically, it seemed now, she'd become strict and orderly. It must have been tough to let Oakley go out alone, and yet as she searched her memory she found no trace of resentment. Perhaps the exhaustion of the early pregnancy made his trips undesirable, and after that it must have been the bulge. She could hardly have been a guitar worth its sound with a melon distorting the strings. So well had she become the conscientious house-wife and mother, washing clothes, cooking meals, and canning tomatoes, that by the time Connie quit nursing, it didn't occur to her to go out with Oakley and drink beer. Staring down their grown daughter, her sudden yearnings for that long-lost carefree life filled her near to bursting.

"How does it feel to be trash?" she said.

Jessamine's face whitened. She stood up, her mouth and fists opening and closing. Paralyzed, yet flaming white, she finally moved in one swift turn toward the door and passed almost invisibly through it. She hooked the knob and swung it hard into the frame, which clapped in shock. The door shuddered.

Hattie's heart was thumping and she felt chilled and she wondered why she was always so hard on her girls. Because I expect them to help me through this life, and they do not. The curtain of sadness finally descended. Oakley was not coming back. Now she was alone, the sole parent.

She tried to figure the quarterly taxes but the numbers swam. She broke her fountain pen in half, watched the ink squirt then pool on her calendar. A dark lake drowned out last week. How nice, obliteration, she thought, and took out a soap dispenser and cleaned her inked fingers.

The door opened and Hattie braced herself for Jessamine's return but it was Gert, whose face was pinkly agitated. "There's a delivery man with tomatoes like to made of rubber," she said and held up her bandaged forefinger, a victim of the shipment's unripeness.

"We'll take them," Hattie said. "We are desperate for tomatoes."

Gert stood aside for Hattie to pass. "Miz Bohannon, if we pile them in paper bags with apples, they'll ripen right up."

"Let's do it," said Hattie, and she followed Gert to the kitchen.

★ ★ ★

Almost boozy with the smell of tomatoes, she returned to her office and glared at the rest of the mail still stacked neatly, waiting for her attention. She pushed aside the taxes and put her head down on her arms. Morning had been years ago.

A tap on her elbow woke her. She grumbled, "Go away." Her eyes registered a masculine hand and followed its curled fair hairs to a khaki sleeve. She sat up and covered her mouth.

Paul Dodd leaned across her desk, fixing her with his eyes, and said, "It's soon to be summer, too hot for much. How about a drive to DeSoto Falls this evening? I can get us in, special privilege."

She felt a sharp sting, as if bitten by a mosquito, when he said *special privilege*. He could be using his special privileges to chastise Richard Reynolds. Yet she truly regretted the answer she had to give because he looked so fine and it had been a lifetime since she'd gone into the woods with a man at night. "I promised Heather I'd help her with her homework. It's a little essay she has to write about her family. Let's do it tomorrow."

He'd shrugged, his shoulders drawing the khaki taut from his waist, the thing she remembered as she fumbled for an answer to Heather's assignment: Write an essay describing your daddy.

The child implored with eyes hazel-gold, not found in the Bohannons. Hattie knew this day would come but, unprepared, she lied. "Title the paper *Oakley Bohannon*. He was a soldier in World War Two. He raised corn and tobacco. Tall and skinny, he laughed a lot." Once she started lying, she couldn't stop. She could not mention the depression that grew as his body declined in the grips of angina and lung disease. Or the last six months at home when he was delirious with memories of the war, or her own exhaustion. Nor could she say he was not Heather's father. "He left you money to go to college with. He is going to be buried in Arlington Cemetery, outside Washington, D.C., a very select cemetery. President Kennedy is also buried there. His grave will be marked by a white cross and I will plant a small bush of pink roses on his plot, in honor of you, because you were such a rosy pink baby."

Heather giggled. "Mama, I can't write that."

Troy Clyde picked Hattie up when there was an hour of sunlight left. The air was still warm and made her yearn for cool sheets and sweet light music, but instead she was wearing grubby jeans and her fingernails were caked with soap. They would plant tomatoes in the low field he owned on the banks of the Ruby River. He'd also bought rosebushes on sale. They stood, prickly and green, above the small forest of vegetable leaves.

"I was fishing in some mighty queer waters the other day," Troy Clyde said, as they drove around the mountain. "On the Chattahoochee with a bunch of them bankers. Reverend Peterson was along, but I don't think he likes fishing much. He wore this big old orange life preserver with fluorescent crosses on it and held on to his pole like it was a lifeline to the shore. I think when he came here was when that church quit having baptisms in the Ruby."

"He's been a constant presence at the truck stop since the fire," said Hattie. "Every day sitting at a table with his papers spread out. Never orders a thing but ice water. Never leaves a tip. And Gert Geurin just moons over him. She's started wearing makeup. I'm surprised he puts up with her. But she sits with him on her break and he seems real interested in her tales of kitchen life. It's beyond me."

Troy Clyde parked at the field. The sky was faded blue and the river a boiling brown. They got out and set to work. "Gert Geurin wearing makeup in your dining room. She's a threat to your business."

"As long as she keeps cooking, I'll keep her." Hattie dunked two root balls in a bucket of water.

"There's too many tents in the trees," he said, pointing his stick at the edge of the forest where soft white nests of caterpillar silk hung on each tree.

"Maybe there's a plague of butterflies in our future. Ready?"

"A plague of fire ants more likely," Troy Clyde poked holes in a furrow. "I hear you been on a date."

Hattie placed a plant in each hole and mounded dirt around it. She nodded.

"You like him?"

"We're not in kindergarten, Troy Clyde."

"I just wondered if I had to beat him up or not."

"That I will not tell you," she said, and soaked the mud off her hands. She recaked her fingernails with the hard little soap.

"That sheriff must have the greasiest knees in town, if you count the number of arms he's slipped away from."

"Every day's a new day, Troy Clyde."

"Is that religion or talk-show talk?" he asked.

She flicked water at him and he asked her to do it again, he was sweating so much, so she didn't. He knelt, in his sleeveless white undershirt, above the small holes while Hattie crouched beside him, a fragile tomato shoot poised over its place in the earth. They worked two rows in silence.

"Well, Hattie, I might as well tell you. I'm a free man."

"A free man? What about Melanie?"

Melanie, Troy Clyde's newest wife, worked at the bank. She was twenty-six years old and seemed to have her life charted all the way to the grave. Last year for their first wedding anniversary she'd bought twin plots in the cemetery. Troy Clyde took off in his jeep and slept in it for ten days, wondering if she'd bought the plots to exaggerate their age difference — he was forty-six — or to announce to the world that she had succeeded where so many others had failed: she was his final wife. A third reason had occurred to him, the one that sent him roaring back home: maybe she intended to shoot him. That was not a challenge he'd run from. From

Hattie's perspective, Troy Clyde came through everything smiling. He didn't believe divorce rescinded conjugal rights and his ex-wives didn't either.

"I ain't never had a wife who worked before, so these obligations seem a little funny to me." He squatted, digging too deep a hole in the furrow. Hattie settled back, cupping the dirt ball at the base of the plant's stalk to keep it from drying.

"It all started last night when I had to go down to the bank's banquet they have every year. First, I had to get on my suit and my tie and my alligator boots."

"Melanie made you wear a suit?"

"I said a suit is only for marrying or burying, some occasion where you got a preacher up front. And Melanie says Reverend Peterson is on the board of the bank and he'll be at the head table, so she won that little skirmish. Anyway, we get there and first they call up the gray gooses that have been at the same position for twenty-five years. The gray gooses wobble up and get their pats on the back. Why, I bet if they give them a pat on the ass they'd work thirty more years at the same position, but then I ain't running the bank. I wish I was, though."

Across the field, the dogwood trees

flared, white and pink, in the shadowy woods. Hattie stretched her legs out in front of her.

"Then comes the sneak announcement of the evening. Melanie has been promoted to branch manager of their sister bank down in Opp. She gets so excited but it is all I can do to keep from going up and saying *Melanie is not going to South Alabama. Her family and her husband is right here and this is where she belongs.* I stewed for hours and that sorry stuff they serve for punch didn't help the situation. You would think that the boys at the bank could spring for shots, but no. They dump all the liquor in the punch and then make it puke-green with lime Kool-aid and pineapple juice. *Blech.* I had one glass and Melanie had many. So I put this silly look on my face and waited until we finally got out to the truck, where World War Three breaks out."

The small tomato plant had dried out and the sun seemed hotter than it had all day. Hattie wanted to touch her brother but he sat so still, as if in mild shock.

"Melanie decides she will go and spend the night with her mother, and I have already turned up the old bird's street when Melanie remembers that her mother doesn't believe ladies smoke, drink, or screw, even after they're married. So we go on home. This morning I figure things will be worked out so I go to get my breakfast, and thank goodness I put on my shorts because there in our living room was Melanie's mother. I took my bowl and my cereal and pretended the old bird was a piece of our everyday furniture. Melanie must have eat early, knowing this fright to the appetite was coming over.

"So I'm sitting there eating my cereal when Melanie's mother starts looking familiar. Then she makes these loud sniffs, like this." Troy Clyde inhaled three doses of pungent air. "So I say to her, 'Miz Killian, what is your real name?' And she says, 'It's Rhuhanna Polk Killian.' "

"I just about snorted my cereal. You know who she is? Remember Pudge Polk from back in school? She was in my class for about two weeks, sniffing the whole time."

"I don't remember her," Hattie said.

"I said, 'Pudge Polk! You sure have changed from our school-days!' Back then her fat red face and body put you in mind of the heap of raw clay next to the brick-works. You should see her now, skinny as a birch twig. She works out at that gym downtown. I've always said some women need to have a good amount of weight on them or they're about as peachy as a block of chalk. Melanie's got this stuff she puts on her face called a mask, supposed to prevent wrinkles, she says. Looks like her mother forgot to wash her mask off. And her eyes that used to be sunk in, now they wobble like egg yolks on her hard cheekbones. You look at her eyes and you think they're going to slide off her face and make a mess on your floor."

"So you kicked Melanie out because of her mother?"

"Naw. When Melanie came into the room I told her to go on down to Opp, meet the people at the bank, check out the housing situation, find out what cultural events might be to her liking, and when she comes back we'd sit down and have a mature conversation and I might reconsider my position."

"Troy Clyde, you didn't!" Hattie crushed the tomato plant. Its leaves broke in a sickening squish.

"Yeah. Melanie gave me the most dumbfounded look I've ever seen on her face, but Egg Yolk Polk sniffed a little higher up on the sniff scale, so I figure she approved."

"Troy Clyde, you can't move to Opp. You can't leave all your kids. Or your farm. You have to stay here." She stood up and slung sticky hair from her forehead. "Troy Clyde. You can't leave me."

He reached toward her shoulder but dropped his hand as if great stones had moved between them. "Look at them two crows. I wonder what they're doing."

A pair of tangled crows tumbled over the bean hills.

"Troy Clyde, I can't go on if you move." Her breath came fast, almost white.

"Oh, I ain't worried one bit. Opp's the hometown of the Annual Rattlesnake Rodeo. Melanie's scared to death of snakes."

Hattie threw the wadded tomato plant at him. It unfolded its bent fibers and clung pathetically to the fine ridges of his undershirt. "I could kill you."

"That's the surest way I know of my leaving here." He kicked a clod of dirt loose and fired it at the squawking crows, who winged swiftly to opposite sides of the field. "Naw, I ain't worried one bit about Melanie. It's the snakes at the bank we got to look out for."

"Tell Melanie their new computer program keeps bouncing my checks by accident. She needs to ride herd until they learn the system." She buried her hands in the dirt. "We better get the roses in or I may never want to go home. It's so pretty out here." In the twilight, the caterpillar tents looked like iridescent diamonds.

"Hattie, I may be married, but you're the only family I got," said Troy Clyde.

"Thanks, bubba," Hattie said. The rose sprig she selected stuck her thumb but good. On second glance, she noticed it held its single thorn out proudly, hooked, green, ready for battle.

Jessamine Bohannon

As Jessamine left the house, Mama and Heather were settling down for homework. The scent of bacon followed her, like perfume sprayed on her wrists and neck. Well, no one was going to get that close to her, and in a bar everyone wore a wrapper of smoke. Smoked sausage. She giggled. Richard Reynolds, the Smokin' Sausage. He always came to mind these days. She took care where she placed her open-toed heels. No dirt ring on her toes, please.

Her white VW looked lonesome at the edge of the parking lot, a marshmallow forgotten at the bottom of the bag while the fire dwindled to embers. She was ready to jump in the fire. Mama must have wondered at her going out tonight, like she had a date, not an illicit rendezvous. Richard had not called. Not once. His loss. She reached across the passenger seat and rolled down the window. Let the fresh air blow over her body. In and out of honeysuckle clouds wove the VW on its way to Bigbees across the Georgia line. She'd known as she pulled on her sleeveless maroon dress that this was where she would go. As she draped her necklace of large blue glass beads around her neck, she knew the bar of ill repute was her destination. She figured out why she was going there too, although she didn't dwell on it. Richard the chickenheart would not dare show his face away from home.

Bigbees promised ugliness, the kind of place she might have endured for years if she'd continued as Richard's mistress. For years, she thought. I could have gone on for years. Thank God I called his bluff. She felt relief now. At Bigbees there was no way she'd find anyone interesting, because — well, she really wasn't interested in meeting anyone. Not yet. This time she would be selective, let her mind lead the way.

She slammed on her brakes. The VW slid sideways, halting as a heavy-duty garbage bag flew by her window and split on the tire hump. She hadn't seen the old pickup truck lumbering up the hill. Its shape was visible for a second against the sky, a floppy hat appearing at the peak, before the dark trees obscured it. She heard a loud squish, the rattle of cans, and the spine-chilling shatter of glass as yet another bag hit the road.

She rolled up her window. A putrid mix of rotted eggs and sweet vegetables permeated the car. She reached over and rolled up the other window but felt like she'd trapped the smell in with her. The VW lurched toward the lip of the ditch before Jessamine remembered she was not straight on the road. *I could have hit that ditch easy as pie.* She roared off, then slowed, looking for the next garbage heap. She yanked down the window. It's got to be nicer out there. Gradually, she increased her speed.

The entrance to Bigbees from the back road was an old lane. It didn't have the gigantic billboard touting a winking woman or a path of lanterns made out of plastic cups advertising the Alabama Crimson Tide and the Auburn Tigers, like the highway entrance did. Jessamine eased the VW around a waterhole that looked big enough to swallow the car. A hand-painted sign said CARS and TRUCKS, with arrows pointing in opposite directions. Lined up like a barrier between the bar and a weedy field were half a dozen tractor trailers. The car lot was three-quarters full. She picked a lighted space between two Chevys.

Jessamine combed her hair. Inside, the bar looked like a bar. Tables. An empty dance floor. Men's haunches hugging bar stools. No one even looked at her when she walked in. Good, she told herself, but she felt like a kid gawking at the circus. She should take a table. One out of the way. Her chair wobbled on uneven feet. She ordered a beer from a waitress wearing a tight gauze shirt. The woman's large brown nipples showed through the sheer material. What's the big deal? Jessamine wondered, although the thought of bare breasts made her a little ill. Yet this was her cure. She forced herself to look at the other waitresses who were similarly covered.

For a long time her eyes made little forays into the room, noticing people but not looking closely enough to identify anyone. After her beer came and she'd drunk most of it, probably too quickly, she spotted Sheriff Dodd at a corner table. She stared. He was talking quietly to a waitress in a very serious manner, the way Richard used to when he told her his mournful life stories.

Jessamine pretended to be impressed by the wall covered with license plates. Apparently truckers left them as tokens of appreciation. She counted the states she saw, trying in her mind to think of something she knew about each one. Virginia — Is for Lovers, Robert E. Lee, Elizabeth Taylor. Dela-where? — must be in Canada. California — Hollywood, Clint Eastwood.

"Howdy." Sheriff Dodd swung his leg over the empty chair and sat down. In one hand was a cold pitcher of beer, in the other several napkins shaped like figure eights. They were pink and she realized what they were — breasts — in his large fingers. He put one down in front of him and placed the pitcher on the warped table. The beer rocked close to the edge but didn't spill. He picked up her empty glass and waved it over his shoulder. A waitress appeared immediately with two iced glasses. He took them both in one hand. He spread a napkin in front of her, making sure the edges were flat before setting the cold glass down on the middle. Jessamine shivered self-consciously but he didn't notice. He filled his glass. Then he tipped the pitcher. A gold stream leapt and crashed against the bottom of her glass, finally subsiding as foam stood on top like icing.

"You get to know a lot of people when you're sheriff," Sheriff Dodd said. "I like to come up here every now and then to relax."

To hide her nervousness, Jessamine drank. Sheriff Dodd's blabbing mouth surprised her. He was so cool and silent at the truck stop. She ought to say something, but everything she thought of drew attention to the fact that she was sitting in this bar alone, which made her think of Richard. She hoped Sheriff Dodd wouldn't tell Mama he'd seen her. She clutched her beer as his questions got more boring.

"It's not a bad place," he was saying. "Relax. Enjoy yourself."

Jessamine sighed.

"You like Eddie Rabbitt or Alabama? I'll tell them to play you a song."

"I don't like them. John Anderson's good."

Sheriff Dodd grinned. There was a slight gap between his top front teeth. "I'll be dogged. You know a real artist, all right. I was afraid you'd like those slick fellas." He called to the waitress and gave her some quarters for the jukebox. He finished his beer and filled both glasses.

The first bars of Anderson's "Swingin' " swept into the club, lifting her expectations.

Sheriff Dodd shouted, "Are you waiting on somebody?"

She signaled him to hush. He sank back in his chair, happy to listen to the music. Jessamine grew sadder as the song played out. It was about cheery love, something so impossible for her now, it made her throat ache. Her fingers kept time on the table-top. As the song ended and "Long Black Veil" began, Jessamine noticed Sheriff Dodd looking at her with interest.

He reached over and wiped her cheek with his thumb. "You had a smudge."

Her cheek burned. His eyes were a burning blue. Feeling his eyes, her body tingled. She missed Richard. "Thank you." She blushed.

He held out his hand. "Let's dance."

Jessamine followed him to the small stage where a few couples hugged under the guise of dancing. The music was incredibly slow. He stepped close and rested his fingers on her lower back where her muscles flowed gently into her buttocks. Her face rested on his shoulder. She inhaled his aroma, the khaki of the law.

The warmth she'd felt at the table became a slow hot fire. He kept them from moving. He kept them slow. He dropped his head to her neck and breathed. A warm stream whistled down to the back of her knees, each fine hair along the way rippling with electricity. His breath continued to brush her as if he were a stablehand with a curry comb, intent on making her shine. *I could love this man,* she thought.

The music stopped. She opened her eyes. They were alone on the dance floor. She smiled at him and settled her head on his shoulder. He didn't sway but stood straight. Then, as the thought crept across her mind, a stinky smoke seemed to fill the bar. *I could sleep with this man.* My mother's boyfriend. She felt drunk. The room swirled. She clutched at his shirt as she tripped over her feet. "Oh, God. Oh, God. What am I?"

Sheriff Dodd said, "It's okay. You're at Bigbees, with me. The sheriff."

"The law," she moaned. "The law."

"I'm not going to arrest you," he said. "I need to get you home."

She let him lead her to the door. Again his presence overwhelmed her. She hung on to his arm, leaned heavily against it. Oh, God, she thought. It is going to happen. I'll leave with him. Her body was not listening to her. The little voice was drowned by a slow-spreading sweet sea that reached the very top of her head.

He pushed the door open.

"No!"

Sheriff Dodd let the door bang shut. He sat her in a chair. "Do you have your keys?"

"Yes. Here." They jangled in her hand.

He reached for them but she drew them against her chest. "*You* can't drive me home."

"I am not drunk like some of us," he said. "Do you want to end up dead in a ditch?"

"Dead would be safer."

"You are a morbid drunk, little girl."

"I won't go with you." She wrapped her legs around the chair and gripped the table.

Sheriff Dodd disappeared through the door marked EMPLOYEES ONLY. In a minute Ash Lee came out the door, buttoning up a hunting shirt that Jessamine recognized as the sheriff's.

"Come on." Ash Lee kicked open the door. Sheriff Dodd took Jessamine's arm and helped her to the car.

"I'll be around to get you," Sheriff Dodd told Ash Lee. "Don't go inside the truck stop. I'll be right behind you."

Jessamine slumped in the passenger seat. Both windows were down. The air felt nice, just the thing she needed to cool off.

"The lady who owns the truck stop, she's your mama?"

"Yes."

"Fuck."

Jessamine didn't know what Ash Lee was cussing about, the jerky way she was changing gears, or what Jessamine had just said. Her head was spinning. The car whined as it was forced to pick up speed. It swerved suddenly.

"Damn sack of shit in the road," said Ash Lee.

Jessamine felt scared by the power of her body's raw hunger. It was beyond her control. She grabbed the dash and pressed her fingers hard into the vinyl. She wondered if Ash Lee's skinny body had a burning desire like hers did and if Ash Lee got satisfaction all the time and if being satisfied made you want less or more. Jessamine compared hair — light and dark; faces —

round and lean; bodies — both slim, fingernails painted in pink shades; shoes — sandals and sneakers. She wondered if anyone could tell which of them was the prostitute.

Ash Lee relaxed once they got on the interstate and had the VW humming like normal. "I was hoping you were going to work at Bigbees. I was real happy when Dodd took a liking to you. Keep him off my back. He makes me work there so I don't contaminate your Mama's place. All the girls used to work that lot, but he busted us and made us work the bar. But I ain't going to stay. Being a waitress you got to punch the clock. I like keeping my own hours. But seeing as your mama's his girlfriend, I guess you ain't gonna be his waitress and still be alive when you get home."

"I have a job," said Jessamine.

"He is a real piece of shit. Pawing all over you and dating your mama."

For the first time Jessamine considered that Sheriff Dodd could take some blame. "God, no. It was me. Dancing with my mother's boyfriend. What am I?"

"You got problems? Go to church. That's what they always say to me. *Jesus will save your soul.* But what about my ass?"

"Sounds like Sheriff Dodd has saved

your ass," said Jessamine.

"And yours too," said Ash Lee.

Jessamine rested her head on the dashboard. She felt like she was being sucked up the grill fan and turned into a swirl of smoke. Unfortunately, she couldn't just disappear.

Hattie Bohannon

Now and then the moon broke through thin clouds and gave Hattie a glimpse of the wilderness as Paul drove down a closed road toward De Soto Falls. Paul had come the next evening, as planned, and now as the landscape disappeared from her sight, she remembered Darla's red bunched-up face when she and Paul left the house. Maybe she should have waited for the ashes to arrive before going out. But no, there was the moon, glossy and grinning, playing hide-and-seek through the trees.

Paul parked the truck on an incline. Hattie was tilted toward the ground. She wore a plum cotton skirt and white Indian blouse with embroidered sleeves that caught on fledgling branches as they dashed down a dim trail. Laughter floated from her mouth. He pulled her along and hissed *hush* every few strides. The path twisted through an arbor of lilacs. It was dark, too dark to see the flowers. As they ducked below the branches, they passed in and out of fragrant clouds. The lilac scent thick across her lips, she followed Paul through a gap in a granite wall.

They stood on a slippery ledge under DeSoto Falls. Mists moved like ghosts, her skin tingling, moist. For several minutes, Hattie leaned against Paul. His body was warm but diminished by the exhilaration she felt for the falls. An invisible cascade, but roaring, oh, roaring with power. Moonlight cast white shadows along the granite floor.

Paul stepped away and placed a bottle of wine in a crevice. Water trickled over it, giving it a hooded robe like a religious statue. He wrapped her up in his arms. They kissed, the kiss sweet as lilac. She felt the power of the falls pounding the pool behind her, the waves gently lapping over the ledge. She was falling.

He thrust her under the waterfall. Water filled her mouth, forced her to her knees. She kicked at the slippery granite, lost her balance. She clutched at him. He whisked her from the brink. She clung, heaving for breath, her heart pounding louder than the water, louder than his laughter. Her knees, formless as water.

He half carried her to a boulder and settled her on it. "I bet wine sounds good."

Her heart slowed but she continued to huff loudly until she realized that the falls drowned her out. Paul rearranged her legs to make room for him on the boulder. She said nothing.

He uncorked the wine, placed the cork in his pocket, and tilted the bottle to his lips. A few drops spilled on her thigh.

"I forgot the glasses. We'll have to share." He offered it as he might a bouquet.

She gulped a swallow of fruity wine. He took a sip, then wiped the bottle's mouth with the hem of her dress. Her second sip was fruity and metallic, wine with a river aftertaste. She thought of Kenny Ranford drinking water from her well. "The taste of metal, the taste of money," he'd said. "This water will make you a millionaire." Hardly.

"You dreaming?"

"No." She spread her wet skirt over her toes. "I'm just thinking about water."

Paul hopped around on one foot, his legs a figure four, as he removed his shoes. He launched into a back dive through the falls. Then nothing but the rush of falling water, shimmering shifting water.

"Hey, hey, hello, hello," he called from the other side of the curtain. "Come on in."

"I can't see what's in the pool."

"That's just like you." He disappeared.

She sipped the wine. He yelled and cavorted like a dolphin in the silvery foam. She caught glimpses of him as he dove through the falls. Just like a kid. Water swept in folds down the glittery black wall. Tingling with a strange intensity, her wet clothes like cool velvety skin, she chose to sit on the granite while he delighted in the rush and power of the water.

He heaved himself onto the ledge, his squared shape distinct against the misty white curtain. His belly button was the size of a quarter. Her face warmed. He shook his head, hit his ear, and shook his head again. He stripped off his shirt and tossed it near her feet, where it landed with a slap, arms outstretched.

She thought suddenly of the way Jessamine talked about the tangle of sex and love and found herself at the same crossroads. It was not love she felt but it felt like love. As Paul approached, she blurted, "What am I going to do about Jessamine?"

"Jessamine. Jessamine?" He blew a sour note across the mouth of the wine bottle. "Not a thing. Have you talked to her about birth control?"

Shocked, she flung her head back, the ends of her hair catching him in the jaw. She'd meant her question as a light thing, or maybe she hadn't, but she resented his assumption of a greater intimacy than she felt.

Paul drew back and slammed the boulder. "Doesn't the moon mean anything to you? Seeing the moon shine through the waterfall? The wine cooling in a natural spring? Our walk in the woods? Just you and me? Every time we are together we might as well be sitting in a booth at your truck stop. You're always bringing your kids along with you. Especially Jessamine. Talking, talking, talking about your kids. Well, I'm not interested in taking your kids on a date. Can't you just be you?"

She listened for the water's roar but it sounded dulled and familiar. "Oakley's ashes have been sent. I'm glad they're on their way. Then, when I have them, I will be ready to . . ." She paused and smiled in the dark and felt her heart step up its pace.

"You're waiting on his ashes?" He picked

up the bottle and took a long drink.

"Yes. It's right for the girls that I wait."

"You're their mother but you have a life." He brushed her wet hair off her forehead. "I don't mind holding out a little while if it's for you, but if it's a screwy reason for your kids —"

"Screwy reason!"

She watched him don his shirt and shoes with detachment. *I am my children. I am my job.* Just as he was his job. He had a written code that determined how he reacted to any situation — except how to deal with an angry mother. Sorry, no rules pertain. Therefore, such a situation doesn't exist.

She could stop him before he buttoned his shirt. They could lie together under the waterfall; her body was ready. But it wouldn't be right. "I'm too cold right now."

"Right," he said. "Let's go then. You can snuggle under a dozen quilts for warmth. I guess that's what you want. Quilts."

Gert Geurin

Church was hot again. It was like Reverend Peterson brought the fire from the Word into the building and stoked it to the rafters. All sprigged out in a purple vestment, he zipped through the devotional and the first hymn and began on all the sins of the world and mainly those right here in Maridoches. He lulled me awhile and my mind drifted and I was having thoughts, which I allow myself from time to time even though he is the authority and God's personal messenger. If someone speaks in tongues, that brings me right back because there is message in the music of the strangled sounds. You're hearing with a part of your not-brain and yet the understanding is clear.

I understand the part about forgiveness of sins, that the Lord always forgives and we should too, but it always seems that women have to do most of the forgiving. If men were made in God's image, why are they needing the most forgiveness and why must we always forgive? Why should Ann Reynolds forgive Richard? Why should Jessamine? Why do we have confession of sins and it's always the men up there? I think it makes them think they can go out and sin again and they will be forgiven. It's too much free rein, if you ask me.

Reverend Peterson impresses me like no other preacher because of his concern for his flock. Some preachers would go into

177

Bible stories or parables, and he just out-and-out states things in a modern way we all understand. Sometimes parables cause people to get off track. Like Gee and Haw setting at the lunch counter arguing about how can somebody bury a talent. I'd like to bonk their heads sometimes, the stupid stuff they get stuck on, but they are just old men with nothing to do but examine all the knotted thoughts in their heads.

Stelle broke out in tongues and woke everybody up and Miz Breathwaite interpreted the words — more about wantonness and temptation, which I thought Reverend Peterson had mighty well covered.

Then Reverend Peterson announced there was a meeting after service for the Board of Elders, a silly name since the elders are not old but are all men, mostly in business and big farming. I'm elder than most. Rumor has it Stelle sends in notes for Reverend Peterson or, rather, the rumor is she writes out his plan — like a good secretary, I say, to whoever thinks she has too much influence, just because she doesn't have the title. She is serving the Lord too. She has duties. Imagine who would pick the hymns and scriptures and do the visitations and the counseling if Reverend Peterson was single. Probably that burden would fall on someone like me.

The ladies meet too, and sometimes I go, although most are younger than I am and live in town so I'm sort of like a potato to their tomato. They want to start an aerobics class in the fellowship hall. That I cannot abide: women in skimpy outfits doing high kicks to modern music in the house of the Lord.

They want to do it on Sunday and Wednesday evenings before service. I can just imagine all those sweaty women sitting in the congregation, their faces flushed and pink, all thoughts on their bodies when they should be thinking of His message. And to say nothing of the men's responses. I know the Lord will put a stop to that.

After the sex sermon, I was fanning myself when Reverend Peterson said something that gored me to my heart. He quoted out of Leviticus: *"Do not prostitute thy daughter, to cause her to be a whore; lest the land fall to whoredom, and the land become full of wickedness."* He said *we,* the congregation of the Church of the Holy Resurrection, could not in good faith go to Miz Bohannon's truck stop because of the evil that was going on there. This nearly made my heart jump out of my body. I felt anger rise up and I liked to stood and give them folks a tongue-lashing like I was Joel or some other wild-eyed prophet. But I am a woman and they stone us who speak in English. I wonder if that is why Stelle always speaks in tongues: because if she spoke in English the people might stone her? So I sat and boiled. We are not bad, the Bohannons and me. We serve food, not smut. I could feel that anger seep out of me and turn to rivulets running down my face and under my arms. Baker Thomas inched his backside down the pew in one direction and Miz Killian pretended to sneeze. She rose up off the seat an inch and sat back down away from me. I got to the point of blindness, where all I could see was dark red out of my eyes. It took so long to get out of the pew and then down the aisle. So many people were congratulating the reverend on this great idea. They actually stopped to talk instead of brushing his hand in passing like they've just played a ball game and were on their way to the snacks. Especially the sinners: Baker Thomas, Richard Reynolds, all of them others holding up the line. A guilty conscience always has a lot to say.

It was like a public atonement but I thought, Just you wait. The minute one of you skunks goes to Ash Lee, I'll find you out. Won't be nothing for me to walk through the brambles and get there, not as often as I'm at work. I'll just go down after my shift and watch. I'll just drive over with a big hamper full of food, stretch out in the back of the station wagon, and catch them. With their pants around their ankles and their eyes dancing the Devil's delight.

Reverend Martin Peterson

Martin was his old self, full of verve, planning a march on the truck stop to protest its immorality. As in the old days when he organized battalions of tornado relief volunteers, he made lists of squads, each with an appointed warden. He assigned four wardens: Ann Reynolds, who choked softly and hung up while he was enthusiastically outlining her position front and center of the marchers, Elise Thomas, Verdena Tannehill, and June Ann Breathwaite. The three who were in agreed to bring at least ten others. They would write Bible quotes on posterboard and staple them to stakes donated by Logan's Yard. They'd meet at 9 A.M. at the ramp and march up the hill, perhaps singing an appropriate song — Martin would ask Stelle to choose it.

He looked up when Stelle came down for tea. She moved on moccasins so soft he had not heard her approach. He looked up and there she was, a long column of white cotton that showed him nothing and everything of her elegant body.

He shared his plan for the march and she broke out in a smile, and warmth moved back into his gaze. "I can't imagine why Ann Reynolds hung up on me," he said.

"She may want out of the spotlight," said Stelle.

"Why? Her husband's back in her bed. That should make her happy."

"That should," said Stelle.

He glanced at Stelle's face but found her eyes closed and her nose happily inhaling the aroma of her peppermint tea.

"I thought I'd give her a chance to triumph over that truck-stop hussy. Make her a warden."

"Oh, Martin," she said, "it's not a war."

He emitted a throttled snort. "It *is* a war. A moral war."

Though she didn't laugh, he felt like she had. He watched her open the freezer and remove half a gallon of Rocky Road ice cream. She scooped three large spoonfuls into a coffee cup and put the box back in the freezer.

Martin said, "No, thank you."

She startled. "I thought you wanted to whittle your tummy down. I was eating it so you wouldn't."

"Always the good Samaritan, Stelle," he said. "But seriously, have you gotten a good look at your rear end lately?"

Stelle carved off a bite and set it in her mouth. She closed her eyes. Her back stiffened. She dipped up another spoonful and lobbed it at Martin. It missed him but stuck on the wall behind him.

"Missed." He grinned.

"No kidding," she said, and walked up the steps to the second floor.

He felt she'd meant something more than she said. He listened to hear her footfalls above him but heard instead her vocal exercises, scales of *la-las*. She'd shifted back from painting to singing, now that there was a church action that required more of her voice. He looked at his list and drew a line through Ann Reynolds's name. He thought awhile and added Rhuhanna Polk Killian, Troy Clyde's mother-in-law. Let the Bohannons fight among themselves. He called Rhuhanna, who gushed through a dozen questions before agreeing to be a warden.

His adrenaline returned. He got up and fixed himself a dish of ice cream. There was only a little left in the box so he added it to the grand mound crowning the bowl, dumped Stelle's melting scoops on top of that, and went out to the deck and gorged.

A very large black ant crawled across the boards toward his foot. He wondered if it could sense his ice cream. He plopped some in the ant's path. The ant circled it and moved away, as if in dread. A weird raindrop, Martin surmised, cold and dark and sweet-smelling.

The sun was still high. His ice cream melted faster than he could eat it until it was chocolate soup with nuts. He looked to the house but couldn't discern where Stelle was so he did an unexpected thing. He walked down the steps toward the water.

The trees were hung with gossamer sacks of caterpillar nests. All through the hot green maze to the lake, cottony lanterns clung to branches. Martin had not seen an infestation like this before. He wondered if the trees would die or if there'd be an overabundance of caterpillars in his woods, crawling in armies up to his house. He wondered if they ate ice cream. Mosquitoes flew by his ears and nibbled his arms. He swatted them and zigzagged his head to miss a swarm hanging out like a mob needing a victim. He moved faster, his shoes slipping on the mossy steps, until he broke suddenly into the clearing and stumbled onto the dock.

Blinded by the flat white surface of the lake, he grabbed at air and fell hard on his knees. At least he'd hit the wood. The dock rose and fell with small waves. His closed eyes bored into the back of his head as he clutched at the splintery wood for a handhold. There was none. Just balance and motion and the smell of hot mud and the sting in his knees. He turned his head toward the dark pines and opened his eyes, then slowly, slowly, brought the lake into his view. He saw ripples on the surface, black hillocks of water, moving away from him like a brigade of soldiers. From his rampart, he smiled. If he gave them the Word, God's Word, they'd be his Army of the Lord.

He crouched on his knees, mesmerized by the waves, and felt a surge of power.

How long since there'd been a river baptism in Maridoches? Years. Yet he believed in the washing away of sins. He lay on the dock and folded his hands and slipped them into the warm water. God would make Stelle right. The promise and relief washed up against his hands. If he could swim, he'd jump in right now and be healed — but he could not, so he let his hands come clean.

On the deck, up at the house, he found his bowl full of drowned black ants. He took it inside and washed them down the drain.

Hattie Bohannon

"Are you kidding?" Hattie said to Gert, who had come all the way into the office and shut the door behind her.

"No, ma'am. They are going to march up here and protest your truck stop on account of prostitutes."

"That's nonsense," said Hattie. Church people were mostly full of hot air. Stupefied on Saturday, sanctimonious on Sunday, mundane on Monday. She wished Gert would go and let her finish the payroll.

Gert shifted from one leg to the other. "Jessamine's just under the influence of bad spirits. She's not trash."

Hattie looked up sharply. "Is this because of Jessamine and Richard Reynolds?"

"Praise the Lord." Gert worked her hands one over the other as if trying to rub them clean.

"Are you kidding?"

"You know about it," said Gert with relief.

"And you know too?" Hattie's stomach clenched.

"I discovered them," said Gert.

Again Hattie was confused as Gert launched into a tale like the one Jessamine had told her that involved the gold chair and cigarettes and Richard Reynolds and underwear hanging on the doorknob.

"Who told Reverend Peterson about this?"

"Richard Reynolds did, at confession during service. He said he'd been with a prostitute up here."

"Jessamine is not a prostitute." She shot Gert a look.

"No, ma'am," Gert insisted. The cook did not go on and defend Jessamine's virtue, which Hattie had hoped for. If she had done that at church, she might have stopped this rumor.

"We have no prostitution here. Shoot, I

don't even sell girlie magazines or allow condom dispensers on the premises. If those folks come, they are going to look pretty foolish, don't you think?" Hattie said. "There's nothing going on in Maridoches this month but hot weather. I wish those churchwomen had jobs. Then they'd quit poking their noses where they don't belong."

"I need that sick day off," said Gert.

"So do I," said Hattie. "They're all beginning to be sick days."

Gert thanked her and backed toward the door, feeling behind her for the knob, which she grasped and turned twice before finding a grip with her sweaty palm.

Hattie had a good mind to call Reverend Peterson and ask him what he was up to. He was a slight man with a pale face who subsisted on ice water. She did not believe him capable of any full-blooded action. And so she returned to signing checks for payroll, relieved that Jessamine had not been publicly named but also despairing for the way bad publicity flew around town for free while truthful advertising cost so much.

As the day wore on, she felt uneasy so she called Paul Dodd. She'd never called him before and it felt strange, but as a businesswoman she'd call. His voice sprang back at hers, eager for contact. When she asked about prostitution in her parking lot, he assured her there was none. She had the cleanest place for miles. She laughed and invited him to come to dinner at her place.

The Bohannon Sisters

That evening Hattie's daughters fled the dinner table, like a flock of startled birds, in a single clatter. They fled, they told one another as they sat on the front porch, eating blueberry pie, so Mama and Sheriff Dodd could have their coffee in peace. They knew Mama's placid face would soon appear and her polite voice would dish out pleasantries. The sheriff would think her remarkably calm, but they knew white anger burned beneath the seamless smile. They had better eat the pie pretty damned fast.

Darla, the pie thief, plowed through her second piece with a relish that matched her enthusiasm for the first. Her legs dangled off the porch. She'd make herself sick on pie before the sheriff got a single bite.

Connie swung listlessly in the porch

swing. Her pie sat on her lap, untouched. "Think of all the calories in one slice of pie."

"Please don't spoil good pie." Jessamine leaned against a pole.

"A pie's for eating. What's the big deal?" Darla said.

"Mama made it for Sheriff Dodd. She hasn't baked a pie in forever. She must be dying in there, right, Heather?" Connie swung forward and rapped Heather's head with her foot.

Heather alternated bites of crust with bites of filling. When her mouth was full, she breathed into the gray tabby's face, then watched the cat's nostrils twitch. "I was only trying to make him feel at home."

"Burping at the table is disgusting," Darla said, through her full mouth.

"He lives alone," said Connie. "He probably burps a blue streak whenever he has to. It's a natural reaction."

"But a burp doesn't become a tarzan yell, Heather dear," Jessamine finished.

They shouted with laughter, then stifled their mouths in fear of drawing Mama outside. For a long while, the sound of tines scraping competed only with the fluttering of hickory leaves.

"What I want to know," Jessamine began

carefully, "was why you sat in Daddy's place, Darla?"

"Well, he wasn't going to sit there. He's not that important."

"God, are you ever dumb, Darla." Connie broke the crust off her pie. "How many men has Mama invited to have dinner with us?"

"At least I didn't lean away from him like he was a leper." Darla glared at Jessamine, who was not supporting her.

"If you hadn't plopped in Daddy's place, then he wouldn't have had to sit next to me," Jessamine said. "And I had to lean away from him. His thighs are enormous. They kept rubbing against my leg. Then Mama would push me back at him with her leg. I mean, his thighs are as big around as the cannon on the square. It was very unnerving." She ate her pie in quick bites.

"I thought when Mama pulled that long blond hair out of her salad that you'd take the hint." Darla eyed the pie tin. A quarter remained. She scarped up the juice on her plate by slanting her fork.

"Hey, Hobart, care to clean my plate?" Connie handed over her pie but pinched off a triangle of the crust for herself. "I hope we didn't spoil it for Mama."

"I wouldn't say mentioning how cheap his deputies tip was a good topic of conversation," Jessamine said.

"If he wants to impress Mama, he'll see that his deputies give me good tips."

"I wish that he would marry Mama," said Heather. She flicked a blueberry at the cat's nose, where it stuck.

"Why would you want that?" Darla said. "Like Mama said. He's nothing but a friend and business acquaintance."

"Because everybody has a daddy except us."

"We have a daddy," Darla said. "Don't you remember him?"

"No," said Heather.

"He used to carry you around when you were little," said Connie. "He kissed your head all the time."

"Yuck!" said Heather.

"That was before he got too weak," Jessamine added. "Before he just went in his room and wouldn't come out. I remember standing outside the door, hearing him choke."

"Yeah," Connie said. "That sound scared me at night. I used to think it was a monster, coming to get me. I wanted him to go away. Isn't that awful?" She wiped her eyes and looked out at the yard.

"Poor Daddy," said Jessamine.

The girls sat in silence, watching the traffic at the truck stop, listening to other families slam car doors on their way inside to eat.

Darla, who had been watching a crow strut up and down the shed roof, leaned toward Heather. "If anybody asks you about Daddy, or if they say anything you don't know about him, which makes what they say a lie, just deck them."

"Okay," Heather said. "I'll just deck them."

"Right," Connie said. "It's important that we help Mama look around and find our daddy. So, we should be nice to any rich man Mama brings home in case he's the right one for us. We wouldn't want to scare him off, would we, Jessamine?" Connie's voice was innocuous.

"Yes, that's right." She stretched. "Mama would be a lot happier if the VA would get the facts straight."

"I'd be a lot happier if we got paid without selling catfish. The damn restaurant smells like fried fish all the time. I think it's the new grease the Inedible Fat man made us buy. It's the worst smell in the world," Connie said. "I say let Mama have some fun with Sheriff Dodd."

"You all are nothing but idiots!" Darla shouted.

The screen door squeaked. Mama and Sheriff Dodd stepped onto the porch.

"Here you all are," Mama said, smiling pleasantly. "We thought we'd find the pie out here."

"Blueberry's my favorite," the sheriff said.

"Yes, Mama, it's hard to resist that delicious blueberry pie of yours," Connie said.

"We thought we'd sit out here for our dessert but all the seats appear to be taken." Mama smiled at Paul.

"I'll go." Darla jumped up from the floor. She and Jessamine were rapidly washing their front teeth with their tongues. Of course, Connie flashed her stainfree smile for Mama.

"You two could stand to be considerate." Mama stepped toward the swing.

The girls rushed inside, Connie first, carrying the pie tin. "Okay," she said, "give me what you got." Thanks to Jessamine's food stretching expertise — blowing air into the pie filling with a pastry puff — and Connie's eye for arrangement, they produced one decent and one mangled piece of pie. They watched through the screen door as Heather presented Mama with the good slice and Sheriff Dodd the wrecked one. "For burping at supper," she told him.

Hattie's daughters decided it was a lovely evening to hoe the garden, an activity that promised blisters, good exercise, and the foundation for a tan.

Darla Bohannon

After hoeing until dark and rinsing the tools under the hose, Darla still felt her stomach grabbing and releasing. The house was brightly lit upstairs where her sisters were laughing about the day at the truck stop. Jessamine and Connie, both dumb blondes in her opinion, seemed to think everything that happened was funny. She was always out of the loop.

She went inside and passed by the kitchen where Mama and Sheriff Dodd were sitting in candlelight, talking softly like two old cousins. She turned abruptly into the living room to keep from yelling the words that had rushed to her throat: Mama was a traitor. She stood in the dark, listening to her sisters laugh upstairs. Mama is lonely, she said to herself, but that was a lie. Mama is making me lie. To him. She walked to the mantel and picked up her favorite picture of Daddy. She held it in the arrow of light cast by the lamp in the hallway. "I'm the only one like you," she whispered. "I'm skinny and I have brown hair. I will protect you and us." In the photo, a very young daddy was leading a mule pulling a load of jugs. His face was squinched up. He was yelling at the photographer, a woman, whose shadow stretched like a tall steeple toward his long bare feet.

Darla felt a jolt of loneliness in her stomach. She placed the picture back on the mantel and went outside. Mama didn't hear her leave, too distracted by the sheriff. She walked down the slope to the garage and worked the stuck doors open wide enough to let herself in. An old dry dirt smell enveloped her as her eyes adjusted. Whiffs of oil and metal and dried hay were what she sensed in the closed-up air. Light from the overheads at the truck stop streamed in through cracks in the plank walls. She could see blankets wrinkling the elegant outline of Daddy's blue Oldsmobile, the Jetstar 88. She flipped the red wool comforter off the roof, sending up a fluff of cat hair, and crawled into the car. Mama had the key so she sat with her hands on the wheel, wishing the windows weren't electric, a fancy extra from a 1965 model. The rearview mirror stretched in staggered panels across the entire front window. Daddy installed it because he kept running into things.

He had always worked on the car on Sundays. Darla remembered watching his blackened hand glide from under the car to lift hexagonal lock washers, which smelled of oil and ranged in color from rust to steel. Using his fingers as measures, he'd slip the washers on, like rings, until he had the one he needed. Sometimes his thumb, sometimes his pinky fit the washer. She could never guess what he sought, though she rearranged the washers, trying to be helpful. Ringed, his hand would glide back and he'd disappear totally under the car.

The steering wheel moved a quarter turn to the left, then locked. She would leave pitiful Maridoches and find Daddy. She did not believe he was dead. It was all so simple. An orderly had screwed up his name and now he languished somewhere as Bohannon Oakley so doped up he couldn't straighten things out. She would drive to Washington. He might not recognize her grown up. There was no way he wouldn't recognize the Jetstar.

Yet as she thought this through it seemed too hard. Mama had tried this herself and had failed. Maybe the only way in was in. Exhausted she fell asleep. When she woke, the sky was dark. It had come to her in sleep that she should join the Army. It was the only way to find him. Outside the garage, the dark house and mountain loomed behind her like immovable weights, while in front of her the shifting lights of the truck stop promised easy motion. She went inside the restaurant and helped herself to a cup of coffee. She was relieved that Gert had not come in yet. Rudy, the night cook, never seemed to remember her. She asked him for a ride to Gadsden, where he lived.

"Sure," he said, rolling down his sleeves and drying his hands on a towel. "And I'll do it for free. I'm too tired to even ask for something in return."

Darla smiled. He really didn't know who she was. They rode to Gadsden in his white Cavalier, listening to Hank Jr. wail about parties and the old days. Rudy dropped her at the recruiting office. All she had to do was wait until it opened.

Hattie Bohannon

It happened as I passed the cross lit with white bulbs, fronting the Church of the Holy Resurrection. I came up Raider's Hill and at the crest there was that cross shining in the dawn light and it was then I felt my self squirm back into my proper body, as if what I'd been doing was astral projection, not making love. I needed that cross to pull me back. Otherwise I would have run out on children and work, abandoned the world I'd put in motion, and existed as a wild licentious being. Instead, the white light cooled me into the stiff form I'd inhabit until the next rendezvous.

On the horizon red brightened to yellow, spreading heat across the sky. All day everything would burn. I eased the VW into our yard and walked casually past the tomatoes as if I'd just risen and was engaged in the usual morning assault on the slugs. There were no lights on in the house. The girls must have overslept. Quietly as a thief, I pushed open the door to my own kitchen.

Heather, hands dug deep in the pockets of a faded yellow dress, looked up, startled. The light made her hazel eyes golden, like marbles of truth. We are blue-eyed people, the Bohannons, except for Heather. She stared solemnly and then said in a tone I recognized, "Mama, where is your other shoe?"

My left foot was bare, clotted with red clay. My right was wrapped in a blue leather sandal beaded with a shooting star. Dampness hugged my hips where the lacy hem of a negligee bunched in my jeans. I crossed my arms over my chest. She could have asked just as easily about my missing bra.

She opened the refrigerator door and struggled with a half gallon of milk. She swung the jug onto the counter and peered around it. "What's that smell?"

"Summertime. It's the smell of summertime." The heat the night had not contained flooded my face as salt, salt filled the room. I hugged myself tighter.

Heather poured milk in a glass. "Jessamine's in the shower. With the door locked. I had to pee in the yard."

"I'm sorry," I said. My mouth was dry. If I had awakened thirty minutes earlier; if I hadn't slept at all. I ground my bare foot into the welcome mat. The rough fibers pricked like needles.

"Can I salt the slugs today?" she asked. She'd been banned from the garden after

I'd found mounds of salt in the rows, little crystal tombs cupped over slug rinds. Salt in large amounts was lethal to vegetables, so I'd swept it out. Thus the slugs munched on. Each morning the yellow blossoms of the pumpkin vine lay shriveled on the ground.

"Yes." I poured all our salt into a yellow bowl and gave her a spoon. "Put the slugs in here."

"They'll drown in all this salt," Heather said. At the door she turned and said, "Maybe I'll find your other shoe."

Standing in the tub, I felt a bead of sweat form behind my ear. It tickled my neck, grew fat and inched, like the tip of a tongue, over my ridge of collarbone before picking up speed between my breasts and slipping down my soft stomach into a tangle of curly hairs, where it sat like a shiny jewel. It fell like a drop of hot wax onto my thigh. I turned the shower on cold, full-blast to douse that voluptuous woman, to tighten her into the serene owner of the truck stop, the starched one, a woman so fine people rarely cursed in her presence. Untouchable. The widow self. That one.

I remembered as I slid my damp body into my uniform that Gert was off today.

Jessamine would have to step in and cook, and Darla would have to stay home from school and help her. Carrying my work shoes, I relished the feel of the cool floor on my bare feet. I knocked on Darla and Connie's door. When Connie groaned, I went inside.

She was sitting up in bed, smoking a cigarette. I knocked it from her hand and slapped it out with my shoe on her favorite pink halter top, which was lying on the floor. Her mouth opened and shut as her skin faded so pale no color was left in it.

"I'm sorry," she said. "I promise I won't ever smoke again."

I glared. I had no time to get into an argument. "It will kill you," I said. "Where's Darla?" Her bed hadn't been slept in.

Connie searched the house while I went out to the garden and then to the garage and down the slope to the truck stop. Maybe Darla was out running as she used to do. But Connie found her running shoes; worse, her fanny pack was missing. I called Troy Clyde and he dashed over in his jeep.

I phoned Paul, expecting something rosy in his voice, an understanding that I needed something from him now, after I'd given him my trust.

But he spoke as if I were any concerned mother. He sounded tired and yawned as I described my worries. He said there had to be a twenty-four-hour wait before he could start any official search for a missing person. Teenagers ran off all the time, he said. How often do they end up dead in a ditch? I asked. Those are just the ones you hear about, he said. Maybe the girl didn't want to be the subject of the church's protest against your place today, he said. Maybe she wants to hide from that.

I hung up, all thoughts of my night with him evaporated. So they were coming. The fools from the church, so blind they followed the cracked minister. If I met them in the parking lot, I could tell them they were wrong about prostitution, but when I thought of Jessamine and Heather and my evening, my resolve fled. I couldn't admit these things in public. I shouldn't have to. My breath came up hot in my throat; sweat bloomed on my forehead. How could I get rid of these crazy folks? What would the truckers think? They'd get on their CBs and tell all, and then the place would swarm with men seeking the wrong kind of service. Why had I given Gert the day off instead of firing her? My mind was moving like a tilt-a-whirl.

Heather came in from the garden, a hand behind her back. "I didn't find your shoe but I've brought you a present."

She held out a small very red tomato, the first of the season. It was misshapen, a deep seam creasing the blushed flesh. "It's a heart," she said. "Can I have some ice cream?"

I took the warm tomato heart and placed it in the pocket of my apron. "Ice cream for breakfast?" I said. Her small face flushed and wisps of her hair clung to her chin. "What a grand idea," I said.

And then I had another thought that was even grander. They say the way to a man's heart is through his stomach. I happen to think that's also true of the ladies.

"Today there's going to be a parade at the truck stop," I said to Heather.

"Can I be in it?"

"No," I said. "But if you can't join 'em, you can beat 'em."

Darla Bohannon

Darla limped along in the hot sun. Only a couple more miles to reach home. That stupid trucker she'd hitched a ride with in

Gadsden hadn't told her he was going to Chattanooga via Highway 11 to avoid the weigh stations on the interstate. He wasn't even a licensed trucker. She should have known from his tight Levi's. When he backed the semi into the greenhouse at the Etowah Garden Center, it was all too clear. She'd hopped out of the seat so fast, she'd hit the pavement running and hadn't looked back. Now she panted. God, if anyone saw what sorry shape she was in, they'd think Coach Hiler was right about cutting her from the track team. The white pavement of the interstate baked hot as a deep fry. She slung the sweat off her forehead. If she wasn't so close to home, she'd hitch. Then Mama would scold her. Not the kind of homecoming she expected. But nothing was turning out as she expected. That stupid trucker.

Things had gone much better at the recruiting office. A clean-cut soldier with sparkling eyes had spent a great deal of time looking at her. He'd wanted to know what her interests were. She could talk to him as long as she avoided his face. Her eyes traced the tailored line from his shoulders to his waist. Not a wrinkle for an extra ounce of flesh. *Did she want to fly?* Hadn't thought about it, she said. She was more interested in intelligence. *Yes, he could see that.* She blushed against her will. It was so cool in the office, her sweaty shirt dried. She'd forgotten she was wearing yesterday's clothes. He talked to her for a long time. He never quit looking at her. At odd times, she felt her blood race from her toes to her neck. She signed the papers. The next eight weeks would be torture. But she had direction now, and she'd taken the first step in finding Daddy.

She kicked at loose gravel. Maybe she should go to the truck stop without showering so they'd be real sympathetic. No, that would just give Connie a chance to talk about stinks. She fixed her eyes on the exit sign and marched woodenly, as she imagined a soldier would. Lots of cars were parked along the exit ramp. Mama's business must be booming. She hoped Mama wasn't too busy to notice she was home. A growing cloud of dust sped down the ramp beyond the sign. When the dust lifted, a vehicle took shape and headed the wrong way up the highway toward her. It was Troy Clyde's jeep. She waved hard and began to run toward it.

"You better get in here, you little weed. I ought to tan your backside for all the grief you have caused your mother," he said.

After she climbed in and shut the door, Troy Clyde jammed the wheel to the left and they spun in a roaring circle.

"It's great to be home," she said.

"Your mother should have spanked your fannies all the way up until you were ready to leave home. If she had, she would have spared herself a lot of heartache in these trying times." Sweat dripped from his forehead. He got the vehicle back on the road and started toward the exit ramp.

"Don't you have air-conditioning?" She hung her head out the window, hoping to dry the top layers of her hair.

"Hah!" He snorted. "You're spoiled rotten. Let me tell you, you picked a hell of a day to run away." He wiped his face with a handkerchief, then offered it to her.

Darla turned up her nose at the damp cloth. *I have run away and joined the Army.*

"If nothing else, clean your face." He tossed it onto her lap. Then he combed his hair down.

Darla took the handkerchief and tied it to the mirror outside her window. She bent and wiped her head on her jeans.

"That's barely tolerable," Troy Clyde said. "Now get a load of this."

A line of women and children trudged up the cracked earth next to the exit ramp.

"Just look at them fools. It must be a hundred and two in the shade." Troy Clyde slowed the jeep to a crawl until he caught up with Gert Geurin wearing an undulating flowered pant suit.

"Oh, Gert, it's you. For a minute, I thought it was the Garden of Eden out for a stroll. Watch out!" He waved at her back. "There was a damned bee going for them jumping tulips on your backside."

She breathed too hard to make out what she said.

He kept pace with her. "You sure are walking a long mile for a Camel."

"What is going on?" Darla said. The walkers had to be dying. She'd barely been able to keep going on the flat part of the highway. Gert Geurin should be working.

"Craziness, just damned craziness. Hold on to your hat!" He sped up to a clump of younger women whose makeup had begun to run. Two carried children, while the third dragged a toddler through the red sand. "Heydee, y'all. It sure is hot."

One flipped him the bird as she adjusted her sunglasses.

"Is the truck stop so busy customers have to park on the highway?" Darla said. She suddenly wished Mama was rich and could get her out of the Army and into the Guards. She shook her head. Mama to the rescue as usual. No. She was going to find Daddy.

"Nuts," Troy Clyde said. "Poor little tykes. They don't know why they mamas dragged them away from the television. This is too much torture for a man to see before lunch." He shifted to second, then whistled. "They even got the wicked witch of the south out of her exercise suit for this one." Melanie's mother marched along in a broad straw hat, a violet skirt, and matching tennis shoes. "Oh, the Lord is good to me," Troy Clyde sang. He inched the jeep up behind her and tooted the horn. She jumped. Her shoulders drew together and rose to protect her neck.

"Hey, Miz Polk Killian, I didn't know you from the back, what with your skirt clinging to your bony heinie like a kid sucking a tit."

Darla shaded her face. Maybe she should jump out right here. She looked at the yards and yards of hot blacktop with its shimmering mirage. No way. She'd survived one weirdo already today, she could put up with Troy Clyde.

Pudge Polk swung her sign up to screen herself.

"CARNAL KNOWLEDGE IS A SIN," Troy

Clyde read. "Oh, Mother-in-law, is that based on your own experience?"

"Quit calling me mother-in-law!" Her nostrils flared and sucked in a good snort of dust. She began to cough. Troy Clyde leaned out and offered to pound her back. She held up the sign to ward him away.

"Hey, I read it the first time. Saw the movie, too. Movie's a hell of a lot better." Their skirmish had slowed the marchers who, eager for an excuse to rest, formed a circle around Pudge.

"You just angry 'cause you know I have carnal knowledge with your daughter ever' night of the week and twicet on Sunday."

Darla slid below the dashboard and thought, Nothing will ever change.

Pudge's bun leaked hair and she wobbled while her audible sniffs rapidly approached hyperventilation. Her lids stretched tight over her bug eyes; she slowed her breath and began to chant, as if casting a spell that would drive him from her sight. *"Understanding will watch over you; delivering you from the way of evil, from men of perverted speech."*

"Thanks for your concern, Mother-in-law, but if I was you I'd head right home to my air-conditioning. I ain't never seen no one hyperventilate through their nose.

Where is your minister anyway?"

Others joined in the chant, the smarter ones sliding into the scraggly shadows cast by tattered leaves.

"My engine light's on. You better watch yourself, Mother-in-law, you just got my jeep all hot." The jeep charged up the hill, raising dust clouds that hung in the air, trapped by the humidity.

"All right, girl, get your ass out of my jeep and go help your mother."

Help with what? Darla thought. She saw a refrigeration cart under the awning out front and Connie waving an ice cream scoop at Heather. I'm supposed to be in school. On the other hand, what was the point of taking another multiple-choice test on the habits of fruit flies? She was going into the Army. "I'll take a shower first."

"Suit yourself, but if you take too long, you'll miss one hell of a show."

She slid to the ground and slammed the door.

"Hey, Darla, you're welcome for the lift."

"Thanks, Troy Clyde." She grimaced. Damn it. She was acting like a kid. She crossed the lot and wished for a heavy downpour that would wash Troy Clyde and the ladies off the face of the earth, one

211

that would cool her through her clothes, a flood where she could rescue only the people she liked — but here her thoughts stopped. Few people would be worth saving.

"Well," Connie said. "Look who shows up." She laid row after row of plastic spoons on the table next to the cart.

"Just in time for dessert," said Heather. "That's not fair."

"What's with the ice cream?" Darla patted her face with a paper napkin while Connie explained Mama's plan to disrupt the march.

"Um, I hate to be obvious, but there are no prostitutes working here," said Darla.

"Watch your mouth," Connie said, and nodded at Heather. "This is an end-around rather than a straight up the middle."

"Oh," said Darla. "A reverse when they expect a power play."

"Yes," said Connie. "Automatic touch-down."

"Go left, Bo," said Darla.

Connie nodded and licked a scoop of lemon sherbet. "I'm betting on Gert to break down first."

"Just don't yell anything, Darla. Mama said." Heather gave her a cone.

"Yeah, yeah." Darla's cone cracked at the

rim. She'd been overly generous with the mint chip.

"How does the sign look?" asked Troy Clyde, who'd just shot staples into a cloth banner above their heads.

The sisters tortured themselves to walk in the sun and glare up at the sign. FREE FROZEN YOGURT. FREE ICE CREAM.

"Perfect," said Darla.

"A little higher on the left," said Connie.

"Here they come." A song wafted along first. The signs, uplifted, were hard to read. Some had moistened and bent. Most were coated with a fine layer of red dust.

"What's a pervert?" said Heather.

"Troy Clyde," Darla answered.

"No, he's a pig."

Troy Clyde carried a mixing bowl half full of ice cream. He ate with a serving spoon. "I tell you what, sherbet wouldn't melt in the old bitch's mouth."

"Troy Clyde!"

"I wasn't talking about your mama, now. I was talking about my mother-in-law. How she ever got Melanie, I'll never know."

"I'm sure she says the same about you," Connie said.

The picketers moved closer, a circle of pairs, walking slowly.

"There's Chase Logan. I bet he's the first to get ice cream." Heather stuck her tongue out at him.

"God, I hope those little kids are big enough to read." Darla shaded her eyes. "If not, this isn't going to work."

"They probably left the ones who can read at home. Look at their signs: PERVERT, CARNAL KNOWLEDGE, THE BREAD OF WICKEDNESS, LOOSE WOMAN, ADVENTURESS." Connie waved her spoon as each sign took a turn facing them.

"I'm about sick of ice cream," Darla said.

"Keep eating," said Troy Clyde. "Them little kids may not read but they can see."

"No, there's Dinky Taylor. He's blind and he's carrying a sign. BE NOT WISE IN YOUR OWN EYES."

"Maybe it won't be a kid. Maybe it will be a hot, hungry, humongous lady like Gert," Darla said.

"She looks terrible."

"She shouldn't be out in the heat."

"Look at old Pudge. She must have hernia of the nostril," said Troy Clyde, as if this was the first time he'd laid eyes on her. A red-orange trickle wet her upper lip.

"It could be a bad lipstick job," Connie said.

"It's not the right color for a bloody nose," Heather said.

"Cocaine," said Darla. "It rots your membranes."

Connie looked at her, annoyed. Just because she'd been out all night didn't mean she could just drop all this knowledge of cool stuff. She'd only been home half an hour and she acted like she knew about everything that was in the papers: country music and AIDS, cabdrivers and cocaine.

The Ladies of the Church of the Holy Resurrection

The marchers had jostled for spots in the inner circle. The distance to cover was not as great as that on the edge.

"Gert Geurin, you should lie down," said the ladies. "Are you sure you haven't perspired too much?"

"I can wait on Reverend Peterson."

"Where is he? I thought he was going to march, too."

"No, you may not have any ice cream. I should have left you at home."

"I left my purse in the car. Do you want to walk all the way down there and back and get my purse? I didn't think so."

"I don't see why we can't just stand still."

"The pavement's burning through my shoes."

"Does that sign say the yogurt's free? I didn't wear my glasses. I thought there was going to be TV coverage."

DRINK WATER FROM YOUR OWN
    CISTERN,
FLOWING WATER FROM YOUR
    OWN WELL.

"Justin! Remember your *attitude!*"

"Well, we got our exercise today."

"Yes, you still have to go to church tonight. You can tell the other kids who didn't come what it was like to be a picket. You can witness."

Hattie Bohannon

They were coming. I could hear them in the distance, gaining the long hill, ready to crucify me, and here I sat, the lights low in my bedroom. They needn't bring knives or swords. The words had been enough. *She that liveth in pleasure is dead while she liveth, a widow indeed.*

I longed for Oakley to be here to help on this day. In the past at times, I had talked with him in my head over the miles and he answered in his smart and funny way. He and I had many conversations because I needed shoring up. Today, though I sat on our bed and waited for his answer, there was nothing. Maybe my own guilt over having spent the night with Paul Dodd blocked him. Weariness rode my blood-stream. I could not face this day, these people.

I looked out the window and saw Darla step from under the awning. She was home. Maybe Oakley had answered me. Good. Good. I turned from the window with a sudden lightness and went to the bathroom and washed my face. I brushed my hair and set out toward the ice-cream cart to greet my returned child, but the parade of pickets wound around the perimeter of the lot, a slow, confident snake. The posters glistened like scales. There must be thirty of them, far too many to be considered only the fringe. I squinted at the words, names of everything I had tried to save Jessamine from becoming. Not one picketer succumbed to the ice cream.

I suddenly lost my nerve. I was not going to fight them head on. That was not the plan. I'd go to Darla later, later when I could both hug and scream at her. Now I felt dizzy. The weariness was gone but air was pumping through my veins. I took the path through the scrub to the garage, where no one would find me.

Inside, in the musty place, I climbed into the Jetstar. The dull red of a gas can filtered through a clump of broom straw waiting, as it had for years, for a broomstick. Oakley never got around to whittling its handle. A hard core of anger in my chest whooshed into a hot flame. He had abandoned me, that was the truth.

Yet I was keenly aware of how I used his absence. The spontaneous way his name fell from my lips when correcting a child. "Your daddy would not" a phrase that made Oakley into Santa Claus with its implication: If you are a good girl, your father will come home. Subtle and mean, or was it my own wish? If I am a good woman, God will send my husband home. I parceled Oakley out in small pieces that made him look like a saint and myself the embodiment of patience. In town, at Fred's General Store, pausing over the men's gray socks or buying mentholyptus drops as Oakley had done, a subtle way to remind the clerk of his absence. How much of this was planned and how much natural? I did not know. I talked about Oakley more in town than I ever did at home. In fact, sometimes months passed without a thought of him, except when his memory pushed itself full-blown across my vision, thanks to the sight of a trucker's yellow fingers or a particular laugh. His laugh was like a fiddle in a beginner's hands, uneven and squawky.

Again anger surged at him for abandoning me. If he was here, they would not dare march. This I knew.

His damned car. I thumped the steering wheel. His pride, his vanity. He was always pounding dents out of it. I remembered the one day I'd asked him to watch the girls so I could canoe the Ruby alone. When I got home, he was pounding a dent, and the girls were drenched in raw eggs. "Cheaper than a babysitter." He'd smiled, his face sooty with grease.

The runty hens I'd scraped up from friends and neighbors. I'd fattened them and they'd produced eggs I was going to trade for blue gingham to make myself a new dress after I'd gotten back to normal size after having three babies. My eggs. My money. True, he'd come from town the next day with a flowery yellow gown he'd paid too much for. Yellow made my skin look sallow and I didn't like florals.

I was the most alone I'd ever felt. The closeness I'd shared with Paul was replaced with sudden shame. I had expected too much from it. He had to have known about the protest while we were wrapped in each other's arms. His deputies' wives were ladies of the church. He had known the tarnished position it would put me in today. I had risked my reputation. Yesterday I could have stood out there and confronted those people, covering for Jessamine, but covering for myself was different.

Here no one could reach me. I felt as dried and battered as the broom straw, forlorn, as it hung, prey for rats, a home for parasites. In the past, I merely had to endure to survive. It had been a matter of getting out of bed every day and fixing breakfast and washing clothes. Any tragedy could be got over by doing housework. You saw dirt, you knew what to do with it. But now, the mundane did not give me strength or keep my mind off failure. My daughters finding danger at every whipstitch. The corroded faces of driven truckers, the shriek and echo of silverware in the ever-needy truck stop. The shrill refrain of the righteous letter writers — a woman's place is in the home, the Bible tells us so. In the purple-gray gloom hung a scythe, a half-moon curve among limp feed sacks and spiderwebs. The air in the closed shed fit like a soft blanket. Soon TV cameras would arrive to humiliate me all across the Smokies. Imagine their shock when they could not find me. I turned the key.

The engine groaned and clicked off. I tried again and pressed on the gas pedal. The chrome on the dashboard reflected, like a dancing flame, the red engine light. Patience. I had driven the car only once in the past year. This time the engine caught but died before I stepped on the pedal. There was a tick to listen for. I cranked the key and stomped the gas three more times before screaming. I beat the steering wheel and mashed the pedal to the floor, then turned the engine on. It sputtered. "You damn car! Come on! Come on and start!"

As my shouts rebounded from the tin roof, I got weak and quiet. Even his car refused to help. Because I had betrayed him last night with Paul Dodd?

Oakley had always cut through my fears with the right note. He would know what to do with a girl accused of prostitution. He had known what to do about a girl pregnant at fourteen. He was right then about Heather and Jessamine. But now I was alone with this same girl who could not corral her sex drive, this girl who expected me to fix her biggest mistakes for her.

Oakley would say, *Let her hang in the wind. She is twenty-one, and while you are her mother you must not be dragged down by it. If I were there, I would not allow it. I would send her out into the world and let her learn to be responsible.*

But Oakley, I cannot do that.

Then you will suffer.

I am her mother.

But her suffering is not your suffering.

She is a passionate girl and I do not want her to lose passion in the face of the mundane.

Cut the cord, Hattie. Cut the cord.

You are not here. You do not see her face every morning, full of promise and need.

Then you decide.

Just like that, I was alone again. There were dark shapes in the shed and layers of dust. He had come. And Paul Dodd had not mattered. I wondered who the man in my head was, whose voice that knew more than I did. It was a voice I'd relied on ever since Oakley had gone to the VA, but now I was startled by the thought that I had made him up. That I was him, and he me. I could barely command my arms to open the door. My knees wobbled as I staggered down the hill toward the large white sign proclaiming free ice cream.

Jessamine Bohannon

I cooked all morning in Gert's place. At first I enjoyed cracking the eggs and watching them sizzle while I stirred them into a soft yellow color. But after four hours of it, I was bored and sweating so much I felt slick as if I'd been dipped in raw egg white. When Mama came in to spell me at the grill, I was glad to go waitress. She said she wanted me front and center today. There was a march on the truck stop and I was to make sure I went out and faced the music, whatever that meant. She looked pretty bad, as if she'd been down on her knees with her head in an oven scrubbing a year's worth of charred grease, and it was only lunchtime.

A trucker whose behind was the biggest I'd ever seen on a two-legged animal sat on a stool at the counter. He wiped his head with a red bandanna and called out, "Hattie, Hattie!"

Mama's face was visible through the window behind the counter. Her hair stuck through her net like tufts of brown grass. She shouted back, "Tohee Hornsby! What a surprise. I thought you'd retired."

She didn't say *or died,* which we had all heard.

Tohee shrugged. "I retired from retirement. The TV couldn't hold my attention like the changing landscape does. No time to think, watching TV."

I could not help staring. He'd make five of me, easy.

Mama cleared her throat so I took Tohee's order. It took two tickets.

He said, "I won't be needing the salad, honey. I'm not out for a gourmet experience. I want a meal."

I nodded, then lied. "But I grew the lettuce myself." Mama and Darla and Heather worked the garden. Sometimes I weeded it, but only to get a tan.

"Ah, jeez, okay." Tohee sucked on a Coke.

I clipped the salad ticket to the front of

the order wheel and kept moving the second ticket back a clip every time I passed it. If he'd eat a salad first, it'd knock out his appetite. Anybody could see he needed to go on a diet right away. This, I decided, would be my first good deed for mankind. I'd been thinking about Ash Lee's idea of going to church, which was impossible for me, living with Mama. My stomach never seemed to calm down, not since I saw Ann Reynolds and especially not since I danced with Sheriff Dodd.

Deep in conversation, Gee and Haw rested their gnarled elbows on the counter. They clinked their cups until I stood in front of them.

"The end of the world is coming," Haw said.

"Sooner for some of us than for others," I said, and tapped my pen against the order pad. They could take all day before they got around to ordering anything.

"I didn't think I'd outlive the time before this civilization perished," said Gee. "Unnatural things have come about."

"No kidding," I said. Out the window I could see the picketers slog into the parking lot.

"It's the end of the world," Haw said.

"No, it's not. That's just some wacko

225

fringe out there. Mama's place is going to survive. We'll be open all day and even tomorrow," I said.

"Miss, we got a clear sign." Gee jabbed at the newspaper next to his elbow. It was from last March. The paper was upside down from my point of view but the lead story was the election, the national primary and county offices up for grabs, which simply meant there was no need to change the cushions in the courthouse. Paul Dodd was still sheriff.

Gee pushed it to Haw. "I just can't look."

Haw opened it to the page that listed the vote results in small print. "There." His finger hovered over the result of one race.

I squinted.

"It says that colored man running for president got support in our county."

"I never thought I'd see the day when everything got tumped over in Maridoches." Gee shoved at his teeth.

"He only got one vote," I said, watching the slow motion out the window. The women moved in a circle, their signs tilted to make shade for themselves. I could not read what the signs said.

"Yep. And we're fixing to find out who done it," said Gee.

"I remember the glory days of voting," said Haw. "It was the biggest horse race day of the year. We'd ride to the polls in Georgia, Tennessee, and Alabama and vote in ever' one."

"Are you going to order any food?" I said.

They sat back as if slapped. "Young people are too selfish these days. You don't know your history."

"I take that as a no," I said. I hated the small-talk part of waitressing. It's what Connie does better than the rest of us, thank God. I went into the kitchen and came back carrying an enormous blue bowl piled high with oak and red leaf lettuce, cherry tomatoes, and carrot curls. I held the bowl out to Tohee, the wet leaves catching light, a vision of health and spring.

"Pickup! Pickup!" Mama slapped the Formica.

I put the bowl down and raced to the window. I ran from one end of the counter to the other putting down plates of fried ham, fries, barbecue, donuts, and greens and picking up dirty plates so fast their clanging sounded like the Hobart dishwasher in mid-cycle. Tohee's order came up. I carried it slowly to him, both my arms loaded with plates. I laid them out like a long train, starting with fried chicken and ending with chocolate pie, a foot of food winding behind the other customers' drinks.

When I'd put the last plate down, I heard Tohee call out. I could taste a ridge of sweat on my upper lip.

"I'd like a large glass of Coke," he said.

I frowned at him.

"Diet."

I filled the plastic cup and put it down in front of him.

H reached for a straw, broke its seal, and dropped it in the cold drink. "Here, it's for you. On me."

"Thanks," I said. It tasted great. Mama would yell at me for making him an extra-big salad, but good deeds often inspired opposition.

Tohee ate the whole salad, quietly resisting the bottle of French dressing within reach. When he finished, he cleared his throat, commanding the attention of all the truckers in the room. He held up his left hand. "See this ring?"

I could barely make out a tiny thread of gold wedged between two fatty pads of skin.

Tohee continued, "When I can slip this

ring off my finger, I'm going to marry that little gal right there because she cares about a man."

I dropped the empty salad plate, which vibrated like a mocking drum roll, and bolted through the kitchen out the back door. My face was hot. I cringed. He'd crush me flat. The sun blinded me, and I felt for the steamy concrete wall outside. I could not lean against it. Even in the shade it burned. I was doing Tohee a favor and what he thought of was getting me in the sack. Couldn't I be nice to a man without him thinking I wanted to screw him? Am I a walking dick magnet? Mama would blame me, Gert would blame me, everybody would blame me. I breathed out and felt tears rush from my eyes. I missed Richard.

He had not called me or come by. It was as if we had never shared love. It didn't seem possible it could just end like that. I wiped my eyes and stood in the sun. This heat reached to my core. My arms shook as I thought of Richard's betrayal, of his blue blue eyes, the way we moved together, his hands on the small of my back. I turned so my back was roasted too. This is what I was reduced to, asking the sun to touch my body, getting marriage proposals from freaks, living with a jagged hole in my stomach.

When I was dry, no sweat or tears left, I opened my eyes and heard the faint sound of chanting. I walked along the edge of the building, my warm pants clinging to my thighs.

Out front, a TV news camera was filming a tall beautiful woman. Her hair, black as a crow's, glistened with deep purple highlights. From its center a white streak rose like a feather. Behind her, the sky was ice blue. Heat lifted off my skin. I held my breath. I could not hear her words but a strange feeling grew inside me. She was cool and hot at once. She was the kind of woman I wanted to be. I had to know her.

The Ladies of the Church of the Holy Resurrection

The women were sweat-drenched. Frozen yogurt had fewer calories than ice cream. Free. They'd probably sweated off tons of weight. Where was Reverend Peterson? Who wanted to look like a wilted rutabaga on TV? Gert Geurin had so much to haul, what with her weight. Go ahead, Gert, eat some ice cream. You look like you're about to keel over. She broke rank. Hordes of children descended on Troy Clyde.

As the midnight-blue Cadillac drove soundlessly into the parking lot, the wave of picketers parted. Stelle Peterson stepped out of the car, her eyes perfectly dry, her lipstick in place, not a speck of red dust on her black heels. The local TV cameras placed her against the soft clouds, giving her height and focus. She spoke clearly on virtue and vice. The cameras swung to the marchers, who ducked away, ashamed of the stains under their arms and their dripping faces. The children had won. One mother had taken a lick off a child's cone "so it wouldn't drip and make his hand sticky," and then the ladies cooled off with scoops of banana and lime and icicle blue. The cameras did not miss this detail.

Only Pudge Polk avoided the free cold treats. The only sweet she ever ate was sliced lemon sprinkled with Sweet' n Low. Her teeth were white as a porcelain sink. She spoke loudly, but in vain: *The morsel which thou hast eaten shalt thou vomit up, and lose thy sweet words.* Stelle Peterson did not offer her a ride down to her car.

Hattie Bohannon was called out from

the kitchen. Stelle slipped back inside the air-conditioned Cadillac, its idle an irritating grate on the ears of the marchers. Hattie Bohannon looked like them, her hair falling out of place, her face moist and pink, a wet ring on her back and water beads clinging to her neck. She simply thanked them for making the trek on such a hot day.

Hattie Bohannon

Hattie took a seat behind the refrigeration cart and watched the largest crowd she'd had since opening day disappear into red dusty clouds. They hadn't spent a cent.

"I believe, sister," said Troy Clyde, "that you have won this battle."

"What good are battles if you lose the war?"

"My God! You better eat something sweet. Here, what's this that's left?" Troy Clyde opened an ice cream carton. "Mississippi Mud. Looks like horse shit in February."

The last straggler was Gert Geurin. They watched her amble off with a tub of ice cream under each arm. "A four-humped camel," Troy Clyde said.

"Gert saved us, you know," said Hattie. "She took the first cone. If she hadn't, I doubt anyone else would. She has pride in her work. I never knew that before."

"Hattie Annabelle, you sound wise in your own eyes," said Troy Clyde.

"Maybe I am," she said. She walked around the back of the truck stop and found Darla emptying the trash can.

"Where you been?" she asked.

Darla's face was flushed and she stunk of old sweat. "I went to Gadsden with Rudy last night. Nothing happened," she said. "I should have called."

"Rudy," said Hattie.

"Don't get on him. I made him take me," said Darla. "We sure kicked butt today, didn't we?"

"Yes," said Hattie. She grabbed Darla in a quick hug, then pushed her away. "Go take a shower. You've been out in the sun too long."

Darla said, "I'm going to clean the bathrooms first."

"Fine," said Hattie, as she opened the back door. The cool air of the office enveloped her like water from heaven. A smile grew on her face. She had won the battle. They don't own me, she thought. They don't own my soul. Or my body. Refreshed, she called the *Maridoches Ledger* and canceled her ad in the Bible Contest.

She passed through the dining room where Jessamine was wiping down tables. Her daughter looked like an ordinary blond girl whose main physical attribute was her youth. She did not carry herself like a prostitute, adulterer, or mother. When did reputation's invisible baggage transform a body? When would she shatter and conform to what others said she was?

Reverend Martin Peterson

In the car on their way to the march, Martin had decided it would be best if Stelle spoke to the television crew he had summoned. Having a woman speak about prostitution seemed right. Women would fall in behind her and husbands could go along with their wives because they had to. It was the southern way.

Stelle had risen like a white column of smoke against the blue sky. Her linen dress flowed as she stood in a breeze no one else felt. The white stripe in her hair flicked like a flame against her black tresses. She was elegant. Martin wondered why God was tormenting him so with fantasies of lesser women. He was confounded by his dreams of Gert Geurin and of the bouncy breasts of the young truck-stop prostitute, and he'd even undressed Ann Reynolds in his mind.

Stelle's words were a simple modulation of Corinthian verses. The marchers were rapt and the cameraman's lens never wavered from her. The reporter nudged him and the lens hastily scanned the crowd of sweaty women, his congregation.

From the privacy of his darkened windows, Martin had watched the cart, hoping to glimpse a prostitute, either the Bohannon girl or the woman from the fire. He looked away from Hattie's irrepressible brother, who apparently had a very active sex life at home. Troy Clyde's mother-in-law, Rhuhanna Polk Killian, was always seeking Martin's counsel, worried for her daughter's soul. Maybe he was given dreams to understand the mind of a depraved man, so he could minister to the needs of his congregation.

Driving home, he felt elated. Nothing galvanized women more than the threat of another woman. It was survival instinct, perhaps. "The scripture signs were excellent," Martin said to Stelle. "Our message will be broadcast loud and clear."

"I expect so," said Stelle. "Did you see the young girls giving away the ice cream? They were Mrs. Bohannon's daughters."

"Yes," said Martin. "You can bet that free ice cream cost Mrs. Bohannon a pretty penny. To say nothing of keeping our folks fed. The Lord does provide for His own."

Stelle smoothed her hair back from her face. A tiny line of sweat glistened along her forehead. "Did you see the truck drivers? All grease and beards, muscle shirts and tattoos," she said. "No wonder the poor girls are tempted."

Martin returned his eyes to the curves of Lily Springs Road. "Girls tempted by men?" he said, as if he hadn't heard her correctly.

"Men who will pay them, Martin," said Stelle. "Prostitution is a degrading business for women."

"Then we have done a service for the community and for Mrs. Bohannon's girls today," he said. "We will save those girls from a sordid life if we shut the place down."

"God willing," said Stelle, and she reached over and laid her hand over his as he steered slowly and surely back to their home. Victory was God's, theirs, his.

The Ladies of the Church of the Holy Resurrection

They'd been had. They looked terrible on TV. Stelle appeared marvelous and talked of walking the right path. She hadn't walked. She had ridden. How stupid did she think they were? It was too hot to go to church this evening. The aerobics teacher had started it all with those talks of the benefits of walking. Yes. And then the business of hydration. Yes. And the importance of a variety of exercises. Yes. No more workouts for them. But there was guilt. It was a habit. They went to the evening service.

Jewell Miller smiled at Hattie's victory but she felt a twinge, like a loose tooth hanging by a thread, only it was hanging somewhere in her midsection, close to the ribs. She always rooted for the little guy and especially for the little gal, but Hattie Bohannon was not little. She towered over Jewell. Ha! The thread snapped. Jewell had something Hattie wanted very badly. She still had some power.

Richard Reynolds

The night after the protest, Richard and Ann lay under a cotton sheet, listening to the air conditioner purr. They'd gone to church, though Ann had chosen to sit in the back and had not touched him the whole time. It was as if he were a leper in his own house. The men at church had kept their distance since his confession as well, though business was continuing as if he was still in the Wheel of Gratitude. He'd given Baker Thomas the planks he'd wanted at discount and had floated the idea of investing in a slaughterhouse past his father, who owned a good head of beef. Business was as usual, but what he missed was more important.

Seated in the pew, it had been difficult to listen to the minister chortle over the ladies' march on the truck stop without being aware of the hard set of Ann's eyes. Her breath had grown fast as the minister gloated in detail about the women and children eating all the free ice cream, taking what was given by the Lord. In His service, they had been hungry and thirsty, and the Lord had provided them with nourishment when their own hands were empty.

As he lay listening for Ann's breath,

which he could not hear, he felt a deep pang. It was a dance, a lullaby, sweetness he had been seeking, not raucous sex. But he had misjudged everything. He had let a young girl fall in love with him and then betrayed her with a confession that turned her into something she was not. Something he was not. But for Ann it was better that Jessamine was a prostitute — because there could not have been love.

He lay still. The sheet was moving almost imperceptibly with her breath, a gentle rise and fall across his belly. That small motion connected them. He quieted his thoughts and became aware of all the places the sheet brushed his body. His knees and ankles felt the breath of the sheet. It was so soft and mild a touching. Soon his privates welcomed the gentle caress. He thought of rose petals, pale pink ones, and Ann's puckered lips when they'd first kissed and of the promises she had given him.

He wanted to show Ann he loved her. He knew their journey would be hot and difficult, but somewhere on the horizon was a lush jungle paradise. He touched her shoulder, his hand cupping the bones in an exact fit. Ann turned, receiving his touch. Her body was strangely new to him. It was not as firm as Jessamine's and it lacked that insane, he now thought, jackrabbit anxiety. He ran his hands down her hips, feeling her softness as if for the first time. He placed his hand on the scar. It was hard and pebbly. He tenderly massaged it with his fingertips and, surprising himself, kissed it, then ran his tongue along it as if it were still a breast. And then he turned his attention to the remaining breast. Its nipple was raised. Something rose inside him. Joy.

Darla Bohannon

Darla stayed home from school. Classes were a joke these days, wasted in planning the prom, and who wanted to go to that anyway? She wasn't going to dress up like a soap-opera star and let some guy with pimples try to unsnap her bra. Mama had just sighed and said, "Senioritis?" Darla was waitressing instead, picking up extra money from Gee and Haw, who gave her fifty cents every time she asked a local who they'd voted for in the primary.

The morning passed quickly. At lunchtime, Jewell Miller came in and ordered a large plate of fish and fries. Carrying the food, Darla sashayed between the crowded tables, in and out of high-decibel conversations, and tripped over Jewell's carry-along stool. The fish and fries slid toward the edge of the plate. Her left hand blocked them and got greasy and burnt. She expected Jewell to chew her out. The old woman never took any slop.

But Jewell merely smiled as she shook out her paper napkin and laid it on her lap.

"Do you need anything else?" Darla congratulated herself for remembering to ask. She'd been forgetting.

"This fish looks very crispy. Often when I come in the food is undercooked." She crunched a triangle of fish between two fingers. "Often I get that waitress over there." She nodded her head in Connie's direction and continued without lowering her voice. "She's usually hungover. A shame for such a young girl, but since her mother owns the place. . . ." She waved her fork in a small circle as if to say Ta-ta.

"That's my sister." So this is what Connie and Mama meant when they said Jewell was a crank, Darla thought, as she cleared the next table and pocketed three quarters sitting in a pool of melted ice. Darla spied on Jewell because she was fascinated by her life. During World War II, Jewell had gone to Europe as a code cracker. It was easy for Darla to imagine the old woman, now intent on her fish, her hands neatly splitting the crust and checking the white meat for bones, steaming open an envelope and deciphering chicken scratches scrawled in a foreign language. But it was hard to imagine that the old face had ever captivated her father. There were deep lines across her forehead and her cheeks fell sharply from her large round cheekbones. Jewell and Daddy had dated way back in the 1940s. One story he had enjoyed telling about Jewell was hearing her holler from the passenger seat as his car zoomed down Raider's Hill after the brakes gave out. He said he'd laughed the whole way while he steered them toward the grassiest grade of the bank so that they slipped gently, like a kiss, into the murmuring creek.

Darla had seen the old road and marveled how any car could have come down the sandstone banks without catapulting into a wreck. But she believed Daddy had done it because he'd said so, and he said Jewell had been with him. Darla longed to ask Jewell about it and more. Was it true she had refused to muster out after the war when the government wanted an all-male army again? Was it true she fought them so well all they could do was transfer her to out-of-the way places like Alaska, Guam, and Ghana? Darla wiped the table clean, trying to get her nerve up. Was it true she had left Maridoches and knew secrets of the world?

When Darla's break came, she walked down the hall toward her mother's office. Her hair was matted with sweat against her neck. No matter how much she tried to rehearse giving her mother the news about joining up, she always broke fresh sweat. Her voice in her mind became tinny and thin. The door was not shut and she could hear them talking, her mother and Paul Dodd.

A surge of anger pushed her forward. She'd march in and butt him out of the way. Just as she reached for the doorknob, she heard her mother say, "Darla," and him laugh loudly — "Darla!" — as if Mama was a silly goose. She paused outside the door, listening hard.

"I knew you were overreacting," he said. "She took off for fun. Kids do it all the time."

"She is not given to that kind of fun," said Mama. "And neither am I."

He laughed again. "Oh, I think I know what kind of fun you like."

Darla felt shame over something unnamed but she could not walk away from the door. Smite him dead, Mama, she thought. Smite the jerk to kingdom come.

"I am not inclined to have that kind of fun again until the damned Army returns my husband's ashes," said Mama.

"That's a mighty tall order to lay on a man who's not in the Armed Forces," said Paul Dodd.

"Let's see how tall a man you are," she said.

Relief slid over Darla as she sneaked up the hall to the kitchen. She watched Gert hammering cube steaks and imagined giving her mother Daddy's remains at the same time she announced her news. Back in the dining room she bussed a few tables and picked up a two-dollar tip left by Jewell Miller, the one person in Maridoches who could help her.

That evening, Darla practically ran Jewell over with the VW as the older woman emerged from her apartment complex and disappeared into a thicket. Darla leapt from the car and followed her. Briars snagged her sweatpants. She tripped into a grassy field, where a barely perceptible path headed downhill. Huffing sounds encouraged her descent. She saw a straw hat ahead. "Hey, hey, Jewell Miller, wait for me!"

"I will not wait. If you want to talk to me, come along." The hat sank to a lower level.

Darla slid down the muddy path into trees, as if she were a slalom skier supposed to bang into the lane markers, not skirt them. When she arrived at flat land,

Jewell was not in sight. If the wind would quit, Jewell's footsteps could be heard. Darla rested. Nothing. She jogged ahead on leaves as crunchy as breakfast cereal. There — the hat moved among a copse of leatherwoods. Darla circled a ganglia of branches and spied Jewell, close now, marching forward, a carved walking stick hacking a path out for her one-speed body.

"Hey!" Darla jumped in front of her, then ducked to avoid the swinging stick. She fell hard on her knees in cracked mud. Jewell kept walking. "Hey, I want to talk to you."

"I will not slow down, so come on." She disappeared behind some white hairy grass.

Darla jogged beside her. "I'm Darla Bohannon."

"I know who you are. Your mother just beat the minister at his game. Body versus spirit. Ice cream versus moral superiority. It was not a surprise to me. Your mother's body always wins."

"I know about my mother," Darla muttered, and pushed back the thought of Sheriff Dodd teasing Mama in the office. "Will you tell me about my father?" she called as she fell behind. Jewell's path took her between twin loblolly pines.

"What do you want to know?"

"I want to know if he's dead."

"Your mother can tell you that." Jewell's gait became jerky.

"I mean, I think he's alive." A small hill appeared and disappeared without changing Jewell's breathing. Darla's lungs stretched toward her lower ribs.

"Why do you believe such a fool thing as that?"

"Because we've never gotten his body from the VA."

"What?" Jewell wheeled around sharply, decapitating a dozen cattails.

For a second, she thought she'd stopped Jewell, but only a second as the old woman paced away back up the path they'd come. She limped visibly but moved fast.

"Mama got a telegram when he died, but they never sent him back to us."

"In the Army, mix-ups are not uncommon." Jewell cocked her head as she passed the loblollies. A tight chin strap secured the hat to her head. "Your father had a drinking problem."

"What?" Darla crossed her arms over her forehead and prepared for the leatherwood assault. Maybe Jewell was as crazy as Mama said.

"Your father would have been a fine man

if he hadn't liked his liquor." She slashed a path through a rhododendron hedge. "But you seem to have a bit of discipline and determination in your soul."

"I don't remember Daddy drinking."

"The closet kind are the most dishonest."

The briary path loomed ahead. Without losing a stride, Jewell snapped her collapsible walking cane down to a height of six inches and hung it on her belt. Quick as a monkey, she leapt from branches to stones and roots until she disappeared up the hill. Darla caught up with her in the parking lot.

Breathing hard, Jewell rested on the stairs. She rolled up her pant leg and removed a hard rubber disk and three cotton pads shaped like half-moons. Darla remembered the amputated leg and felt her own knees buckle.

"I never slow down when I'm out walking. Never. Rain or ice. I never give up. In the very cold winter, I do it barefoot."

"Doesn't it hurt?"

"It hurts with an intense pain that you have never ever felt."

"Then why do it?"

"Because I am strong. I can take it." She

flexed her artificial shoe. "Your father and I used to roam these hills back when I had two whole legs. No man loved the lands of Maridoches more than he did. Actually, that's why he and I split up." Jewell wiped sweat from her forehead. "But you can't be too young to know about sex."

Darla shook her head, impressed with her self-control.

"Quite frankly, I would not grovel in the mud. Your mother, however, had no qualms about using the forest floor as a bed. Which was your father's style."

Her entire body blushed for Mama. She could feel her toes grow hot. Jewell was crazy, a crazy liar. The dried mud on Darla's clothes weighed against her skin, smelling of truth she tried to deny. She drove home in a blur of browned pines and pale grasses. When she got home, the sheriff was on the porch. She didn't even say hello.

Connie Bohannon

"So, sheriff, what's eating you?" I say, as a way of taking his order. He's alone, without his squad, and I already know he wants country-fried steak and greens with vinegar and bitter tea.

He looks at me carefully — like, Can he trust me? — and I stand there as blank and friendly as I can look. "Did your mother truly love your daddy?"

"Sure," I say, without thinking. I'd never considered it before.

"She's still hung up on him. It interferes with her present life."

"That surprises me," I say, considering how public she'd gotten in the past year. Before Daddy went away, she stayed at home taking care of us. "She's happy now. Happy to be seeing you. It's the only thing she's happy about." I think awhile longer. "Maybe you're a little scary."

He laughed. "Evidently I am. But seriously, she has asked me, in not so many words, to help get the ashes returned. Then she'll have to decide if the past or the future matters the most."

I fell silent thinking of the ashes out there somewhere in the world. And Mama, as she waited for them to come, keeping Sheriff Dodd at arm's length, holding the future away. I wondered how Sheriff Dodd could find those ashes when Mama couldn't. It seemed an impossible task she had laid on him. But that is Mama, in love with the impossible.

Darla Bohannon

On the third day she skipped school, Darla came down from her room and went outside when her mother called her. She'd felt strange for a long time now, as if her secret was a kicking baby in her stomach, eager to be born. Somehow she figured Mama knew what she'd done. Mama was in the front yard, hanging laundry on a clothesline that Sheriff Dodd had strung up to screen the house from the truck stop. As if the ladies of the church could be stopped by white sheets.

Darla picked up a pin and clamped it on a corner of Mama's bedspread. Sheriff Dodd was mowing the grass. Their conversation proceeded in fits and starts depending on his proximity.

Mama secured the other end. "Jake Hiler called to see if I wanted to run an ad in the yearbook. I know you despise him, but did you see the paper this morning?"

Darla shook her head.

"Where our ad used to be is a big blank square. Somebody paid for that and it's intentional, as if I've been wiped out of existence. And the Bible quotes under the other ads were all pointed at women: *The hands of the pitiful women have sodden their* own children: *Lamentation 4:10*. And *Give not thy strength unto women, nor thy ways to that which destroyeth kings*, from Proverbs."

"Jake Hiler doesn't let girls run on his track team," said Darla.

"I need all the local advertising I can get." Dodd's lawn mower followed an elliptical path around the line, with three small jags to the right for Hattie, Darla, and the laundry basket.

"Don't get grass on my sheets!" Mama yelled.

Darla pulled the clothespin from her mouth and attached a pair of pale blue boxer shorts, her pajamas, to the line. It was strange to listen to Mama and not get all uptight about the truck stop or even Coach Hiler. "I don't care about track anymore," she said, startling herself with the truth of her statement. "I joined the Army."

"You are not joining the Army." Mama flapped the pillowcase she'd dropped. "The Army took Oakley, and he's still not back."

"Jewell Miller came home."

"With half a leg." Mama viciously pinned the pillowcase.

"That was wartime and it hasn't slowed her down. I've been running with her and she's fast."

"Jewell Miller runs?"

"No, she doesn't run. She walks an eight-minute mile, which is a lot faster than most two-legged people can run." Darla flopped white socks across the empty line like she was slapping paint on a fence. Mama followed, sticking a pin in the middle of each sock.

"In the Army, you get to travel and do stuff like spying. Daddy said one time Jewell carried electric wires in her suitcase rolled up like hair curlers. She told the French inspector she wanted to look like Betty Grable and he tried to pinch her but he let her pass. They used the wires to set up a wireless in Normandy to get messages from London. Jewell got seasick on the English Channel."

"How fascinating," Mama said. "But, Darla, you have a problem with authority, and in the Army if you don't respect authority you earn nothing but grief."

"In the Army there's discipline, and I think that's a virtue." She reached into the basket and was mortified to find her white hip-hugger underwear on top of the pile. She bunched them up and stuck the wet ball in her pocket. Next were Connie's bikinis, which she squished into the other pocket. She blushed, knowing Sheriff Dodd was within feet of their undergarments.

"Jewell has really been filling your head with bunk, hasn't she?" They were on the third and final cord of the clothesline.

Dodd cut the engine, stuck his nose in a wet towel, and inhaled. "Sweet lemon freshness."

"Jewell said Daddy was a drunk."

"That woman exaggerates everything. One beer a day and she thinks he's an alcoholic. One slight sway out of line" — Mama rapidly pinned the remaining towels; she bent and raised like an automaton as she spoke — "one step off the obsessive track, and you're condemned for sloth or weakness."

Darla held the last wet garment, Hattie's bra. "She said Daddy broke up with her because she wouldn't grovel in the dirt."

Mama snatched her bra and hooked it over the line. The cups filled in the breeze. "Exactly. And look where it got her. You are not going into the Army, and that is the law." She turned to Dodd. "Would you please finish cutting the lawn? I can't stand the silence."

"If you'll get me a drink of well water."

"Fair enough." Mama marched up the

porch steps. "Perhaps you should move into town and live in an apartment near Jewell. Grovel in the dirt indeed." She cranked the bucket up the well. Paul Dodd, waiting at the bottom of the steps, laughed.

Darla ran, her pockets bulging and wet, into the kitchen. The only place safe from that man was her bedroom. She raced up the stairs and pulled out the underwear. She hung a pair on each bedpost. That man acts like he owned Mama and the house and us, she thought. She watched from the window as he got closer, marking the territory as he mowed down the grass, clipping nearer and nearer the clothesline with Mama's underwear on it.

Jewell Miller is the only one who understands, thought Darla. Mama said I can't join the Army but I did. She cannot stop me. Now I will have to find Daddy by myself. I'm the only one who still loves him. Except Jewell.

Wearing yellow shorts and a long-sleeved shirt, she drove to Jewell's apartment door, climbed the stairs, and knocked on her black door.

"Come in," said Jewell, as if she was expecting company.

The door swung open on the living room. Along one wall rested a metal contraption for weight lifting. Next to it was a couch of hard flat cushions. The couch faced a metal bookcase painted industrial gray. It was the kind of shelf Darla had seen in shop class, where drills and goggles and bits were stored. The books, though, had either red covers with black lettering or black covers with red lettering. What a strange way to pick out a book, she thought. Unnerved, Darla stepped inside and squinted at the bookshelves. The covers were hand-lettered. She smiled, satisfied. False backs.

Jewell fidgeted with the dials of an enormous radio. A static buzz whined for a few minutes until she clicked it off. "I can get stations all over the world on that thing. I like to keep tabs on the whole planet."

Darla nodded, then grew self-conscious in the ensuing silence. She couldn't blurt out that she had joined the Army. "Do you have anything I could drink?"

"You don't pussyfoot around, do you?" Jewell said. "I like that. Most women spend half their lives talking all around what they want to say." She pushed back an accordion wall. A jungle seemed to flood into the living room. Jewell disap-

258

peared among some woody vines.

Darla walked closer to the bobbing foliage. She heard water running and saw grapevines staked in rattan buckets. She squeezed between them. The rungs of a wooden ladder held trays of short cornstalks and cherry tomatoes. Cucumber vines sprawled across the floor. Strawberry leaves clung to the granite countertop. Two spikes of sugar cane stood aloof in the midst of the jungle. Along a vast window spread an array of potted lettuce, its wrinkled leaves ranging from russet to lemon-green. Thick green ivy covered the unseen kitchen walls. Jewell turned away from the sink, over which an iron pipe jutted.

"Your plants are green," Darla said.

"They're supposed to be."

"There's a moratorium on water." Darla inhaled the lush smell and was immediately wistful for her early morning runs in the spring when the dew-moistened soil gave off a sweet scent.

"Nobody can see what I've got in here. I learned many years ago, in a drought before you were born, the importance of inside gardening. That year my garden was half an acre of sticks, thanks to a moratorium. It was the sickest year of my life. Take a look." She snipped off a tiny ear of corn. "I was growing miniatures long before they became vogue." She popped it in her mouth, then pointed to a cup on the counter.

Darla drank cautiously. Grape juice, sweet and fresh as she'd never tasted before. "Wow. It's delicious. You ought to sell it. You'd make a lot of money."

"I am not interested in becoming a businesswoman. There's others quite willing to do such things." Jewell rinsed the cup. "Did you come to spy on me?"

"No," said Darla, as Jewell's clear hazel eyes probed her face. Couldn't Jewell see that they weren't enemies?

"Well," Jewell snapped, "I suppose us weirdos must stick together."

"That's why I came to you." Darla tugged at her shorts. "I mean, you're a vegetarian, right? And you're probably the healthiest person around and I want to be that way."

"No, I'm not a vegetarian in the strictest sense. I enjoy fried catfish. I was raised here, you know. Come along. I'll show you another secret." She swept back a wave of greenery and stepped through a door.

Darla followed through the exotic forest, her heart pounding. A leaf grazed her hand. Her palm began to sting. "What's that?"

"Sorry, I forgot to warn you about that one."

They stood in the bathroom. Jewell drew the shower curtain back to reveal a growth that resembled a massive ball of dewy spiderwebs, threatening to overflow the tub.

"Sprouts." Jewell picked a clump and began to chew. "Excellent source of protein. Have some."

Darla'd heard of sprouts. They felt wetly tender. She could not imagine what they tasted like. "Where do you bathe?"

"Hah! You're afraid these greens are unsanitary. Don't join the Armed Forces."

Darla squeezed the cool crisp fibers into a ball.

The older woman leaned forward. "I'll reveal how I keep myself clean if you say why you came to visit me."

"Deal," said Darla.

"Out back, there's a shower head, left over from the days when this place was a boardinghouse. Every night around twelve, I go down and shower. There's a light on the lot so I can see anything coming my way." She laughed, then tightened her lips. "Why are you here?"

"Well, I wanted to tell you I joined the Army," Darla mumbled at the linoleum.

Jewell grasped her chin and raised it. "Speak up. Be proud of your actions."

"I said, I joined the Army."

Jewell's fingers tightened like a slow vise. "Why did you go and do a fool thing like that?"

"I want to find my father."

"Crazy!" The old woman gave her neck a twist and disappeared back into the jungle.

Darla tossed the wad of bean sprouts onto the white pile. The thorny plant raked her legs as she plowed through the grapevines. She knew who was crazy. She had to get out quick. She banged into the ladder, knocking the bottom trays to the floor. "Shit!" She scrambled to scoop the dirt back onto the corn plants. The shoots of cane were broken off, ruined. She stood up and brushed her hands on her yellow shorts. A dumb color to choose, it turned out.

She emerged to find the older woman perusing the book spines, as if she were in a library on a quiet afternoon. "Don't leave yet, young lady."

Darla wanted to race away and forget everything she knew about Jewell. She feared her life in the Army would be plagued by nightmares of this apartment.

It suddenly seemed hot with the smell of overripe vegetation.

"Sit down." The strong command in her voice made Darla obey.

So what if her shorts were muddy? The ugly couch would absorb the dirt. Maybe Jewell slept on it.

"Now," Jewell still faced the books. "Close your eyes."

Anything was better than staring at the escape door. "Okay."

"Now, I don't happen to believe that you joined simply to find your father. I believe there was another reason. Think hard." The voice glided close. "Here," Jewell trained Darla's hand around a cup. "This is more grape juice. Drink it while I tell you what I think. You felt lonely. You hated your job. You had run into problems at home. You walked into an army recruiting office."

"Yes," Darla hissed.

"You stood around in the office, looking at brochures. In about five minutes, a very handsome young officer came out and introduced himself."

Darla refused to nod, although she could see Will Alton Russell clearly as he smiled and held out his hand. She remembered the long handshake because her hand was suddenly chilled when he let go and led her over to the chair in front of his desk. She sipped the grape juice.

"This young man was remarkably fit. He had an intense stare. He listened to every word you said. He complimented your intelligence."

Darla winced. Somehow she didn't mind letting Jewell tell the story. If she'd tried, she would have been too embarrassed to breathe a syllable of it.

"Shysters!"

Her eyes flew open. She gulped the juice.

"I can't believe it," Jewell said. "Well, yes, I can. There's not much opportunity in this county for a young woman, other than the ancient choices. Don't be mad, young one. I saw the world, too much of it. No, I know all about recruiting because that was the job they shunted me into after the war. Because I was southern and female and had such a seductive little voice and trim little body," Jewell said, "they let me recruit the black boys in this region, the immigrants in the Northeast, and the farm boys of the Midwest." She slammed her fist on the table. "But I learned about sabotage then. I'm just sorry I didn't get a chance to warn you."

Darla crushed the cup. "You shouldn't use Styrofoam. It's bad for the environment." Standing suddenly, she was dizzy. Then blood pounded her temples. "I am going to find my father."

"Yes, I think you will. You are so determined to do just that. Sit down." Again the authority in Jewell's voice stopped Darla from moving toward the door. She closed her eyes and concentrated on slowing her heartbeat.

"I have more to say about that foolish notion but I will not bore you with all the entanglements you would run into, trying to retrieve lost military information. You look ill. I've got something that will cure you."

Darla sank down on the couch. She heard Jewell cluck over the broken cane shoots. Maybe she'd bring out raw sugar. Next she heard the clack of tin snips cutting through the cane. Silence followed. Darla considered her options. If she left now, she'd miss out on Jewell's promise of more information. A soldier would not wimp out.

"Close your eyes," Jewell called out. Her irregular soft footfalls approached the couch. "Wet your finger."

Darla closed her eyes and stuck her

finger in her mouth. She could feel Jewell's closeness. "This isn't sprouts, is it?" she said, lightly, hoping the older woman would laugh.

Jewell jabbed Darla's finger into something powdery, like confectioner's sugar. Darla's mouth watered. Her finger tasted like a cigarette, gritty and ashy, much worse than the chewing tobacco Daddy'd given her once. She spit it out. "That was a mean trick! You should have told me the cure would make me sick!" She took a step forward, her fists clenched.

Jewell held up a red box like a shield. Stamped in black letters were the words REMAINS OF LT. OAKLEY BOHANNON, U.S. ARMY. Darla brushed past the old woman. She just made the stairs before she heaved. At the bottom of the steps, weak and nauseated and dry, she crawled outside and somehow got herself home.

Connie Bohannon

Darla wasn't at the cash register and I had to use my break to find her. Nothing was right about this day. Mama was mad as hell at Jessamine for causing the protest march and tired of waiting for Daddy's ashes. They hadn't come in the post this morning and the Army didn't know where they were — again. No special delivery; they'd sent him regular mail. Mama had a date with Sheriff Dodd tonight, so the timing was bad.

I went up the hill to the house and lit up as soon as I opened the front door. Calling for Darla, I carried the burning cigarette up the steps, daring her to get on me about smoking.

For some reason, our underwear was hanging on the bedposts like there'd been a panty raid. I figured my secret boyfriend, Darryl, had done it. A lump stretched under the covers on Darla's bed. I pulled them back and breathed smoke into her face, "You're supposed to be working."

Darla shivered. Her face was an exotic lime color. She heaved, such an agonizing sound that even I felt pity. "Darla, are you pregnant?"

She covered her nose and mouth and gasped. I put out my cig.

"Do you need a Coke?" I asked.

Darla opened her eyes. They reminded me of the drying ponds around Maridoches whose banks were littered with carcasses of little spiny things. "Jewell Miller has Daddy's ashes. She got the

267

Army to send them to her."

"That goddamn old bitch. They belong to us!" I said. Jewell never overcame the fact that Daddy didn't marry her. Maybe it was cruel of him to dump her after the war but she only had one leg. How could she have raised chickens and had babies? Besides, Daddy loved Mama. Lord knows, she can work like a mule. Daddy was pretty smart to have married a much younger woman. But now it was Mama's turn to have some fun. If I gave the ashes to her, she would mourn, but if I gave them to Sheriff Dodd, she might recognize him as her future and leap happily into his arms.

I was halfway over to Jewell's when I remembered Darla's Coke.

"All right," I yelled, as I pushed Jewell's apartment door open, "where are they?"

A strange pink light poured from a half-open accordion wall and settled gently around the old woman, sitting in a rocker. Her hair, a fresh set of wispy curls, cushioned a green felt hat with an awning of black net. A yellow ball of yarn and two shiny needles lay in her lap. Jewell looked like a sweet grandmother. What a trick. I closed my eyes to picture what a nasty customer the old woman really was, always demanding to know if the salt was from the sea or from a lick.

"You are rude and impertinent," said Jewell. "You will go far."

"You can't boss me."

Jewell's needles clacked away. "I have been semiretired against my will. The telephone company will only let me work weekends now, thanks to the wonderful world of computers. So I knit."

I put my hands on my hips but stayed just inside the door. "Where are my father's ashes?"

Jewell raised her lined face. Two round spots of blush dusted her cheekbones, the color horribly unnatural on faded skin. I started; my father would be an old man.

"Would you like something to drink? I understand it's never too early in the day for you."

"Don't try to pull anything or I'll call the sheriff over." I gulped, afraid I'd let out Mama's business to the telephone operator. To cover, I said, "This is a nice place."

"Your sister needs a lot of help."

"They all do." I sighed as if deeply concerned.

Jewell stamped her wooden leg. "The one that joined the Army."

"Darla joined up?" I said. "The Army sounds like a great place for her. Lots of sweating and horrible clothes that make you look like sticks and stones."

"Young lady, this is a serious matter. Your sister is a tomboy who doesn't see many choices for her in this town so she made a very poor one." She shook her needles. "She hasn't the sense to help herself."

Jewell was right on that one. Darla's pale, weak face peering from the covers flashed into my head.

"You, however, are overendowed with self-interest."

"I want my father's ashes."

"I want, I want. See your greedy self?" She aimed the pointy end of the needles at me. "We will make a trade. The box for a promise. I am taking all the risk since you are a known liar."

"Look, you old biddy, you can just cut the shit."

"No, you cut the shit."

I was shocked and pleased. She was showing her true awful self. The rouge circles were the palest spots on the old woman's face. "You have to tell me what the promise is."

"That you will help your sister get out of the Army."

"But she doesn't want to get out."

"This is a rescue mission."

"Get real," I said.

Jewell sucked in her cheeks and clacked off two rows.

I looked around the ugly apartment. Goddamn her. The more she knitted, the sweeter she appeared. How could I get to her? "I am sure my father would want to rest near my mother."

"You are? And just what do you know about your daddy?"

"Well," I paused. I remembered once walking in the woods with him and my foot had gone to sleep. Daddy said to take a stick and whack it. I winced and my eye fell on Jewell's false ankle. Another time he'd given me a plug of tobacco and told me it was chewing gum. I remembered the bitter shock in my mouth and then I wondered if I smoked now to bring him back. "Well, he wasn't a saint."

"You've got more on the ball than the rest of your family," Jewell said. "That's why the burden of saving your sister falls on you."

"And just how am I supposed to do that?"

271

"There are ways." Jewell bent her head over the yellow yarn as if the matter was finished.

Her pink skull showed in patches through her white hair. For the first time, I felt I was seeing someone completely naked. I would never, never, never let myself go nuts over one man, especially a man who went away. Not even Darryl would turn me into this. Poor Mama. My heart shifted into high gear. Mama was my rescue mission. "I promise I'll do it. Tell me how."

"Substituting a pregnant woman's urine is an old tried-and-true method, but they're on to that one. Homosexuality is another. Hepatitis, but your sister looks fit as a horse."

There was no way I could fake any of those things. "I'll try."

"Good," said Jewell. "When she's discharged, you get the ashes."

"No. I need them tonight," I blurted, and regretted the crafty look that pulled the edges of her face toward her nose.

"Tonight? What about tomorrow or next year or after I pass on to the great sisterhood in the sky? What difference, tonight or ten years from now?"

"The difference," I said slowly, as the

words took form in my mind, "is that you return them to me now or I'll tell the Army you stole my father's ashes. They want to know where he is."

"Young lady, remember I know where you live and who you love." Jewell stood up and limped into the pink light. Tendrils of ivy seemed to spring from the wall. I wondered if Jewell had escaped through a secret door. But soon she returned, carrying a red box. Her hands wavered as she held it out.

The box was surprisingly light and its contents rattled in a creepy way.

"Are you sure they're all here?" I didn't trust the old lady not to substitute rocks for the real ashes.

Jewell nodded. Her brimming eyes were too bright, magnified by the tears.

"They better be," I said, deliberately looking into the wild tangle of plants. It would be just like the old coot to use ashes for fertilizer.

"I could have been your mother," she said. For a moment I saw her as just that, a kindly old lady with a kind old heart, and I felt like saying something sweet that would bring her into our family, but then I remembered how she had stolen Daddy's ashes from Mama. She was mired in a love for him too heavy and thick.

"I'll get Darla out of the Army. I promise," I said, then ran down the steps and leapt into the car. "See you later, jail baiter," I called to the gray bun in the window. How weird, I thought, as I put on my seat belt, that there is such a thing as the right amount of love. With the box stowed safely under the seat, I drove straightaway to Fred's General Store, where I located a dusty little urn. It had a lid and molded roses running down its sides. In candlelight, the roses would deepen with shadows, just the kind of thing Mama liked. I called Sheriff Dodd from a pay phone and told him I was headed his way. My own evening would be wasted trying to convince Darla to break her leg or poke her eye out or do some other hideous mutilation to herself. Too bad Darla wasn't a boy.

"You caught me just in time," Sheriff Dodd said, when I drove up to his house. It was small, a dull yellow. He was washing his RV, which he was going to use for his rendezvous with Mama. "I was getting ready to take a shower."

"Everything all ready?" I asked. I tried to peer past him into the window. I wanted to see if the setup was romantic enough. Inside my chest a large happy face was smiling. I wanted Mama to have some fun.

"Food's all set. Wine's cooling. Did you get them?"

I gave him the sack from Fred's and the box.

He carefully placed the box on the ground, then opened the bag. "Pretty little thing." He handled the urn with an ease that showed his hands were comfortable with delicate objects.

"Mama likes roses."

He nodded. "I got the flowers taken care of." A little gold tab stuck to the urn. He peeled it off. "Damn it, girl, this would have ruined everything."

"Made in Japan." I shrugged.

"Don't you know your daddy was fighting the Japanese in World War Two?"

I shrugged again. "I dropped out in tenth grade." I patted his sticky arm. "Now calm down. Mama will be nervous enough without you being all jittery and spoiling everything."

"Out of the mouths of babes," he said.

I smiled widely at his compliment. "Well, have a good time, Sheriff Dodd."

Hattie Bohannon

Paul Dodd's RV cab was navy blue with a silver stripe zooming across its door. The back end of the stripe puffed up like a cloud, the dust raised by his blinding speed. Before Hattie knocked, the cab door opened. She stared at his white-stockinged feet. Awfully casual, she thought, and regretted her lace collar and upswept hair. "I hope you'll take us somewhere with a pleasant view."

She accepted his hand but was annoyed that she needed help up. Aloft, she found herself pressed into him. "Please." She pushed him away, although they were cramped by the seat and the roof. "You'll wrinkle my dress."

He grinned. "This view doesn't please you, then?"

She sat down on the seat and said, "I'll tell you when it does."

He drove out of the lot and took the old road. The thick canopy of leaves threw shadows into the cab. She pointed at a clearing, the entrance to an overgrown wagon path. The camper hummed slowly through the high grass and stopped beneath tall pines. She wondered what he was planning, since she had told him

276

over the phone that the ashes had not yet arrived. She glanced at his pleased face.

"I'm starved," she said.

"Well, come on back to the dining room." Paul nodded at dark curtains behind the seat.

"Do I have to climb over the seat?"

"I invited you special 'cause I figured if any woman would know how to get from the front seat to the back without climbing, it'd be you."

"If you insist on making rude remarks about me, I will leave."

"The door ain't locked." He stepped over the seat and parted the curtains.

Her flat shoes were a help. She walked on the seat then swung over the backrest as if it were a fence.

"I can see where you've done this before."

"Not exactly. When I was growing up, my jeans had a little hole on the inside right cuff where I always caught them on barbed wire. That's how my mother could tell them from my sister's."

His hand swept across her waist for a thrilling second as he moved toward a tiny round table, the kind where knees couldn't help but meet. He lit a candle and dripped the wax on a saucer to make it stick. On the ceiling, shadows, like fleeing clouds, beckoned. Instantly the dark space became a small charming private booth. He pulled out a chair for her.

"Wine?"

She nodded. He disappeared in the shadows.

A cloud of burnt spices lingered. Aftershave, an insidious invention. Until you slept with a man, the smell was false and even offensive. Then afterwards, because your nose had the best memory of all the senses, the smell made you think of him naked in your bed. Hattie hoped this evening would be pleasant. Otherwise she'd be stuck forever with the smell of rotten memory. She wanted to move toward this man, to enjoy the scent of his soap, but she had promised herself for her daughters' sakes not to slip up again.

"Like my home away from home?" He bent over her glass, then his. The clear wine gurgled like a fresh spring.

"It's quite a surprise." She'd almost forgotten they were inside a camper at the edge of the piney woods.

"This is where I keep my lobsters." He nodded at a tank full of green liquid, secured to a shelf. He rapped the wall. "This door falls out and becomes where I lay my head. Ironing board, too. Got good little greens in this basket from North Carolina. I have a refrigeration compartment where I keep the best surprises."

"Where do you keep your condoms?"

"Shit, woman, I don't keep my condoms."

She filled her mouth with wine. Paul became a low gentle voice, cooking in the dimness. Steam rose from the stove. He wore an apron and wiped his hands. Low flames under a cup of butter set in front of her. Artichoke leaves. Peel and dip. She bit the leaf and chewed. Thorny rough spikes. One caught in her throat. Discreetly tore and swallowed two rolls and drained her glass. Still there. Stuck. She smiled and clinked his wineglass. The men these days cooked with more attention and technique than she did. A bonus.

She smiled and felt something like love.

He licked the butter from his lips. "Look, you been king of the hill for a long time. And if that's what you want, you can be as lonely as a mountain goat. But I like a connection, something soft and reliable, something I can count on. I'm beginning to count on you."

She sighed and turned away so he

wouldn't see the upstart smile flitting across her mouth.

"If you don't want to hear it, then this just isn't going to be very satisfactory for either of us."

"I suppose I will adjust."

"I figured you might." He poured more wine and sat back down. "I got something for you." He held out a lidded vase with a flower on it.

"Thank you." How quaint. Perhaps she'd stick some real flowers in it and keep it at home. It wasn't professional enough for the office. Not really her kind of thing. She set it beside the candle.

"Take a good look," he said.

She obliged him. It was weighted. She hefted it. Held it up. Set it on the table. Cocked her head. Said cute things about it, feeling the romance of the evening slink away. By the time she had admired each of its sides, it seemed as if someone had turned on the lights. She settled her mind. They must go on.

"I'd like some more wine, Paul."

"Yes, ma'am." He looked at her, not with soft eyes of love but like he was taking an exact count of her facial flaws.

"You got any music? A second course or dessert?"

"Something better." Cold air trailed in his wake.

She felt to see if her bun was still in place and debated whether she should let her hair fall.

Paul held a cold peach-colored rose to her lips. "I want you to breathe out like you're fogging a mirror."

She touched its cold petals. Slender lines of frost sparkled as she twirled the stem. She breathed out. The yellow-pink tips wavered. A silver drop ran down into the melon-pink center. Slowly, as her breath warmed them, the stiff petals quivered. Moist and luminous, the rose glowed like a cup of peach brandy. The candlelight stretched into the points of stars.

"You're some damn woman," he said, as he breathed down her neck.

"Mmm." She blinked her eyes and lifted her shoulders. "That is a nice vase. Maybe I'll put some frozen roses in it."

He laughed. "You better not do that."

"Well, why not? You gave it to me."

"It's not very respectful, that's all." His chin rested gently on her shoulder.

She tickled his ear. "I thought you wanted me to be disrespectful."

"You don't have to be disrespectful ever again," he said. "That urn is holding your husband's ashes."

She pushed at his face and wrenched her shoulder free. Somehow her voice came out even. "That is the cruelest thing you have ever said to me. What is this whole setup? You've been making fun of me and my feelings all along. And then, right when I'm finally letting go and trying only to think of right now, you got to come out with his name and accuse me of betraying him?"

"Oh, Jesus. Oh, Jesus."

"You better pray." She stood up and clawed at the curtain.

"Hattie, listen. This is your urn. And your husband's ashes are inside it. I thought that's what you wanted. It's all I've heard about from you." He held out a red box. In the dimness, it looked like a candy box, lettered with the words REMAINS OF LT. OAKLEY BOHANNON, U.S. ARMY. "I'll open the urn if you like."

She marched over to the table and picked up the urn. "Thank you for the evening, Paul Dodd. It was nice. And thanks for returning my husband. Sometime you can tell me how you did it. Someday you will be telling the law." She paused and was struck by how ordinary he looked out of uniform. "Telling the *U.S. Army* how

282

you stole him." She grasped its slender neck and, with as much dignity as she could muster, climbed over the cab seat and down the running board.

Hattie fled through the woods, willing the sun to dive headlong into a distant ocean. But the slow twilight made her path all too clear, her moving figure an anomaly among the shafts of withered plants. Her flat shoes chafed in the dry dust of pine straw.

How could there still be daylight? Paul's cab had been dark and close. It had even smelled of evening. How had he done that? The frozen roses, the lobster in its battened-down tank. And then the surprise, he'd said. She had imagined — what? Some exotic fruit that hinted of smuggler's hands, a powerfully sweet drink native to a Pacific island? But the ashes.

She focused on the scaly trees, the dusty feeling of brown, the smell of dry grass, the heat. She must slow down before the pulses of pain in her head formed a knot. Out here there was no water, no cure for a headache. She'd go to the river.

It was only after a half hour of walking that her thoughts began to cohere. Everything else since he'd said *your husband's ashes* had been pure body response. An awful confluence of past and present slamming head-on into each other: who she was, had been, was about to be. Her body had turned tail. Around her, disembodied advice and rules had floated, then spun, growing tighter and smaller and faster until they torqued inside her skull, threatening to explode the bone. Her breath rasped. She barely saw the narrow deer path as it wound through the pale forest grasses.

But she held the urn in a tight grip. As she slid in her good shoes, she kept the urn close to her hip and let her left hand flail and steady her. It was a fragile thing she carried and yet so heavy, like an infant, or a tablet from God, or a vaccine. It was herself embodied in it, a genie Paul Dodd had hoped to call forth by rubbing the urn with his hands.

The sun dropped. It would soon be dark, and who would she be, out in the woods at the edge of the river at night? Could she find Troy Clyde's raft in the dark? She wanted to drift without aim, not face who she was now. No longer Oakley's wife; that was past. Even the night she'd made love to Paul Dodd was past. It had happened too fast, Oakley gone, Paul there. Her stomach rose, wine and the prickly piece of artichoke. This was madness.

After the urn, she could no more have stripped down with Paul Dodd there in the privacy of his RV than she could have at Oakley's funeral with a hundred witnesses. Paul had spoken of connection, but she'd felt sheered off from him as if by a heavy blow. Walking in the dim light took all her concentration. The river was too far away. She had to get home on her own accord.

The Ladies of the Church of the Holy Resurrection

As it was their duty to keep perversion in its place, the ladies forbade their children and husbands and beauticians and recipients of charitable donations to brighten the doorway of the truck stop. They took some satisfaction in knowing the dust on Hattie's driveway lay undisturbed for days at a time.

The ladies spent all summer sweating. In church, their paper fans, depicting a dole-eyed Jesus cuddling a hot woolly lamb, fluttered so much their wrists thickened. They sent fumes of prayer heavenward for an air conditioner. Water beads, strung like pearls, glistened on their foreheads. They didn't dare go without pantyhose — too tacky. Up front, Reverend Peterson raged with fire over the sins of the flesh. The church was hot as hell.

The gym on the town square sweated through its cinderblock walls until stopped by external pink baked-on paint. The sweat seeped back into the gym, which smelled like an unfinished basement. One by one, the ladies discovered that a certain leg-lifting exercise, reputed to flatten their stomachs, caused the liveliest little shivers to race along their pelvic floors. A few braver ones actually allowed the shivers to build to a crescendo. They modestly turned their faces from the huge mirror. Such a sight was far too intimate in a large writhing room of pink and purple.

Jewell Miller munched her bean sprouts in stealth as the pitch of conversation whined against her eardrums. She missed Oakley's box, now safely in Hattie's hands. Jewell had transported it to and from work for several months, in order that she might share her day with him. Often she held the earphones up to the box so he could share her dismay. She had replaced him with a clever automatic redial attachment, a small humming box that was more companionable. She hadn't been in the Army for nothing.

IV

Connie Bohannon

Mama didn't come home the night she went off in Sheriff Dodd's RV. Afterwards in the light of day she looked pale and talked as if all her energy had leached out. She didn't mention Daddy's ashes but I saw the urn on her dresser when I went in to put a sachet in her underwear drawer, for the next time she went out with Sheriff Dodd.

I spent a lot of time working, covering for Darla, who slept late. Mama didn't make her get up and go to school, so what could I do? One day I got a phone call at work from a high school boy, which was a first.

When the voice said, "This is Kyle Childers," I didn't say anything back. He probably thought I'd fainted because next he roared, "And I am asking you to the prom."

My mind was sorting through heads in a yearbook trying to recall which one Kyle was. "When is it?"

"May thirteenth," he said, like I was retarded.

Then I remembered him. He was so

291

huge that if it wasn't for football he'd be in a sideshow at a carnival.

"Well?" He sounded like he might hang up.

I wasn't sure how Darryl would feel about me going to the prom with another boy. Darryl is my uncle's stepson, and we've been friendly since last Fourth of July. Real friendly. I'd gone to the barn that day to get a mess of hamburger patties from the freezer and was cooling off in the chilly steam when Darryl saw me. He was smoking dope behind the old baptismal font they use for saving dying sinners in the winter. Darryl said he saw me standing over that freezer in my short shorts and my yellow tank top and saw my nipples turn hard and he knew what that meant. He came up behind me and touched my waist real easy. My whole body went on fire from my ankles to my head. I didn't have an orgasm the first time but I had enough hot shivers to go back for more. I'd been having orgasms all my life. I just didn't know you were supposed to have them during sex.

Darryl is married, besides.

I could see Kyle's impatience weighing down the telephone wire leading to the truck stop. He cleared his throat and three finches burst off the line. I remembered Dear Abby's advice to the Other Woman: Get on with your own life. He will never leave his wife.

"Okay," I said.

"Okay? Okay?" Kyle sounded mad.

"Thank you very much," I said, just like a Dear Abby teenager.

Out front, I wiped a table clean and thought, I don't even know Kyle's phone number if I want to cancel.

I couldn't get my mind off the prom even with Darryl's hands running all over me in the garage behind the truck stop. I hadn't been to County High for a year. My exit had been grand. Ninth grade was finally over — I'd passed everything, even algebra — and I was skipping toward the open door and the blue suntan sky above the tennis courts. In my joy I didn't wait until I was outside before lighting up. Mr. Hitson, the principal, burst like a bull from the classroom at the end of the hall, his face as red as Mama's tomato aspic. He stormed down on me and grabbed my wrist, like to broke it in two. The cigarette fell into his hand — what did he expect? — and ash burnt a hole in his black polyester suit sleeve.

"Turn me loose," I shouted, right up in his face. Not because I was brave but because I was scared.

That's when the cigarette burnt him and he rared back like he was going to hit me. If he had I could have sued and then not worked until I was maybe thirty years old. But he didn't. He said, "Connie Bohannon, you are suspended."

I couldn't help myself. I said, "Whoopee ding-dong. I'll just take the whole summer off."

I walked out that door with my head up and I was fine, watching the group of instant admirers I had just got, and I was cool all the way to Jessamine's car — and then I thought about Mama and what would happen to me next.

But Jess and I were going to the lake for the afternoon so Mama was put on hold. Instead I recalled every step I took and the appreciative glances I got from kids who wouldn't give me the time of day even though I had been in school with them all my life. They were the kids who lived in town. They acted like us kids from the county had lice and wore the stupidest clothes. It was the only time I ever saw Daniel Warner look away from Marylou Dearing for a second. Usually they were

Velcroed together.

As I passed him holding open the door to Marylou's gold Camaro, he smiled a real-person smile. It said, *Good going!*

I floated toward Jessamine's Bug like I was riding the jet stream.

Daniel Warner was not my type at all. He seemed more like a model for JC Penney than a real boy. He's cute but I'm not into cute. And he wore khakis and colors boys aren't supposed to wear. But I hated Marylou Dearing. Mr. Briggs, the bachelor high school teacher all the girls loved madly, said once, out loud, even though it was a private thought, "Marylou Dearing wears the nicest clothes."

I was so mad I told Mama and she got her tight-lips look on her face and I was real sorry then. I was afraid she'd go storming into school. But she said, "If Mr. Briggs makes another statement like that, you call him on it right out loud."

Mama has been fighting battles all her life, and as Troy Clyde says, she's finally learned which ones she can win.

After I got off work — it was a busy day, with busloads of tourists heading to or coming from Noccalula Falls — I looked at the calendar. The prom was only one week away. Kyle Childers was desperate for a date. Every other girl at school must have turned him down and he had finally got to the dropouts. I hadn't thought about school much this year. Once I turned sixteen and started waitressing, I knew I wouldn't go back. Being in the world with real people was too interesting. There are truckers who send me postcards from where they've been.

Now I have postcards from every state, even some you never hear of, like Delaware and South Dakota. The truckers are mostly nice men who like to talk to a pretty girl. I am pretty. I take care of my looks even though I am in the prime time. I like to try on different makeups — you know, make Monday a peach day, Tuesday raspberry, that kind of thing. I have to do something when things get dull, which they can.

Mama watches me like a hawk and she watches the truckers like they are about to commit a crime. I've learned how to be friendly but not suggestive: Mama's word. I've learned that when they say they want to show me something in their truck, it's not what they say it is. Lord, some of those men are so old, forty even, and they want to show me something. At their age.

I can't get over it.

As I sat looking at my calendar, I got a good idea, a very good idea. I would go to the prom and everyone, even Mr. Hitson, would have to be polite. I would wear the most fantastic gown there ever was. I would go up and speak to Daniel Warner and Marylou Dearing and all those idiots and I would make them talk to me. Kyle, being a football player, wasn't such a bad date after all. No. He would be the perfect prop.

"What if I get pregnant?" I asked Darryl once.

"I know someone who will take care of it."

That seemed too simple, but Mama didn't tell me anything about the facts of life. I learned about love from Darryl.

Mama's talk went like this: "These are the pads you use when you need them. Do you have any questions?"

"Is white the only color they come in?" I mean, why not a dark color?

"Good heavens," she'd said, and left the room, the big box on my pink bedspread.

With only a week to prepare for the prom I was in bad straits. First of all, every beauty salon in Maridoches County had been booked for months. I called around and got an eight-thirty in Gadsden, 52 miles away.

The dress was the most important thing. I had made such a grand exit from County High that I had to come back even better. I had to show all of them I was high class; I was somebody. Of course I could not afford $400 to buy the beautiful black sateen cigarette dress I wanted. And I didn't want to buy one that was advertised for a hundred dollars in the newspaper's bargain basket. If someone had worn it to last year's prom, my stock would fall faster than a stone drunk from a bar stool.

I was so nervous about the dress I kept mixing up food orders until Gert looked across her broad blue shoulder and said, "Is it your time of the month?" real loud so the whole kitchen could hear. She always shouted everything. "Scarlupt potatoes and hambuggars up!"

I told her my problem, and much to my surprise she said, "Don't worry, Connie honey. I sew real good. I was the one what made County High cheerleader uniforms before they got X-rated."

My dress turned out beautiful. It was made of emerald-green satin that shimmered every time I breathed. The bodice was shaped like a green heart, with a curve over each breast. Gert had sewed black lace between the cups and collar, a bit of modesty I could have done without until I saw how mysterious my skin looked beneath the dark roses. Jessamine lent me a pair of black high heels and she and I actually worked together one whole night without fighting, gluing paste emeralds from toe to heel. My stockings were black lace, expensive. It took half a day's tips to buy one leg. I thought of that as I put them on, hoping I wouldn't snag them on my sparkly fingernails.

My hair was done up like a Gibson Girl's, all butternut curls, and my face had turned out perfect. I'd practiced it a million times, but I'd never had the proper accompaniments before. I couldn't stop staring at myself. Even Mama and Darla, for once, were struck dumb. I couldn't believe the beautiful young woman was me, Connie Bohannon, in this one-of-a-kind dress.

I imagined the other girls would look like Barbies in dress-up clothes, or guides for a gardenia tour, and I would be a woman. That was it. I looked like a woman.

The doorbell rang and it was all I could do to keep from running to get it. I listened for the call to come down the stairs, and then I heard Darryl ask for me.

My heart leaped about a mile in the air.

"Why?" said Mother.

"I brought her something for the prom."

I felt sweat begin under my armpits. Cigarettes?

I could hear Mother's foot tap the floor. I heard the steps squeak as she came up.

"You have a visitor," she said.

"Oh, wow." I primped.

"It's not your date. It's your married cousin." Mama spoke evenly so I could not tell what she knew or what she thought she knew. I played dumb.

"What is he doing here? Gee whiz."

"That's what I want to know," said Mama.

"Okay, Mama. I've been letting him get away with not paying for his meals and he owes me. I told him I needed the money tonight." My face flushed.

"Oh, dear," said Mama. "You're beginning to glow under your arms." She unsnapped my buttons, dabbed me with Kleenex, and rolled my armpits with Sure. "I'll send him home."

"Okay." I struggled to rebutton the bodice.

300

Next thing I knew Darryl was stepping into my room.

"What?" I said, crossing my arms, forgetting I was beautiful.

"You're — wow, you're not Connie."

"Screw off." I went to the window and looked at the truck stop, lit like a flying saucer in an empty field, and hoped one of the cars turning up the lane was Kyle's.

"No. You're so gorgeous it scares me. I mean, some guy going out with you —"

"Screw off, Darryl. I'm supposed to be gorgeous. I'm going to make them all bow down before me." I beamed with the thought.

"Yeah." He fiddled for a cigarette in his pocket.

"No smoking in here," I said, even though I did it all the time.

"For you." He cupped his hand so I couldn't see what was in it until he opened his palm.

It was a small velvet-covered box, a ring box. "Darryl," I whispered and looked at him, all hunky and tall and dark.

He smiled, then shrugged like he didn't care.

Downstairs the front door opened and I could hear Mama introduce herself and ask Kyle how the air was, like she hadn't had her head stuck out the window for the past half hour watching for him.

"See you," Darryl said.

He clumped down the stairs and didn't say a thing to Kyle but "Hey." Didn't bother to check him out, he was so quick out the door. I could tell. His engine roared before Mama called me down the steps.

I yelled, "In a minute!" which I know I wasn't supposed to do. Holler like I was at a ball game. So Darryl wanted my loyalty. I felt like I was already at the prom under the crystal ball. I swooped around the room, imagining Darryl, Darryl pressed close. I opened the ring box. Inside were three silver foil packets. Three! I crushed them.

I went down the stairs in a blur. The flashbulb from Mama's camera erased the rest of the false cheery scene, me and Kyle as a couple. I couldn't see right until we sat down to dinner at Romeo's Ristorante.

Kyle squared his sloping shoulders against the chair like it was a big effort to hold up so much flesh. He would have looked better if he'd worn his football shoulder pads under the tux. As it was, I was on a date with a sack of sand. But he had nice eyes and one of those open chubby faces so common around here, the kind that gets jowly and growly around age thirty. He'd already taken the best picture of his life and I was in it, back home in Mama's camera.

All the prom couples went to Romeo's because they let kids bring booze inside in paper bags. Kyle had pink Riunite for me. I ordered 7-Up and mixed the two whenever he went to the men's room, which was a lot. He'd brought himself a six-pack and drank it all.

On the table between us a candle burned in a glass covered with fishnet, which cast weird shapes all the way up his neck, reminding me of heat rash. I blew the candle out. In the dark, I covered my mouth to hide a yawn. Good Lord, boy, think of something to say.

He banged his fork about twenty-five times on the table. "Why'd you quit school?"

I stared at him. How could he not know about me telling Mr. Hitson off? He began to bang his fork again so I said, "Intro to Business One was typing and Business Two was more typing. I learn lots more about business working at the truck stop." I tore my hard little roll in half and smeared the pat of real butter out to the edges, then left it sit on the bread plate. "I'm not going to talk about work anymore. You got to say something. This is prom night."

"I guess it would be easier if we were in love." He sighed. At the next table, a couple I thought I recognized were buried in each other's necks. They made Kyle and me seem even more like total strangers.

As we ate I checked them out and it was Marylou and Daniel. Kyle accidentally kicked over his sack of empties, which rattled across the floor. I saw Marylou Dearing flinch. A can rolled under her enormous southern-belle skirt. She reminded me of dolls with crochet skirts propped up by a roll of toilet paper. Daniel Warner smiled at me and I smiled back. He was dressed as a Confederate soldier. Kyle was having a time chasing the empties around the floor. As he bent to pick them up I got a good look at his blue tux. It clashed with my dress. He was probably color-blind.

Outside I made myself smile at Kyle and he grinned back. After all, next year I would be too old for the prom, or married, and I didn't want to miss it.

"I'm getting a new car," Kyle said. He

opened the door of his yellow Gran Torino and slid across the seat and unlocked my door. I got in and said, "Nice."

"Now that I signed with the Tide, Mr. Walker is loaning me a convertible. Pick it up next week. A blue Trans Am."

"Mr. Walker's the only Auburn fan in Maridoches. Why's he lending you a car?"

"Maybe he's seen the light," said Kyle, as he sped up the hill. Then he talked more about the convertible and all its features, which I couldn't give two hoots about.

Drowsy from the wine, I leaned against the car window as the headlights swept the road. Every star in the sky was shining on us. The night was so beautiful. I thought of the old ladies at the beauty parlor this morning and wondered why the word *prom* had made them froth at the mouth.

I giggled, remembering one woman, wrinkled as a pachyderm, squawking over and over, "The prom is the first step to the altar," as if she were a talking doll with a pull string.

"What's so funny?" Kyle asked.

"Old ladies."

He sighed and kept driving and driving.

"Are you lost?"

"No," he snapped. "I know the territory."

I slumped in the seat and almost said, Wake me when we get there, but I could tell he was annoyed. Finally the car stopped. I recognized the scenic-mountain view marker and broken railing of Pealiquor Ridge. Beyond the hood, the lights of the town seemed farther away than the stars. "What are we doing here?"

"Prom goes on all night." He looked at me like he wanted something, something I knew about. "You're so beautiful."

"Thank you," I said. "Can we go now? I can drive us straight there."

"It lasts 'till eleven. Then there's the after-prom. We got plenty of time." He pulled a bottle of Rebel Yell from under the seat and set it on the dash. I looked over the ridge and listened as he uncapped the bottle.

"I want to go right now."

"You're so beautiful."

His hand fell on my forearm. I stiffened. His fly was open and there, like the water tower outside of town, stood his dick, curved and gleaming in the moonlight.

"That's against the law," I said.

"Aw, truck-stop girl, you're so beautiful."

He lunged and I was being squeezed, choked it felt like, mashed. He held me so

306

tight I could not breathe. The air smelled too much like a locker room and I was drowning in it. He kept saying, "You're so beautiful, truck-stop girl. You're so beautiful." The power in his arms shocked me. He was like a giant vise. I felt small, very small. There was so much fabric around my face.

I heard ripping. "My dress!" I fought him, twisting, flailing, wriggling my legs. "I'll take it off. Let me!" I screamed.

I found the door handle and jerked it and the door opened and I fell out and the air seemed cool. Kyle flopped across the seat, looking down at the gravel. Sweat glistened behind his ears.

My hands flew to my head, my beautiful hair, which dangled in stiff clumps. Kyle raised up and watched, like a fish inside a tank. His eyes seemed large, his mouth hollow as a coal shaft.

I breathed deeply and stood up. Slowly I lifted my elbows above my head and reached for the first button of the high neck. All the while I was thinking, *This is not supposed to happen. What next? What can I do?* I was shaking inside, like I might get sick, but afraid that if I did I'd lose everything. I had to say to my fingers, *Grab the button, push it through the hole. Now the next one.*

Kyle moved. Toward me. I sprang against the door. I felt the jarring crack as his head went backwards. I leaned into the door and dug my shoes into the gravel and pushed and pushed until my sweat broke and turned cool. He wasn't going to get out of that car for anything.

I pressed against the door a long time. My legs cramped and my arms felt more tired than they do after a ten-hour shift. There was no sound from the car, no movement either. I peered into the shadows of the front seat and saw Kyle's tux rise and fall as if he was asleep.

I had started around the car when I felt a sharp tug on my dress. I yanked at the cloth, convinced Kyle had come to. But he hadn't. My dress was snagged in the door. I pulled it out. A dark stain grew near the hem.

I danced around and around but the wet fabric wouldn't swing free. I twirled and spun, lost my shoes in the gravel. I ran, the dress slapping my legs, down the warm blacktop road until I was winded.

Self-defense. I'd walk to town, which was a long way and might take all night, and call Sheriff Dodd, who wanted to get back together with Mama after their fiasco of a date. My ruined dress would tell everything, the blood and rips. Gert had worked so hard to make it perfect and I still owed Mama eighteen hours of overtime to pay for it. My stockings were run, my unpainted toenails sticking through the lace like the long toes of a rat.

I wanted to kill Kyle. If we never showed up, everybody at County High would think we were screwing. Even without us doing it, they'd think I had screwed that big fat freak-show freak. I cried and cried and followed the center line through the dark woods.

Why did this happen to me? I'd been beautiful. Like a bride. No, prettier than a bride. *The prom is the first step to the altar.* They'd warned me, the old ladies at the beauty parlor, Darryl with his condoms. Now it seemed the condoms were an act of love. Sadness welled again and I thought of Kyle undressing himself. Truck-stop girl, he'd called me. And then I knew what he meant, what he'd expected. Kyle had invited me so his buddies would know he got laid. The church ladies' march had tarred all of us. Mama should have taken them on directly, not with ice cream but with words. She should have smashed their signs and sued their lying butts. But she hadn't. Around me, crickets sang, high-pitched and shrieky.

The road dipped and curved. The line turned yellow and doubled. The lines meant nothing. Any car, anytime, could and would cross it, no matter the curve, the hill, the darkness. On I walked in the middle of the road, beyond the crickets, shivering against the silence.

A car roared near, and when its headlights swept into view I hunkered down in a ditch of wet leaves. As the car passed, I hid in the earth-scented shadow, where it felt safe. I couldn't trust anyone.

I rested awhile and thought about staying there until sunlight, but what would Mama think? She'd go out of her mind. I could see her slowly parting the lace curtain to peer at the truck stop, watching first for Kyle's headlights and then, as the hours passed, hoping to see the car parked down below the honeysuckle hedge, hoping then at that hour that we were making out, giving that up in order to see me safe. I stayed a long time in the ditch, imagining Mama and her coffee and her soft blue gown. I sent her messages through the air. But still she sat by the window and cradled her coffee cup. Slowly my body cramped. I looked up through a clearing of loblolly pines at the starry sky. Oh, Darryl, I prayed, come and look for me. You know Pealiquor Ridge is the parking spot. I wished, wished, wished he'd come.

I walked a long time before I heard music. It pulled me like a lure to a long low building with a tin roof. A sign painted on the wall said THE GENTLEMEN'S CLUB. Between the road and the dirt parking lot, a strip of grass sparkled like an open treasure chest. The boys at school called this a jive dive and bragged about throwing empties into the parking lot after evenings on Pealiquor Ridge.

I didn't dare go in.

I stood in the road looking at the building, wishing I could. I moved a half step forward and felt something crinkle under my foot. It was a pack of Marlboros, with four inside, one of them crushed. A book of matches advertising Dreamland in Tuscaloosa was jammed under the plastic wrapper. I should have been grateful, but I was in no mood for gratitude. I jabbed inside the pack. Bits of tobacco clung to my fingers and as I lit up, crumbs on my lips, I thought suddenly of Daddy. I remembered his yellow-tipped fingers teaching me how to lace my shoes, his rich scent of soil and beer and smoke and his patience as he retrieved again the black-and-white saddle shoe I'd kicked under the couch. I had not cried when Mama said he was dead. No, I had finished eating my jelly sandwich and cried only after Darla punched me for getting butter in the jelly jar.

Smoke curled from the cigarette. If Daddy were alive, he would come find me. Walking tall like a skinny tree, he would appear, his straw hat a little crooked. He'd sit on the log and take my hand in his yellow-tipped fingers. I would ask him about love and soak his shirt with tears. He would murmur songs into my hair because I was the youngest and always came in last.

He'd point out the animals made up of stars overhead and name the fat bugs scurrying over the log. And that odd tree over there, the one whose bark reminded me of a knight's club, spiky and hard, Daddy would know its name. My tears were warm and slow as a summer river. If he were alive and with us, Mama would not have the truck stop and I would not be stranded right now. One by one I smoked the three cigarettes left in the pack. Their stubs, clustered together, white in the darkness, reminded me of a family of soft mice.

A car was coming but my legs stood still. As quick as that, my body turned to fear. Blinded by the headlights, I skittered across the strip of broken glass and tumbled under a fig bush, balled up tight to keep from screaming.

Blood branched across the arch of my writhing left foot. The flow would not stop. I scattered a small red rain on bobbing ferns, then hopped toward the smoky building. Fear couldn't touch me now. Fear operated when you had options. The Gentlemen's Club was fixing to see an entrance like they never had before. A drunk, dirty, insane white girl was coming to call.

Feeling my way like a blind woman through a sea of metal dinosaurs, I lurched from car to car. I limped to the door and then, not knowing if I should push right in, knocked, which seemed silly. Knocking on the door of a bar. Who could hear me?

A man bathed in the red of the exit sign peered out. He thrust his face into mine, his eyes deep, black, and pointed. It was like I was staring into a double-barreled shotgun. He said, "Who you know in here? This a private club."

"I'm bleeding. I need to call an ambulance."

The man just stared. "Why don't you white kids leave us alone? All the time coming up here and causing trouble. Daring somebody to ask for a drink. You ain't going to get the law up here, ambulance or no." The door swung at me.

I thrust my foot into the disappearing slice of the Gentlemen's Club.

"You *are* bleeding." His voice softened. "Go around to the back. We only got one toilet so you can't come in."

I must have looked really desperate because he sighed, then half smiled. "I'll send somebody back there what can help you."

I hopped around the building, my foot gone numb, and sat on a stump. Minutes later, the blackest man I'd ever seen appeared, carrying a glass of whiskey, a cloth, and a pan of water. His head was smooth and bald and sat like a gigantic egg in a nest of wrinkled neck skin. "This gonna hurt." He poured whiskey on the cut.

I gritted my teeth and felt my spine collapse. In a moment I was sturdy again, sitting up, reaching for the glass.

"Here." He put it to my lips. "For medicinal purposes."

The whiskey rolled down my throat,

whetting my lying voice. "I killed a man."

He looked at me out of the corner of his eye. He took in the blood and dirt on my dress and the smell of Rebel Yell.

"Up there on the ridge." I shifted. "We were supposed to go to the prom but he tried to get me drunk and took me up there. He just wanted. . . . He didn't want to take me to the prom." My voice rose and fell and in an odd way caught the melody of the music. "So I broke his head open with the car door."

"Pipe dreams," said the man.

"It's true. I cut my foot running away from him."

"A girl out alone at a club for gentlemen only." He shook his head. "Mighty peculiar."

"I just killed a man. What could scare me?" My voice wobbled.

The man cut away the stocking and put the strip in his pocket. He swabbed my foot with the cloth. "We can't keep you here if you're running from the law."

"I'm not running from the law. I just need to call home."

He shrugged. "You got to take care of the feet." He began to rub my foot, to probe little bones I didn't know I had. Starting at my heel, he rubbed small circles

315

on my skin, his touch soft but firm, stronger in some places but never painful. I sank into the music. I saw it dance across the starry sky in colors. Peach melba drifting lazily along like a river. Large magenta stones tippling into the water, dissolving, spreading magenta ripples. Then the yellows, sharp bars of lemonade ice, marching like piano keys, leaping high and turning translucent before slipping below the surface without a splash. The tinkle of purple fish as they swam upstream.

The man sank sharp fingernails into my left ankle. With a pocketknife he made two quick swipes across my foot and with a pair of nail clippers pulled a sliver of metal, half a beer tab, from the gash. He sewed up the cuts with fish line.

"Tender feet." He said it as if it were a disease he'd diagnosed. He guided my foot until it pointed straight at the moon. "I'll be back."

I felt indecent, leaning back on the stump, my foot aimed at the moon. I gathered the long skirt between my thighs. A couple of men poked their faces out the back door of the Gentlemen's Club.

"Whoo. Check this, Joe. We got a statue in the woodpile."

"Damn, that's powerful whiskey. I mean, damn," said the second man, rubbing his eyes. "Give me some more of that shit."

"Shut up," I said, wanting to drop my foot but unsure if it was good health or not. "I'm waiting on the foot doctor."

"Hey, Joe, she can talk."

"Never mind," said Joe. "I got plenty of women that run their mouths."

The men came out into the yard. They each had a small bottle of liquor, which they raised and clinked. "To you, princess of the stump," said the squatty one.

I laughed, woozy, near tears.

"Cheers," said Joe, and they clinked bottles again.

The men lurched along the back wall and urinated, hiding nothing from me. The foot doctor returned.

He held up a jar of cobwebs. He reached inside and wrapped the sticky silver strands around my foot. "Took me awhile to find these. Housekeeper come yesterday."

My white foot draped in a sandal of cobwebs gleamed in the moonlight. "You have beautiful midnight color up here," I said, as a flush of well-being returned. "I wish I could put it in a bottle."

He continued to wrap my foot as if he

hadn't heard me.

"And the music," I said. "The music would be like an egg, all beautiful sad blue on the outside but on the inside veins of Emperor's Gold and Peach Melba and Burgundy Rust. What glorious colors this place has."

"Dr. Feets, this girl done lost it," said one of the urinators, shaking himself.

"She just been through surgery," Dr. Feets said.

I rode with Dr. Feets in his old van and relished the dingy, dusty smell of hunting dogs it carried. Inside I was bursting like a sunbeam, because the world wasn't mean and ugly but had good people in it, strangers even. The prom seemed like a dress-up game for kids compared to my visit to the Gentlemen's Club. I wanted to tell this to Dr. Feets, whose neck shook with every bump, but he'd ignored everything I'd said so I simply grinned at him. We drove pretty fast for the curves and hills yet I trusted him completely.

"About that dead boy, if there is a dead boy: if he died up to the ridge, we're going to get the blame," Dr. Feets said, as he barreled up the spur toward Pealiquor Ridge.

Kyle couldn't be dead. I'd seen him breathe. As we drove up the hill, the odor of persimmons crowded the van. My stomach tightened as if I'd eaten every unripe fruit in the forest. What if Kyle demanded that Dr. Feets hand me over? Never, never would I get out of this truck. I hoped Kyle was dead. I prayed that Kyle was dead. I even skipped over all the things I had to be forgiven for first and prayed mightily for that burning love God kept in his fingertips ready to zap the most undeserving of us all.

I wanted to appeal to Dr. Feets, to say, Please don't make me go with Kyle. Light spread across his bald head. He looked as cold as the moon. The truck churned up the gravel of Pealiquor Ridge.

Dr. Feets strolled to the Gran Torino and peered in the side window. A bright star, alone at the edge of the sky, blinked. Alive or dead, what was my wish? I wished I was at the prom.

I heard a grunt as Dr. Feets prodded Kyle. "Hey. What the hell?" Kyle's speech was loud, too loud, and the words slurred together: *whatthehell.*

"I'm calling the cops," Kyle shouted, and slipped when he tried to stand up.

"You out of luck. The cops don't have

this address on their radar screen," Dr. Feets called over his shoulder as he came back to the van. He climbed into the driver's seat and glanced at me. I'd prepared myself for any news, my hands folded, my eyes on the shining star.

"That boy has a head like a rock."

I laughed, silly and ridiculous and relieved and crazy, all at once. "Oh, Dr. Feets, I was safer at the Gentlemen's Club than I was with Kyle."

"It's a club for gentlemen. Why are you surprised?" His voice was sharp and his pen jabbed the pad he wrote on. He tore off the top sheet and said, "Fifty dollars for the surgery. You can pay on the installment plan." He turned the key. "Your boy ain't dead. Run along as best you can."

"You can't leave me here. You can't." I thrust my face up to his. I was right under his nose, his smoky mouth above mine. "Don't leave me."

He turned his head away. "You're a pretty woman. You probably think your nose is too big but it ain't."

I let myself out. God! I wanted to scream. I crumpled his bill and threw it over the railing.

Kyle was propped up on the hood of his car. I stood like a statue where I was. Dr.

Feets drove away, his engine fading like my last hope.

Kyle came toward me, letting each foot drag through the gravel. "Look at you," he said. "Look at you. Stockings ripped to shreds. I saw you kiss that jig in the truck."

He didn't hit me. I guess he didn't know me well enough for that. I couldn't even run now. I shook as I felt him circle and kick gravel at my bare feet.

"You are the only girl who would go to the prom with me. You are the first one who ever said yes. And look how it turned out."

Part of me started to say, I'm sorry, but Mama's voice rang out clearly in my head: *Never apologize for something you did not do.* So I said nothing and shivered at the memory of his strength.

"We were all supposed to meet here but none of them came. My buddies, all supposed to come up here to show off the chicks."

They'd probably seen the car and thought what they wanted to. I knew then that Darryl's condoms weren't enough of a show of love. He had to do better than that. "You are not my love life," I said to Kyle.

"I hate this damned monkey suit," he

321

said, ripping open the vest and clawing off the tie.

We heard a car coming up the road. It was Sheriff Dodd. When I didn't get home by curfew, Mama had swallowed her pride and called him up in tears, insisting something bad had happened to me and she was not about to hush anything up.

We looked like we'd been attacked. Kyle's forehead had developed a large purple bump and blood had dried on his upper lip. With my ripped stockings and falling-down hair, mascara smudged on my cheeks, I was a mess.

I was so numb I stayed silent while Kyle tried to answer questions he didn't know the answer to. Me, who could lie to my mother's face about Darryl and to Dr. Feets about murder, and me, who could scream at the principal, I said nothing.

Sheriff Dodd left us in the patrol car while he investigated the Gran Torino. He picked up one of my shoes and hooked the heel over his belt. When he slipped into the shadows, I could see a bobbing cluster of stars, the paste emeralds shining for all they were worth.

"Connie, I'm sorry what happened to you," Kyle said.

"Sorry? Are you apologizing?"

"Yeah."

"For what?" I wondered how far he'd go.

"For that black guy."

"You're apologizing for *him?*"

"Why you keep asking me questions? Aren't you right in the head?"

"We both wanted something different, Kyle, and neither of us got it."

"Ain't no girl would go with me," said Kyle. "Why did you?"

I didn't answer.

"If I didn't have football, nobody would like me," he said.

"Football doesn't mean you can rape girls," I said, not in an angry way. It just popped out of my mouth like a solemn truth.

"I didn't rape nobody."

"You tried."

"But you aren't a virgin."

"So?" I said. "Are you?"

Kyle studied his hands. He looked like a fat kid alone at a swimming pool with his stomach drooping over his trunks, pretending his body was okay to him. It was like I was seeing what he thought without any words being spoken. And then I thought of Darryl at the creek, and the smooth line of his belly and the curves of his shoulder blades, those nice triangles like small wings. I wanted to get my dress back perfect and go to his window and call him out and lead him to the cliff and let the moon be our crystal ball and let him and me dance and dance forever.

Darla Bohannon

Everything I eat tastes burnt. My father is in my mouth and on my tongue. Every day I retch and retch, but the big bar in my stomach does not come out. It is like living with a brick inside me; it blocks everything. My breath is short. I feel constipated. Cleaning a bathroom is impossible with its associations. I cannot eat or breathe or move. Mama tries to have me drink broth, every day thicker and thicker, and I try for her sake, but she does not ask me what is wrong. She feels my head and puts a thermometer in my mouth and says if I want to join the Army we must talk about it. Maybe it is not a bad thing for me, after all. She brings me apple juice and even the newest blueberries, which I love, but they just wither and die.

Connie Bohannon

Sitting in Sheriff Dodd's office, surrounded by paneled walls reeking disinfec-
tant, the yellow sun baking her bare shoulders, Connie felt like a Lysol can under
pressure. Her stomach threatened to flee
toward her mouth every other minute. So
this is the after-prom, she thought. She
was hung over and the damned chair was
metal and one leg rickety, which made her
seasick if she shifted an inch. Behind his
desk sat his empty wooden chair, carved to
fit a flattened-out behind. At least she
didn't have a ridge of wood poking up her
ass.

She craved a cigarette. It would settle
her stomach and help her figure out why
Mama had hauled her out of bed so fast
this morning, practically slammed her into
the car, and rode hell-bent-for-leather
down to this hotbox. Actually, Connie
hadn't minded the ride. She'd stretched
across the backseat and lifted her injured
foot to the open window and enjoyed the
dancing wind. Mama kept twisting to stare
at her, as if she were a werewolf ready to
sink teeth into Mama's neck. At least
Jessamine, who was driving, had her sense
about her. She pointed out that Mama's

rear end mashed against the front window was getting a lot of honks from passing cars.

Maybe if she puked she could get out of here and go home to bed. She considered rummaging through Dodd's drawer for cigarettes. What power he had. If she swiped a cigarette she could be charged with a misdemeanor, but if she took one from anybody else, they'd get pissed then buy some more. Maybe that's what Mama saw in him, the great hunk of morality. She gagged. Mama deserved better, even if she wouldn't admit it. Connie leaned too far back in her chair. The room jumped like a startled horse and the puke rose dangerously close to the top of her throat. She gripped her knees. A cool wave rose from her spine and washed up over her forehead.

When she raised her head, Sheriff Dodd towered over her. He had snuck into the room. She eyed him, a sneer raising her left nostril, as if he smelled of some disgusting odor.

"Did you take a shower?" he said.

"Did you?" she said, and smirked when his set features slipped, for a moment, out of their detached-inquirer mode. He marched around his gray desk and sat in the ass-hugging chair. From a drawer he took a crime report, a pretty stack of pastel paper, and a black pen. He wrote some things down, then smiled at Connie. "Would you like something to drink?"

His voice was pleasant, as if they were sitting around Mama's table for Sunday supper. But she felt uneasy, aware of his size. "What kind of drink?"

"Water."

"Oh, yeah, I forgot. This is the jail."

"I would offer you coffee but Heloise, that's my secretary, goes shopping on Saturday for office supplies and she won't be in with them until tomorrow." He nodded toward a coffeemaker and Styrofoam cups resting on a file cabinet.

Connie willed herself to smile. "I hate coffee."

Sheriff Dodd patted the report's edges, pretending to straighten them. Connie looked at his thick fingers with their clipped nails. Poor Mama, they must feel like tapeworms inching up her leg.

"I want a cigarette."

"Young girls shouldn't smoke. It's a dirty, nasty habit."

"You're not my father."

His eyes slowly perused her outstretched legs, then moved up to the straps of her sundress slipping off her shoulders. "That's right. I'm not your father."

She met his marble-blue gaze and drew it above her shoulders, where she knew it would stay. Then, "Fucker!" burst from her mouth. She wobbled and covered her lips and closed her eyes.

"Being an instant dad would be hard," he said, his voice a little softer. "I'm sorry. I'm just used to looking at a pretty girl."

She held herself as still as a column of stone and felt at the top of her head a small irritation, a flutter inside her skull. She clenched her hands and eyes tight. She would not cry.

"Tell me what happened last night, accurately and in detail."

He probably gets his jollies this way, Connie thought. She looked at his hulking shoulders and shuddered.

"I know this will be hard for you and I know it must be a tremendous disappointment for your prom to turn out so badly."

She'd tried to keep her mind off the disappointment of last night. "Are you going to arrest me? If you are, you need to tell me first before I say anything to you." What a sneak. She'd tell Mama about this cute little trick. She crossed her arms.

He quit tapping the pen. "Arrest you for what?"

"Well, I am certainly not dumb enough to do your job for you."

"Look, there are enough laws on the book to get anybody any time. You're underage and you're nursing a hangover. *Right!*"

She smoothed the yellow dress over her knees, forcing her fingers not to shake. "There's no law against being hung over or throwing up in the sheriff's office on a day when the secretary is out."

He sighed and looked at his watch. "Okay. Okay. You and Kyle Childers were parked at Pealiquor Ridge. What happened?"

Connie was dead tired. He wouldn't arrest her if she told the truth because Mama would drop him in a minute. And, she reasoned, he must know that. "Listen, I'll quit smoking tomorrow if you just give me a cigarette. I really feel like I'm going to puke."

He walked to the coffeemaker and opened the lid to the water compartment. It hid a pack of Salems. He popped one out and offered it to her. She lit it. He opened the window and said, "Move your chair over here and direct the smoke outside, will you?"

Connie took several drags before she risked getting up. Dodd pulled her chair abreast of his desk. She smothered a snort. He didn't want his secretary to know when he'd had a smoke.

"Well, Kyle was drunk as a skunk. I mean *drunk*." She rolled the tip of the cigarette in the metal coaster he'd taken from under his chair leg and inhaled before speaking. She felt smoother inside and took another drag. "I was in a pretty desperate situation. You know how *big* Kyle is."

Dodd had quit writing and was watching her closely. Yet Connie felt her confidence return. "Well, you know how boys are." She waited until he nodded. "Well, I was able to get out of the car still — ummmmm, still —"

"Undamaged — unhurt," Dodd said.

"My dress was wrecked. It's at home. It's filthy with alcohol" — she curled her lips and held the cigarette away from them — "and blood."

"Whose blood?"

Connie inhaled and took her time exhaling a thin stream that was swept out the window. "Kyle's."

"Kyle's?"

"I smashed his face with the car door." She offered Dodd a simple smile.

"Did you hurt him in any other way?" Dodd shuffled through another pad of pastel papers.

"No. That's when I left."

"Alone?"

"I had no choice. I was scared, considering he tried to rape me." She felt a chill, remembering the dark woods.

"He tried to? What about the gang of black men?"

"I wouldn't call them a gang. There were a lot of them at the Gentlemen's Club but I didn't see but a couple of them."

"Something's not right here. Did the black men touch you?"

Connie stubbed the cigarette out. She pushed her chair back and tried to read Dodd's curious face. What was going on here?

"Honey, I know this is a real traumatic thing for you. I hear there's all kind of psychological damage done, but we want to punish them that have done wrong. Here, have another cigarette."

She took it and spent a great deal of time lighting it, slowly blowing out the flame, twirling the thing in her fingers before taking a drag. "Why am I here?"

"Are you okay? Would you like a physical? I think you should have a physical because you're all shook up. You're blocking things out. It's real common."

Connie stood up. "Look, Sheriff Dodd, if this is some excuse to play hugsy-feely with me, I am going to tell my mother. Physical, my ass." She walked quickly to the door. Her sudden rise had upset her stomach. She reached for the doorknob.

"Were you raped?" Sheriff Dodd called.

She swung around, her mouth gaping with denial, when a flood shot out across the sheriff's floor. Her stomach heaved and heaved until it was dry. Sheriff Dodd froze at his desk. Then, he began to swallow vigorously.

Connie stepped over the puddle and returned to the desk. "I would just love a glass of water right now. And if you have a little squirt bottle of mouthwash —"

He opened a desk drawer and produced a vial.

"Thank you." Connie sprayed her throat and swallowed the mint aftertaste. "Sheriff Dodd, I have told you the truth."

"There have been charges filed against a number of black men for attacking the two of you in Kyle's car, beating him up, and taking you hostage. The Childerses have been to see me already today."

"The Childerses'!" said Connie. "It's because he plays football, isn't it? Because he signed with the Tide."

Sheriff Dodd moved closer to the open window and breathed in a lungful of air.

"I tell you what. Kyle won't be able to identify any of those men. If he does, he's lying."

"Can you identify them?"

"Yes," she said, and then realized she'd answered too quickly. "The guy at the door —" she thought of his dark eyes but skipped over the urinators, because that would help make Kyle's story truer — "and Dr. Feets."

"Dr. Feets?" said Sheriff Dodd, unbelieving.

"The guy who bandaged my foot and drove me back to Pealiquor Ridge. Dr. Feets." As she said the name, she began to giggle. How brilliant. Dr. Feets was a code. The sheriff couldn't go to the Gentlemen's Club and ask for Dr. Feets. He'd get laughed out of there, men claiming to know Dr. Lung or Dr. 'Sophagus but not Dr. Feets. She laughed and felt the room sway.

"The law defines rape as against your will. It is obvious to me from this interview that nothing done last night was against your will."

"Everything that happened at Pealiquor Ridge was against my will. Kyle Childers almost raped me. Write that down." She stood up and reached across the table and grabbed his pen. She scribbled words onto the crime report. "This is what happened. Nobody beat Kyle up. Go smash your face with the front door and see what it looks like. I tell you what pisses me off. I was robbed of a chance to go to the prom. Put that down. Kyle robbed me of that. I want him arrested."

"Get ahold of yourself!" he barked, and grabbed at her, wrenching her fingers as he snatched his pen back.

She cupped her hand and said quietly to his flushed face, "You hurt me."

He gathered the papers to his side of the desk away from her and clicked the pen several times. "We are still investigating this incident. You had better watch yourself. Drinking underage is a crime."

"There are worse." She limped away, circled the puke, and walked out the door, leaving Sheriff Dodd shaking. Damn, she thought. Mama materialized in the gray light of the hallway. She looked drawn as a dried apple but her arms were strong around Connie.

"It's okay, Mama. Nothing happened last night. I wasn't raped by any black men. Kyle made that whole story up so he wouldn't look like an ass. I admit I'm hung over, but all I need is sleep. And" — she squared her shoulders — "I think Sheriff Dodd is a fucking pig."

Mama slapped her face hard and then spun around abruptly. Mama's sniffles came like a weak cry in the tunnel leading to the far-off door of sunlight.

Connie was too shocked to yell. She counted out loud until Mama's footsteps quit.

Jessamine emerged from the shadows in the hallway. "Come on. Mama didn't mean it. It was probably the word *fucking.*"

"Why did she slap me?"

"God, Connie, she thought you were raped. I mean, your clothes were torn and bloody. She was probably relieved you weren't."

"I don't believe that. It has to do with Sheriff Dodd," Connie said. "He's a fucking prick. I thought he'd be on my side, after what I've done for him and Mama. But there he sat, not believing me. I love the Crimson Tide, but goddamn, it doesn't mean I have to service their players. And there was a minute in there when I thought he was checking me out, you know what I mean? If he's that kind of shit, Mama doesn't need him."

"I don't think he's the right man for Mama," said Jessamine.

"I wonder what happened on their last date," Connie rubbed her smarting cheek.

"Come on. Maybe you should apologize."

"Screw that. First I get dragged out of bed because someone says I've been raped. Then I have to put up with Dodd's eyeballs, and then Mama slaps me because I wasn't raped, and on top of that I am supposed to apologize?" Connie hobbled to the car. The pain in her foot reminded her that she needed fifty bucks to pay Dr. Feets and sixty bucks for the beauty salon. She couldn't get her hands on that kind of money, especially since she only made tips. That pissed her off even more. She got in the backseat, slammed the door hard, lit a cigarette she'd swiped from Dodd, and blew the smoke at the back of Mama's head.

Hattie Bohannon

Her first reaction to the fiasco had been anger at her daughter. Why couldn't Connie go to the prom and return without scandal? As the pieces of the story came out and she understood Connie's fear and courage, she felt ashamed of herself.

In the afternoon, Hattie climbed the steps and went into the girls' bedroom. Connie was asleep on the lower bunk, her face scrubbed and pale. Hattie bent to touch her forehead and kicked an ashtray hidden under the bed. She pulled back, gritting her teeth. It took several minutes of strong breathing to dissipate the anger she felt.

Why was it so hard to simply hug this girl? She leaned against the top bunk and willed her hand to brush Connie's brow. Warmth spread across her palm where they touched. Her anger softened.

Connie's eyes opened and she did not protest but lay under Hattie's hand. "Kyle called me truck-stop girl."

"That's not a bad thing," said Hattie.

"Yeah," Connie shrugged.

"I'm sorry," said Hattie.

A long sigh came from Connie. "Mama, are you going to kick their ass?"

"Yes," said Hattie. The church had started this holy war. The next move was hers.

Paul Dodd came over that evening doused in the same aftershave he'd worn in his RV. The scent formed a small cloud on her porch, where they sat silently in the amber light of the fading day. Hattie closed her eyes. She was an overloaded electrical outlet, with cords crossing and burning, and here came a hand with one more wire, the wire that would blow the whole system to bits. Her eyes flew open and she breathed in Aqua Velva man. In the corner eave swayed a magnificent spiderweb, three feet across. The fat spider rested, the dark center of calm silver lines. It too had worked hard today, adding a foot of web, securing a large horsefly that hung like a ripe grape.

"If Connie says nothing happened last night, there is no case," said Paul. "As a mother, you wouldn't want it otherwise." He left his rocker and moved behind her and nuzzled her ear.

It felt like a buzzing mosquito, something that would prick and draw blood and leave a demanding itch. Instead, she wanted a man who would police the world

338

so her daughter could go to the prom without being attacked by a teenage boy. She wanted him to protect the truth, not merely the law. But he was a man, she realized, with flaws and scratches and itches. It was more than she wanted right now — to be his salve. What she wanted from him was unfair. To make her world right, safe, honest. To hold and protect her, to lift her when she was tired, to laugh at her jokes, to share her children's woes, to offer solace and intelligence, guidance and help. Good Lord, she thought. What a price to pay for good sex.

"I can't see you anymore," she said, with clarity.

His hands fell to her shoulders, then commenced to squeeze them. He worked at the knots there, and she felt relief.

"Paul, don't."

He heaved a sigh. "I must," he said. "Can I keep working your shoulders? I need to believe this."

"Please, don't," she said, her voice thin as a spider silk.

He quit kneading but rested his heavy hands on her shoulders. "I did what you asked. I brought you your husband's ashes. Did you love him so much you'll always be his?"

She was staring out at the truck stop and thinking of Oakley's tobacco barn, tall and gray. Its planks and beams were stored under a tarp behind the garage. She'd burn them soon, in a memorial service for him. That would be fitting. Maybe after that she'd be ready for Paul Dodd. "I am so emptied out. I can't love anyone right now," she said.

He moved away and leaned on the porch rail, the white web above his head like a halo. "I intended to marry this year."

She heard in that a further plea and turned this over in her head, but her heart did not jump-start. It beat on normally. "It's only May," she said.

"So it is," he said, and clomped down the steps. He bent and measured the grass, which was past the third knuckle on his middle finger, ready to be cut.

She almost expected him to wrestle the mower from the bed of his truck and power it up. The mower had a light in the front like the old super-deluxe-model vacuum cleaner Oakley had inherited from his mother. Oakley's mother had traded two of her husband's hunting dogs for it when a traveling salesman happened by, after the Tennessee Valley Authority brought light to Alabama. But Paul Dodd climbed into his truck. Fireflies dizzy with the dark flashed and dove above her overgrown yard. His headlights blasted them into obliteration.

Gert Geurin

After the protest march, Miz Bohannon seen the error of her ways and broke it off with the sheriff. What a dog he turned out to be. He quit bringing his squad up for weekly breakfasts at the truck stop, and that hussy Ash Lee came back to work her wantonness in our parking lot.

On the last Sunday before revival week, it was so humid everybody just wanted to ooze until fall, Reverend Peterson got hetted up in the pulpit about working for the Lord and wanting those of us in disreputable reputations to cease and desist. I studied on this but took my cue from the Lord God Himself. I had been given a mission and I was going to follow it through. My doctor said my blood has dropped down near normal, thanks to me getting off cigarettes.

By the time I reached Reverend Peterson at the back of the sanctuary, I was bright with plans. The poor man had snakes in his own house but he did not know it. "I ain't going to quit my job," I said.

He looked puzzled, like he couldn't place where I work, and then said, "Of course not. Labor is a gift to God."

I gave him a big powdery hug that left him gasping and sneezing. Lord, I felt powerful.

It was time to take action, what with the protest and Jessamine's soiled reputation and that wild animal that attacked our dear Connie and ruined her beautiful dress. Miz Bohannon was too sunk in herself to defend her family. She said to me, "Gert, I watch those men playing video games in the back room of the truck stop and I just don't get it. If they want real bloodshed in life, they ought to try being a single working mom." This worried me as to her state of mind.

Now I was not right in my heart about Reverend Peterson anymore — he pushed things too far at the truck stop. There was evil in his flock and I intended to root it out. So that's when I went searching for my Polaroid. I haven't taken many pictures in my life. You have to be able to see more than what you do. I might see a pretty blue jay pecking at the yellow grasses so I shoot it but what comes back is a picture of weeds with a speck of blue. I do not know why I have this calamity with wildlife but it happens all the time. So I gave up bothering.

I cotched that hussy in her lair. She camped out in the woods near the truck stop, under an upheaveal of rock that made a cave, and inside there was soft moss and dirt and leaves and a chair and an air mattress, and some pillows and blankets. It was the sheets hung out to dry on a pine that caught my eye in the first place. She was asleep. I shook her awake roughly.

She had no place to go. The rock wall was behind her.

"I know you," she said. "You're the maid at Dollarskin."

"I am not," I said, "but I recognize your face. Your chest has been subjected to Miracle-Gro since our paths last crossed."

She shifted. A blue bracelet sparkled on her right hand as she moved to a sitting-up position.

"You are going down the wrong path."

"Oh, fuck off," she said tiredly.

"I'll offer you a better life."

"Don't talk church to me or I'll blow your head off," Ash Lee said, and showed me her little revolver.

I could tell she had not the energy to use

it. "Look here," I said. "I want you to tell me if you've had commerce with any of these men." I opened the church yearbook. Every year we each get a turn to set for the photographer from Atlanta to document our membership in its best light. He makes a yearbook of the Church of the Holy Resurrection. We are fine-scrubbed and beautiful, if I say so myself. It hurt me to foul this book with these doings, but I could not stop now. I flipped past the picture of the church cross at night. I showed Ash Lee first the intact families in alphabetical order, the men in suits, the women all in flowerdy dresses with bows and poufed-up hair, the children grinning like jack-o'-lanterns, powdered and dusted like they belonged on a wedding cake. I am in there, lumped with the older unattached folk, Gee and Haw on either side of me like bookends. I wore my lilac dress and gloves. It was a good likeness but for the knobs beside me. I suddenly thought I didn't want to know if Gee and Haw were active in Ash Lee's way. We passed over the Toller Odoms, the Baker Thomases, the Reynoldses. I was watching to see if any pictures caused her to light up or get gloomy, but nothing showed on that foxy face. She touched the women's dresses as if she could feel the raised roses or the starched bows.

She held the picture of the Childerses close to her eyes. "That's the guy with the bruises. Football player. He's got a new convertible, but he is so strange," said Ash Lee.

"Upon my soul, I do not need to hear these confessions," I announced. "Do you know him, yes or no?"

"He treats me like I'm his date," said Ash Lee. "He never does anything. We go to the drive-in and watch the movie and drink Coke and I eat caramel corn and Jujubes and then he brings me back here and I kiss him on the hairy cheek. He gave me this bracelet." She shook her hand and the blue beads shone. "He is really strange. I wonder if he just takes me around to hide something else. Like he's a fag, maybe."

I had no advice for her on this account.

She snapped the book closed. "What are you, the God Squad?"

I laid it out straight to her then. Yes, I was the God Squad and here is what she must do. If one of these churchmen came to her in a compromising position, she was to whip out the Polaroid and take his picture.

"Like, do you want to watch? I can get

345

you moving pictures if you're into it."

Dear Lord, I am in the wilderness here. Please keep me from busting out in anger and murder at her words. I am a Christian woman, not to be subjected to this kind of whoremongering. My face was warming up like an electric burner.

"I'll feed you," I said.

"Food?" Her eyes grew luminous.

"Three square and dessert too." The child was hungry. She'd been putting the wrong thing in her mouth; there was no sustenance in it. She just wanted to be fed. "Where do you live in the wintertime?"

Ash Lee shrugged. "Wintertime I travel. I like this place, though. I'll be back. I'm saving money for a Jim Walter home. It'll have a kitchen and two bedrooms and a living room that's separate and a hall. I've been collecting ducks." She pocketed her revolver and rooted around in the cave and brought out some white fabric with blue gingham checks and waddling ducks on it. "Could you put these in your house? I'm afraid the rain'll ruin them. It's my curtains."

I did not want anything of hers in my house, but in that moment she looked very young and true and dim, like Jessamine often does, and my heart softened, and I took the curtains. I wondered if this made me an aider and abettor, or if it made me more like Jesus who talked to the harlot, or if I was like Martha the housekeeper, and then, if I was, shouldn't I be the better one, the harlot? This was getting too complicated, and here I was in the woods with a hussy with a gun.

I handed her the camera. "Just push the button."

Ash Lee peered through the lens at me.

"Don't!" I said, too late and then was blinded.

She looked at the developing film. "These men, it's not what you think. They talk and all I want to do is get them off. I'd like to tape their mouths shut. It ain't sex they want but to feel loved and I ain't got that. But they pay and that's all I care about. My mother told me the most important thing was getting a man. Hell I get five–ten men a night if I want."

She handed me the photograph and it was a big blur of light, that's all, that's me. I was on the right path.

Reverend Martin Peterson

"Why do I deserve this?" he said, as a big old Oldsmobile nosed like a shark into the church parking lot. He had no idea who it was, perhaps some very old lady who just remembered she'd been a Christian once and wanted a checkup. He rolled his eyes. These women always wanted to reveal their deep, mostly imagined sins. They'd read something in the Bible, usually from the letters of Paul, that made them think they'd boil in hell forever. Sometimes they wanted an immediate baptism, citing a collapsible lung, a herniated heart, or a liver psychosis as their expected death du jour.

The big ones were the most difficult. He'd wade into the baptismal font with them and wait in the waist-deep water and they'd go under and lash about, all that pink flesh visible under the white filmy baptismal robes, while he held on to what he hoped was an arm. They came up, water pouring off their faces, like great falls over serrated rock; then the two eyes would flash open and he'd startle and look away, expecting that his revulsion was clear. These women were not mountains, Stelle had told him, when he complained, but humans with souls. She was disappointed in him for this, but she was not the one in the font with these big bags of flesh.

Martin decided he'd pretend to be busy. He took out a handkerchief and began polishing one of the lightbulbs on the cross. The car door slammed and he heard a woman's voice.

"Look, here, little man," she said. "One of your church boys tried to rape my daughter because of your lies, issued from the pulpit as if from God Himself. And it's just you, you little man, thinking big —"

Martin turned and was shocked to see Hattie Bohannon in her blue work uniform, her face distorted and deeply colored. Usually she was pleasant when serving biscuits or taking his cash. But that was a long time ago, it seemed to him. *Little man!* he heard her say again.

"Prostitution will not be tolerated in Maridoches!" he shouted at her. Suddenly he felt small, standing on flat ground. He could not lean against the wall of the church because of the lightbulbs.

"There is no prostitution at my truck stop," she said, coming closer. She carried a leather purse, and she was sweating. Curls clung to her face while the rest of her hair rose about her head in wild waves.

Her eyes were incredibly blue and he noticed her breasts and the pink lipstick on her mouth. "Harlot!" he shouted.

She picked up a rock and threw it at him. He watched as it hit above his head and he felt a strange urge to unzip his fly, much like soldiers were wont to do in face of fire. He stooped and found a smooth stone and hurled it in her direction. It flew toward the silver expanse of the car's windshield and he waited in horror and happiness for the crash.

Mrs. Bohannon swung her purse by its long strap and knocked his rock out of orbit, sparing the face of the Jetstar. Martin stood agape at this feat of coordination. The Devil invested his workers with strange powers.

Hattie Bohannon became a hurling machine, scooping up rocks and throwing them with accuracy, shattering the lightbulbs on the cross. "I'll call the police!" he shouted as he ducked, and was horrified at his physical reaction. He was so taken with her body in motion, he thought, I'd like to ride her to Galilee. The bulb directly above him broke and splinters of glass rained down.

He dared not move. Above him glass explosions, poofs of surprise, then bits falling like confetti around him.

He watched as her color changed, lightened, and her face smoothed out from the exercise. She seemed to grow taller. The purse hung like a tiny sack. Whatever she'd come to do was done.

She climbed into the car. The headlights came on when she started the ignition. The Jetstar reversed as if sucked away from the church by a great force. Martin smelled something burnt in the air. The car disappeared in clouds of red dust that lingered like tumbleweeds along the road. He still heard lightbulbs plinking — but it wasn't glass falling, it was rain. Holy rain. Prayed-for rain. He opened his arms. He was so parched, he opened his mouth and felt fat water dot his tongue. The stiff grasses opened up and drank, and the landscape reveled in the winds, long grasses twisting, twirling, swirling in the cool caress of rain. Release begun with a shower of glass turned to rain.

I have been praying for the wrong miracle, he thought, on the verge of an understanding — something in the torrent of water, light and then heavy, brisk and cold, soft and wet, the spectrum of sensation, grace. And then a horrible thought: she had caused the rain. The devil woman with

351

her attack on his lights, she had brought down the rain.

Hattie Bohannon

Rain beat on the windshield in sheets so white she could not see, and Horseshoe Bend was coming up soon. The mountain hugged the road on her right, leaving no room to pull the big wide butt of the car out of the lane. Ahead lay the threat of wet curves and a slippery slope leading toward the river, which surely churned with this welcome rain. Hattie used the granite cut as her guide.

The rain slowed her, made her drive safely while her wild blood demanded speed. It had taken all her self-control to aim above Reverend Peterson's head. How dare he spew lies that put her daughters in danger! Now she regretted missing him. Now she regretted not taking knives.

The wipers clacked back and forth like a train on the track. Moisture filmed the windshield. She pressed the button to open the side windows. The rain, heavenly rain, came in and slicked her arms and bounced in her lap. She wiped the windshield. She could see. She fell in love with the low gray

352

sky and the wet scent of the pine boughs, the rising odor of blacktop, the temporary coolness, and now, in the tapering rain, a fine mist, ghosts rising off the road. The air grew heavy as the sun broke full and glittering as if it had not rained. It was hot again, so very humid that her dress hung on her like a damp extra skin.

But it is only the heaviness of home, she thought, as the truck stop and house came into view. As soon as I get close, I feel the weight. I come up the drive and the yoke settles on my neck, two buckets of milk balanced precariously with each step. Why do I live this way, when what I want is to throw rocks and shout and run and drive fast? Pummel the lying man as a man can do? Dance in the rain? Sing? Love lightly and fully?

And then there is this: against the dripping-wet roses, on a path of pale petals strewn along the grass, a small blond girl in a bright blue dress, yellow plastic sandals, holding a basket of red tomatoes, waving, calling, "Mama, Mama."

Jessamine Bohannon

Each morning during the drought I watched Heather unroll the hose and water Mama's tomato plants in the garden. She would wear only dresses, this child of mine. The thick air was yellow and the beans and shriveled cornstalks curled and yellow too. But the tomatoes stood sturdy, flush and green, the spiky leaves dotted with small yellow flowers like butterflies alighting. Firm green fruit hung among red globes while Heather carefully placed the hose at the roots. She conserved water in her own way. She let each plant drink until a saucer-sized collar of mud surrounded its green stem. While the water trickled, she plucked off slugs, bare-handed, and dropped them in a can of salt.

That toughness must come from her father. I felt a pang of sadness, not for him, whoever he was, that boy in the river, but for my lonely existence. Mama and I had lied about Heather's parentage and I lost my daughter. I told the truth about my love for Richard and I was labeled a prostitute. Nothing was fair or right. In both instances, Mama blamed me and carried with her a deadly weapon, painful words that could cut me down quicker than any handgun. They did not kill me, the words, but they kept the wound of me raw and alive.

I dreamed of a new life.

I'd have a new boyfriend and Heather and my own house, maybe, and Mama would treat me good. I could go out on a date in public. I watched couples when they came to the truck stop. Some were old and tired and even fat, but there was something in the way one would order for the other or reach across the table and wipe a chin. To be half of a couple like that was my dream.

But it didn't seem that a man would date a suspected prostitute. I was ruined as far as Maridoches was concerned. When I thought of my prospects, that's when I got very angry at Richard. I had called him once and said, "I am not a prostitute," and he'd said, very softly, "I know, baby, but you're not married. You don't understand," which had stung so hard my whole body felt numb as the venom from the sting worked its way head to toe. I never called him after that.

So June was drought again, hard on the rainless weeks of May. It was unpleasant and parched outside, and I didn't care if it ever rained again. Let the calves die and the cattlemen go bankrupt. Let the vegetables dry up and the whole world starve. Let the church be hit by a tornado. Let the truck stop fail. Let the lumberyard combust. Let an earthquake spew Alabama into the sea.

These were my litanies. This is what I thought at work while Gert was talking miracles and revival and assuring me I was a good strong young woman, a follower on the right path. Little did she know I had cooked up many murders in my mind, starring hers truly as she talked. She liked me now because I let her do what she wanted to in the kitchen. She wanted to dump Worcestershire sauce in the hamburger meat, let her. She wanted to lard up the vegetables with butter after they'd been cooked with a hock or rind, let her. I am not the one to prevent heart attack or burn. I am not even I.

One day in the midst of her garbled singing, "We must be born again," she mentioned that Stelle Peterson was a regular songbird at her church. I imagined the magnificent woman in a small gilded cage, a bird with sleek exotic feathers, singing music so beautiful it broke your heart. Of course, Gert's song, "We must be born again," got caught on the record player in my head and I was humming it all afternoon. Every time I sang it, I pictured Stelle at the protest, cool and elegant, and everybody listening to her. She had them all in the palm of her hand.

In the morning, I passed Heather crouched in the garden singing to the slugs and told her to tell Gert she was in charge until I got to work. Settling into the VW, I felt as furtive as if I were going off to see Richard in our hotel in Georgia. My stomach rose in the same way, and I turned Z-95 up so loud the steering wheel was vibrating. Just like old times. I drove up Raider's Hill, going slower and slower toward the Church of the Holy Resurrection, until it seemed I was not aiming for it but being dragged there by a dying engine.

The sunlight was glancing off the white church walls and glinting off the cross. My eyesight was pretty patchy as I walked to the door marked CHURCH OFFICE and pushed it open. Blinking in the dimmer light, I must have looked addled to the person behind the desk. She was not the first thing I registered. Behind her, a long cloth hung from a pole near the ceiling. The cloth began pale at the top, then flowed down through blue tones to a dark hem, nearly black. The fabric was like a waterfall, undulating, silk.

When my eyes found the woman, Stelle, dressed in purple, her glossy hair caught at the base of her neck with a white clip, I said, "I'm Jessamine Bohannon."

To my relief and dread, she said, "Come in."

She smiled in a way that meant she'd hear me out, and yet I sensed she was glad to see me. "I need to change my life," I blurted out.

"In what way?" she asked.

"I did something bad and I don't want to be always marked by it," I said. I thought of Heather in the garden keeping the tomatoes alive and wanted to rush home and hug her. But I knew I was not ready to tell Stelle the truth about Heather.

"What is your purpose?" Stelle asked gently.

My purpose. My need. What I sought. I'd never been talked to like this before. It was embarrassing and hard. I became aware of an undercurrent of sound, a very low modulation of chords, what a slow-moving river would sound like if it were notes. "I need a new life," I said. "So far I've messed things up following my own way. Gert says that God can help."

"God is forgiving," said Stelle. She pressed a button with a click, and the noise of a tape rewinding came up from her desk.

"He is?" I said. I'd never been forgiven anything. In my chest, a dark hard knot, weighty and familiar, contracted. For a second or two, the knot dissolved. "Your revival is for forgiveness and new life?"

She did not answer right away and I felt mistaken. The knot returned and I lashed out. "It's bullshit, you know. This church stuff, all those hateful ladies making up lies. Is Richard Reynolds forgiven for lying about me?"

Stelle placed her hands together as if in prayer. She held them to her lips in an attitude of thought, but really she was hiding a smile. "I don't know who God forgives or why. I just know He does."

A little smile grew on my face too. Maybe Richard was not forgiven. Maybe he was going to Hell.

"Forgiveness and rebirth are the way of the Lord. I believe He has led you to our door."

Sunshine swelled through her stained-glass window, muted reds, blues, and golds, draping us in soft color. The river tape clicked on again and gentleness slipped into my ears. "Can I come tonight to the revival?" I asked.

"Yes," she said. "I will give you a ride."

Reverend Martin Peterson

Thirty minutes from now Stelle would arrive home. Martin bathed his face in water he had delivered in blue four-gallon bottles. Stelle drank it. She didn't know he washed in it.

He toweled his face and then went for the concealer, yellow to cover the purple shadings under his eyes. "Purple mountains' majesty," he sang, as he dabbed on concealer. He took a mascara wand, dark black, and touched up the gray hair around his ears. It wasn't much, a strand or two, but he couldn't stand to pluck them out. Last he found Stelle's eyeliner pencil and drew in brown lines to make his brows fuller. The revival required more from him than usual, more vigor and stamina, more sermons, one for every night of the week.

Last night after the service, Stelle had come down hard on him. He'd been feeling tiptop and exhausted in the rightness of his message, Eve's great transgression in the Garden.

Stelle had not hummed them home as she usually did. Instead she spoke to him unmusically, as if rocks had taken up residence under tongue. "Adam ate the apple too. You cannot blame it all on her."

Martin sighed. "If she hadn't eaten it and tempted him, he would not have done it."

"Oh, Martin. This man who was made in God's image doesn't have to take responsibility for his own action? If he hadn't eaten the apple, he wouldn't have been cast out. Adam had plenty of ribs. God could have made another woman more submissive than Eve, while Eve could have been cast out as Cain was."

Martin was too spent to argue this basic Bible lesson. He did not understand why all of a sudden he and Stelle had to read the Good Book as if for the first time. These conversations were tiresome and counterproductive. The precedent of the biblical temptress was the central theme of the revival's sermons. It related well to the truck-stop situation, which, since God had not sent the rain he fervently asked for every Sunday from the pulpit, was a good way to keep the faith going among the congregation. It rankled that Hattie Bohannon had made it rain, and briefly at that, like a taunt from God.

Ten minutes until Stelle arrived, enough time to put on his clothes.

He was fairly uninspired in his garments. For work, in the pulpit, he wore a robe. Underneath it, black pants, a white dress shirt, a navy blue tie. His shoes were black. His socks were black. Black made him disappear.

On Stelle, black was glorious.

What to do with Stelle? Her study of Eve had changed her. She was determined to stamp out prostitution. This was the only link in their marriage now. Her passion was not for marital sex, it was for stamping out extramarital sex. Maybe it was truly driven by a desire to stamp out all sex.

After their last lovemaking, a celebration of the successes of the protest march, she'd said, "I'd like to see a snake handler."

"What in God's name for?" he'd asked, his hand curved on the firm rise of her hipbone.

"I'd like to go to Kentucky and see a snake handler. The snake was a friend to Eve."

"No, it wasn't."

"Without the snake, we wouldn't have knowledge. Without it, Eve would never

362

have gone outside her home."

"The Garden of Eden, the paradise to which we have never returned?" He dropped his head gratefully to the dip in her waist.

"Whose paradise, Martin? God's? Adam's?" She sat up, his head tumbling into the covers. "How did Eve feel, being an afterthought?"

"Snake handling is illegal."

"Of course it is."

Thus ended their evening of triumph after the truck-stop protest.

Stelle had not seen a snake handler but she had gone to the rattlesnake rodeo in Opp and bought a nonpoisonous snake. She kept it in the living room in a large glass terrarium, on a bed of sandy-colored pebbles. She fed it grasshoppers and toads. She became a regular at bait shops and vending machines.

"I do not think," Martin had said, "that a minister should have a pet snake in his house."

"Why not? Anyone else can have one. Why not you?"

"The symbolism of it."

"You mean, like a snake equals a penis?"

"No! Like the snake in the Garden of Eden."

But Stelle did not remove the cage. This afternoon, however, Martin had taken action. He'd pushed the terrarium over to the front door and gently lifted the lid. The snake slithered up the side and flicked its tongue, taking in the new smells. It fixed its eyes on Martin's. They stared at each other for several minutes.

"Tell you what," said Martin. "I saw a nice fat mouse running up the walk earlier today. Had your name on it."

The snake swiveled its head, its tongue flicking at the open doorway. It craned its neck, slid up and over the glass wall, and disappeared down the brick walk.

Martin moved the terrarium back in place and left the lid open a crack. He doubted St. Patrick felt like this, stealthy, guilty of a gesture of secret pleasure. He sat down next to the empty cage to pray.

When nothing but mirth filled his head, he'd begun dressing. Now for some reason, his tie would not sit right on his neck and he thought of not wearing it. The air was pregnant with moisture it would not release. Headaches were common afflictions these days. What they needed was a river baptism. He swallowed and imagined the low brown water rising to his waist. As long as his feet were planted into thick river mud, he could overcome his fear of a sudden wave.

The front door slammed.

"Look what I've brought," Stelle called.

Martin ripped the tie off and threw it over his shoulder. It landed on the TV antenna. "Swiss cheese?" he said hopefully.

"No, silly, look."

Martin came down the stairs as Stelle held out a perfectly ordinary pinecone.

He said nothing.

She waited, then dropped it in the soil of their lemon tree.

"I don't mean to disregard it. You don't have to throw it away," he said.

"I'm not. I've learned that pinecones keep cats from playing in the plants," said Stelle. "I need to change."

"I'll wait," he said. Forever, until you change into the Stelle I know.

She came down plainly dressed, gray cotton slacks and a fine-ribbed coral T-shirt. "The Bohannon girl has been to see me. She wants to come to church."

"Richard Reynolds's prostitute? That one?" Martin asked.

"I think she's sincere. She talked of wanting a new life, to be born again."

"Did her mother send her? She can't come," said Martin. He shuddered, thinking of Mrs. Bohannon armed with rocks, entering his church in an attempted rescue of her daughter. He thought also of the men's Sunday school class and their dependence on him to keep the truck stop under the gun, and of the good feeling he had now when he entered their room, the slaps on the back, the discreet increase in offerings, the deal he'd gotten on the new Buick, which meant little except that he'd found acceptance.

"She can't come, Stelle, it is not —" He hated to admit how much he missed the truck stop. He had loved their liver and onions, the apple pie, the fresh-cut hash browns, overhearing truckers talk, the welcome feel of seeing familiar faces, of Gee and Haw always ready to chat.

Lord knows the Bohannons never gave him special treatment. He snorted. Beneath the good-mother smile of Hattie Bohannon was the heart and mind of an amazon harlot. Her daughters prostituting for Richard Reynolds right there on the premises. And Gert Geurin, a regular maypole at the revival, telling him she'd stay on and steer the ship of vice back to clean waters.

"But Martin, there is room in the church for forgiveness," said Stelle.

"What's to say this isn't a ploy? Prostitutes have always tried to work both sides of the issue." Martin glanced at the empty snake cage and felt stronger.

"But if we bring the prostitute to the Lord, won't she go and sin no more?"

He wanted to tell her why that was too easy. Years ago they would have discussed a church problem with intelligence and generosity, but now there was a gulf between them.

"Isn't that what we are about at the Church of the Holy Resurrection?" She was so gentle and sensible, she could convince the men's Sunday school class that a Christian steak house was an un-Christian idea if it required routing out an earlier establishment.

"Oh, Stelle," he said. She is my angel of the Lord.

"Martin." Her face grew cold, as if sensing his warmth.

"You'd think prostitution was a man's issue," he responded.

She shut her jaw and her eyes became hard. Clearly he'd stepped into one of those gaping holes that lay hidden everywhere between them now. "You'd better not say that publicly," she said.

"Well, I'd just like you to consider what

Ann Reynolds might think if we allow that young harlot to come to church. Think of her pain."

"Ann Reynolds," said Stelle, "should have taken a red-hot poker to her husband. Maybe Miss Bohannon's presence will inspire her to new enlightenment."

Martin shivered, all thoughts of tonight's sermon gone. "I must get some air," he said, and walked out into the heat in his suit and made-up face. He stepped onto the deck, hoping for a glimpse of the snake, but it was not there. He went down the dry steps through the woods where the caterpillar tents had hung. The insects had eaten wild cherry leaves all over the state, fallen to the ground, and been consumed by brood cows and pregnant deer. All across Alabama young calves had drowned in their mother's wombs, cherry poison liquefying their hearts. Where was God in this world?

Martin ate a meager supper of fruit and salami while Stelle was showering. She said she'd drive herself to the revival and meet him there. He undressed and put on blue cotton dress pants and a white shirt and skipped the tie. It was his duty to call Richard Reynolds and warn him that the girl would be at church so he picked up the private line in his home office, feeling nervous as he had as a teenager, calling to make a date.

Richard answered the phone. Martin rushed past any common pleasantries and explained briefly his dilemma. "Stelle is insisting we let the girl come to the revival. She's claiming it is an opportunity for forgiveness, but I'm not sure if it's humanly possible to meet Stelle's standards."

Richard Reynolds sighed. "You got to keep the wife happy."

Martin felt a bond with Richard, a wee bit of camaraderie. He'd never discussed his marriage with anyone else before. With God, yes, but no one who answered him directly.

"Ann's feeling poorly in this heat. Her stomach's upset most days. We won't be coming to the revival. She'll be glad to know you asked about her."

Martin's relief was so great he barely kept the word *good* from escaping his lips. "Many blessings on you and Ann, Richard."

"Thank you, Reverend. It's good to hear your voice," said Richard.

Martin grinned as he put the receiver back in its cradle. He expected the girl to be scared off by the ladies. He expected her to be run out on a rail.

Jessamine Bohannon

The revival sounded like a dance party. The lights in the church blazed while the band, two drummers, three trumpet players, and an electric guitar wizard made everybody crazy to dance. Stelle and I stood shoulder to shoulder near the back. She swayed and erupted with a sharp "Jesus!" every time the drummer clapped his copper cymbals. I snapped my fingers, saving my breath for a faster number. Down front, Gert rocked on her knees.

I kept my eyes open for Ann Reynolds. Stelle had said in the car on the ride over, "Ann Reynolds is on the verge of forgiveness." She said Ann Reynolds was a proud woman, and admitting your husband had taken up with someone younger was not something to tell the world if you are a proud woman. The longer Stelle talked in her musical voice, which made words like *adultery* and *fornication* sound melodious and pretty, the better I felt.

Gert was the first one to the altar. Flinging her arms in the air, her prim hair tossed free, she twisted, a spinning flower. The bright shine in her eyes lit on something heavenly and not on us.

The last chord hung in the air when free-flowing syllables poured out of a woman's mouth. I did not understand a single sound. But I believed the emotion they came from was honest because I had the warmest feeling inside. The woman stopped in mid-cluck. Reverend Peterson appeared at the front of the church. He seemed as fragile as a child with a terminal illness. Not a soul sat down during his long ascent to the lectern. Reverend Peterson interpreted the woman's message in a speech as inspiring as the incomprehensible language of God.

The band started up again, really rollicking this time. I bopped and twisted and yelled "Jesus! Sweet Jesus!" with Stelle. Then, drawn by the driving beat, I danced down the aisle, swishing my hips back and forth and stamping my feet on the thick red carpet. I stopped in front of a layman who was shaking with the music himself. We shook and shuddered, the two of us. Stelle and her friends from the choir surrounded me and began to pray in loud voices. Gert held my hand. Then I sort of lost my mind. My tongue got thick and stuck in my mouth while I tried to say something, even though I didn't know what words they were. Someone pushed me into the pool beside the altar.

After the third time I was dunked, I realized I was being baptized while everyone else danced with joy. They blurred into a writhing mass of colors in my water-filled eyes. I heard hard, clear sounds coming from the preacher's mouth, as he told what God had said through me.

God had spoken through me! I had received the Holy Ghost. I was washed clean and I could see that Heather was an angel child, a gift from God, not an embarrassment or a lie. Around me was light. The faces were fuzzy, at the edges of my vision, but there was still song, quieter now, almost hushed.

In a daze, I walked with Stelle up the aisle to the door, two words running through my head: loving tongue. Outside, the congregation gathered in the parking lot, waiting for Reverend Peterson to switch on the lights of the cross. It wasn't night yet; the mild blue of evening darkened the edges of the sky. I sensed people watching me but it felt nice, not nasty. I was relieved Ann and Richard weren't there.

The lights came on and the cross looked like a crooked smile, one missing teeth. All over, lights were out. A gasp rose from the crowd.

"This is what the heathen have done," said Reverend Peterson. "They have tried to blot out our light. We must be vigilant and root out all forms of evil in our midst. We must reclaim the way."

Stelle slowly drew me to the back of the crowd. "He's going to ask for volunteers to sweep up the glass and replace the bulbs. He said he discovered the damage the day of the cloudburst."

I liked the warmth of Stelle's arm on my shoulder through my wet clothes. I was still a little delirious.

"I am so pleased for you," Stelle said, as we walked to the Cadillac. "I'll get Martin to give you a date to join the church."

I started. Join the church? This new life was happening so fast. I slid into the passenger seat as Stelle opened her own door.

"You'll want to bring your mother to that service, of course." Stelle started the car. "Do you recall what the Lord said to you?"

"All I can remember is loving tongue."

"That's what I thought you were saying. Once you get on the wavelength, it happens all the time. Soon your whole life is telling people what God says. I prefer singing." Stelle opened her purse and took out a purple scarf and tied it around her head. "I have to tell you something that's not for sharing with anyone."

"Okay." My voice had changed register and was pleasant and smooth.

"I tape myself at rehearsal so I can practice on the way home. I have a slow memory for notes and my tone is really not good. Nobody knows how much time I spend on my tone, and I am embarrassed to say anything to anyone about it, but I had to tell you because I have to practice all the way home on account of the Ladies Circle meeting tomorrow, and they often ask me to sing a song I don't know, and it must be perfect. I have to sing at least two hours a day away from rehearsal to keep my tone right." They were driving a bit erratically now, as Stelle appeared nervous about losing time.

"Oh, please," I said. "I would love to hear you sing."

Stelle wore the scarf to hide the earphones plugged into the Tape of Perfect Pitch. If her pitch wasn't already good, her staggered singing might have been irritating. I shut my eyes and listened while tickly bubbles rushed through my veins. My life was new. God had forgiven me.

Stelle rolled down the windows. She hit high A.

We barreled into the truck-stop parking lot, the car skidding to a stop, spraying both Sheriff Dodd and his patrol car with a wave of gravel. Stelle quickly unhooked her earphones and drew her scarf back over her ears. "Hello, Sheriff Dodd. We're having a revival. Would you like to come?"

He leaned down into the car. I tried to peer through his reflecting shades but all I could see was Stelle's lips distended and enlarged on them. I burst out laughing.

"Good heavens, Paul Dodd. Are you going to come or not? I'm making my list," said Stelle.

"A list of what?"

"Men who might like a ride to the revival."

I covered my mouth but it did no good. Laughter spilled out bright and brassy as a trumpet solo. Paul Dodd looked at me. I felt his gaze, coming through the lips even though I could not see his eyes, and deep down inside me, I remembered our slow-dance dance at Bigbees, and something dangerous turned over.

"Thanks, Mrs. Peterson. But I've got more vehicles than I know what to do with. Besides, if word gets out that I'm at the revival, all hell will break out over the rest of the county." He chuckled at his own joke.

"As long as you're on our side, sheriff."

"Yes, ma'am." He saluted and walked to his car.

Stelle drove slowly up to the house. "Pshew. Did you see the big dent one of those rocks made in his car door?" She nosed the car as close to the porch as she could before braking. "I'm so proud of you." Stelle leaned across the car and took my face between her soft hands. "So proud." She kissed me gently on the forehead.

I paused on the porch and looked out over the valley, which spread like one gold sheet from the foot of the purple mountains to the edge of the plateau. Gilded clouds billowed white, and rosy streams of light fell from them like curtains. What would I wear to church on Sunday?

Connie Bohannon

Connie was eating a hot fudge sundae in the porch swing. She saw Stelle kiss Jessamine, and thought, *Oh, my God!* What was wrong with her family? She was too shocked to say anything to Jessamine, who walked by looking dreamy. A jealous surge lifted inside Connie, but she fought it down.

She slurped the sweet white liquid in the bottom of her bowl. Maybe she should join the church and steal the collection plate. There had to be a lot of money in that business, considering how fine and large the Petersons' house was. It had a two-story glass wall looking over a lake. It must have cost a mint. Maybe she could be a church secretary. Naw, it would take too long, snitching a little here, a little there. Besides, she'd never learned to type. There had to be more to getting rich off Jesus than rolling on the floor and feeling the money rain down. If that's all there was to it, there'd be a church on every corner. Actually, on Main and Court in Maridoches, churches did hog three corners. She looked longingly in the direction of the drive-in theater where she and Darryl had spent so many nights of love. Spots of light filtered through the million trees separating her from it. Friday night in Maridoches. Here she was thinking of going to church. Pitiful.

Hattie Bohannon

She pushed the door open and walked gently into the bright room. Darla lay under a sheet on the top bunk, her dark hair a nest of sweat. Hattie had brought shampoo, a bucket of water, Darla's gold towel. The girl had refused to get out of bed for nearly two weeks, despite Connie's cajoling and Hattie's threats.

"Darla, I'm here to wash your hair," said Hattie. "Please sit up."

Darla did not move so Hattie rolled the sheet down and touched her daughter's shoulder. She took a brush and began to stroke the girl's hair. "I'm not my best self these days," she said. "Receiving your father's ashes, ending it with Paul, constant surveillance from the church, the drought, Connie being attacked. I'm going under. I went over to the Church of the Holy Resurrection and threw rocks at their lighted cross."

Darla tossed her head and sat up. "Did you break any?"

"Dozens."

"That's cool, Mama."

"Cool?" said Hattie. "I threw rocks at the minister too. Missed him, though."

"You missed on purpose. That's even

cooler," said Darla. "What's with the bucket?"

"I'm going to wash your hair." Hattie lifted the bucket to the top bunk then climbed up the end rail. Darla dipped her hair into the water as Hattie cupped up handfuls to wet her whole scalp. She thought how pretty Darla was, with her slim features, fine narrow nose, deep blue eyes, and ridges of cheekbone. "I went after him because Paul Dodd wouldn't support me against the lies. I am not a madam. I despise prostitution. I don't want it here and Paul Dodd told me it was gone. Don't choose a man that adds to your burdens."

"I don't know that I want a man," Darla said.

"That's an option," Hattie said. "I'm sorry I'm not a good nurse. It's why Oakley had to go to the VA. I couldn't nurse him and raise you girls."

Darla sat up and shook her head, spraying Hattie and the room with water. The bucket spilled, soaking the bed and splashing onto the floor.

"What's wrong with you?" Hattie said, and regretted it.

Darla covered her eyes, her knees pulled up to her face. "I don't want to go in the

Army!" she cried out.

"You don't have to," said Hattie.

"Yes, I do. I joined up the night before the protest. I'm supposed to be there the end of July."

Hattie mopped up the floor with the towel. The Army could not have another one of her family. "You can't go. I won't let you. I am sorry. I will send you to Canada or someplace. It is impossible." She put the towel in the bucket and carried them into the bathroom. She filled the bucket again and took a fresh towel and sheets back into the bedroom. "You'll have to change the sheets," she said.

To her surprise, Darla tossed the covers to the floor and stripped the bed. She tucked in the clean sheets and lay back down. "Will you still wash my hair?"

Again Hattie climbed up the end rail and placed the bucket on the bed. She laid the towel under Darla's wet head and lathered her hands with shampoo. It smelled of almonds, and this improved her mood. She worked the lather hard into Darla's rat's nest, massaged her head, then rinsed her fingers in the bucket.

"You've missed weeks of school," Hattie said. "I doubt you will graduate."

"Oh, who cares?" said Darla.

"The Army cares," said Hattie.

Slowly Darla raised up, her hair a white sculpture of foam. She looked girlish, an ad for shampoo and luscious hair. "If I don't graduate this year —"

Hattie broke in. "I will go in to school next fall and talk to Jake Hiler and see that you run on his cross-country team. After all, there is Title Nine."

"Oh, Mama," Darla said, "that is so great! That is the best." She jumped down from the bed and danced around the room. "Yay! Yay! Yay!"

"Rinse your own head — okay? — but come to my room. I have something I want you to do," Hattie said as she walked down the hall. The light in her bedroom was warm and soft. The urn looked out of place, something she'd never choose, Oakley either, she realized. He needed something green from the 1950s. She sighed and lifted the urn and recoiled when she heard it rattle. That always unnerved her. Ashes contained bone. It was time to plan the memorial service, time to end this marriage. High under her sternum, there were little flutterings, as she thought, *I am an unmarried woman.* How strange those words, how defining. Was it freedom or fear that made her nerves flutter? Like the *whoosh* down the roller coaster — you went because you had faith in the machine, but still that taste of imminent death coated your mouth. This is what it felt like. Unmarried woman.

Darla came in, her face clear and eager, her wet hair pressed to her head.

"I'd like to have a memorial service for Oakley and I'd like you to be in charge. I want you to build a bonfire out of the wood from his tobacco barn." In Hattie's eyes were tears and in her throat a lump was lodged.

"Yes, Mama," said Darla. "I can do that."

Jessamine Bohannon

Jessamine stood at the back of the church in the white baptismal robe. She hadn't invited her mother to see her join. She wanted this day to be her own triumph. Under her robe, she was sweating. Finally the music started. After the march down the aisle to "Let Us Walk Together," Jessamine paused to loosen her sandals. Barefoot, she followed the carpeted slope at the front of the church to the lip of the baptismal pool. The silvery-blue water shimmered, then stilled. It was more than water, it was the clear coating of God's love.

Reverend Peterson entered the pool from the side reserved for church members. She glimpsed his white veiny feet below his own white robe and had a moment of recoil. She took a deep breath, then eased down into the warm bath. The water had a thick viscosity. She thought, If love has a physical body, this is it. Reverend Peterson took her hand. He chanted the Covenant of Membership.

"Yes," she said. "Yes, praise Jesus." Tears rolled down her face. She took her eyes from Reverend Peterson's face, which was wreathed in light from the candelabras, and looked out at the smiling congregation, singing for her grace.

Holding her firmly around the waist, Reverend Peterson pushed her head underwater. The sudden violence of the baptism scared her. She churned against the water's resistance as she climbed the stairs. Stelle Peterson and Gert dried her with rough towels before wrapping her in a white robe. The people who left their pews to give blessings seemed of a single heart that opened to embrace her. She wiped her eyes to catch the picture of the happiest moment of her life.

Afterwards, a lightness radiated in her chest. Instead of going home where everything was practical and tense, she sped up a winding mountain road, passing black-eyed Susans and Queen Anne's lace swaying like hands. The car zipped higher. It rode perfectly on the grade through the pines. She flew, faster and faster to the top of the bald mountain where the sky was open.

As she rounded the last curve, a siren shrieked behind her. Red beams swept through her car. When she pushed on the brakes, she was surprised how far the VW slid. The sudden stillness gave her vertigo. She wondered how fast she'd been going.

In the side-view mirror she watched Sheriff Paul Dodd walk down the middle of the road. His approach seemed slowed by the amber haze. He walked hard on his heels. She watched as his head evaporated above the mirror, as his boots and knees disappeared, as his thighs advanced toward her car, as he stopped suddenly, giving her a postcard-picture of his crotch.

She stepped out of the VW, her white cotton dress dry and light in the dusty breeze. She shook her hair out of her eyes. She felt the thick red sand lap her toes as she raised her face to his. They kissed. Jessamine felt, in the eerie color of the sun, what was normal — green grass and blue skies — change to more comfortable tones: dusty rose and orange and golden-brown, the subtler shades of feelings, unexplainable, colors not found in children's drawings.

Paul Dodd grabbed her up against his chest, where his heart was beating at a frenzied pace. He buried his tongue between her lips. A simultaneous tremor passed between them. What she felt was almost as powerful as God had been this morning in the font, this shaky feeling that gilded everything she saw. Paul's rough hands squeezed her bottom. She drew back to breathe. He sought her mouth again, this time with less passion, with the curiosity of exploring a new place. She, too, relaxed as he lifted her skirt and ran his rough hands on her thighs. She began to explore inside his shirt and cupped his round biceps, his tough hard shoulder muscles. Then he slipped a finger inside the stretch band of her white underwear, inside her thigh. She drew back but then took his mouth in hers and let her hands run down his body and push open his leather belt.

Afterwards, she felt limp and giddy. All her senses had been filled and overfilled and she no longer had a mind and a reason for things. Everything in the universe had changed, and nothing was important anymore. They hadn't spoken a word. She watched Paul rearrange himself back into his pants and could tell her gaze embarrassed him.

He choked on the dust, or pretended to.

Jessamine noticed concrete things: his hand bruised above the third knuckle, the pulsing light on the patrol car, the dry field behind them, the warmth of the VW's door against her legs.

Paul Dodd looked over her head, not at her, even though she searched for his eyes. "Let's go on a picnic," he said. "I got sandwiches."

This sounded sensible. She nodded, then swung down into the road, raising dust that settled on her toes and ankles. She ducked into the VW and took out her purse and her church bulletin. For a minute she hesitated. Should she leave the car here on the shoulder of the road?

He was watching her, she could see in the side-view mirror, looking without shame at her bent over rear end clothed in white, at the small beads of sweat running down her hard calves, streaking their powder of red dust. Just for fun, she wiggled her butt, but his expression didn't change. She reached back and straightened her underwear, running a finger around the elastic leg band, pulling it straight and smooth. Still his face merely framed his eyes, a wooden mask with two peepholes of moving blue. There was nothing in the car of value. When she turned around, he was wearing reflector sunglasses.

Hattie Bohannon

Gert Geurin marched into the truck stop, flew past the employees only sign, and strode into Hattie's office. Hattie raised her head from a blissful sleep. Her eyes were ringed with purple, the corners of her mouth drawn tight.

Gert announced, "Miz Bohannon, Jessamine joined the church this morning, and you were not there to share in the most joyous occasion of her young life."

Hattie never figured she'd witness Jessamine's most joyous occasions. "She did what?" Surely she'd heard Gert incorrectly. "They just let her join?"

"Before you join, you get baptized when

the Holy Ghost speaks to you."

Hattie wanted to ask how you knew when the Holy Ghost spoke to you and especially how this miracle had happened to Jessamine, who seemed a very unlikely candidate for divine dialogue.

"I was blessed today to see Jessamine join. I seen the rapture on her face as she came streaming out of the font, the cleansing water pouring from her eyes. She looked so fragile in that little white gown. You could almost see angel wings on her back. Blondes make beautiful church members."

Hattie's head hurt more than ever. It dawned on her that she had missed her chance to get the business back on track. If Hattie had gone to the church, they would have taken her in with open arms if it was with the aim of supporting her daughter's choice to join.

"Jessamine never said a word to me about the church."

"Miz Bohannon, this is a miracle day. I am happy to know she has beat back the devil and will be the kind of daughter you deserve."

"Why, thank you, Gert," said Hattie.

Gert smiled and bowed her head, then raised it and marched out, humming a tune of celebration.

Hattie felt something new creep into her bones. A wisp of air had uncovered the long-dying embers of a fire and, for a second, blew the coals into a yellow flame.

Still at her desk, reworking numbers that showed the profit line was barely skirting red, Hattie nursed her seventh cup of decaf coffee of the day. It was already after 11 P.M., and she wanted desperately to sleep. The door opened and in stepped Jessamine, whispering over her shoulder. She was wearing a blue sleeveless dress that made her look younger than her years. Her hair hung down, uncombed. It reminded Hattie of dried weeds.

Biting her lower lip, Jessamine shuffled up to the desk. "Mama, I have something important to tell you."

"I know, I know. Gert told me."

Jessamine froze. Gert had spied on them? She imagined Gert following her for some reason, a new group to join or a job in the chorus, Gert driving like crazy on cruise control up those winding turns and coming up suddenly on Paul's car with the light flashing, and then getting out to see what was wrong, her high heels sinking up to her ankles in the red sandy road, which prevented her from yahooing before she got to the scene because she'd hate to fall in the red sand and soil her green chiffon dress and matching lime heels. And then, when she did make it to the patrol car, white gloved fingers scratching at Paul's car for balance while Jessamine's own fingernails were searing marks of passion into his back.

Jessamine gripped around for the extra chair. She sank into it, her face the same ashen-gray as the vinyl upholstery.

"You don't have to be ashamed, Jessamine. There've been church members in our family before. If you'd told me I would have gone with you to see you become a member." Hattie thought, *With my pockets full of stones.*

"What else did Gert say?"

"If I wasn't off duty I wouldn't waste my breath." Hattie swirled her coffee. "She said your face glowed. Tears streamed down your face. You were wearing a beautiful white dress. You looked young, fragile." What else? She didn't pay any attention to Gert's gilt descriptions. "Jessamine, are you ill?"

"Yes, Mama. I've had a long day, and if you don't mind, I think I'll just go home and go to bed." She blushed bright red.

There was a cough in the hallway, throaty, low, and familiar. Jessamine blushed again. She slid out the door and pulled Paul Dodd into the office. His face was expressionless.

Hattie glared at Jessamine. She had no interest in making up with Paul Dodd. Why couldn't he just leave her alone? Here he was using her daughter to get in to see her. "Jessamine, Darla and I have been planning your father's memorial service. I am too tired to discuss anything else tonight."

The long happy sound that issued into the room came from Paul Dodd, which surprised Hattie, as if he was the one under pressure. She watched his shoulders relax and his face soften into friendliness. Maybe Jessamine had set him up too.

"Have a good evening, ladies," he said, and tipped his hat as he left the room.

"Well, good night!" Jessamine called after him and frowned.

The Ladies of the Church of the Holy Resurrection

What bothered the ladies most about the Bohannon girl's presence during service

391

was where their husbands' eyes and minds would be. They knew their husbands well. The summer sermons, with all the focus on lust, kept the men stirred up. So the ladies went as a committee to Reverend Peterson and expressed their fervent desire: that he pray for rain, that he pick sermons about water, the parting of the Red Sea, Moses in the bulrushes, Noah and the Great Flood. It was what Maridoches needed, now that the harlot had been saved.

But if she came around too much, too many Sundays and Wednesdays, the ladies decided they would simply not speak to her. It was a tactic tried and true, the only way to keep themselves untainted and superior. Imagine God looking down into the church and seeing the tart in their midst. They trusted God would know whose souls were white and whose were scarlet. The church could forgive and they would as members of the church forgive, but, they could not, as individuals, consort with a girl with a reputation.

Jessamine Bohannon

She was so happy. She had passion and love was its reward. She thought of Paul and her heart beat quickly and a smile grew and grew across her face. There was no place for the ordinary — the stuff that brides plan forever — their china, their patterns, tablecloths. This was not about silverware, it was about feeling at home at last.

When she rode in his truck, her body relaxed, even though she knew she should not be seeing him. How could she deny this relationship? Everything was sky blue: his eyes, the Ruby River as they shot around Horseshoe Bend, clouds forever, the days long as Mardi Gras. They rode into DeSoto Park and walked hand in hand under the trees. There, up high, it was actually cool. He would take her wrist and nuzzle it, pull her close, and then they'd be lying on pine straw, his eyes looking, pleading — she knew she could say no but she never did. Always yes. This is what her life had become with Paul. The undersides of leaves were beautiful.

At night they went to the river, to a place where the ferry had operated a hundred years ago. There was a short rocky beach and often teenagers who needed to be chased away. At times she and Paul listened to the drone of all-terrain vehicles, illegal at night on the hills, but Paul was occupied, his tongue on her. The picnic table became their bed; her back was chafed near her backbone. She looked over her shoulder in the mirror at those two scraped spots with pleasure. Would they linger? How could she explain them? It was clear, very clear, that when he gave her a ring she would have to tell her mother.

They talked of it, she and Paul, how to tell Hattie, though she could not see him as the man who'd been courting her mother. He was hers, new, a different soul altogether. He raised herbs and made his own pizzas; she doubted her mother knew that. He liked to throw steaks on a grill and buy tomatoes and fresh corn at road-side stands. He knew how to clean up after himself: her favorite view, Paul with his fair-haired arms up to his elbows in bubbles at the kitchen sink. Was there ever a man such as this? A man who vacuumed his house every Saturday, who routinely hauled his bound bags of garbage to the dump? Everything Paul did was remarkable.

The night of the ring he took her to Birmingham to Copa Cahawba, the fanciest place she'd ever been. In his blue cotton work shirt, he seemed awkward at first, surrounded by men in suits, but he was the law and rose above discomfort. The glances of appreciation he got from the other men, because she was so young and blond, put him at ease. She relished this and held his arm as if she needed his support as they were led to their table. Jessamine had eaten nothing all day and fell upon her salad, despite its strange leaves, like a mountaineer on greens after a long winter. Purple and bitter the lettuces were but she ate them all and then, too, the nut-crusted trout, the curled carrots and apple slivers, a hill of sliced cabbage. For dessert, key lime pie, so rich and creamy it made her blush. Happiness looked like Paul Dodd, and he was looking at her. She wondered how they'd ever last the two-and-a-half-hour drive home without making love.

He saved the ring until it was past dark and they were on the highway alone, heading north to Maridoches. He pulled over at a scenic mountain view. Clouds had come in and covered the stars. He got out of the truck and flashed his badge at several vehicles occupied by men, which screeched out of there fast. When it was quiet he came around to her door and opened it and held out his hand, warm and strong.

She walked with him in the sweet summer air to the guardrail and looked out into the dark. He got down on one knee and held up the small box. She clutched it in both hands and stepped forward, pulling his head to her belly. She stroked his head, the short bristly hairs so fine on her palm.

He lifted his eyes and said, "I want to see your face."

She smiled down and held the box in her left hand and opened the lid. Light sparkled in the dark box, light from somewhere, her eyes perhaps. A small shining diamond that was bigger than the dark valley behind them.

"Yes," she said to his two bright eyes. "Yes."

He stood and embraced her. Their mouths met, but it was different now. She could wait until they got home, until they told Mama. She could and would. His grip on her was less intense, more settled, relieved. He picked her up and spun her. A car slowed and caught them in spotlight: Jessamine lifted high above his shoulders, her hair and skirt umbrellas of flight.

Reverend Martin Peterson

The next week in the men's Sunday school class, the Wheel of Gratitude spun lackadaisically as the men brooded over the need for rain, an aspect of life they could not control via gifts and favors. Finally, Toller Odom spoke up, "Reverend, explain to us the mysterious ways of the Lord regarding that Bohannon girl joining our church."

"The Lord forgives those who want to be washed in the blood of Jesus. She spoke in tongues. She was saved, her sins washed clean," said Martin, managing not to choke over the words that Stelle had uttered.

"That's all well and good," said Toller Odom, "but it interferes with our other holy purpose of establishing a Christian steak house on the site of former sin. We need the Lord to understand that our work is like reclaiming toxic landfills, rooting out what is poison and returning the land to proper prosperity."

"Let us pray on that," said Martin, and bowed his head. Around him, he felt the men shifting their bodies to an attitude of prayer. No words came to him so he let the silence grow and grow until it seemed the room was about to combust. "Amen," he said, and the chairs squeaked and the men glanced around at one another.

"I believe," said Baker Thomas, "that even though the young girl has reformed, the taint of her past will linger at the truck stop."

"And," said Martin, surprising himself, "there is still her unredeemed mother."

"My wife does not like to share altar space with that girl," said Toller Odom.

"Ask her to pray for a forgiving heart," said Martin. "After all, the girl has not sinned against your wife."

Toller Odom's open mouth clamped down on his prepared reply. In a moment, he said softly, "No, Reverend, my wife has no truck with that particular girl."

"I would like to raise another issue," said Ed Wohlgemuth in his raspy voice. "Where is our steak going to come from since the plague of caterpillars has annihilated this year's crop of cattle?"

"I wish Richard Reynolds was here to give us a report," said Baker Thomas. "Then we'd have a better sense of what a good steak will cost next year."

"We may have to go outside the state of Alabama for beef," said Toller Odom.

The men sat in solemn silence at this prospect.

"Well," said Ed Wohlgemuth, "we might could try Texas."

"You addled old man," cried Toller Odom, "have you forgot the 1980 Cotton Bowl?"

"Nothing good has ever come out of Texas," said Baker Thomas. "We ought to try South Alabama first — get some of their beef. It's been done before."

"And Warner Robins, Georgia wasn't hit by the plague."

"It'll cost us. It'll cost us."

"Trust in the Lord to find a better way," said Martin.

"Reverend, I'd appreciate it if we prayed long and hard for some rain. It seems the only place rich in vegetables this summer is the truck stop, and I am sorely needing some vitamin C," said Toller Odom.

The men bowed their big heads in prayer, and this time Martin issued a call for rain to end the drought and for patience in the face of unforeseen obstacles, such as the caterpillar plague and the unlikely being saved.

The men seemed cheered by the prospect that their prayers might be heard and moved happily out into the heat of the parking lot. In a few minutes the lot was empty but for Martin's Cadillac and a VW.

He went inside to his office and had swabbed his face with a baby wipe when there was a knock on his door. Before he could say anything, Jessamine Bohannon came in.

"Reverend Peterson, hello. I'm sorry I missed church this morning but I have something important to tell you."

He hastily dropped the wipe into the trash can and pointed at the chair in front of his desk. His mouth had gone suddenly dry. During the revival and baptism service, he had been surrounded by so many people, Stelle, and music, involved in the ceremony, that his mind had stayed where it should regarding the girl. But now, with her in his office, alone, her face fresh and pretty, her breasts cleanly outlined by her small pink T-shirt, he was overcome. He sat down and swallowed.

"Is it about your mother?" he asked, trying to calm himself. "Or Gert Geurin? She works with you?" Suddenly an awful thought flashed through his mind: Gert Geurin a prostitute, the reason for his dream of her?

"No," she practically yelled. "This is about me, just me, or rather" — she smiled and held out her left hand, where a small diamond sparkled — "me and my fiancé."

"Your fiancé?" he said as the chill of disappointment flushed through his body.

"I want to have my wedding in the church. A white dress, bridesmaids, music, and you to marry us. I want to plan it with you." She smiled again, like a child preparing for a slumber party.

"Well," said Martin, "let me see what papers we have about weddings." There were no papers, just a list of suggested donations for the minister and the pianist as well as places to shop for wedding needs, stores all owned by church members. He wished to call Stelle and ask her advice. "Just a minute."

He left the office and went into the sanctuary and stood above the baptismal font. He did not believe that praying among the wives would bring the church together on the issue of this girl joining the church. His control was slipping away and God was not helping him. Where is my salvation? he asked his pale reflection in the pool of water.

His face rippled with light coming up off the white bottom of the pool: a swimming face, indistinct, backed by the darkness of the ceiling. There was no answer in his face. He stirred the water until his face broke into tiny leaves of light and went back to Jessamine.

"Who is your groom?"

"Sheriff Paul Dodd," she said proudly, and lifted her head as if she wore a crown.

He gazed for a moment at her smooth forehead and felt a force in her that he would turn back. "Paul Dodd is not a member of the church. You can't marry here."

"Is that a rule?" she said, her jaw hardening, reminding him of her mother.

"I doubt your husband-to-be would take the plunge into salvation. What do you think?"

She stood above him, red color washing up her face. "You're against me too."

She turned and dashed out of his office. He heard her shoes slap the corridor and the door groan as she slammed into it. Next, rocks of gravel thrown by her tires, a long hard blast of her horn, grinding gears, and then quiet.

He carried his weary self into the sanctuary for the third time that morning and dunked his head in the holy baptismal water.

Hattie Bohannon

The food was beautiful and illegal, bounty of Troy Clyde. He'd brought it to my kitchen at home in crates: striped cucumbers; red, gold, and green peppers, skins smooth and clean, jalapeños and redhots, like tiny Christmas lights at the top of a package; corn husks upright in a crate, the soft yellow silks a crown of ribbon; red potatoes and yellow potatoes promising firm buttery mouthfuls of pleasure.

Jessamine came into the kitchen and began poking around in the crates. "More gifts from the hose monster," she said. "Sunday supper will be pretty good."

Although no one had ever talked about it, we both knew that Troy Clyde was siphoning water from the river with long hoses. The plot he and I had planted with tomatoes was in the flood plain. He'd added the other plants as an experiment. Usually the river ran over the bed, but this year the drought proved it worth his gamble. Hence I could serve fresh local vegetables at the truck stop, circumventing Kenny Ranford and his Vegetables of the South.

I plucked a tomato from the basket on

the table, Heather's contribution. I bit it. Fresh flavor bloomed in my mouth and made me bite again and again. Firm flesh from my own backyard.

"Mama," said Jessamine, her back to me, hands testing the vegetables for firmness, "I'm going to cook your breakfast from a new recipe." She picked out a jalapeño and washed it in the sink.

"How nice," I said. Here was my born-again daughter, the one Gert said I deserved, cooking for me. I watched as she took down an onion-soup pot I'd picked up at the outlets in Boaz. I hadn't used it but once. No one liked the dollops of parmesan clogging up the thin brown soup. They'd just as soon eat their onions raw, they'd said. With a tomato and corn bread and some black-eyed peas. That was a good dinner, they'd said, my girls. So away went the onion-soup pot, banished to a high remote shelf.

Jessamine sliced the jalapeño. She put the pot on a burner and melted butter in it. She cracked an egg on the rim of the pot. I heard it crackle as it hit the hot butter, a second crack for another egg. I began to have a little déjà vu. Paul Dodd had made me eggs in a red clay bowl the night I'd overslept at his place. He had a hot green sauce, made from tomatillos and jalapeños, that he put on the eggs.

The diced pepper went into the pot.

"Would you like orange juice and coffee, Mama?"

"Juice," I said. "But don't bother shaving chocolate into the coffee."

"I wasn't — wouldn't do that," said Jessamine. "It's not wintertime." Her voice grew thin and a little higher. She moved very quickly. Sweat showed under her arms, and then I saw it: a diamond ring on her left hand. She'd turned the ring so the diamond was on the palm side, to hide it from me. I watched and waited to see if cream was the next ingredient.

She placed the hot little pot in front of me and opened a new carton of cream and poured it on, stood back, and looked at my face, hopeful for praise, I saw.

I picked up my spoon and ran it under the crisp edge of the egg, letting the cream saturate the whole dish. Then I ate it, because it was good, the sting of the pepper mellowed by the cream, the egg a neutral solid. My firstborn, cooking up treachery and betrayal, offering it as love. My grip grew tighter on the spoon as I scraped up the cream and egg cracklings. How many times did I have to suffer birthing pains with this daughter? The truth was too awful. It was there on her finger, twisting.

"You're fired," I said.

"Fired?" she said. "But where will I go?"

To hell, I wanted to say, but did not. "I don't need to tell you."

"Oh." She stumbled over a few more words but then relief bloomed on her face; it was a pretty color, the lovely tone of a peach just where the deep red begins. "Pshew," she said. But then, because she is Jessamine and has to push, "Heather —"

"Don't even think about it," I said.

A sob broke from deep inside her, the sound of a wounded animal. Her shoulders heaved and she slapped the orange juice to the floor. She ran out of the kitchen then, leaving me in shock, with dirty dishes. I threw the soup pot in the trash and poured the good cream down the sink. It was strange to be up and moving when I wanted to smash Paul Dodd over the head, crush his skull, pound his bones to powder, and condemn Jessamine to eternal fire. Dangerous thoughts were flying around in my head, given that there were knives on the cutting board. I could not see what my body was doing, but after a time, the kitchen was clean and shining.

I aged suddenly. My softening thighs, my squinting eyes, my lowered center of gravity, a wisp of gray in my hair — all of it the look of an old woman. Paul Dodd and his lie about preferring a woman his age. This is my reward for saying no to a man who was not right for me. This. To Paul Dodd:

I feel as if I have been murdered, by you, man of the law, and by her, daughter of my body; blow by blow, you killed me. You killed me in secret when I did not know it, every time you met. Together you murdered me. And when you would not kill me fast enough, she delivered the final blow.

But I am alive, my body shattered. I lie smashed, bloodied, no longer a shape recognizable as me.

Connie Bohannon

The Sunday Jessamine moved out, the rain came down so hard it struck the dry ground like pebbles flung on tin. Mud slopped up on her shoes and on everything she carried out of her room — her pillow, clothes, makeup case, yearbook, tapes — all her junk. Nobody helped her. I was at work and so was Mama. Darla told me

407

about it that night. Her room seemed hollow when I went into it. My name echoed when I spoke it out loud. I'd thought I'd ask Mama if I could move in there, but the room gave me the creeps, like she'd died or something.

On Monday, it was raining hard when Jessamine called me and asked me to meet her at the courthouse. I told her I was watching Heather. She said to bring her and a pair of boots because Jessamine had none. I borrowed Darla's combat boots; mine leaked. Heather and I splashed to the Jetstar and got in. It smelled like slick plastic, an odor I hate, but I had to keep the windows rolled up all the way to town. We drove slowly on the highway, flashers blinking, because truckers will barrel along as if it's sunshine all the way to Hawaii.

I parked next to Jessamine's VW on the square. She jumped out in the rain, opened the door, and slid next to Heather. She looked great: her makeup was done and her hair was very blond on the dark day. "Where are the boots?" she asked.

I gave her Darla's. "Shit," she said. Then, "Oh, well." She slid her stockinged feet into the army surplus boots, the kind of thing Darla loved, and told us to follow her. We ran in a pack of yellow raincoats up the gray slippery steps of the court-house. Inside, it was cool and dark and carpeted. I followed Jessamine to the office of the Justice of the Peace.

If I'd known she was getting married, I would have worn something other than my jean shorts and tube top, but — hey, what could I do? At least I was not a bride wearing combat boots to my own wedding.

When it was determined that I was six-teen and could not sign as a witness, the sheriff called Heloise, his secretary, down-stairs to stand up for them. She was what I expected: a wrinkly lady wearing lipstick in a red shade that was popular before guitars were electric, someone who'd swear the sheriff didn't smoke even if she found his cigarettes in the coffee machine. Poor Jessamine, I thought. Where was she going in her new life?

Towering above Jessamine and Paul, the Justice of the Peace asked for objections. I resisted the urge to shout the list of very reasonable objections that had appeared like the Ten Commandments in my head. Paul Dodd is a prick, for one. Mama would go to jail for murder, number two, probably on two counts. I looked at Heather and thought, Maybe three counts if she included me as well. Paul Dodd is so old. How could Jessamine do anything with him, like kiss that hard-ass mouth or let those wormy fingers anywhere close to — well.

Jessamine's dress was white, sleeveless, its sash light blue. Paul Dodd wore his khaki uniform, fresh-pressed, his boots blacked and shiny. It was like witnessing the wedding of a war bride. When he turned to kiss her, his gun butted her stomach and she flinched.

Heather, who had spent the ceremony swaying from one foot to the other, said, "Your gun's hurting her, Sheriff Paul."

He moved the holster around to his back. "Hold tight till I give my wife a wedding kiss."

He made an enormous smacking noise that caused me to blush.

"Girls," said Heloise to Heather and me, "look what I brought." She opened a sack. Inside were tiny rice bags made of pink, yellow, green, and purple pastel net. She hurried us up the stairs and back to the entrance.

We stepped through the groaning metal doors into the sunshine. Blinded and expecting rain, I didn't notice the large crowd lining the courthouse sidewalk.

"Move, please," said Heloise, tugging on

my arm. "The photographer needs a clear shot of Sheriff Dodd and his wife."

"What photographer?" I said. *The sister of the bride wore a tube top and short shorts and carried a yellow raincoat.* No wonder maniac football players can't keep their hands to themselves.

"The one from the *Ledger*. It's not every day the Sheriff gets married." Heloise pointed and flashed a grin at a man with a bazooka-type lens before pulling me out of the way. She hustled down the steps, insisting people take a rice bag.

Catcalls came from the barred cell windows in the basement of the courthouse. I ignored them. Heather stayed up on the top step, where it was drier. I guess she was dressed fine enough for Heloise, but then, Heather always wore dresses. Most of the crowd on the steps were women wearing bold designs. The mix of diagonals and dots, stripes and florals, all in primary colors made me feel like I was on the Ferris wheel at night during a firecracker display. Then, like I'd been jerked to a stop, I realized they were Paul Dodd's former women, witnessing their loss. They were the secretaries and the clerks, the saleswomen and the tellers, all of whom worked less than a minute from the sheriff's office.

Jessamine and Paul came out. Jessamine was so right in simple white and blue; she wasn't trying too hard. She was just beautiful. But still, she should have gotten married in the church. After the ceremony, we should all be going to a fresh-mown field where long tables in red-checked tablecloths offered good country cooking.

Jessamine and Paul Dodd ran through the rice to his patrol car. Jessamine, in her stocking feet, scooched inside the car, the red light rotating above her head.

The courthouse clock chimed. Polka dots and stripes disappeared into the numerous glass doors reflecting the square. The siren screaming, Paul and Jessamine circled the courthouse three times.

Heather chased tumbling bits of pink net while I gathered up the pastel ribbons scattered across the steps. These seemed so sad a memento of a wedding, just ribbon and net. Maybe I could make a picture frame out of them — or a G-string. Shouts from the underground prisoners kept coming at me.

"All right!" I yelled in the direction of the barred window. I marched over to the basement panes and let out a torrent of the ugliest words I had ever strung together.

V

Gert Geurin

God answered our prayers for rain with a mighty downpour that lasted the whole week after Jessamine got married. It could have been Miz Bohannon crying, is what I thought, when I heard the news of the wedding: all them tears from Heaven. Red mud washed up on everybody's shoes. We looked like we'd walked through blood, all of us beings in Maridoches.

The downpour kept the sensible at home. Only travelers and truckers sloshed into the truck stop. Even the old fools, Gee and Haw, knew enough to stay out of the rain. In the weeks following, God rearranged the weather patterns of the earth, prayer is so mighty. Ever' afternoon in July, it rained short and sweet, like He'd moved the tropics to the mountains. There was no heat relief from the rain of July, but the ornery Alabama crops revived. Thank the good great Lord. He got me some fleshy produce to work my culinary wonders on.

As usual, God's way was a mystery to me, as far as how things were working out. I was mighty pleased that Jessamine was touched by the Spirit and joined the church. I had completed my mission with her. Even though she absconded with the sheriff right afterwards, at least she was saved.

Now the hussy, Ash Lee, though, she was still unredeemed, and I fixed my eye upon her. It took me awhile to catch her because I was frantically trying to plan a fish fry. Kenny Ranford told Miz Bohannon she needed an event to surge sales, since hers had dipped after the protest. She explained that most businesses don't last out two years so this summer was real important to our survival. That was troubling my mind when Ash Lee come in one night to eat — breakfast at 11 P.M. I said to her, "You're not in the family way, are you?"

She had plumped out some in her legs and arms and face, since she'd been scarfing down my cooking.

"No, I need some more film," she said, eating french fries with her fingers.

"I haven't seen a picture at all," I said. "Why you be needing more film?"

She shifted her eyes to the two pieces of fried chicken on her plate as if deciding whether I'd snatch the food back when her answer came. "I tried the camera out on some truckers, just to practice for when a church man came, and" — she slurped her Coke — "they liked the pictures so much, they bought them from me. And soon, they all wanted a picture of me on 'em, so I made some money and ran out of film."

"That is not what that camera is for!" I shouted. Something of mine used for smut and profit. I would trash that camera's eye when I got it back.

"I need more film," she said. "Those men in that church book, I seen them before. They'll get the itch sooner than later."

"Well," I said, "you know you could just come to church with me. Jessamine Bohannon was saved."

Ash Lee said, "Saved from what? Not heartache, that's for sure." The chicken crunched in her teeth and she swallowed noisily. "I wasn't surprised she run off with the sheriff, seeing how they was carrying on up at Bigbees awhile back."

"The sheriff and Jessamine? You lie."

"Naw," said Ash Lee. "She got drunk and was dirty dancing him, and he made me drive her home. I ain't surprised they run off, I'm just surprised he married her. He ain't the marrying kind."

"Shows what you know," I said.

"To each his own," she said. "I'm moving to Tuscaloosa myself."

"What in tarnation for?" I said, but I was happy with this bit of news. The Lord would move her away from here and Miz Bohannon could hold her head high without worrying that someone would cast rotten tomatoes at it.

"Kyle wants me to get an apartment."

"Don't let that sod think he's going to make money off your labor," I said, suddenly fearing that scads of college boys would be seeking her out. Poor child would suffer pestilence and disease. I had to move fast to bring her into the fold.

"No," she said angrily, "to be his girlfriend. He wants a house with columns and skylights, something bigger and finer than a Jim Walter home. Ain't nobody down there gonna know who I am."

"When is this going to come about? He's already left for fall practice," I said.

"I'm saving my money and he's saving his. He sold his car, the Gran Torino; now he's driving the loaner, a black convertible. I'm moving down at Christmas."

So I had a few more months to work God's word on her. She'd have a new bright beginning. Tuscaloosa was her glory road.

I got her more film for the church men. "Why those truckers want a picture of you?" I asked her, her with her buck teeth and that clacking blue bracelet.

"In my bidness, you ain't got to be pretty, just open-minded," said Ash Lee.

Darla Bohannon

In June it was too dry to burn Daddy's barn wood. The grass might catch and the house and the truck stop and even the side of the mountain. Then in July it rained every day, soaking the boards so they'd need to air. It never got to where we could burn them and that is what Mama wanted, the way we should pay our last respects: with a bonfire at night, the air tobacco-tinged because Daddy was. We could cry in the dark and no one would be embarrassed, especially not Mama. We could sing and tell stories about Daddy and drink Mountain Dew in his honor. That was what I had planned and Mama approved, but the sky did not cooperate.

Heather and I tested the boards every day. "Damp or crisp?" I asked her.

We carried the crisp ones into the shed and repiled the damp ones, turning the darkest to the sun. I told Heather about fire-curing tobacco in Daddy's barn. How I sat with him when I was her age and kept the low fire going in a trench, while above us the tobacco sticks heavy with leaves cured in the rafters. I showed Heather how to squat flat-footed like Daddy and I used to as we sipped thermoses of ice water and tended the fire. He'll always be with you whenever you smell this odor, I told her, lifting a board to her nose.

My fingers came away black on the tips and I was reminded of Jewell Miller and the ashes. I breathed out slowly, thinking as I held the old board that she missed Daddy terribly or else she wouldn't have gone crazy trying to keep him. I tried to hate her but I kept seeing her as pathetic. If she hadn't made me taste the ashes, I would be in the Army right now. I felt like Daddy was there with me. I knew he would want me to treat Jewell right.

From watching this family I've learned that love is a lot like the Ruby River — sometimes it runs straight and true but sometimes it shoots out in a new direction, and when it does you best just ride it. That's what Daddy always said, "You best just ride it."

I couldn't ask Jewell to our family

memorial service. So I picked out several crisp planks and thought she could make a new bookcase from them. I'd take them to her apartment. She'd have a memento too.

When finally the rains stopped coming every afternoon, it was August. The wood dried out, but there was the still problem of inviting Jessamine and Sheriff Dodd to Daddy's ceremony, which Mama could not do. It seemed Daddy would always be with us, waiting for a proper acknowledgment, stuck in a purgatory of our minds and memories.

Hattie Bohannon

Troy Clyde sat at a stool at the truck-stop counter, reading the newspaper, waiting on the rain to quit. Hattie manned the cash register.

"If you keep that anger all wrought up inside you, ain't no room for nothing else," said Troy Clyde. "I learned that a long time ago, with Darryl's mama. It was like I had a iron lung instead of a heart, heavy it was, like to dragged me under the ground. It was like I was walking with my ankles just breaking the soil, and every next step I'd sink back under again. Heaviness didn't suit me, and it don't suit you neither."

She looked at him, her eyes wild and blue. "I like feeling angry."

He turned back to his reading material. "You know what makes me angry," he said, "it's this newspaper. Every time I read it I start to sneeze." He balled it up. "They're using a different kind of ink, even though they'll deny it when you call them up to complain about it."

"Nice try," said Hattie, as she took the wad from him. "I already saw their picture." She smoothed out the crushed photo of Jessamine and Paul descending the courthouse steps, Heather behind them, floating, it appeared, like a small cupid. "How can he just up and marry her, of all the women in Maridoches!"

"He married her 'cause he couldn't have you and she's the closest thing."

"She's not the closest thing." Hattie balled the paper up and tossed it into the trash can behind the counter. "She's not like me at all."

"Well, I was talking about him," said Troy Clyde. "Remember back when I was all hot-to-trot with Maybelline McCormack and she dumped me, and then I ran to her sister Jodine and married her up real quick? If it weren't for Cher and Greg

Allman beating us out by one day, me and Jodine would have had the shortest marriage on record. 'Course, me and Jodine got twins out of it; Cher and Greg Allman only got one little'un. Anyway, Jodine was the closest thing to Maybelline, but she wasn't Maybelline."

"Are you saying Jessamine will be back?" This thought panicked her. There could be no reconciliation, no homecoming. "I am afraid the next time I see Paul Dodd, I will pound his head until his neck collapses and then grind his bones under the tires of an eighteen-wheeler," she said. Her eyes were far away and her voice was distant too.

"Lord, sister," said Troy Clyde, "you need a man for a whipping boy more'n ever. I better just light out till another day comes."

"Don't go," she said. "Troy Clyde, don't go."

"You want me to take care of the sheriff for you?"

"No," she said. "No. I want you to take care of me."

"All right," said Troy Clyde, "but I'm going to get some pancakes."

A few truck drivers came up and paid their bills. She didn't even notice them —

what they were wearing, which state their accents had come from.

Troy Clyde came out of the kitchen with a stack of pancakes tall as a top hat. "Pays to know the cook," he said, as he took out his hunting knife and sliced the stack into quarters. Strands of syrup as long as spaghetti noodles oozed down the sides. "What you need is a hobby," said Troy Clyde. "Or something to take your mind off yourself, like fishing."

"How does sitting in a boat for hours take your mind off yourself?" she said.

"Well, go out on my raft and just float along under the sky, then," said Troy Clyde. "It's what I do when I'm in the doghouse. I seen a cloud rotate once. Now that is a rare sight, rarer than a comet that comes around every eighty-five years."

"Troy Clyde, watching clouds do flips will not help me in the least."

"Well, you ought to do something for that briny tongue."

"Thanks, but I'll stay home."

"Just don't wallow in it."

"I don't wallow."

"That's my girl." Troy Clyde punched her shoulder as he left, an empty pool of syrup on his plate.

She did not understand how, when she needed sleep more than anything else, she could not do it. Her nights were a torment of displaced rage and ridiculousness. It was utterly peculiar to be herself, to follow the turns of her mind.

Try as she might, she could not keep her thoughts off Jessamine and Paul cavorting through the night hours of their honeymoon week while she roamed her dark kitchen. She opened the refrigerator, its light a shock to her mole eyes. Maybe she should bake them a cake. Aha, it was her Betty Crocker personality tonight, thought Hattie, powerless to combat it. They hadn't had any kind of real celebration, thought Betty/Hattie. She counted her eggs. Tomorrow she would arrive at their kitchen door, bearing a flat yellow cake spread with shaved coconut and white icing, and Jessamine, already awake, would say, "It's just the thing. Our cupboard was bare. We needed something to go with our coffee." Little bluebirds would tweet. Then Paul would come in, buck naked, see Hattie, and flee from the room. Hattie shut the refrigerator door.

When her eyes readjusted to the dark, she spied the old cutting board, a wedding present from Oakley's mother. Hattie ran her hands across its rough surface. Now it was more a cradle than a board, with one corner curving upward, a testament to its age. It was heavy, a two-foot slab of hickory one inch thick. All her friends and aunts and female cousins had given her heavy things for wedding presents — an iron skillet, a butcher knife, a meat tenderizer — no lace doilies or tablecloths or embroidered napkins, nothing to make her kitchen pretty. She figured that out later when tales of marital strife echoed about the mountain. Ruth Hiler brained Ezra with her rolling pin after he traded her Singer sewing machine for a tractor wheel. Hattie had never had to do that with Oakley, but a strong clobber on the head was what Paul Dodd needed.

Good. Molly Hatchett had replaced Betty Crocker. This felt more like it. She hefted the cutting board. A useful wedding present with a tradition. It was better than a cake that would crust over and make bird food. A light rain pattered against the window. Perhaps this was the end of the strange summer weather. Hattie opened the back door and sniffed, a wash of oak and pine. The rain came down heavy. Hattie thought of the stuffed moose head she'd seen lashed to a Trukbox in the back of a pickup as she'd left work. Now the trophy would be pelted with rain, riding on to West Georgia, defiance prickling his antlers. Behind the truck Hattie imagined a man driving a car, its windshield wipers whipping through sheets of water, then a bolt of lightning illuminating the outraged moose head, the terror of its godlike face driving the poor soul off the cliff into the Chattahoochee River. It was nice to be inside when it rained.

In the day she affected brightness and cheer so well no one knew that her heart had shrunken to a dried prune or that she did not give a hoot about missing silverware or ads with Bible verses about wanton women. To her daughters, she showed that the will marches on, despite missing a heart or a brain or a leg. On you go, pain not altering your stride in the least. This was not said to her daughters, Connie and Darla, it was implied, shown in her kindness to the Inedible Fat man when his overly solicitous inspection of the fat pipe dislodged it the day before the fish fry.

The Ladies of the Church of the Holy Resurrection

When the front-page wedding picture of Sheriff Dodd and Jessamine Bohannon appeared on the ladies' breakfast tables, they quickly dropped a serviette on it to spare the children. They thought it was a prostitution bust. Later, in secret when they read the caption, they fanned their faces to keep from succumbing to shock. Paul Dodd had married *her!* By the second hour of cocktails, they felt gladness in their hearts. They called each other and said, "Have you heard the good news? Hattie Bohannon's daughter has married the sheriff!" Meaning they could pretend to be happy about the news but really they were happy for Hattie's comeuppance. But at 3 A.M., tiny pinches of sympathy entered their hearts. They were, after all, Christian women. Nothing could be worse than what her daughter had done. Nothing. Now they could pity Hattie Bohannon, and from that position of elevation they made kindly remarks among themselves about her trials and tribulations.

Reverend Martin Peterson

He'd write a quiet considered sermon, one that took nothing from him. The relief of the rain had stemmed some of his pent-up feelings. He wanted to ease the congregation into the mass baptism, now that the river was flowing clear again. Until the rain had raised the water level, it seemed the baptism would be more like mud-wrestling than an opportunity for spiritual salvation. Now it would be sweet relief to rejoice in the aqueous bounty of the Lord. And thanks to the boycott and the drought, he knew, the whole county knew, and even Hattie Bohannon had to know that the truck stop was permanently doomed. The sheriff was not going back up there, not after marrying Jessamine Bohannon, who had had the sense not to return to church. There was general relief all around, a sense of victory.

Stelle was painting again: snakes, always snakes that looked strangely and accurately feminine. Long and tall, a flow of sensual curves and knowing eyes, hooded with gold like the eyeshadow of tarts. This is what saw him at breakfast; this is what he saw as he wrote.

Stelle herself came in wearing a drab

olive blouse and matching pants, carrying a Bible with her finger marking a passage. Martin stole a glance at her eyelids and was relieved to see they were unpainted.

"I'm writing the sermon," he said. "It's on an even keel, the obvious verses to prepare for the river baptism. What have you found?" he asked tentatively. In the past, she'd discovered unremembered gems of startling clarity that added to the breadth of his sermons. Perhaps she'd done the same today.

"Yours first," she said.

"And if a man take a wife and her mother, it is wickedness: they shall be burnt with fire, both he and they, that there be no wickedness among you (Leviticus 20:14)," he read.

"That is distortion," said Stelle.

"It's an interpretation." He shrugged.

"And so is *To avoid fornication, let every man have his own wife, and let every woman have her own husband (First Corinthians 7:2),*" Stelle countered, her face cool, lacking even a hint of humor. "Martin, do we want to lead a congregation that thrives on hate?"

"We are servants of the Lord. We follow His design. We are not to force the congregation one way or the other based on our interpretations of the Bible," said Martin.

"Martin, that is what ministry is and always has been."

"What has happened to you?" Martin shouted. "Where are you anymore? You are not here for me. You are not here for God."

"I don't believe that tolerance and forgiveness and taking care of the weak are antithetical to Christian doctrine," Stelle said. "I do not believe in a military church."

"So what am I, Hitler?"

She fixed her dark eyes on him and he held their gaze steadily, her doubly dark pupils emanating a cool disgust. She flicked her eyes away from him. The Bible lay open between them, the verses she'd quoted underlined in red. If she wanted to, she could find passages to justify anything. But, he thought with a sudden surge, so could he.

If it was forgiveness she called for, then let her own be the cornerstone in the new house of the Lord.

Jessamine Bohannon

Every afternoon at five o'clock, after the showers, the sun blazed back in the sky and steam rose from the pavement. We lived in a ghost land. Blacktop had breath and it was warm and smelled of tar.

I marked my days by the rainfall, the sunshine, the tiny beams of stars light-years away. I had never been so bored in my life. Paul went to work in the morning and often in the night as well, while I hung around the house, his house. It didn't seem like mine.

He had ways of doing things that seemed to be written somewhere in iron. The first week I found little squares of yellow paper, crammed with instructions and admonitions, stuck to things all over the house. *Use 409 to shine the front of refrigerator, dishwasher, and stove. Lemon Pledge* ONLY *on cabinets. Hang my shirts so they open on the left.* The one that burned the most, on the end table, the yellow tab with a large red arrow aimed at a water ring that obviously I was responsible for. *Please don't stain the furniture when watching TV.* USE COASTERS! *There are forty-three in the china cabinet.* Why couldn't he tell me instead of writing notes, as if I were a housekeeper he never saw?

I think he was surprised by how fast he had a wife living in his house. Most days I was going out of my mind waiting for Paul to come home, nothing to do but invent worries. Sometimes I called my sisters but they seemed nervous talking to me, like I was a big disgrace. But my wedding picture had been on the front page. My reputation was wiped clean. I imagined Richard Reynolds seeing how good and happy I looked and his stomach tightening and then throwing up because that could have been us. Not that I wanted him anymore, but I would have liked him to suffer some, too.

It became clear that it wasn't me and my life Mama had been saving, it had been Heather's all along. But I can't believe it's true that Mama is the best mother. I seem to be the only person who knows her flaws. Paul won't entertain a single bad word said about her, and he is my husband.

About ten days into my married life, I stared into the green refrigerator. It was hard to dredge up energy to cook supper. Maybe I should order a pizza in Gadsden. Then I could drive around for an hour. Hah! There in the meat compartment was the missing ham Paul claimed was stolen last night. I couldn't understand how a man who had lived in this house for a dozen years suddenly couldn't find things in his own refrigerator. He was so orderly. I felt like hanging the ham on the front door. Next time he woke me up in the night, lost and confused, I'd tell him to keep looking. The doorbell rang before I found the car keys.

It was Stelle Peterson, our first visitor. I thought of pretending I wasn't home because I hadn't been to church since Reverend Peterson refused to marry us, but I was lonely. I opened the door.

"How's married life?" Stelle asked. Her skin was clear but it looked like it had been recently shrink-wrapped around her strong cheekbones. Maybe it was the vermilion scarf she wore, pulling everything tight, her white streak of hair a wide part, the rapids through granite.

I smiled and nodded at our small yard and house and let the domestic scene do the talking.

"How's your mother?" she asked.

"The same," I said. Even though I should have felt grateful to Stelle for taking me into the church when I needed it, I held a grudge against her husband. It put a damper on my belief in their brand of God. I always thought God forgave. I had prayed long and hard one day, asking to be forgiven for having Heather without being married, and the lightest, happiest feeling had filled my heart. My child was supposed to be in this world. I expected forgiveness from the Church of the Holy Resurrection.

"Guess what?" Stelle said.

"What?" I asked, crossing my arms. I feared a spontaneous devotional meeting coming on.

"Ann Reynolds is pregnant. I knew you'd be delighted to hear the news. And" — she lowered her voice as if afraid the hydrangeas would hear — "she's going to breastfeed."

"What, with one tit?" I said, and wished I hadn't.

"Now, Jessamine, that's not very nice." Stelle colored. She'd seemed on the verge of saying something welcoming, but now her cool smile stretched into a haughty arc.

"My word." I guess Richard hadn't suffered much at all. I pulled the door shut behind me. "We're out of food. I have to make a quick run to the store. Sorry, Stelle."

"I'm in a hurry to get to rehearsal anyhow." Her shoulders straight, Stelle walked toward her Cadillac, which blocked out the setting sun. Dangling from her scarf was the thin cord that would connect her to the

Tape of Perfect Pitch.

That night, pretending my restlessness was the fault of pepperoni pizza, I was plagued with dreams of a single enormous breast, attached to Ann Reynolds like a hot air balloon. Poor Ann would be known as the one-breasted wonder and her child would be judged too. Then I imagined bringing Heather here, giving her the front bedroom, the two of us reading bedtime stories, picking out cool clothes. I would go to parent-teacher conferences and give my opinions. I would help her learn to multiply and teach her what an offensive tackle was as opposed to a defensive end. We'd be, mother and daughter, a lovely complement to Paul in his uniform. I wouldn't be lonely anymore.

On his side of the bed, Paul snored. Nothing bothered him at all. One would think a sheriff would fear for his life or at least have dreams about being shot. But no: snore, snore. Our ceiling was clean and white. I believed mightily in God. I'd thought God and Paul would take care of my problems with my old reputation. Perhaps they had.

I turned over and looked at Paul's profile, his smooth forehead. He didn't seem attracted to Mama anymore, not that I could tell. He'd planned a delayed honey-moon trip for us to Atlanta. But I couldn't shake the feeling that somewhere a connection wasn't hooked up right. Paul groped my thigh in his sleep. Resigned, I reached for him.

I spent the next day in preparation for a serious talk with Paul. All afternoon I had imagined what it would be like to have Heather here with us. I figured two parents in the house would outweigh one working mother, if push came to shove. I prayed that Mama would see this as a chance to move ahead with her own life.

After my shower, I cleaned the kitchen and decided to cook a meal without burning anything, and to have the place nice when Paul got home at ten.

Candles flickered over our dinner plates. The wine was chilled, the chicken tender, the salad fresh and pretty, with onion curls and bacon bits sprinkled among fresh leaves of spinach. Paul gazed at me over the food with his familiar longing. I chose to concentrate on his fine chin.

After supper we sat on the front steps. He popped open a beer can.

"Paul," she said, "I need to know some things."

He swallowed his beer and waited.

"Do you go up to the truck stop?"

He pressed the can so it clicked. "It's my job, Angel."

I leaned my cheek into his shoulder. "Have you seen Mama?"

He pulled a long draft of beer. His arm clutched my hip. "Honey, that all happened before I met you."

"Before we decided to get married," I corrected, and then felt very sad for Mama. I reached for the beer and took a sip. If I brought Mama into our talk, I'd have to ask questions that I should have thought of before I married him.

"I never loved her like I love you."

I put the beer to his lips. "I had lovers too, Paul." I didn't understand his attitude but I didn't want to hear anymore about him and Mama. I shivered. Paul stroked my bare arm.

"Honey, I heard tales about you. I trust they are not true."

I was glad we were looking at the half-grown pine trees in front of the house instead of each other. Paul crumpled his beer can and threw it at the trash can beside the road. It clanged.

"A three-pointer." He grinned. "That was a real nice dinner you fixed us tonight.

It makes me real happy we shucked the other folks and found each other."

He nudged me to sit in front of him. Ensconced by his thick thighs, I let my head drift back to rest on his chest. Together we stared at the white impatiens in the yard. Overhead, moths swirled around the yellow light next to the front door.

"Paul. I have a child." Did his chest tighten and slide away from me for a second or did I imagine it? A button on his shirt rose against my skull with each of his slow, deep breaths.

"I wish I had brought another beer out here," he said.

I pushed my elbows into his stomach.

"Don't hurt me, Sugar. I don't know what you want me to say. I don't know what to say, Jessamine."

I looked up into his face. His cheeks sagged and his nose twitched in a brief second of uncontrol. His eyes fell on mine as he said, "Honey, this is what I feel. I feel that we both have pasts."

My fingers tingled like someone was stabbing me with pins. "It's Heather, Paul. She's my child. I mean, she's Mama's now, but I had her."

He cupped my breasts with his hands

and tweaked my nipples. My big secret had only turned him on. I wanted to push him away. He was always turned on, even when I woke with sleepy breath and tangled hair and eyelids stuck together. I wriggled my head out from under his chin and twisted my breasts away from his hands.

Despite the dim yellow light, I could see his neck darken and color rise on his cheeks. He clasped and unclasped his fists. Several times his jaw opened but no sound came out. His breath got faster until it was audible, the short grunts of a sweaty runner. Air choked him. He was hyperventilating. I pushed his head between his knees and raced inside for a brown paper lunch bag.

I slipped the bag over his head. Gradually its loud, violent flapping subsided. Paul sat in the porchlight, his shoulders broad, his fists tight, the bag his protective helmet. I placed my hand on his forearm. His muscles were tight as a spring. He was embarrassed. I slid my fingers under the bag and stroked his ears, then inched up into his hair as his chin emerged from the bag. I kissed his chin. With slow exploratory fingers and lips, I nudged the bag up and off his head, as if it were the wrapper of a delicious present.

He raised his hand, slow, as if he feared an electric shock, to touch my face. He rubbed my cheek and sent shivers up my neck. It was the only way he could show his love for me.

"Paul," I said. "Let's hug. Let's just go to bed and hug all night." But the words I breathed through his hair did not convince me of the limits of my own desire. "Let's just hug all night."

Hattie Bohannon

Alone and overwrought, she went to the river, pushed out Troy Clyde's raft, and glided into the stillness. It was warm, as night is in Alabama in August. She docked at the tomato patch and, in the dark, pulled weeds, losing herself in the sensual feel of the dirt, the pungent odor of the lush plants. Under the sky, there was peace. Crickets chirped in the high grass and the Ruby rolled on, gently brushing the river reeds. It was a place to sleep. Finally, she'd found a place to sleep.

When she woke on the soft grass mat her body had made, she rolled over and looked at the stars. The bugs had hushed. There

441

was the good iron smell of the soil, a hint of tomato in the air. She breathed deeply and rested and thought of the long-ago frozen nights she'd roamed the house disturbed by dreams, drawn by the silence of the night to thoughts of peace in death. I like being alone, she thought. I need to be hugged as the earth is hugging me, in this darkness that is peace.

When her father died, she had understood that it was not God but living that was so hard on him. It was the bad market prices for crops, the uncertainties of the weather, the things he could not control that inspired his helpless rage. Living is hard, she knew first hand, and yet there were times of respite. *All I want is to feel like this, free and rested. My own place, uninterrupted.*

She thought of her mother, long gone from Maridoches, living a new life. Sadness welled as the wave of abandonment washed over her but ebbed. She understood now a little better her mother's need to flee. Maybe it wasn't a bad thing to change course. Maybe it had been a triumph for her mother, made at great sacrifice, to leave her home and two older children. Maybe she'd felt she had no choice.

Uneasily she let her mind return to the

truck stop. Here, in the starlight, it seemed to exist in another dimension. An alien world of dangerous situations; a place ruled by public scrutiny; requirements and rules she did not believe in. *I bet those church people are dancing with joy.* She'd read the letters to the editor, letters foaming with rage so blind it made her want to carry a gun in the glove box to protect herself. A world with that kind of hate was no place to raise children.

Why should I stand in the doorway awaiting a bullet from a mad fundamentalist, thumping his Bible as he shatters my windows and molests my children? I cannot let my daughters work there any longer. I must protect them. They are too young. I was the naive one.

But who would come work at a place where there was perceived prostitution? No one, she thought. I can hire no one. It would be Gert and herself and Rudy the night cook.

I can quit this business. She watched the lights of heaven clear and unblinking above her. I can. I can sell the truck stop and walk away. Oakley left, my mother, my father. I can too. Maybe there is virtue in change.

Why should I be the one who must live

by the rules? The good mother, the celibate widow, the one who overcame the new business odds? Did I make the truck-stop world? Or was I merely the support, the tent pole holding up the sky? I'd rather lie here on the ground and see the sky stretch out by itself. It's doing fine without me.

She sat up and inhaled air thick as a warm wrap. Her heart beat a little faster. How embraced she felt by the humidity as she stood up and stepped through the grasses. How pretty the black sky was, the white trunks of sycamores, the shadowy outlines of water oaks. When she got to the river, she slid down the bank and stood at the edge of the dock, took off her shoes, then lowered herself into the cool water. She ducked below the surface and came up doing the breast stroke. The river held her, a natural element of love.

Reverend Martin Peterson

After a series of gnashingly unsatisfactory prayers, Martin acknowledged his bared soul. He'd seek out the prostitute, sin, and afterwards rededicate his life at the river baptism, which would require standing in deep water, a perfect penance. If Stelle learned of his transgression, she could exhibit forgiveness, and become a pillar of tolerance. Maybe then she would gather him in her arms again, triggering renewed love as had happened with the Reynoldses.

When he left the house that evening, Stelle called out, "Have a good time," before dipping her paintbrush in a pot of ochre. He drove the long way to Bigbees and pulled onto the shoulder to stare at the bar's sign, a bare-breasted neon woman with winking eyes and flowing hair, the same silhouette truckers affixed to their mud flaps.

He grew suddenly furious with Stelle. *Have a good time.* Is this what she meant? Take your needs somewhere else. Where were the words of God now? He could not believe Paul and Jesus, that celibacy was the true way to spiritual attainment, even among married people. Martin was shocked at the distorted face the rearview mirror showed of him in the light of the blinking woman: now her shirt was on, now it was not. "I was not born to be celibate," he said calmly to the God of darkness and temptation. "I was born a man with a man's needs."

Out of the night, in the beam of his headlights, a woman appeared. Hippy in a short jean skirt and a skin-tight shirt, she approached, swinging a large bag on a strap, until one headlight was completely blocked out by her body. A young woman with a mass of brown hair and a pleasant if narrow face. She smiled and knocked on his window. He hesitated. What if she poked a gun in his face? She'd kidnap him and away they'd go. She was young and forceful and he'd be — not dead, but oh, so alive.

"Need some help?" the young woman said. Her breasts practically asked the question. He recognized Ash Lee.

His voice abandoned him. He swabbed his face with a Kleenex.

"Oh, it's you, Reverend Peterson. Thank God." Without asking she slid around the car and got into the passenger seat.

Martin swallowed. Was this a gift from God?

"I think it's safe to park here on the highway," she said. "Unless some dumb trucker rear-ends us. That sign is an awful distraction." She frowned as if in distaste.

He nodded at the sign. "Do you work there?"

"I'm a waitress, there, yeah, sometimes."

She twirled a bracelet of glass beads as if getting up nerve to make her next move. "Reverend, can somebody's soul get clean after it's been dirty?"

"Yes." His very thought.

"How does one get clean?"

"By prayer. By asking the Lord for forgiveness. Forsaking unclean ways. By penitence," he croaked. These were not the words he wanted. They bound him like a life jacket.

"Can you pray right to God?"

"You have a personal relationship with God."

She went pale. "A personal relationship?"

"He knows who you are. When you address Him, He hears you and answers you." Martin blew his nose and surreptitiously dabbed his eyes again.

"Wow. This is cool." She leaned back in the seat. "I just ask and He forgives me?"

"There is also penitence and forsaking your wanton ways."

"What's penitence?"

"It's an unpleasant task you do to make up for your sins."

"Like giving a blow job," said Ash Lee. "I've been doing penitence and sin at the same time. Thanks, Reverend. You've made my day." She opened the car door and bounded away into the darkness.

Martin's teeth were grinding. Free blathering advice. That's all she wanted from him. He honked the horn and Ash Lee turned around. He waved for her to come back and she did. This time there would be no mistaking his desire. "Get in," he said. "I have some business for you."

She stood outside the open passenger door, light flooding the front seat.

"Hang on," she said, as he unzipped his fly and freed his twitching penis. "I have to put something on that." She opened her big purse and, quick as a snake's flickering tongue, snapped a picture of him. Ash Lee disappeared in the flash of light, a large red cloud hovering where she'd been.

Martin spent the night in the church. He lay on the carpet and felt the stiffness of the concrete floor it covered. It was chilly and bad for his bones. He had finally called Stelle and told her he was working on his sermon. Now that the men's Sunday school class had lost faith, he needed to get his message exactly right, he'd said. But in his heart, he knew he'd never be exactly right again.

Light had just begun to color the

stained-glass windows when he heard the door of the sanctuary slam shut. He sat up as Gert Geurin, sweaty in a flowered dress, bore down upon him. He had no stomach for anything she had in mind this morning. He needed a day of fasting from the congregation, from humanity. He needed to prostrate himself on his dock and lie without sunscreen from now until dusk, making of his pale skin a hair shirt, each breath a knife of pain.

Gert sat in the first pew as if waiting for the Call to Worship.

"It's not Sunday, Gert," he said kindly.

"I know what day it is, Reverend. This is an urgent matter. Come over by me and hear me out," she said.

Martin stretched as he rose and felt a twinge in his back. He joined Gert in the pew and smelled Lily of the Valley wafting off her person.

"I feel my presence here is the Divine Will incarnate. You have no idea how long I have harbored this pain in my breast."

"Have you been to a doctor?" said Martin, hoping to ward off an impending confession. He recognized the religious bent seeping from her like ink from an octopus.

Gert twisted her hands in her lap. "Reverend Peterson, this is a pain no earthly doctor can cure."

Martin waited as she opened her purse and sank one hand inside it.

"My time has come to confess to another victim of fleshly desire. I am glad it was you."

Martin started. Had she been having a version of the same torrid dream he'd been having, the one of her naked in the snow? Women had flirted with him before but he'd recognized it as a misplaced need to love an authority figure. It happened to all preachers and teachers, through no fault or virtue of their own. "Gert, I am not the victim of fleshly desire. I am the victim of a conspiracy. There's that family at the truck stop operating under your very considerable nose that is trying to ruin me. Those women!" he said. "Remember the passage that warns of wolves in sheep's clothing?"

"Oh, Reverend Peterson, that is the good God's truth. I thought he was just a lamb with soft brown curls, but behind that handsome dimpled face, inside that perfectly sculpted human anatomy, lurked the rage and desire of a wolf!" Her fingers sank into Martin's arm.

"Who are you talking about?"

"Oh, Reverend Peterson. It shames me

so. But I must go on." She loosened her fingers and placed her hands, folded, on her lap. Her voice grew high-pitched, as if she were a witch narrating a child's puppet show. "I was very young when I married Floyd Geurin. I'd just graduated high school, and Floyd was so sick."

"And much older, I believe," Martin said, before he could stop himself.

"I know there's them that wonder why I married a man sicker than my grandfather and older, too. But I had met him through the youth group and he was lively and smart; it was after our engagement that he began his decline. We were in love, and I mean in the pure holy sense, unlike what passes for love these days." She cast her eyes at him. "It was the warmest feeling I had when I was with him. After the wedding, someone had to put his right leg in the car for him because he'd lost all feeling in it standing up during the ceremony. I can remember that because a look of shock traveled from one face to another down the whole row of well-wishers. Instead of saying those funny honeymoon things, they all just stared. He never got use of that leg back."

Martin turned his face to the stained-glass picture of the Sermon on the Mount.

The details of Gert's honeymoon embarrassed him, nothing more. He was relieved. Maybe his humiliating encounter with Ash Lee had driven all the perverse images from his mind.

Gert continued. "He took to his bed as soon as we got in the door. Then the doctor come out and fixed up a nose tube so he could get oxygen, and I took care of him. The thing was, I didn't mind. I really was happy." Fat tears brimmed in Gert's eyes. She dabbed them with her handkerchief. "Floyd's youngest boy, James, came home from the University down in Tuscaloosa for a holiday. He was a nice boy but real impatient with Floyd. It hurt him to see his daddy lying all day under a white sheet. Or I thought it did." She gulped and took a deep breath.

"I don't remember a James Geurin."

"Oh, I wish I didn't!" She sniffed, then held her head high.

Martin wished her a failure of nerve.

"One night I was taking my shower, a real hot one to open my pores and let the impurities out. My skin was as red as the devil. I put on a white filmy nightgown someone had given me for married life. It was all pleats and had large loose arms, kind of like angels wear. I felt very pretty

452

and took to admiring myself in it, even though I knew pride is a vice. I reasoned it would be nice for Floyd to prepare him for sights in the afterlife."

Martin licked his lips and kept his gaze on the carpet.

Gert jostled his arm. "You must hear this, Reverend Peterson, you must."

Martin nodded, his teeth pressed against each other as hard as he could manage.

"I had finished brushing my hair out — shiny and gold it was then, before it salt and peppered — and I turned to find James standing in the bathroom door, wearing a bathrobe, open." Gert shook. "I couldn't look at his face for shame and instead found myself looking at this snake that rose up to greet me. I don't know what happened. He — he touched my breasts." The word came out *bray-yests* and sent Gert into convulsive tears.

"I hardly think a little fingering is a major crime," Martin said, and winced, recalling how he desired just a little touch from Ash Lee. "But any mingling of flesh is a transgression," he decided.

"Oh, Reverend Peterson. I can't go on."

"That's fine, Gert. I'm sure that all is forgiven," he said; he found this experience excruciating, now that he harbored guilt.

"We shall pray and you will be baptized in the river."

"Since when do you presume to speak for the Lord?"

Martin lost his voice. The great question he'd been struggling with since spring. He could not presume to speak for the Lord now, even if no one but Ash Lee ever knew of their encounter. He would know that he was insincere, flawed with sin. He could no longer mask his pain. He wanted to throttle this woman.

But Gert's voice flowed steadily, with no modulation. "I found myself prone on my very own bed. The wind blew in from the open window and the long curtains shook in the strength of the breeze. But I was not alone. James was scenting me with English Leather. He worshiped my feet with his tongue, then my knees, my thighs. He rose as the wind blew chills across my naked body. We cleaved and cleaved again and again. I was resisting. I moved my head away from his hot mouth and I spied Floyd's cot just six feet from my bed. Floyd's head was half sunk in the downy white pillow and his blue eye shocked wide open."

Gert swallowed as Martin shivered. She had seen the eye of God, the judgment in the cold blue eye. Martin had seen nothing but a flash of blinding light.

"At that point, a pain pierced my heart and I stopped struggling. Every inch of me was burning with pleasure and shame at the same time. And the better I felt the worse it was, and vice versa. I struggled long into the night, and finally the golden rays of the sun touched my bed and opened my eyes that had been shut in shame. I was an instrument that night but I still am not sure exactly who was doing the playing, if it was God or the Devil himself."

Martin's mouth hung open. "How could you?" he sputtered, although the question sounded more like desire for advice than moral indignation.

"For years I have puzzled that myself."

"What did Floyd say?"

"Floyd never said another word until he died two months later. I believe that I have been punished with knowledge for forty years because Floyd had an attack and never saw another thing in this world. I wrote James and told him never to come back. And he didn't even come to the funeral." Her voice was wistful. "Reverend Peterson, will I be forgiven?"

"For adultery, enticement, exhibitionism, lust, perversity!" he shouted. "There is no way that you will ever be forgiven. Lust of the flesh despoils the spirit. You will flame in Hell for eternity, and Floyd will look down upon you with his blue eye and laugh. I am not surprised that you were drawn to work in a house of prostitution and that you have continued to work there under the evil influence of that Bohannon harlot and the harlots who work for hire there. That Ash Lee." Spittle flew from his mouth and hit her face.

"You hypocrite!" Gert spit back.

He saw the photograph in her hand as she turned and fled.

Now the news would be out. Stelle would know his transgression, and he expected she'd ring his death knell in the service of the Lord. It was too late, all too late. He tried to pray but nothing came to him. *If I don't believe, I cannot be redeemed.* There was only one thing left to do. He had his body to give. If that is what the Lord demanded, then that is what he would give in exchange for his everlasting soul. When the river baptism came, he would offer himself up, and she, the self-righteous old bitch Gert Geurin, would have a much worse crime to torment her. To her grave she would take his last breath.

Gert Geurin

There was nothing I could do but leave that picture in the mail slot of Stelle's office as I fled that damaged church. I had gone to Reverend Peterson with my soul in my hand. I had offered it to him as a way of allowing himself to confess to me. I shared, but he did not redeem himself. He is not worthy of God's name.

I should be washed in the Lamb's blood, my suffering brought to peace. Instead I feared condemnation, and yet, as I drove away, my voice gave way to songs, verses I invented. I sang recipes to the tune of "We Gather Together." Was this new prayer?

Soon I felt better. I did not need Reverend Peterson to confess to. I could talk right to God, and so I did all the way back to my house. We got it resolved, there on the highway, me and God. Reverend Peterson had been my challenge, but I had not succumbed to his passion of misinterpretation. I had confessed in church. I would take baptism and come clean.

Then I went to work, still humming, and Miz Bohannon had a smile on her face, the first in a long time, and she brung up Jessamine and what a relief, she was surprised to say, it was to have her out of the house. In her home there was more laughter now.

Hattie Bohannon

The next morning I went to work. I thought I'd be sad looking at the kitchen or upset sitting at my desk wondering how many more days I'd be filing papers. But I didn't have any of those feelings. Instead I thought of Jessamine and wondered how she was doing.

I pictured her in Paul's small yellow house with the blue-checked curtains, surrounded by squirrels and pine trees, the graying yellow linoleum in the kitchen, the peppy pink tile in the guest room, the thin plasterboard walls. I wondered if Paul had fixed the hole near the closet. At first the house seemed nice with its dark wood floors and bamboo curtains in the large front window. But the closer you looked, the more flimsy it was. The window frames were stained to a sticky finish, and none of the shades worked. The cabinets were large and painted off-white but there was no cloak closet, and the bathroom closets fit awkwardly into corners and smelled of cedar-stained plywood. But then, had I ever imagined a future for Jessamine? No, not really. My oldest daughter seemed ageless, cutting pies in the kitchen. I'd pictured new stainless steel mixers, a gleaming new Hobart, a silent garbage disposal, and always Jessamine cutting pies and Gert rolling biscuit dough.

But that vision was not our future. Jessamine had absconded, altering the picture. I remembered Jessamine's cry as she fled this room. That's what this room held for me now, that breach between us: not the first month I recorded a profit, not my numerous business coups, but Jessamine's cry. It was losing Heather that made her cry out. We had both lost daughters in that moment.

Her desire to mother her own baby: I never saw it before. I saw only that I was sparing her grief and shame and hard work and a diminished future. I never understood her loss of love, the joy in caring for a sweet young child, of claiming it as yours. It was no wonder she was desperate for something of her own — Paul Dodd, who had temporarily been "mine." A great sadness infiltrated my breath. I wanted to touch her, my daughter, and hold her again, and tell her she was perfect the way she was.

That afternoon I worked out front, bringing drinks, bussing tables, taking payments. I was testing this job to see what gave me pleasure.

Troy Clyde sauntered in and wiped his head. "Blacktop's so hot it was burning my feet through my boots." He helped himself to two cold drinks and sighed as if he'd watched a rerun of his life and figured the star of the movie was a sad sack. "I came to tell you that you can beat the tar out of the Jesus brigade. I'll help you string them up."

"There are things bigger than a person sometimes. Staying in this business isn't worth it."

"Those are quitting words, woman. You better stick them back in your mouth because you are not giving up." Troy Clyde placed the drinks on the counter. "What will happen to your girls? You going to stick them in the welfare line? I swear, Hattie, your cracks are showing pretty bad."

I hated him, his little dark-gray eyes, his free-swinging limbs. This was not love. I needed to be gathered up and encouraged, not pummeled for what he took to be my crime: walking away from a killing situation.

"Look, you already got the lights turned down like a damned funeral parlor. There's people coming up to see you." He stepped out the door, then came back in. "Hattie Bohannon, you are the best dang woman in all of north Alabama and south Tennessee. If you wasn't my sister, I would have married you myself."

A physical jolt traveled the length of my body. "Don't you leave yet. I am not finished talking to you. I want you to know that I am tired of putting up with your foolish schemes and your damned heartaches."

Troy Clyde shifted from one foot to the other, his bill cap in his hands. "Hattie, no one admires a business failure." He slipped outside and roared away in his jeep.

I stared a long time at the salt shaker. Troy Clyde should have married a woman he could talk to, but why? He had me. And did he take care of my needs? No. He rarely listened. He brought me vegetables and game and tribulations. He cared about me in his own way but I gave more. Now I'd run him off. And damn, did I feel glad about it.

That evening I watched the truckers eat. They tucked into the hot food on the white plates with pleasure. I smiled, knowing that this work I did was good. As they came and went I knew, of course, that they could find food somewhere else, or maybe even here, under different management. This was my place but it was not me. Other people were invested more in its success than I was.

Even though it was nearly midnight I called Kenny Ranford, who was awake. He'd had an offer for the franchise from local businessmen who wanted the property for a steak house. He had intended to visit next week and tell me in person. He had not anticipated the community's resistance to the truck stop and to me. The best thing was to dissolve our franchise agreement and sell. He recommended I take the offer from Steaklords.

"But how can I live in my home and see them down there every day selling steaks?" I asked.

"That is not my problem," said Kenny Ranford.

Could I plant a fat hedge or build a wall to keep a steak house out of my view? What of the smell of burning meat? The animal lard congealing as it waited on the Inedible Fat man? Would he be so frequent if Gert wasn't in the kitchen ready to stanch his ardor? I'd probably have to sell my house, too.

Gert Geurin

The day of the baptism in the Ruby River I had the worst migraine of my life. We were in the midst of hundred-degree August days. The pain started at 2 P.M. and I fought it by sitting in the meat cooler. Miz Bohannon came and cooked up the few orders we had. She was a regular Jacqueline of all trades now that Jessamine was gone.

I had to think of quiet things, like little Miss Ash Lee telling me she had enough money saved up now and she was quitting the harlotry. She felt bad about taking the Reverend's picture because she had seen the light right before she done it. I do believe she grew a conscience in that moment. She showed off a new black and red dress she was going to wear for Kyle when he came home later in the fall. And she had her hair streaked so now she's an ashy-blond, and she was getting skinny again, maybe thinking of all those cheerleaders down in Tuscaloosa who are so tiny and baby-voiced. So she was a good calming thought and I did okay for long periods of time. But then it got on near 6:30 P.M., and I had to go and meet the Reverend.

I was befuddled when he asked me to be his rower, knowing what I did about him. I figured he was keeping me from the congregation as best he could. But then I saw the hand of God in this duty and I sighed and said, Yes, Lord, I accept this mission too.

Stelle would lead the songs from the riverbank. "Let Us Gather at the River," "Michael, Row Your Boat Ashore," "I Will Meet You on the Other Shore." After the dunkings, the congregation would each receive a candle and they would shift to glory songs, so that after the sunset there would be a big blaze of light and sound that could reach up to the heavens.

If Reverend Peterson came from out on the water, he would be clean when he got to the shallows and could step from the boat unsoiled by red mud. He wanted to look like what he was representing, since this was a spiritual event, not a bodily one, he'd said on the phone.

I set out in my car, driving to the river. My head almost quit throbbing. It goes in remission, this pain, and you think it is over but the smallest thing can start it up again. Reverend Peterson, in a white robe, was on the launch, the boat tied to a post. I got in first and took up the oars. He made a strange gravelly noise as he got situated in the bow and his end of the boat sank as deep as mine. I wondered had I lost some weight.

He did not say a word, just turned and faced the other side of the river. I rowed away from the sun but it glared hard at me. I chewed on my cheeks. I did not want to ruin the baptism. I could see only shimmery water and Reverend Peterson, a white hot fire in the bow of the aluminum boat, my head a magnet for all that light, about to blow a fuse.

Hattie Bohannon

I had to get away from the truck stop to think about selling it. There was heat in my blood when I thought of the churchmen owning my place. My impulse was to fight to the last dime, but at what price, my daughters? With less than twenty-four hours to make my decision, I went to the Ruby River and sought Troy Clyde's raft.

He'd built a seaworthy one this year. In the past he'd chosen young trees that sank with the weight of their sap, but this year the poles were light and dry and strong. I took off my shoes. My dress clung with sweat and I wished to take it off as well, but the sun still burned orange. I hadn't swum naked since Oakley. I thrust my head into the brown water, lifted it, and swung droplets all over myself.

Tall willows grew from sinister twisted roots. Turtles slid off fallen trees into the water as I poled to the middle of the river. A gentle current ran, rocking the raft like a cradle. I lay down, looked at the pink sky, and closed my eyes, deliciously alone.

I must be practical. Not get lost in thoughts of Oakley and his home place. It wasn't his home place any longer. His barn was gone, his fields paved with blacktop.

Tension ebbed out of my back as I drifted, the sun's warm rays on my face. I'd buy a houseboat, float and rock in the evenings, dock at the river-bottom fields in the day, work. The solitude of the plan made me crazy with happiness — just colors and smells and physical work. It's all I need. It's all I want. Relief was as big as the deep blue sky.

Gert Geurin

I never saw it coming. We hit another craft and Reverend Peterson was flung off the bow onto the other boat and took it down under. He came up, two heads came up, then one went down. My eyes were squinted to slivers as the rowboat rocked. My stomach rose and then I seen him thrashing around, grabbing ahold of the other head, shoving it under the water. I had moved my oar over to him, but when I seen him do that I pulled it back to me.

His robes was spread on the surface like spilt paint, and him the center of it, heavy, going down, but he had the other person in a headlock and was taking her or him down too. Then I seen a flash of her face, peering up at the sky from underwater, wavery and soft — her eyes the look of dreams. It was Miz Bohannon.

There they were, fighting each other in the water. Lord, I prayed, Lord. I could barely keep my eyes open. I rowed closer to the thrashing and gulping. Neither one was doing good. He had her around the waist and was pulling hard at her shoulders, and all she was doing was keeping her head above the water.

I was so weak with the migraine. I could

save only one: Miz Bohannon or Reverend Peterson, no time for prayer. When I saw his head come up by itself, his eyes locked onto me like my old husband's had the night of my biggest sin — it was stare and demand in one look.

I bumped the boat into his head and reached down in the water and searched out Miz Bohannon's shoulder and wrenched it up. Her arms came next and she nearly tanked the rowboat getting her legs in.

Hattie Bohannon

She was roused by the fluttering of huge wings. Shouts came from the frantic white creature as it danced above the water. It was human and it landed on her raft, capsizing it. Arms clawed at her dress as she was spilled into the river.

The white robe wrapped around her legs and pulled her under. She felt a great rising in her chest while bodily sinking at the same time, an exhilaration with calm at the edges. Above, a circle of rippling light, amber in color. Weeds ran like ribbons around her feet, soft caresses. A storm of mud to her side, a whirling of clay, a sienna cloud. She fastened her eyes on the amber circle.

Her left breast was seized and twisted. She gulped water as she cried out, fought, kicked against the flailing arms. An underwater face of desperation, Reverend Peterson's, appeared, long and fishlike. She kicked his stomach, kicked his head, propelled herself to the surface. He clung to her leg. She kicked his head again. Still couldn't get her foot free. Water filled her mouth. Gagging, twisting, reaching up inches per stroke, slowly working head and shoulders up to the light, taking forever, him dragging.

A strong arm lifted her free of suffocation. Air, sweet air. She cracked the surface with her legs, kicking herself into the rowboat, where Gert Geurin sat, stoic and pale, holding an oar.

He hadn't come up. She tugged on the heavy robe but Peterson was still submerged. The robe must have snagged something, an old tractor, a twisted tree, barbed wire. She leaned out of the boat and reeled in the white filmy cloth. Peterson bobbed up. She rolled him into the bow and drained water from his mouth. His eyes opened with a flicker of contempt. She closed her own and knelt above him.

His lips were cold and clammy, yet his face had a faint warmth. She blew gently at first, then harder and harder, getting dizzy each time she forced air into his mouth. His arms were outspread, his cold white gown an icy bed she knelt in. She felt like shaking him. *Come on. Come on. Breathe. Breathe.* In her head, the voice would not hush. *Stop, fool, stop,* it commanded. *A delicious luxury to let him die at your feet.* She pressed his chest, blew hard, yet the warmth receded. *I am good,* she said to the voice, *I am good.* She became crazed and rhythmical as she forced breath. *Take it. Take it. Breathe. Breathe.*

Gert vomited over the side of the boat, unbalancing it. The sun sank and darkness fell on the river. Onshore, hundreds of small flames bent to the left, then adjusted themselves upright, but Hattie felt no breeze.

She heard voices around her, she didn't know how close. Paul Dodd in the sheriff patrol boat, the motor a long time coming.

"I lost him," she said to Paul, her eyes unseeing in the dark.

"You done what you could," he said. "Get in the boat. We'll take care of —" He jerked his head at the white mass of linen.

"He's gone," she said.

"Leave him to my men." Paul clasped her arm. "Step up. That's right, now sit still. We'll be out of here in no time."

They put Peterson in the motorboat. Already oxygen snaked into his lungs from a heavy tank.

"He's ticking," said a medic.

Paul Dodd expelled a long sigh of relief. "Good news," he said to Hattie.

"Where's Gert?" she said.

"She insisted on rowing to the church side to deliver the Reverend's last words. I believe she will make it," said Paul Dodd.

The candles on the shore had been tossed into a huge bonfire. It was night now, and the single huge flame was the only living thing she could see. The fire seemed so distant and she so cold. She'd felt death claw at her legs, try to pull her under and smother her in its deceptive white wings. She began to shake. Her teeth chattered.

She was a tiny speck in the inky night. The water black, the sky black. Even the stars had dried out. There was only the large licking flame on shore.

The Ladies of the Church of the Holy Resurrection

The ladies of the church could not shake that sight from their heads: in front of the most glorious sunset, the silhouette of Hattie Bohannon bending over Reverend Peterson, their mouths locked, their movements rhythmical and frenzied. It was a blessing the sun went down when it did. There was no mistaking the passion because, as they witnessed, Reverend Peterson was not yet a brain-damaged man. On the contrary, he looked very much brain-engorged. She'd drug him up, a wet dragonfly, and pressed her mouth to his.

So Hattie Bohannon was a hero in town. Her bravery was cited at the Reverend's bedside, which showed that forgiveness was indeed God's way. It seemed to the ladies of the church that it had been the summer of forgiveness. After the prayer service for the return of the Reverend's speech and sanity, struggling across the gravel in high heels to their cars, they heard Rhuhana Polk Killian say, "I am going to switch membership if we have to forgive one more person."

Stelle Peterson offered herself as the new minister, in the manner of Lurleen B.

Wallace, she liked to point out, who served when her husband was barred by law from running the state government. But that didn't sit right with the ladies, to have a lady lead them. Lurleen had just been a bust-head anyway. Everyone knew that. Her husband, with a new wife by his side, had later run again and won again, disabled as he was. But Reverend Peterson had lost the ability to speak, and how could they know that Stelle was really telling his message or His message? She might be making up her own thoughts, and that was surely not the way of the Lord.

Reverend Peterson himself continued to haunt them. They tried to revise the image of him and Hattie fused at the lips. They had never seen pornography. A few of the braver ones went so far as to appear suddenly on top of their startled husbands in the privacy of night. Maridoches burned with a wildfire that neither the Gayfer's fall catalog nor the heavy fall rains dampened. The ladies of the church grew to prefer the rain. It kept the hunters home and the wild game safe.

Connie Bohannon

After Mama and Gert saved Reverend Peterson from drowning, Mama changed. She sold the truck stop to some men from the church. They renovated it to look like a Crimson Tide museum. Everything is red inside: the booths, the bathroom tiles, the chairs, even most of the steaks. There are pictures on the wall of football players. The napkins are red-and-white houndstooth check.

After they bought it, they hired a company that replaces burned-out houses to take everything down to the foundation and walls, just so people wouldn't be reminded of what it had been. They didn't save anything of Mama's. There is nothing that looks Jesus-y either in there, although Gert is the queen of the kitchen, in charge of everything.

I heard that Kyle Childers had some problems with double vision, but that didn't keep him off the football team. He doesn't have to see very far anyway. He's a lineman, and all they do is push other big beefs around and maybe once in a while a football bounces off their heads. Sometimes they catch it and if they are on offense it is a penalty. I'm betting Kyle will be that kind of offensive lineman, clueless. I'm not sure if he can drive or not. It would seem not.

Mama is building a house for us in the woods above the tomato patch. Our front view will be the Ruby River. She wants to watch it flame like fire every night before the sun goes down. I am going to school and so is Darla. We are both a year back from our classes but that's okay. I never liked the people in my class. I need a new boyfriend, a real one this time. I know from watching Jessamine that it is better to be able to hold hands in public than to get orgasmic in a shed.

So I get another shot at the prom, and I've decided I am going to be prom queen next year. I'm betting I know a hell of a lot more than anybody else at that school. Plus I already have two votes: mine and Darla's.

Jessamine Bohannon

Darla invited me to Daddy's ceremony. I hadn't been home since Mama made me leave. It was strange to ride up the driveway and not see the Bohannon's sign or the truck stop surrounded by semis

475

lined up like cattle at feeding time. Paul drove and he looked good, in a crisp blue shirt. I laid my hand on his arm. He patted my thigh.

We parked in front of the garage. I could see Mama had set the picnic table with an old cotton tablecloth and our good dishes. Connie was pouring drinks into the green glasses. Darla was rearranging the barn-wood bonfire and ignoring Troy Clyde's suggestions.

I got out and carried the watermelon I'd carved like a basket and filled with berries and cut fruit.

"Hey, Jessamine," said Troy Clyde. "Nice fruit."

Paul joined me. He kept putting his hand on his hip to feel for his missing holster. It was funny to see him out of uniform.

Connie sidled up close and whispered, as she took the watermelon out of my hands, "Do you use his handcuffs, you know, like in private?"

"Shut up, Connie," I said. "Where's Mama?"

Troy Clyde came over and shook Paul's hand. "I'd stay away from the woodpile if I were you," he said, and gave Paul a significant look.

Paul smiled. "I don't think anyone's going to catch me on fire. I'm ninety percent water. By the way, you don't know anything about night hunting, do you, Troy Clyde?"

"Is the answer hunting done at night?"

Paul smiled again, using his friendly I-gotcha voice. "Night hunting is a crime."

I nudged Paul. This was supposed to be a family event, not official business.

"Get off the horse, sheriff," Connie said. "Your badge is no good here."

"I think I need to find something else to drink, in the house," said Paul, and he walked away from me. So there was going to be shit to get through. Everybody was tense. I volunteered to help Darla but she said the bonfire was done. Connie was off smoking behind the shed. Troy Clyde asked Darla what kind of starter fluid she was using and then argued that newspapers soaked in vegetable oil would never create enough combustion. I picked up two glasses of Mountain Dew and walked toward the house.

When I reached the porch, I could see Mama and Paul through the living room window. Alternating sips, I drank from both glasses. I watched Paul and Mama argue. They were doing a dance but probably didn't know it. Mama would pick up a newspaper article — our wedding announcement — read it, and drop it like a handkerchief on the coffee table. He'd scoop it up and follow as she turned the corner. She'd spin around, take it back, read it again, step away from him into the center of the room. Again and again, arguing all the while.

Mama looked best when she argued. Her face seemed collected, all her features aimed at one purpose behind that blue stare I had not inherited. Only Connie's eyes were as blue. Paul's face was hard too, but his eyes didn't have the usual reading-them-their-rights look. No, there were sparks. I put the glasses down on the porch rail and balled my hands into fists.

Mama glanced at me in the window, ran to the front door, threw it open, and grabbed me in her arms. "Jessamine, I missed you," she said.

I stood stiff as a board. She hugged me very close. There was a barrier in my chest that was big and heavy, and my heart was on the other side of it. I could hear her words, understand them, but they could not reach my heart or unlock the fence around it. It was strange to have wanted this for so long and then not to be able to accept it.

"Is Paul Dodd treating you well?" she asked, releasing me.

I blushed and nodded.

"Go in and get the cake," she said. "It's in the kitchen."

It was a yellow sheet cake with coconut icing, my favorite. I slid my hand under the cool glass serving tray and lifted it, the smells bringing back long-ago birthdays, when we were small and Daddy was here, laughing and relighting the candles as many times as we wished, until they burned down to nubs. Cigarette burns on the frosting, Mama had always said. Today we'd do that. For us and for Heather to know that part of our family history.

I scrounged around for candles and found a box in the drawer with the rubber gloves and new sponges. How many? It didn't matter. All of them. We'd need all of them to burn away the bad air, to get clean to the surface and start anew.

We ate our fill and everyone was pleasant, although there was one more tense moment between Troy Clyde and Paul. Troy Clyde acted like he was the bull goose of our family, and it bothered him that my husband was both his age and the law.

Troy Clyde asked me where I was working. My mouth was full of mashed potatoes so Paul answered.

"I don't know that I like my wife to be working," he said. "It would keep her from getting the housework done."

Darla stuck her finger in her throat and mocked a gag.

"I reckon you had the time to do the housework before you married. Where did all that time go?" Mama said, filling Heather's cup with water.

He glared at her. "Do you really want me to answer that?"

She cracked her jaw and blushed. Troy Clyde slid around the table and clamped his arm around Mama's waist.

"Let me tell you something, sheriff. It's a good thing you laid off my sister, because I was getting ready to take you on if you pushed her where she didn't want to go."

"Shoot him, Mama," whispered Connie in a not-whisper.

Troy Clyde sighted Paul down his pointing finger. "I want you to know, sheriff, that having a working wife is like finding methane gas under your pasture. It's an unknown fortune. Take it from one what knows. She don't bother you about fixing the toilet or asking you why the paint is still peeling off the north side of the house or tell how the baby had diarrhea at the checkout counter. She don't care if you watch ball games or go hunting. I think she likes hunting season so she can have some time by herself, and that's okay by me. So if you want to look out for your future happiness, you will do everything in your power to keep that little lady employed."

Hattie wriggled free of Troy Clyde's grasp. "Time for cake."

I lit all thirty-six candles. My sisters and I bent over and blew them out. Then Darla lit them and then Connie. By then, they'd melted down and we began to tear up. We let Heather light the last round, which took a long time but we didn't want it to end. Tears had streaked our faces. We watched each little light go out and waited for Mama.

"Cigarette burns on the frosting," she said.

Heather looked at us, wondering why we were so sad. I hugged her to me and held her very close, and she hugged me back.

Darla, who was shaking, went to the bonfire and lit it. It took awhile but slowly the paper caught and even more slowly

Daddy's barn wood. Heather sat on my lap a long time. Mama moved into the chair next to us as the sun set, oranges and blues and pinks beyond the dark mountain. Soon smoke curled into the picture, pale and present. And it did smell of tobacco, the best-smelling wood in the world. My daddy's ghost hovering near, and yet he was going away, too. I felt him smiling.

In the swirl of smoke, I reached out and touched Mama. We do share a daughter and a life, and I think — I really do believe — that she loves me.

She said I ought to look into the community college and she might too; then we could go together. But I don't know. I fought hard to be me and I don't want to blur the lines again.

But I can't tell her no. She has come so far to reach me.

Darla Bohannon

Darla and Jewell Miller poked around under the hood of the Jetstar. They talked about compost heaps and Jewell's new bookshelves as they changed the motor oil. Jewell tightened rings and replaced hoses. They cleaned their hands and then Darla drew the car keys from her pocket. She pressed them into her palm. They were light and thin, small as her pinky, colored silver and gold.

Jewell climbed into the passenger seat. "I'm not used to being the passenger."

"You'll learn," Darla said.

She took the old windy road. The car was exactly as wide as the blacktop. The trees leaned close, their branches holding back crowds of wild weeds. Leaves fell like ticker tape. The Jetstar eased through noisy swells that rose with vigor and ended with the gentle pattering of more brown and orange-flecked leaves.

A space of sky appeared and a white cloud was reflected across the hood of the Jetstar. Darla pulled off near a fence post with only a single rusted wire curling around it. "This is where we need to put the marker for my father," she said. "You can tell there used to be two posts and a gate. Daddy'd unhook the wire and drive the mule team through and go to work, and the dog would ride on the wagon with him."

Jewell nodded. "I remember this field."

They got out. Darla opened the trunk and wrestled a posthole digger out of it while Jewell pulled the smoky barn post from the backseat.

Darla ran her hand over the post and got stuck by a splinter. "Shit." The splinter was soft and broke, half embedded in her skin. She decided to leave it.

They worked an hour twisting the digger into the soil, lifting it, and dislodging the red dirt into a nearby pile. They took a break and drank the grape juice Jewell had brought and bemoaned the lack of shade. When they began to dig again, sweat rings appeared on Darla's T-shirt and on Jewell's pale surgeon-style blouse.

When the hole was deep enough, they dropped in the pole and heard its satisfying thud. Jewell fought to hold it upright while Darla packed the dirt tight around its base.

"No one's ever going to notice what a good job you've done," said Jewell.

"I'll know about it," said Darla.

"You are your mother's daughter," said Jewell, and Darla blinked through sweat at the high praise.

"Institutions crush people," said Jewell. "The wise get out before they're mashed."

Darla tamped the dirt high above ground level, "In case there's a gusher," she said, but really she was imprinting the ridges of the post on the memory of her fingers. The last touch. She stood and smelled rain in the air and carried the digger back to the car. She looked away to the pattering leaves, flipping their pale sides in the swelling wind. She'd let Jewell make her peace with her dad.

The first raindrops plashed down fat on the hood of the Jetstar. Darla got in and reached across the seat and opened the door to let the bustling Jewell in. The old lady smelled damp, of sweat and dirt. "Tut-tut," she said. "Looks like rain."

Hattie Bohannon

A charred circle in the middle of the old wooden bridge slowed Hattie's purposeful gait. The burnt planks were coated with carbon silk that some mild winter wind would pry away. In these woods, abandoned buildings mysteriously burned, sacrifices, she supposed, to saints or the perversity of pyromaniacs. She thumped the bridge. It was still solid. Come spring, only a shadowy patch would remain of the burning.

She walked on, shifting her backpack to scratch her shoulder blade.

Under the influence of the gray sky, shocks of dead grass became a brilliant orange sea in the field on her right. Soon she passed the rise of an old cemetery. As children, she and Troy Clyde had joined hands and run shrieking past it all the way to the bridge. Brown cords of Virginia creeper lashed the five angular headstones, each pointing heavenward, to the earth. The cemetery looked forlorn.

Hattie cut through two fields and a stand of pines. Majestic and green, the pines seemed an artificial bright spot against the pale hues of the rest of the landscape. She realized, though, that the pines had been managed and would soon be harvested for timber. Next year, oval stumps would peer like rain puddles from this field. Hattie tramped on. She came upon the hackberry tree alone in a fallow field. Brown leaves still hung from its branches, making it harder to read the names carved in the bark. Troy Clyde's name was the lowest, but it was beyond her reach. Birds probably nested among the first letters carved on the tree, now hidden in curled leaves eighty feet from the ground.

She shaded her eyes. Troy Clyde + Viola + Mary + Martha began a long list. At least Troy Clyde hadn't x-ed any girl out. Instead, he'd carved a huge heart that encompassed all their names, Troy filling one hump and Clyde the other. Above the heart, she spotted her father's name and her mother's initials, scraped out in a moment of passion, perhaps when they moved into the house. Names of cousins and people she'd heard of disappeared up into the branches and the glare of the white sky. She walked to the back of the tree, where her name appeared twice. She'd scratched it there when she was eight, missed the bus to school, and spent an agonizing day in the woods, hoping Mr. Hiler wouldn't look up from his corn and see her.

Oakley had hiked to this tree the night before they got engaged and set about adding their names to history. The awkward stripes spelling out Hattie Annabelle Dameron Bohannon started large, about ten inches high, and sloped down to a respectable four by the end of her name. She took Oakley's old penknife out of her backpack and cut his name and the date into the tree at chest level. Although twenty feet separated their names, she felt they were connected, a feeling that got stronger as she struggled with all the curved lines in OAKLEY and BOHANNON. Her hands puffed and raw, she blew the splinters away from his marker.

The sky was unchanged. She could not

judge the time but had an impulse to hurry away. The ground sloped gently up through what used to be a tobacco field but now was dotted with the smooth fingers of young dogwoods. Spindly pines, their needles appearing wet as a young chick's feathers, advanced from the woods, dragging lines of rattan and honeysuckle with them. Hattie followed the path, an old wagon road, cluttered with beetle-dead trees and wooden carcasses from last year's ice storm. She climbed higher into the sphere of the hardwoods, the leafless, gray, serrated maples, oaks, hickory, and sourwood. Layers of leaves lapped over her ankles, her motion a *shush-shush.*

If it hadn't been almost winter, she might have missed it. In the spring her mother's native azaleas and hydrangeas would have lit the old yard, now a tumble of bushes and brambles and upstart magnolias. The chimneys, victim to high winds, lay in heaps of brick secured by poison ivy. In a way, it was a relief not to find anything memorable in the vines. A stranger would have thought it just another lumpy hedge in the forest. She climbed over the bricks and foundation stones, pausing when rock clinked rock and gave off a false metallic ring. Hacking through briers, she found the slate floor, cracked into slabs, like a natural outcropping. Then she knew where the kitchen had been and where her father most likely remained. She was an hour ripping back vines before she had a clear patch of dirt. It was strange to stand in a place so empty of human life and remember her impressive home and see only broken slabs and twisted weeds, as if she had invented her whole childhood and the people in it.

Suddenly aware of a chill setting in after hard exercise on a cold day, she took a small collapsible spade from her pack. The top layers of dirt were black with decayed leaves, the kind of soil that would have made her father a successful farmer. Several inches of obstinate dirt yielded to grainy red clay streaked with black ash. She stirred the clay and ash together until the shovel clanged against something metal. She rooted out a flaky piece of rusted pipe. It crumbled under the blows of her shovel. When she had a brownish mix of iron, clay, and ash, she scooped it into a pound coffee can she'd brought.

Hattie carried the can in one hand, a box with Oakley's remains in the other, to the granite ledge jutting above the swirling river, glad she came before ice crusted its edges. The drop was fifty feet. Across the river, rock cliffs loomed as monuments. She had planned no ceremony, and the chill in her bones made her act quickly. The coffee can, her father, fell straight into the river. Its white spray disappeared into the lead-colored water. Hattie hoped the can settled on the bottom of the riverbed in cool depths undisturbed by the fast current. Given the blankness of Oakley's hospital room, Hattie wished the woods were bursting in fall reds and yellows, and that he could float away on Indian blue breezes, but shades of black and gray would have to do. She opened the box and took out the pretty white urn, trailing roses from spout to bottom. He had loved wild roses, even when they took over fences and sprawled into lanes. She should plant wild roses around his fence post and let them roam across the whole field. She might start some to edge the tomato fields.

Hattie opened the urn. She lay flat on the ledge and shook the urn hard. The gray ash fell like dust swept off the porch. She faced the urn's mouth into the wind for it to take the last bits of Oakley and let him sail and swirl all over the lands he loved. Still, some ash clung to the insides. Hattie did not want to take the urn home and wash it out in the sink. Clean, the urn would bring a quarter at a garage sale. She scolded herself for thinking such a thing at this moment but realized that Oakley would have gotten a kick out of it. She was a businesswoman. She had loved him as best she knew how. The urn was light in her hand, a little too light. She scraped up some stones and added them for ballast. She threw the urn in a magnificent slow arc. It spun, a pink and white pinwheel, across the sky and the river before smashing against the granite wall on the other bank.

EPILOGUE

Reverend Martin Peterson

He was born with a hole in his heart. When the wind blew he could feel it gush deep in his chest, a sound like green hush. If he was working the water on a Sunday morning, always a Sunday morning, he heard the wind play as a harp, the ripples on the slow river like the notes in his heart.

Townsfolk thought he was crazy. But he kept the channels clear of dead trees, errant logs, trash, even automobiles that shot like divining rods off the Lotus Mill Bridge or through Horseshoe Bend high above the river. There were never survivors. The townsfolk, in times of such waste, were grateful for his madness — his doggedness in locating the remains, going at times for weeks on end, poking among the cottonmouths, prodding slippery rocks into underwater avalanche, sometimes firing gunpowder to get a stubborn body to rise. It took persistence and often a clear day of radiant sunlit circles lying on the surface to draw the body up after its spirit had already split the seam in the sky.

It was a Friday, three days of working the

water and no sign of the girl he hoped to find. Blue shadows draped the bank and lay a thin hem at the water's edge. He'd rescued a kitten on Tuesday, a marmalade bone-thin scratcher that had been put on the river in a Styrofoam cooler. The kitten sat at the bow, hitting the water to catch its own reflection.

What he knew of the girl was this. She was slim, which made it difficult to find her. A small body could lodge in a crevice of shale or a cage of brambles or snag on a root. As days passed, she'd bloat and perhaps float free. He'd left the young man's sports car embedded in the bank. The boy's heavy body had hit dry land and scattered and been gathered, but the frail girl had flown from the car, the impact of air enough to dislodge her from the passenger seat of the convertible. He wondered perhaps if she had jumped.

He steered the boat to a cool cave marked by a ghostly sycamore. The kitten batted at tendrils of leaves hanging at the cave's entrance. A half pint of Old Grand Dad floated on its side. He rescued it and unscrewed the lid, put a drop on his tongue. The seal had held. He took a long draft.

The girl had ash-blond hair, blue bracelets, and a black and red dress, according to the people who'd seen her last. The colors meant little in water. He thought of her parting from the car, long hair splayed, arms wide, her body too full to fly. Her cry as the car flew forward, as she floated, then dropped like a stone to the surface hard as concrete, bones driven through the skin. He was looking for bones.

He took off his cap and drank more, then put his cap on backwards. A bracelet could chain her to a root, and though flesh would want to rise, bone would hold her down. He heard the wind in his heart, a sigh, hollow and free as her bones would be. One day she'd sink, become a white pile in the brown depths. He knew he would not find her.

He laid up in the cave and drank for three days. The kitten caught a frog and ate its face and legs. It purred as it crunched the bones. On the fourth day, he pushed the boat into the slow current and let it take him to the site of the crash. The car was gone, but the hole it had bitten into the hillside remained. A small oak, its top sheared off, stretched toward the water. The grasses arched slowly toward their natural height. He passed without reverence or thought.

A glimmer of light drew his glance to the shadows along the bank. Blue jewels winked, a blue bracelet on a white hand, held up as if waiting to be called on. He touched the kitten and felt it tense. He waited for the claws, but it stayed rigid. Gently he rubbed its bony neck. Gently his boat approached the hand. He was sure she was underwater, sure she had been blessed by a baptism of light.

Acknowledgments

I am grateful to the women at Charlie Brown Daycare in Tuscaloosa, Alabama, Greenhill Development Center in Takoma Park, Maryland, and Growing Together Preschool in Lexington, Kentucky, who shared the care of my sons while I developed as a writer. For their generosity, faith, and friendship, I thank Doris Stinson, Nanci Kincaid, Rebekka Seigel, Annie L'Esperance, Nina McCormack, Diane Dennis, Barbara Hausman, Pat Zeilen, Lynn McCune, Lynne Houldin, Deborah Isenstadt, Deborah Reed, and Gurney Norman. My perspective was shaped by my family, Carolyn Geurin, Ann Tahir, and Margit and Tom Pruett, with whom life is always an adventure. For years, David Lee Miller has provided enthusiastic support and encouragement. My son Jack's keen wit elevates all occasions. I thank Truman and Sam who help me focus and keep me laughing.

I have been blessed many times by my association with a wonderful group of writers, the Kentucky Book Mafia, (Ka-BooM!): Mary Alexander, Susan Christerson Brown, Pam Sexton, and Crystal Wilkinson. The Kentucky Arts Council, the Kentucky Foundation for Women, particularly the Hopscotch House residency program, the Kentucky Women's Writers Conference, and the Barbara Deming Memorial Fund all provided timely support.

Special thanks to my favorite cousin and traveling companion, Michael John Ross. *Merci beaucoups* to Rosemary James and Joe DiSalvo of the Words and Music Faulkner Festival in New Orleans, to Tim Parrish, a model of charity, and to Bruce Tracy, who aided and abetted. I owe a mountain of chocolate to my agent, Amy Williams, for her passion and wisdom, and a lifetime of gratitude to Elisabeth Schmitz, my editor, who knows all the right words.